EVERY LITTLE PIECE OF ME

ALSO BY AMY JONES

We're All in This Together (2016)

What Boys Like (2009)

EVERY LITTLE PIECE OF ME

AMY JONES

McCLELLAND & STEWART

McClelland & Stewart and colophon are registered trademarks
of Penguin Random House Canada Limited.

Library and Archives Canada Cataloguing in Publication data
is available upon request

ISBN: 978-0-7710-5067-1
ebook ISBN: 978-0-7710-5069-5

This is a work of fiction. Names, characters, social media handles, companies,
places, and incidents either are the product of the author's imagination or are used
fictitiously. Any resemblance to actual persons, living or dead, organizations,
events, or locales is entirely coincidental.

The epigraph from Anne Carson is taken from her preface "Tragedy:
A Curious Art Form," which appears in *Grief Lessons: Four Plays by Euripides*
(New York Review of Books, 2006). Copyright © 2006 by Anne Carson.
Reprinted by permission of United Talent Agency.

"Piece of Me" Words and Music by Christian Karlsson, Pontus Winnberg and Klas
Ahlund Copyright © 2007 by Crosstown Songs UK Ltd. and Universal Music
Publishing MGB Scandinavia AB. All Rights for Crosstown Songs UK Ltd.
Administered by Music Of Windswept. All Rights for Universal Music Publishing
MGB Scandinavia AB in the U.S. and Canada Administered by. Universal Music—
MGB Songs International Copyright Secured. All Rights Reserved.
Reprinted by Permission of Hal Leonard LLC.

Text and cover design by Kelly Hill
Cover images: woman © Jeff Bergen/Getty Images;
flare effect © I am Kulz/Shutterstock; frame © Milos Djapovic / Shutterstock;
texture © Here/Shutterstock.

Typeset in Berling by M&S, Toronto
Printed and bound in Canada

McClelland & Stewart,
a division of Penguin Random House Canada Limited,
a Penguin Random House Company

www.penguinrandomhouse.ca

1 2 3 4 5   23 22 21 20 19

For my husband, Andrew F. Sullivan,
who lived with me while I wrote this book
and somehow still wanted to marry me.

Why does tragedy exist?
Because you are full of rage.
Why are you full of rage?
Because you are full of grief.

—ANNE CARSON

You want a piece of me?

—BRITNEY SPEARS

Mags

November 2014

———◇———

"Barometer"

Mags hadn't expected the club to be so crowded. The band's previous shows in New York had been sparsely attended. But Align Above's new album had dropped a few weeks before, and tonight there was an electricity in the air, something that she couldn't explain. In the green room she drank half a fifth of whiskey and smoked three joints before stumbling on stage in a haze, her body hot and cold at the same time, her skin sweaty and goose-pimpled.

"I'm fine," she told Emiko, her manager, who held Mags's face in both her hands and stared into her eyes like she was trying to see into the future. "This is what I need. This is what I do."

She sang. She knows she must have, because people were cheering—so many people, the audience a big blur of colour in front of her, pulsing with vague outlines of human forms. Adrift, she locked eyes with a beautiful Asian boy while she was singing "Barometer"—a song she had written about Sam, so new she had only ever played it live once before—and she was surprised to see that he was singing along, gazing at her with such naked adoration that it made her shiver. "You will rise, I will rise, we will rise, like a barometer," she sang, and his mouth moved with hers, almost as though he was claiming her voice somehow, making the words his own in a way that momentarily startled her, her hand dropping from the mic, her voice fading out before the end of the line.

After the show, she found him in the hallway outside the green room, waiting for her. He was just a kid, a scruffy teenager with doe eyes and expensive sneakers, a forelock of hair sweeping down across his brow. But she could feel the relentless pull of the pit, that gaping maw of a comedown she ran from at the end of every show, so she pressed herself up against him, the contours of his body meeting hers in a way that was familiar and yet unfamiliar, like wearing someone else's shoes.

"Do you have somewhere we could go?" she asked, lips inches from his ear, which fluttered almost imperceptibly as she breathed against it.

"I have my own place," he said, and she could feel the newness of those words in his mouth, how good it felt for him to say them.

They were in the Uber by the time she started second-guessing herself, realizing too late he wasn't even close to what she wanted. But it wasn't until they got to his apartment and she saw all the video cameras that she knew she'd made a huge mistake.

"I'm not a pervert or a weirdo, I swear," he said, his doe eyes clouding over with worry as she inched toward the door. "It's this stupid reality show I'm on. They leave the cameras set up all the time."

"Reality show?" Mags was sobering up, and all she could see were blinking lights, red and green and blue, cables tangling across the floor like tussling snakes. She suddenly felt as though the entire world was watching her, as if they could see through the eye of the lens right into the depths of her soul.

"They're not on right now, I promise," the boy said. "See?" He picked up a cable attached to a camera and showed her the dangling end. Mags realized the blinking lights were all in her head. "There's a schedule. They're only on when the crew is here."

Mags stepped toward the camera tentatively, as if it were a wild animal she wanted to feed from her hand. She touched the top of the lens, which was coated with a fine layer of dust, and blew the dust away gently. "That doesn't seem very real," she said.

The boy laughed nervously. "It's not," he said. "There's nothing real about reality television, trust me."

She moved around the room, feeling the boy's eyes on her. At least the reality show explained the apartment—sparsely but tastefully furnished, with high ceilings and exposed brick, a pool table at one end of the living room and an entire row of expensive guitars lining the opposite wall. She wandered over and picked one up, strumming it before realizing it was a vintage Gibson Les Paul Standard Sunburst. And it was signed.

"Eric Clapton," the boy said, shrugging. "I got it at an auction last year."

Mags ran her fingers over the strings. It probably cost more than all of Align Above's equipment combined. But the boy didn't seem to care—he hadn't rushed over to grab it from her, hadn't kept it under lock and key. "Do you actually play this?" she asked.

"What's the point of a guitar if you don't play it?" He took it from her and began strumming softly. *Oh no*, thought Mags, *please don't*. But then he started singing, his voice soft and earnest, and she could do nothing but sit there, helplessly listening, not knowing whether she should laugh or cry. At least it wasn't one of her songs—from what she could tell, it was something he had written himself, probably during a period when he was listening to a lot of melancholy stuff, Bon Iver or The National. When he stopped singing, she smiled at him, and before he could launch into his next number, she kissed him, the guitar pressed between them, the strings mashed up against her belly.

3

Later, Mags got up from the boy's bed in the dark and walked naked to the bathroom, keeping the water cool as she splashed it over her face, avoiding her own red eyes in the mirror. Walked back through the apartment, head jumbled, running her hands over the exposed brick, heading toward the balcony to see those lights of Tribeca, wondering what it must be like to live here, to live this life.

Before Mags made it halfway across the living room she saw her, through the glass doors of the balcony—a woman wearing only a T-shirt and underwear, climbing up onto the parapet, her pale skin scraping across the concrete as she stood up on the ledge. Mags grabbed a blanket from the couch, scratchy and wool but big enough to cover herself, and rushed to the balcony, the wind hurtling itself at her as she hauled open the doors, all rust and smog.

As soon as the doors opened she realized she had no idea what to do. She tried to remember how high up they were—four storeys, five? Surely high enough.

"Hello," Mags said quietly.

The woman turned to face her, and Mags realized she was still a girl, really, barely out of her teens. There was something vaguely familiar about her. Her eyes were a startling blue, her hair white-blonde and cut close to her head in a haphazard way that made Mags think she had done it herself. Her T-shirt had a picture of a fairy on it, possibly a cartoon character from a television show Mags had never seen. Even as she balanced there on the parapet, she stood with her back straight, her hand on her hip, her head angled at a perfect, fashion-model 45 degrees as she regarded Mags through mildly inquisitive eyes.

"It's you," the woman said. She dragged both her hands down her thighs as though she were drying off sweaty palms. For a moment, Mags thought she was going to reach out to shake her hand, but instead she crossed her arms over her chest, cutting off the head of the cartoon fairy. "What are you doing here?"

4

Mags didn't say anything for a minute, afraid the truth might push this woman over the edge. "Are you planning on jumping?" she asked instead.

The woman dipped her toe off the ledge, her eyes drawn to the street below. Then she pulled her toe back and turned to face Mags again. "Are you naked under that blanket?"

Mags glanced down at her round calves and bare feet sticking out of the bottom of the blanket, which hung just above her knees. "I guess when I saw you climb up on that ledge, finding clothes wasn't exactly my first priority."

Narrowing her eyes, the woman crossed her arms tighter over her chest. "You slept with Val," she said.

Val. Mags knew the boy's name, but it was so much easier to think of him as "the boy," as if he were the only one. But now. Val. She nodded.

"Good for you. My brother loves you, you know. The show tonight was the only thing he could talk about for weeks."

"He's your brother?" Mags asked.

"We're both adopted," the woman said. "Everyone knows this. You know this." She paused. "Or maybe you thought I was his girlfriend."

"No," said Mags, realizing she hadn't. But she didn't want to talk about Val anymore. And she was sick of talking about herself. Sick of herself in all kinds of ways. Maybe just sick. "Can we get back to talking about why you're standing on that ledge?"

"I'm pretty sure I'm going to jump," the woman said, without drama, without pathos. *I'm. Going. To. Jump.*

"Pretty sure?"

"Very sure." She spread her arms wide, an eagle about to take flight.

Mags thought about all the things she could say. *No. Don't do it. You have so much to live for.* But did she? How could she know? "What's your name?" she asked instead, stalling.

5

The woman stared at her, her body silhouetted against the New York skyline, backlit by the lights from a thousand different windows, a thousand different lives being lived. Then she started to laugh, a huge, aching belly laugh that Mags worried would propel her off the edge through the sheer force of its kickback. When she finally stopped laughing, she looked out over the city again. It was like a switch had flipped, and she was back to thinking about whatever it was that called to her.

"It's Ava," she said. "You might be the only person in New York who doesn't know that."

Mags moved toward the ledge and hoisted herself up, swinging her legs over, sitting next to Ava's feet. "Do you smoke, Ava?" she asked.

"Gross, no."

"Too bad," said Mags. "This would be a good time to have one. You know, one last smoke before . . ." She gave a low, descending whistle and made a diving gesture with her hands.

"Wait," Ava said, balancing herself on one leg. "Isn't smoking bad for your voice?"

Bad for your voice. How many times had Mags heard that over the past few months? And not just about the smoking, which she had only recently taken up again, but about all the other things she had recently taken up too. As though her voice was the only part of her worth preserving, the only thing that mattered. "My husband died four months ago," Mags said, fingering the edge of the blanket.

"I know," Ava said. "I read about it somewhere."

The back of Mags's legs were cold against the concrete ledge. Below her, she could see a couple standing by the curb, their arms wrapped around each other as they tried to hail a cab. It seemed like such a mundane thing, standing on a street corner, going out together, going home. How little she had thought about those things when she had them. "His name was Sam. He was our bassist."

Ava brushed her toe against a pebble on the ledge, sending it down to the sidewalk. The couple, still locked in their embrace, didn't notice as it landed a few feet away from them. "How did you get through it?" she asked.

"I didn't," Mags said, without hesitation. "I've basically been drunk since the funeral."

"How inspiring."

"I'm not trying to be inspiring, I'm just telling you the truth." Mags pulled the blanket tighter around her. "My husband died and I wanted to die too. But I didn't. I went back to work. Because that's what people do. Put one foot in front of the other and keep going."

"So you *did* get through it," Ava said.

Had she? "I'm not sure I did."

"You're here, though."

"Yeah." Below them, the couple disentangled, the woman laughing at something the man had said. "I don't know. I'm not sure you ever get over something like that. It becomes a part of you. The grief will just always be a part of who you are. I'll always be the woman whose husband died of cancer."

"At least you'll be *something*." Ava began swinging her leg like a pendulum over the parapet. Mags's stomach swung with it. "I am *nothing*. I don't even exist without those." Still balanced on one leg, she turned and swept her hand back to the row of cameras standing sentinel on the other side of the glass door. The momentum caused her to stumble, shuffling sideways on her standing foot until her swinging one found the concrete once more.

Almost involuntarily, Mags reached out and grabbed Ava's ankle, the skin surprisingly warm against her hand. "Will you sit down? It would make me feel a hell of a lot better."

"I'm the one trying to kill myself," Ava said, lowering herself down onto the ledge. "*You're* supposed to be making *me* feel better."

With Ava sitting beside her, Mags could finally see her face. Wide-set blue eyes, tiny nose, reddish cheeks. A baby. Someone whose heart could be crushed by the slightest touch, a fontanelle not yet closed over. And yet, as Mags studied her more closely, she saw the firm set of Ava's chin, the glint of steel in her eyes, the rigidity of her fingers as she gripped the edge of the parapet. Even shivering there on the balcony, Ava was so much stronger than she first appeared. Still, something had broken through all of that.

"You're not nothing," Mags said. "You can be anything you want to be."

Ava laughed. "Come on. Don't sell me that line. You're not a network executive."

"Sorry, I've never tried to talk someone down from a literal ledge before." Mags paused. "Is it a guy?" she asked, somehow already knowing the answer.

Ava didn't say anything, just pulled her knees up to her chest. Along the top of her left foot, Mags could see more than a dozen cuts in varying states of healing, too perfectly spaced and measured to be anything other than purposeful. Higher up, on her shin, just above her ankle, was a much more ragged gash that appeared to be brand new.

Ava caught Mags's gaze and covered the top of her foot with her hand. "Can you pass me my wine?" she asked, nodding toward a glass a few feet away on the ledge. Mags passed it to her wordlessly, with a vague hope that she might drink enough to pass out. But instead, Ava took the glass and overturned it, pouring the wine over the side of the balcony.

"What are you doing?" Mags said.

"It seemed like the thing to do." Ava motioned toward the couple, who were now getting into a cab, oblivious. "But I missed." She contemplated the glass in her hand as if she might throw that too, but then she put it down. "They're probably both cheating on each other anyway. Love doesn't actually exist." She pressed her hand down harder against her foot. "Love is just a word that people use to manipulate you. They pretend love is real so they can get what they want from you."

Mags shivered. "Jesus. Who hurt you?"

"Everyone." Ava removed her hand from her shin, where her gash had reopened, streaking her palm with blood. "It's okay. I probably deserved it."

"Do you really believe that?"

"No. I don't know." She poked listlessly at the gash. "I haven't been very good to the people in my life. My parents, my sister . . ." She trailed off. "But they haven't been very good to me either."

The air around them seemed to pick up a little, a breeze floating the fringe of the blanket over Mags's thighs. "Do you want to talk about it?" Mags asked.

Ava shook her head, snaking her hips forward on the parapet until she was balancing on the edge.

"Don't," said Mags, her heart spinning circles in her chest.

"You know, you won't just be the woman whose husband died of cancer. You'll be the famous singer."

Slowly, Mags began inching closer to her. "And you'll be Ava."

"Ava isn't real. Ava only exists on television."

"No, it's television that isn't real. *This* is real."

"It doesn't matter."

One foot scraped down against the wall, and Mags heard Ava's breath catch as gravity started to take her forward, her fingers scrabbling against the concrete. Mags saw the whole thing play out in front of her: Ava teetering over the edge, Mags watching in silent horror as Ava's body slipped out of view, a hand shot out too late, a scream. Her broken body lying on the sidewalk below, splayed out at odd angles, her heart smashed to a pulp in her chest.

But there they still were, the moment hanging by a thread in front of them, a split second when everything could change.

Mags caught Ava's arm with both hands and pulled back, sending them both tumbling across the balcony. Then Mags sat up, stunned by the violence of what she had done, by the brute force that had bubbled up from inside her. Ava had been a rag doll tossed into the toy box when playtime was over.

Mags exhaled a long breath and climbed to her feet, her veins pulsing with adrenaline. "Ava?" She peered down into her face, but Ava's eyes were closed, her breath coming in shallow bursts. "Shit." She unwrapped the blanket from around her shoulders and spread it out over Ava's limp body, then, with more effort than she'd expected, picked Ava up in her arms and carried her to the couch. She wondered briefly if she should call 911, but then Ava's eyes fluttered open.

"Your boobs are smaller than I thought they'd be," she whispered.

Mags put her hands on her hips. "A camera trick. You should know all about that." Her gaze fell uneasily on the nearest video camera, but it remained dark, lifeless. She turned back to Ava. "You know, I'm so sick of it being about a guy. If you're going to try to kill yourself, it should at least be over some kind of deep, existential dread, an inner war between dark and light or whatever. That shit is at least interesting."

"I'll keep that in mind for next time," Ava said.

Mags picked up a phone from the coffee table between them. "Is this your phone?" she asked. Ava nodded. "If there is a next time, call me and I'll remind you."

As the phone came to life, she expected to see a cute lock screen, a burst of notifications, at least a background photo. But there was nothing. Ava's phone was almost factory-preset pristine. Even her contact list was nearly empty, with fewer than a dozen names listed, most with the words *LifeStyle* after them. Mags entered her own name and number and then opened Ava's camera roll. There was only one photo in the folder: a much younger Ava and Val, along with another girl and two older men, standing on a rocky beach with the ocean behind them. They looked as though they had just gotten off a roller coaster—wind-blown, a bit apprehensive, perhaps slightly nauseous. But happy.

"I knew it wasn't really about a guy," Mags said. But Ava had fallen asleep, one arm flung over her face, her chest rising and falling softly under the blanket.

Mags turned and walked back down the hall. She had planned to slip back into her clothes and leave, stuttering back to her hotel in sky-high platform boots along unfamiliar New York streets. But the coolness of the room hit her as soon as she walked in, and she found herself drawn into the quiet and the stillness—the curtains gently moving in the breeze coming through the windows, shadows dancing across the walls, Val's muffled breath. For this one night, she'd let herself sink into the stillness, wrap herself in that feather duvet and melt into this perfect, beautiful boy. She'd let herself think about someone else's pain—Ava, sick inside because of another boy; who would someday find so many other things to be sick about, and yet still be able to go on.

Tomorrow, she would curl up her edges again. Tomorrow, she would go back to steeling herself against all the tender, delicate, beautiful things that threatened to undo her.

But tonight, she would stay.

Favourite Dave
@davIddave
Align Above are killing it at the Davenport tonight. If this is what having your bassist die of cancer does for your band, then I'm recruiting at the chemo clinic.
11:23 PM – 12 Nov 2014
28 Retweets 113 Likes

xAlign Abovex @samsgirl213 47 min
Replying to @davIddave
You sick jerk, Sam Cole was the heart of @alignabove and they will never be the same without him #RIP #wemissyousam #samsquad #fuckcancer

Favourite Dave @davIddave 23 min
Replying to @samsgirl213
Mags Kovach sure doesn't miss him, I just saw her leave with some Korean guy.

Allison Jean @icepack78 21 min
Replying to @davIddave @samsgirl213
OMG you mean that Japanese guy???? I saw that too!!!!!!!! Was that Val Hart?????

Favourite Dave @davIddave 17 min
Replying to @icepack78 @samsgirl213
THAT'S who that was. I thought he looked like a little dickless bitch now I know for sure. Guess that's how she likes em tho

xAlign Abovex @samsgirl213 14 min
Replying to @davIddave @icepack78
Your just jealous you can't even find your own dick #loveyousam #samsquad

Jessica Parker Loves Sam Cole @jessikittiy 14 min
Replying to @samsgirl213 @davl ddave @icepack78
Her husband barely in the grave, Sam Cole deserved so much better than
that skank!! #samsquad

Taylor's Ghost @tayser298 13 min
Replying to @samsgirl213 @davl ddave @icepack78
Val Hart!! He's not Japanese, he's Filipino. I saw Ava Hart there too, she
is a #fucking #goddess

Allison Jean @icepack78 10 min
Replying to @davl ddave @tayser298
OMG I love her!!!!!! I can't believe I missed her!!!!!!!!!!!!

Favourite Dave @davl ddave 8 min
Replying to @icepack78 @tayser298
I can't believe you missed her either, she had her weird pointy tits out in
everyone's face.

Taylor's Ghost @tayser298 3 min
Replying to @davl ddave @icepack78
Pig

Show additional replies, including those that may contain offensive content
SHOW

PART
ONE

Ava

March 2009

———◇———

"There's something we want to tell you guys," David Hart said, draping his arm on the back of his husband Bryce's chair.

Ava took a sip of her water, glancing suspiciously at her dads over the glass. They were at her favourite restaurant, Smalls, which served very tiny versions of regular food items. She had ordered her favourite dish, the Micro-roni and Cheese, which was served in twenty bite-sized portions on twenty ceramic spoons. She loved the precision of it all, the predetermined portions, the perfect containment. Twenty complete miniature universes of cheese and pasta. Plus, she never had to worry about making a mess.

Val and Eden, her younger brother and sister, loved Smalls too, although Val always complained that there was no way his four little hamburgers added up to one normal-sized burger, and they always forgot to leave the onions off. Her dads, however, hated Smalls—David liked things to be big, loud, and messy, and Bryce just thought the whole idea was silly. But Bryce was now nibbling

17

carefully around the edges of his Oreo-sized pizza on a stick, and David had already gulped down his first three shot glasses of Petite French Onion Soup, calling out "*Santé!*" before knocking each one back, thin threads of cheese clinging to his beard. What could it all mean? Ava had wondered. Now, as she saw the apprehension in Bryce's eyes, the hopeful optimism in David's, she knew. It was bad news.

"It's good news!" David said. "We're moving!"

All three kids groaned.

"Aww, *moving*," said Val. "What a pain in the ass."

"Yeah, a pain in the ass," Eden echoed. "A *major* pain in the ass."

Ava said nothing. David's face was a comma, not a period, and Bryce touched his wrist with his long, delicate fingers, waiting for the next clause. She knew they weren't just talking about a move to another penthouse, or to another building, or even out of the Upper West Side—somewhere Ava would have to take a car to meet her friends for gelato after school, which was currently the most important thing in her twelve-year-old life. She picked up her fourth spoon of Micro-roni and began waving it through the air like a conductor's stick, willing David to get on with it.

"Here's the best part," David said, leaning back in his chair, placing his hand on his wide Midwestern belly, the fake joviality on his face enough to tell Ava that whatever he was going to say was not, in fact, going to be the best part at all. "We're also starting a new business."

"What kind of business?" Ava asked.

A dramatic pause. Then: "A bed and breakfast," David said in a booming stage voice, puffing out his chest the way he did when he was about to put it on for them. This was Broadway David, song-and-dance David, the-show-must-go-on David. Ava hated that David. She much preferred Sunday-crossword-in-his-pajama-pants David, super-competitive-*Mario Kart*-racer David, re-enacting-*Lion King*-in-the-bathroom-with-decorative-soaps David. *Dad* David.

18

"A bed and breakfast, can you believe it?" he continued. "It's in a beautiful historic old home that used to belong to a wealthy shipbuilder. The previous owners recently passed away and it seemed like a fantastic opportunity for us."

"You're quitting acting?" Ava asked skeptically. It seemed unthinkable. David had finished a successful run as Brick in a Broadway revival of *Cat on a Hot Tin Roof* a few months earlier, and Bryce was coming off several weeks of guest-hosting a late-night talk show whose host had been at rehab for the seven-millionth time. They had been on the cover of *Celebrity* magazine last year for three weeks in a row, for god's sake—once with their family, five shiny, happy, multi-ethnic faces pressed together in front of the New York skyline, a beacon of hope and acceptance in a cold, cynical world. At least, that's what the writer's tagline had said, even though she had spent all of three minutes with Ava, Val, and Eden.

The air between her dads fizzled with tension. "Not exactly," Bryce said, folding his hands in his lap and gazing over her head, an old interviewing trick that made everyone around you think you were completely engaged with the interviewee when in fact you couldn't even look them in the eye. Ava had helped Bryce practise it before he guest-hosted on *The Cynthia Show,* so she recognized all the signs: the cock of his eyebrow, thin lips pursed, his back straight as a pin in his chair. Neither of her dads could pull anything over on her. "It's a bit of a long story."

"I've got time," Ava said, putting down the spoon and crossing her arms over her chest. Val and Eden, taking a cue from her, did the same thing. Her dads surveyed the three of them around the table, then let their gaze settle back on Ava, knowing that where she went, her brother and sister would follow.

"We didn't exactly buy the house ourselves," David said slowly. He glanced around the restaurant to see if anyone was paying attention, and then leaned in. "You kids know the LifeStyle Network, right?"

"The one with all those shitty reality shows?" Val asked.

"Valhalla!" Bryce said. "Watch your language."

"You let me say 'ass,'" Val said, peeling the top bun off his remaining burger and making a face. "I *knew* there were onions on here."

Bryce turned his head sharply to his left to glare at David over the rim of his glasses—his *how dare you* stare, which was usually reserved for the kids. "I told you 'ass' was a gateway swear," he said through clenched teeth. "Before you know it, he's going to be punctuating his sentences with f-bombs."

"What's an f-bomb?" Eden asked, concerned.

"Nothing, sweetheart," said David. Then to Val: "Yes, the one with all the . . . *crappy* reality shows." He took a breath, and Ava felt like he was sucking the air directly from her lungs. "The executives at the studio have made the wise decision to stop making crappy reality shows and start making *excellent* reality shows. Including one about a fabulous New York couple who decide to give up their acting careers and open a bed and breakfast with the help of their three adorable children. It's *Jon and Kate Plus 8* meets *The Simple Life* meets *Queer Eye for the Straight Guy*. It's a feel-good family show for the modern era!"

From a bag hanging over the back of his chair he produced a thick stack of paper, placing it on the table in front of him with a flourish. On the front page was a picture of what might have been the world's ugliest gingerbread house, pink and cream coloured, with a huge tree off to one side, a wooden swing hanging from a large branch. Across the top were letters so looping and cursive that Ava couldn't even read them. At the bottom, in regular typed letters, it said *Season One, Episode One*.

"It's *Home Is Where the Hart Is*," said David proudly, his face breaking open into a grin.

No one said anything. Val and Eden, still with their arms crossed, sat motionless at the table. Ava uncrossed her arms, picked up a spoon of Micro-roni and shoved it into her mouth, allowing her teeth to scrape loudly against the ceramic as she slowly pulled it out again, staring at her parents.

David smiled wider, circling his hands over the papers in front of him like a show model, then raised his eyebrows. *"Home Is Where the Hart Is?* Get it?" He clapped his hand across Val's back. "Get it, son?"

"I think they get it, David," Bryce said.

"I don't," said Eden, staring at Bryce, her eyes wide and confused. Ava reached out and squeezed her hand, felt the skin on her thumb where she had sucked it into a permanent clammy and wrinkled state, sucked through thumb gels and finger covers and bandages and palatal cages until the act was such a part of her it became invisible. "Papa, I don't get it."

Val leaned back in his seat, puffing a lock of hair off his forehead. "A reality show? Seriously? They're going to, what, like, film us 24/7?" He stuck his finger into a pool of ketchup congealing on his plate, then licked it off. "Even at school?"

"That's up to you all," Bryce said, folding his hands in his lap again. His body motionless, only the tiny twitch of an eye betraying his air of calmness. "You can be involved as little or as much as you want."

"Well, within reason," David said. "When you're at home, they're going to expect all access."

"All access? Like in the bathroom and stuff?"

"Like I said, within reason."

Ava let go of Eden's hand. She swallowed her Micro-roni, which she'd been chewing all this time, in a way that she hoped was menacing. "So what's the sweet potato?" she asked.

"Oh, honey," David said. "It's nothing." He reached over and patted the back of her hand.

Ava cringed and snatched her hand away. "I said, 'What's the sweet potato?'"

Her fathers hated giving bad news, almost as much as Ava hated sweet potatoes. Ever since she was little, it had been their code word for the thing they hated to tell her—usually hidden, as the sweet potato was, in something creamy or deep-fried, something delicious, although sometimes it was slipped in behind the other, less offensive vegetables. Her fathers had given away the news of the move and the show too easily. There had to be something more.

"Well, it's . . ." David tried to catch Bryce's eye, but he was staring at his plate, brows knitted together, a deep gully of worry slashed across his forehead. "You know, saying it this way makes it sound like it *is* a sweet potato, when really it's a beautiful vibrant radish, carved into a delicate rose—"

"Oh my god, Dad, just say it!" said Ava.

David leaned forward across the table, drawing them all in to him as if he were about to reveal the secret ingredient in his mother's *köttbullar.* "The bed and breakfast," he said, in a practised stage whisper, "is in Nova Scotia."

Crickets. From around the table, three questioning faces gazed at David and Bryce as if they had snakes coming out of their ears. Ava blinked slowly, feeling her eyelids scratching over sand-dry eyes. To her right, she could hear Val flicking his fingernail, making a *scritch-scritch-scritch* sound, and her arm eventually shot out to cover his hand with her own. David smiled even wider, making small, encouraging circles with his still-outstretched arms.

"Oh, for heaven's sake, David," Bryce said. "They don't know where Nova Scotia is."

David dropped his arms. "What is wrong with our school system . . ." he bellowed, his shoulders pulling back in preparation for an indignant speech. Ava rolled her eyes.

"Dad. Papa. We know where Nova Scotia is." She did, vaguely, insofar as she knew that it wasn't New York, or L.A., or even New Hampshire—was actually, possibly, could it be, in *Canada*?

"I don't," said Eden softly, and then she began to cry.

"And how is everything?" their waiter said, sidling up to the table.

"Great," said David and Bryce simultaneously. Ava looked down at her plate, which still contained twelve spoonfuls of Micro-roni. *Twelve*, she thought. *The same age I was when my life ended.* She narrowed her eyes at her dads and vowed to remember this day forever.

—◇—

Two weeks later, they re-enacted the scene at Smalls for the cameras, doing take after take as Ava's Micro-roni grew cold in front of her. "It doesn't have to be exactly the same as it was," said Antonio, the show's producer, pulling his ball cap lower over his eyes. "Just see if you can capture, like, the feeling."

Like, the feeling. Ava felt her ribcage tightening around her last bit of goodwill like a jaw. She hated him already, him and his trying-too-hard, cool-dad vibe. "This is *stupid*," she said. "I thought this was supposed to be *reality*."

"It *is* reality, honey," David said. "This happened, remember?"

"Oh, sure," she said. "Like I totally forgot about the moment you ruined my life."

David opened his mouth, then closed it again as Antonio came over to them, writing something down on a clipboard. "One more take. We want to get it from one more angle. Let's take it from Valhalla's line."

"Just Val," Val mumbled.

"Sorry, *Val*." Antonio patted him on the shoulder. "I should get that straight. Val, and Eden, right? Just Eden?" Eden nodded, giggling. He turned to Ava. "And it's Ava, right?" He pronounced it with a short *a*, like he had forgotten the second syllable of her name.

"*Eh*-vah," she said, exaggerating the long *a* sound. "Like the way any normal person would pronounce it."

He raised an eyebrow but didn't say anything. "Back to Val's line." He turned to Javier, the cameraman—"Rolling!"—then swept his finger toward Val.

"A reality show?" said Val, his voice stiff and unnatural. "Seriously? They're going to, what, like, film us 24/7? Even at school?"

"That's up to you guys," Bryce said, patting Val's hand, a monument of nurturing parental concern. "You can be involved as little or as much as you want."

"Well, within reason," David boomed, in a voice trained to reach the furthest corners of a cavernous theatre. Ava cringed. "When you're at home, they're going to expect all access."

"All access? Like in the bathroom and stuff?"

"Like I said, within reason."

Ava chewed her Micro-roni methodically. "So," she said dryly. "What's the sweet potato?"

"Cut!" called Antonio. "Ava, sweetie, we changed that line. We need you to say, 'What's the catch?'"

Ava put down her spoon. "It's not a *line*. It's what I said. I said, 'What's the sweet potato?' That's the way it happened." She glared at David, who was inspecting his beard in the front-facing camera on his phone. "That's *reality*."

"That's also something that's not going to make sense to our viewers," David said, slipping his comb into his pocket. "And we don't have any opportunity to explain it right now."

"Why not?" asked Ava. "Why can't we do one of those dumb on-camera confessional thingies?"

Antonio had explained this was going to be part of the show: short segments where they would talk directly to the camera, giving context for some of the "real life" action. For Ava's first on-camera confessional, she had tried to recite Sylvia Plath's poem "Daddy" in its entirety. When she got to the line "Every woman adores a Fascist," Antonio made Javier turn the camera off. In retrospect, she might not have been doing herself any favours.

"It's not that," said Antonio. "It's not something that will track well."

"*Track well?* What does that even mean?"

He shrugged. "It's too cutesy," he said. "It's babyish."

Ava clenched her fists, trying to contain her rage. "Right, because this whole thing is such a mature expression of artistic relevance."

"Young miss," David said, his voice low. "Watch yourself now."

"It's okay," Antonio said. "We've got to let her be herself. If she wants to be a smartass . . ."

"Smart *aleck*," Bryce said, glancing at Eden.

"Sorry, smart *aleck*."

Ava sighed, moving a strand of hair off her forehead in what she hoped was a casual, non-committal kind of way, even though inside she was seething with anger. How dare he try to erase a part of their actual real history as a family? And how dare he call her babyish? If anything was babyish, it was this whole reality *farce*. "Fine," she said. "If you think television viewers are too stupid to understand things the way they really played out, I'm happy to dumb them down for you."

"Great," said Antonio. He turned to Javier. "Let's get another take."

Ava closed her eyes. Here she was, at one of the trendiest restaurants in New York, re-enacting the moment she found out she was never going to go back to the trendiest restaurant in New York. And there was nothing she could do about it.

"So," Ava said quietly, making her voice as low and powerful as she possibly could. "What's the *catch*?"

Later that evening, Antonio took David, Val, and Eden back to the apartment in the LifeStyle van, and Ava rode home with Bryce. "We can swing by that bakery you like on Columbus and pick up some dessert, if you want," he said as the driver pulled the car away from the curb, slipping effortlessly into the line of yellow cabs, a fish in a stream.

Ava glared at him, sinking back into her seat. "Bribing me with cupcakes will get you nowhere."

"It can't hurt to try," he said. He smiled, but there was no mirth behind it. Ava felt a twinge of anxiety—Bryce was a calm lake in the centre of their chaotic family, so on the rare occasions he did get upset, the waves crashed against everyone—but she pushed it down. She wasn't going to feel sorry for him. She was the one whose *entire world* was crashing down on *her.*

Ava waited in the car while Bryce went into the bakery, then they ate the cupcakes in the backseat as their driver slid them down Broadway toward home, rain skittering across the roof like little animal feet. Ava stared out the window, her lips slick with icing, and watched a sea of umbrellas undulating beneath the bright lights of the theatre marquees, their reflections dancing in the dark pools of rainwater puddling in the gutter.

"You know," Bryce said, flicking a crumb from her cheek, "I think if you read up a little on Gin Harbour, you might discover it's not that bad of a place."

"*Not that bad?*" said Ava. "Way to sell it." She reached into the box and pulled out another cupcake, peeling the wrapper away and letting it fall.

Bryce glanced at the wrapper on the floor, his body tense as a coil, ready to spring. But he remained still. "There's a lot of interesting architecture there," he continued. "And I think you'll find that the area is quite rich in history and culture. Did you know that in 1997 it was designated as a World Heritage Site?"

"Ooh, someone's been on Wikipedia."

"Avalon." Unable to hold it in any longer, Bryce leaned forward and snatched the wrapper from the floor, folding it carefully and tucking it back into the box. "Please give this a chance. Dad and I have worked very hard to get this opportunity for you three."

"For *us?*" Ava kept her gaze focused out the window, but she could feel Bryce's eyes on her. "You did this for *us*, did you? You thought, Oh, hey, let's take our kids away from the cultural capital of the entire world, move them to Canada, and make them do reality television. That would be good for them. That will turn them into bright, upstanding human beings with something meaningful to contribute to society . . . That's the most insanely delusional thing I've ever heard."

Bryce was quiet. "I know," he said finally.

Ava turned to him, startled. "What? What do you mean, you *know*?"

His eyes flicked away quickly, but Ava could see his shoulders were slumped, his neck muscles tense under his collar. "It's horrible. Every morning I wake up and think, *What have I done?*"

"Oh my god, Papa, seriously?" Ava shifted in her seat to face him. "We don't have to do it, then! We can still get out of it! You didn't sign anything, did you? Please tell me you didn't sign anything."

Bryce folded his hands in his lap, straightened his back. "Ava, we're broke." She blinked at him. "As in, give-up-the-apartment broke. As in, Dad and I doing local dry-cleaning commercials broke."

Dread crept up Ava's limbs, numbing her skin as it travelled across her body. "How?" she asked, digging her fingernails into her palms, trying to make herself feel something.

"It just . . . It goes, Ava. The jobs go, and then the money goes." Bryce sighed. Ava had never seen him so defeated. "David hasn't worked in months. None of those talk show guest-host spots I did turned into anything. The work dried up." He patted her hand, smiling sadly. "No one wants to hire a couple of wasted old queens."

"Papa, it's . . ." She didn't know what to say.

She should have known. David, he was Minnesota-rugged, with a shiny optimism and a wholesome lilt underneath his practised New York accent. But Bryce, he was born and raised in the city. He had grown up with its subway tunnels and alleyways, its bakeries and pizza joints, Madison Avenue and Central Park, the Rose Reading Room and the Met. The same way Ava had. And leaving was breaking his heart, the same way it was breaking hers.

"You're not wasted, Papa," she said. She moved across the seat and curled herself into him, feeling his heart thumping beneath the fabric of his suit jacket. Her papa. Her papa. "It's okay. You're not wasted. You're not wasted. You're not wasted."

—◇—

That night, Ava dreamed a vivid, candy-coated dream that sent her bolting upright in bed, her whole body shaking from the cupcake sugar rush. She could feel eyes on her, eyes everywhere—in the corners of the room, on the ceiling, under the covers, under her nightgown. Eyes in the back of her throat, snaking down her esophagus, skimming up her spine and into her brain. A camera switching on, a blinking light in the shadowy corners of her mind, illuminating her darkest thoughts.

She slipped out of her room and down the same hall where she'd learned to walk as a baby, running her hands along the walls that guided her as she stumbled through the dark to her dads' room after a nightmare, tiny toes catching on the edges of the throw rugs. How many times had she taken these same steps? Thousands? How would she learn to walk through new halls, to negotiate the creaks and groans of new floorboards, the particular height of new staircases, the curves and edges of new rooms?

In the kitchen, she opened the fridge, unsure of what she wanted, just needing something solid in her hand. She stared blankly at the shelves of food, finally pulling out a box of cherries. You probably couldn't even *get* cherries in Gin Harbour. Especially not in March.

As she closed the door, she heard a breath behind her.

"Hi," Eden said, the word tripping out over her thumb.

"Hey," Ava said. She held out the box. "Want some?" Eden

pulled her thumb out of her mouth and replaced it with a cherry. "Here." Ava held out her hand as Eden finished chewing, and the pit dropped from her sister's lips into her palm. "Maybe we should get a bowl."

"We could spit them off the balcony," Eden said. "Remember, like we did last summer?"

"We got in a lot of trouble for that," Ava said with a smile. She tossed Eden's pit into the sink and wiped her hand on her pajama pants. "Come on."

They stepped out through the glass door and onto the balcony. It had always been Ava's favourite place in the apartment. She loved being so far above everything, being a part of the world yet still removed, still somehow separate. The rain had stopped but the furniture was still wet, little puddles in the seats of the chairs, water pooled in the hammock. She wiped off the patio table with the palm of her hand and placed the box of cherries on top. "Okay. Lock and load."

She and Eden popped cherries in their mouths, then once they had sucked the flesh from the pits, put their hands on the railing. Ava glanced sideways at Eden. "One . . . two . . . three!" They both leaned back and spat, and Ava watched as their cherry pits vaulted into the air in identical arcs before disappearing into the darkness below.

"I think mine won," Eden said, grabbing on to the railing. "It went a tiny bit further, didn't it?"

"I think you're right," Ava said. "Let's do another one."

"Hey, remember when we had the funeral for that sparrow?" Eden asked, pulling apart two cherries that were attached at the stems.

"Of course," said Ava. The bird had smashed into the glass doors while the family was at the dinner table. Their dads hadn't even made them finish eating before planning the funeral. "Remember the little coffin that Papa made out of that tissue box?"

29

"And then Dad sang 'Amazing Grace' so loud, and the neighbours upstairs got mad and started blasting their television."

"Even David couldn't compete with the screaming on *Dr. Phil.*"

Eden giggled, then stopped. "What did we do with it, after? The bird, I mean."

Ava thought about it for a moment, rolling her cherry pit around on her tongue. "I can't remember," she said. She felt the pit slip down her throat. What else were they going to forget?

As she glanced back into the apartment, she realized that all their stories were locked in those closets, tucked into these cupboards, circling this bathtub drain. Everything that made them who they were was here. Without that window seat they would fight over, without this fridge with the squeaky door, without the corner of the balcony where Charlotte their pet spider lived, how would they even know who they were? And how could they be the same family in a new house, in a new city, with the whole world watching them? How could they still be the Harts?

She didn't know. She just knew they had to try.

Reality Check
Reality TV Writing for Reality TV Fans

LifeStyle Announces New Reality Series,
Home Is Where the Hart Is

Lex Jackson, staff writer
03/15/09 9:00 am Filed to REVIEW

A new reality series starring *Celebrity* magazine favourites David and Bryce Hart is in development at the LifeStyle Network, *Reality Check* has confirmed.

David Hart might be familiar to viewers for playing Findley MacLean's father on the teen drama *Findley's River*, which ran on the DX for 5 seasons, beginning in 2002. Following that show's cancellation in 2007, he returned to his stage roots, most recently performing as Brick in an all-queer off-Broadway musical re-imagining of Tennessee Williams's *Cat on a Hot Tin Roof*. Bryce Hart, David's partner of 20 years, is an award-winning African-American journalist and the former host of Channel One's popular morning show, *American Wake-Up*. Ever since his dismal two-month stint at the *Late Night* desk in 2006, where he was eventually replaced by Zoe Conrad, he has been cycling through guest-hosting gigs on the late-night talk show circuit.

According to the logline, *Home Is Where the Hart Is* will be a fly-on-the-wall series "combining the fish-out-of-water motif of *The Simple Life* with the feel-good family tone of *Jon and Kate Plus 8*." In it, the Harts, along with their three adopted children—Avalon (12), Valhalla (11), and Eden (10)—leave behind their cosmopolitan life in New York City to run a bed and breakfast in the historic fishing village of Gin Harbour, Nova Scotia.

"We chose Nova Scotia because it has an undeniable exotic appeal, while still being culturally familiar enough to remain relevant to the average American viewer," says Bob Axelrod, president and CEO of LifeStyle. "We think audiences will love the picturesque landscapes, the friendly, down-to-earth people, and the heartwarming family dynamic the Harts will bring to the town." LifeStyle has confirmed an eight-episode run for the show's first season.

Home Is Where the Hart Is will premiere on Thursday, July 9 at 8 pm EST, following the season 12 premiere of *Hot Dog Vendors of Atlanta*.

Mags

January 2009

———◇———

"White Lies"

"**G**et the fuck out of here," Frankie Kovach said, as she lit the bowl of her bong and took a long inhale, regarding Mags with narrow eyes, before expelling the breath in a loud exhale that dissolved into a cough. "We're busy."

Mags leaned against the kitchen counter and stared back at her sister. Their apartment was so small that the kitchen and the living room were the same room, a small counter separating all the broken appliances and the cracking linoleum floor from the pull-out couch and the television. This charming kitchen/living room combo was, unfortunately, also Mags's bedroom. "Where am I supposed to go?" she asked. "You're sitting on my bed."

Frankie sat back on the couch, pulling a limp, tattooed arm over her shoulder and nestling into the body it was attached to. In her other hand she held the television remote, and she ran through the channels aimlessly. "Do I look like I care?"

Normally, Mags would be at the library after school, but it was closed for some literary event, and she didn't have the energy to go to any of her regular haunts—the hotel lobbies, the 24-hour laundromats, the mall food courts. "Come on, Frankie. I need to do my homework."

Frankie laughed. "Oh, honey. No you don't. You really, really don't."

The body on the couch stirred. Elias, Frankie's boyfriend. Mags could see his eyes trying to focus on her face through an alcoholic haze, and she felt a thread of revulsion unspool in her stomach. A skate punk who broke into cars to steal butts out of the ashtrays, Elias had been homeless before he met Frankie. He was basically a human cockroach—impossible to get rid of. "Is that Maggie? Why the hell is she here?"

Mags turned to him sharply. "Shut up, you piece of shit. I *live* here. I should be asking *you* why the hell *you're* here."

"Jesus, Maggie, you need to chill out. Here, have a hit." She nudged the bong forward on the coffee table with her toe.

"Hey, what are you doing? You think that weed grows on trees?" Elias reached over and tweaked Frankie's breast, then leaned in and stuck his tongue in her ear. Frankie giggled, running her hand up his thigh as she curled back into him, shutting Mags out.

Mags closed her eyes. Elias was just the latest in a long line of boys with their tongue in Frankie's ear. With their piercings and tattoos and hoodies they might as well have all been the same boy, but Mags remembered each and every one of them. She remembered Nate and Jonas and Jimmy and the one who just went by Bug, remembered their dirty fingernails and bad teeth, the smell of their shoes, their slack-jawed faces glowing pale and haggard in the light from the television. She also remembered their hungry eyes following her as she moved around the apartment, their bodies pressing up against her in the narrow hallways, their faces too close, their hands finding their way into secret places in the dark. As though they were entitled to take whatever parts of her they wanted. As though she owed it to them.

She never said anything to Frankie, though—Frankie with her too-wild laugh, who made her own body fit perfectly against each boy's body, conforming to each new shape as easily as water flowing into a glass, their words becoming her words, their thoughts her thoughts. Frankie needed a vessel to pour herself into, and when she didn't, she spilled out everywhere, flooding their apartment with her rage, her need. Mags never had any doubt whose side Frankie was on.

It had always been that way, would always *be* that way, Mags knew, no matter how much she wished it weren't true. The problem was, Mags had nowhere else to go. So she stayed trapped in their stinking, suffocating, broken life, eating her peanut butter sandwiches and sleeping in her clothes with a kitchen knife shoved in the crack between the couch cushions, staying away from the apartment as much as she could. Not letting herself think about the future, even for a second, never pulling her focus from the mere act of survival—of getting through each day, each hour, each minute—for fear of stumbling, of losing what little she had. For Mags, there were no big dreams or dark nightmares—just this endless tightrope, which she walked without looking down on one side or the other, constantly moving forward. One foot carefully in front of the other, never knowing when it would end.

"You can't have everything you want all the time," Mags's mother, Karolina, always told her when she was growing up. But to her mother, "everything" meant "anything," and "all the time" meant "ever." Karolina worked as an orderly at the hospital, and spent her days mopping up vomit and emptying bedpans, stripping soiled sheets and getting yelled at by nurses, doctors, and patients alike. She had grown deathly afraid of disease and wore a paper mask over her face everywhere she went, even to the grocery store or to Mags and Frankie's school, which mortified the girls. When Karolina got home from work, she wouldn't let her daughters touch her until she had showered with her disinfectant soap, coated her entire body in hand sanitizer, and put on clean clothes. Mags supposed it was ironic that Karolina ended up slipping and falling in that shower, knocking herself out and drowning in the water that had pooled in the basin that never seemed to drain properly.

Now, as she sat on the floor of the bathroom—her math textbook open in front of her, listening to Elias and Frankie laughing in the next room while a heavy bass beat shook the floor—Mags thought about her mother's words. When Karolina died three years ago, it was up to Frankie, then just barely eighteen, to make sure that Mags got everything she needed, and nothing she wanted. Frankie had managed to get herself on disability, but that barely covered the rent, and the government cheques that came for Mags once a month evaporated in a literal cloud of smoke. At first, Mags had walked dogs, shovelled snow, raked leaves, but her money disappeared from her piggy bank while she slept, so after a while she didn't even bother. For Mags's thirteenth birthday, the first one after she had lost her mother, Frankie gave her a box of Froot Loops. She took it out on the fire escape and dug the cereal out of the box with her hands, eating it by the fistful while she watched the buses careening down Barrington Street, splashing pedestrians with the water that was perpetually gathered in the gutter, regardless of how long ago it had rained. It was the first time she had eaten cereal that wasn't oatmeal, and it was the best thing she had ever tasted. It hadn't occurred to her, then, that cereal wasn't a normal birthday present, that she might have asked for more.

None of this made Mags sad—it just made her angry. But anger wasn't an emotion Mags had the luxury to feel. So she swallowed it down, feeling it bubbling under the surface, trying to escape. It woke her in the middle of the night, her feet pressed rigidly into the arm of the couch, back sweaty against the scratchy upholstery, ragged breath squeezing through her lungs. But in the morning, she would feel her aching jaw, her throbbing head, and know she had won, the pain her prize for keeping the anger locked in, her prize for surviving.

From the next room, the bass beat transitioned into a steady, rhythmic banging that Mags realized was the couch against the wall. She grabbed a bath towel and pulled it down over her head, trying to block out the sound. Against her leg, she felt her phone buzz. A text from Sam.

Wat u get for 4?

Mags consulted her sheet, then typed $N = 5$.

No. How

$N + 1/N = 78/15$. *Multiply all values by N, form quadratic equation, solve.*

Ughhhhhhhhhhhhhh, Sam replied. Mags smiled, the sex marathon in the living room temporarily forgotten. Being with Sam had given her a tiny respite, a moment of ease in her world of constant vigilance. They had only been dating for two months, but in that time she had allowed herself to take a breath, to let her guard down, to raise her eyes from the tightrope, if only for a second.

Should have studied instead of playing with ur dumb boys

She waited until Sam's :-| appeared on the screen. Sam had met Paul and Zac, the guitarist and drummer of Nietzsche's Watering Can, at rock camp the previous summer, and when their bassist quit a month ago, they'd asked Sam to step in. Paul and Zac were both twelfth-graders from Halifax West who were obsessed with *Star Trek* and *World of Warcraft*. In 95 per cent of the possible universes out there, Paul and Zac were not even a little bit cool. Sam resided firmly in one of the other 5 per cent, and Mags knew he would do anything to be a permanent part of the band. Including let her beat him at math.

It was cool tho, he added. *We wrote a new song. It's in Klingon.*

Super cool, Mags typed back, adding a :-/. Mags liked Nietzsche's Watering Can—she did. She thought they were as solid as any of the bands she'd seen in town, and if they had a real singer rather than Paul and Zac just trading off tentative verses between guitar solos, they could actually play some gigs. That's if they stopped writing songs in Klingon. That was probably the clincher.

How dare u, Sam responded. *I'm going to sing it to u later. Over and over and over.*

Suddenly the bathroom door opened, hitting the back of Mags's head. "Ow! Watch out," she said, turning around.

"Christ, Maggie." Elias leaned against the doorframe. "What are you doing down there? I gotta take a piss."

Mags tried to shut the door, but Elias held it open with his toe.

"Do you mind? I'm trying to do my homework."

Elias laughed. "In the bathroom?"

"I don't have a room, remember? You and Frankie are on my bed."

"Oh yeah." Elias gave a half-smile, exposing a mouth full of chipped grey teeth. She could feel his eyes on her, as tangibly as if he were actually touching her with his grimy little hands. "You should come out and join us."

"No thanks. I think I'll pass." Mags grabbed her books and her phone and stood up as slowly and calmly as possible. No sudden movements, no loud noises, no aggressive comebacks, nothing to draw attention. She had been here before, knew every possible outcome of this encounter like she knew her own skin. "I'll wait in the hall."

"Hey, wait." Elias blocked the door. "Your sister's right, you know. You need to relax." He reached out and touched her cheek with one finger, drawing it down over her jawline and onto her neck.

She cringed at his touch but didn't move. "The bathroom's all yours, okay?" She fixed her gaze past his head into the hallway, her destination. Then she felt his finger drop down to her clavicle, and she instinctively flinched, her shoulder jerking upward, shrugging him off. Big mistake. She quickly tried to move around him, but he caught her by the waist.

"Come on, now," Elias hissed into her ear, reaching his hand up over the front of her shirt and cupping a breast. "Don't pretend you didn't like it."

With one swift movement, Mags brought her knee up between Elias's legs. He made a sound like a balloon slowly deflating, his eyes bulging comically, his legs clamping together, pinning her knee in place.

"You bitch," he breathed, grabbing her leg and pulling her toward him. Mags clung to the sink behind her as he pulled, and when she finally wrenched her foot free, she drove it into his crotch. This time he slumped to the ground, his face turning a pale shade of green.

"What is going on here?" Frankie said, pushing Mags aside as she flew into the bathroom and crouched down beside Elias. "Maggie, what did you do?"

"What did *I* do? *He* grabbed me. Your disgusting boyfriend tried to feel me up!"

"I didn't do nothing," Elias moaned. "*She* grabbed *me*. When I told her to get off me, she kicked me in the nuts."

"He's lying!"

"*She's* lying! Look at her!" Elias motioned up and down with his hand. "She's like a nympho or something. She couldn't keep her hands off me."

"You wish, you disgusting piece of trash." Mags turned to her sister, who was still on the floor, her arm around Elias's shoulders "Frankie, come on. You know he's lying, right?" But as she spoke she saw the fear flicker in her sister's eyes. It had been there even before she stepped into the bathroom. It had probably been there since the day she was born.

Frankie jumped to her feet. "You pathetic bitch!" She began pummelling Mags with a shower of frenzied fist falls that sent Mags stumbling backward through the bathroom door.

Mags held her arms up in front of her face to ward off the blows, her anger giving way to disbelief. "You're going to believe him over your own sister?"

But Frankie kept coming at her, a blur of red face and red hair, the dark maw of her mouth, the milky whites of her eyes. "I always knew you were a little skank who just takes everything she wants!"

That's when Mags felt something come undone inside her, the dam she had been holding up since her mother died, every muscle in her body engaged in keeping her anger from flooding the world. Why that was the moment that pushed her over the edge, she couldn't say. But she felt it, so viscerally, a steaming geyser erupting from deep within her gut and blasting out of every pore. "You're the pathetic one!" she yelled, pushing Frankie back through the bathroom door to tumble over Elias, who was still lying on the floor. "If I wanted to date a slimy little weasel-faced drug-dealing subhuman, I could go down behind the Dairy Queen on Spring Garden and find my own!"

For a split second, Mags saw Frankie falter. But then her face hardened once more. "Get out!" Frankie screamed. "I never want to see your face again, you fucking whore."

Mags grabbed her backpack and ran out of the apartment and into the elevator without looking back. As the doors closed, she slumped to the floor. She couldn't say how long she sat there, head bowed over her backpack, before getting to her feet and pressing the button for the lobby. She had to go down; that much she knew. Beyond that, though, she was lost.

At least it wasn't raining anymore. But the rain-slicked streets had frozen as night fell, the sidewalks coated in a sparkling film of ice that could take your feet out from under you and the breath from your lungs. Mags made her way carefully down Barrington

Street, which was deserted except for a small, middle-aged man pulling a suitcase behind him, likely heading for the bus station. Mags thought briefly about following him until she remembered the city had taken out all the benches at the station, hoping to stop people from camping out there.

She had two dollars in her wallet and two minutes left on her cell phone.

Mags had never asked for help before. She had always prided herself on being able to make it on her own. But now, it seemed too overwhelming, too impossible.

Two dollars and two minutes. Enough for bus fare and a phone call. And for the first time ever, she knew someone who might actually pick up.

"Don't worry, my parents are never home," Sam said as he ushered her through the door. His bass was still strapped around his neck, hanging limply in front of him as he led her through the cavernous halls of his empty house. "When they are, they never come down here."

It was her first time at the Coles' house. Mags had never even been in this neighbourhood before, with its wrought iron and brick, and its wide, manicured lawns that swept down to the Northwest Arm. She had known Sam was well off, but she hadn't really registered that he was *rich*. He seemed embarrassed about it more than anything, so she kept her questions to herself. What would she have said, anyway—*hey, you're rich, why didn't you tell me?* Rich people never thought about money. The more you had, the less important it seemed to become.

As he led her down to the basement, Mags immediately started to relax. It was clearly Sam's space—bare walls, clothes and papers littering the floor, an old wooden dining room chair in one corner with a quilt draped over it, his bass stand next to it.

"Is there a bed under there?" she asked, pointing to a pile of books and sheet music in a corner.

He swept the sheet music onto the floor. "Sorry. I guess I should have cleaned up a little." He sat down on the spot he had just cleared, and Mags sat next to him. Other than the chair and the bed there was no furniture, but it felt homey, real. It felt like Sam. Out of the detritus he fished out a speaker, which he propped up on the bass stand. "Can I play you this song I found today?" he asked. "It made me think of you. Like, the singer, I mean. She reminds me of you."

Mags nodded, and Sam began fiddling with an iPod he produced from under a mountain of clothes. After a moment the song began to play, the singer's voice filling the room. "I like it," she murmured. "It's really good."

"Wylie Daniels. She used to be the singer for Open Curtain. Remember them?"

"I think so." Mags noticed Sam's jeans had a hole at the knee and she stuck her finger through, moving it in a circle over his kneecap as the song kept playing.

He scraped a nail lightly against one of the bass strings, and it sounded like the noise an insect would make. "I'm thinking of naming my bass."

"Like a girl's name?"

He shrugged. "I guess. Jaco Pastorius called his bass the Bass of Doom."

"That's pretty badass," she said, her finger spelling out the words on Sam's knee as she spoke them. P-R-E-T-T-Y B-A-D-A-S-S.

"Yeah. I guess you can't really top that." He plucked a string. "Did you know that Jaco Pastorius was killed by a security guard at a club when he was only thirty-five?"

"You've told me about a million times."

It was actually the first thing he had ever said to her, sitting on the steps of their high school one afternoon, him smoking, her drawing on her backpack with a Sharpie, kittens with daggers in their teeth, skulls with flower crowns. He was an odd, skinny kid—T-shirt sinking into his concave chest, a little ratty moustache struggling on his upper lip, but with a subtle swagger in the stretch of his legs as he slid over to her. And when his shoulder brushed against hers she felt a fizz of heat rising in her belly. *Did you know that Jaco Pastorius was killed by a security guard at a club when he was only thirty-five?* She took his cigarette from him with a shaking hand. *I bet you say that to all the girls.*

"That fucking guy," Sam said now. "Imagine what he could have done if he had lived another fifty years."

"Maybe nothing," said Mags. N-O-T-H-I-N-G.

"I don't know whether that's a silver lining or super depressing."

"Let's say silver lining," she said. "That way we can believe we're not missing out on anything."

"I'm sorry about your sister," Sam said. He turned to her, and his eyes were so blue she was momentarily speechless. Had they always been that blue? Had she just never noticed before?

"Yeah," she said finally, breaking his gaze. "I mean, it's okay." They both knew that it really wasn't.

"Okay." He paused. "It's weird that you're here. But I'm glad you are."

Mags didn't reply, but her fingers traced out I L-O-V-E Y-O-U. Sam's head twitched, and she wondered if he had been able to feel her words on his kneecap. "So, let's hear the Klingon song," she said, pulling her finger back, flustered.

Sam shook his head. "No. It's bad." He picked up the iPod again. "It's so depressing. This whole thing is full of half-finished tracks."

"So? Finish them."

"But writing is *hard.*" He stuck his lip out in a mock pout. "The music is okay, it's just the stupid lyrics. You know, hence the Klingon. And the grocery list." One of their songs was literally a grocery list they had found on the floor of Zac's garage. "Apples, bananas, skim milk, popsicles," Paul would mumble tunelessly through some extensive feedback. "Toilet paper, chicken wings, fabric softener."

"No song should have the word *toilet paper* in it." Mags lay back on the bed, letting herself sink into Sam's clothes. "You can't sing any old words over the music and have it be good. You might as well just sing gibberish at that point."

"Lots of hit songs are gibberish. What about, like, 'MMMBop'?"

"Your standard for musical integrity should not be *Hanson*." She breathed in deeply, the smell of Sam's laundry detergent causing a twisting in her gut that she couldn't name. It was as if she missed him even though he was sitting right next to her. "Also, you should get more current references. Have you even listened to any music made in this decade?"

"Nope. I am confounded by you kids and your crazy rock and roll." He stood up. "Are you hungry? I'm hungry. I'll go get us some food."

"Don't change the subject," Mags called after him, but he had disappeared up the stairs. As she watched him go, she felt panic rising up in her chest again. Being with Sam, she had felt like a normal kid, and this was just a normal night, hanging out in her boyfriend's basement. Instead of, well, what it really was.

To keep the terrible thoughts out of her head, she picked up Sam's iPod and pressed play on one of Nietzsche's Watering Can's unfinished tracks. Immediately the music washed over her, and she began to relax, the panic breaking up and drifting away like lake ice in spring. She listened to the first track all the way through, then started it again. "My love is with you wherever you go," she sang softly under her breath. "But my weakened voice can't tell you so." She frowned, restarting the song. "My love is with you wherever you go, but my broken voice can't tell you so." She pulled a notepad out of her backpack and began to write.

By the time Sam came back downstairs, arms laden with ham and cheese sandwiches and blueberry yogurts, Mags had filled

44

three pages. She tucked the notebook back into her bag as he spread the food out on the floor. "You really need to get some furniture in here," she said, sliding off the bed to sit next to him.

"That would ruin the ambiance." He handed her a sandwich. "Don't worry, when we get our own place I promise there will be chairs."

"When we get our own place?" Mags felt that twisting in her gut again. "Like an apartment?"

"Yes, like an apartment. Unless you thought we were going to live in my parents' basement forever."

"No, I guess not forever." They chewed their sandwiches in silence, the word hanging in the air between them.

One foot in front of the other, Mags thought. *Keep focus. Don't look forward.*

But it was too late. She was already looking ahead.

Bandwidth Forum
Songwriting Chat
All users can post to this forum on songwriting topics

Moderators: bandwidthmod1, johnnysocks07, purple_rain

52 replies Page 1 of 4 >

SONGWRITING ADVICE
by MagsK Mon Jan 17, 2009 4:15 pm

I'm just starting out with my songwriting
and I was wondering if anyone had any tips?

user: MagsK
posts: 1
joined: 01/17/09 4:11 pm
location: Halifax, NS

Re: SONGWRITING ADVICE
by Phildaddy Mon Jan 17, 2009, 4:17 pm

I've got a tip for you, honey. It's in my pants.
***
*This life is like a swimming pool. You dive in the
water, but you can't see how deep it is.*
– Dennis Rodman

user: Phildaddy
posts: 117
joined: 03/30/07 6:30 am
location: Philadelphia, PA

Re: Re: SONGWRITING ADVICE
by guitarmike112 Mon Jan 17, 2009 4:19 pm

"Phildaddy wrote:
I've got a tip for you. It's in my pants."

user: guitarmike112
posts: 967
joined: 08/18/07 1:14 pm
location: San Diego, CA

Dude. Come on. She's just starting out. You don't want to give her the
wrong impression. Most tips are way bigger than yours.

Halston Market Research Group
Focus Group Discussion Transcript and Analysis – *Home Is Where the Hart Is* Pilot
LifeStyle Network, 2009

Total participant time required: 43 minutes + 20 minutes
Total number of participants: 6
Moderator: Jensen Lee

SECTION FOUR: CHARACTERS

Moderator: Okay, let's talk about some of the characters on the show. Which one of the Harts did you find most relatable?

A: I liked the little one . . .

C: Oh, me too . . . what's her name . . .

Moderator: Eden.

A: Right. What's with those names, anyway? You should change them.

D: Those are their real names, they can't change them. These are real people we're talking about.

A: Do you live under a rock? Everyone knows there's nothing real about reality TV.

Moderator: Does anyone else want to add any thoughts on how they felt about the Harts as characters?

B: I liked the Chinese kid. Val. He's cute.

C: Ava seemed a bit standoffish. Kind of cold. It was almost like she was bored by everything.

D: Yeah, I agree. Like in the scene where they're leaving their apartment for the last time. They're saying goodbye to everything they've ever known, and Ava looks like she wants to get it over with.

C: Yeah, like she just doesn't care about anything. No emotion at all. I mean, come on, even the dad was crying.

D: She's spoiled, that's what it is. A prissy little princess.

A: Thinks she's too good for TV. They should recast her. Find someone else to play her part.

D: Oh my god, seriously? What is it about *reality* you don't understand?

Ava

June 2009

———◇———

HIWTHI S01E02:
Follow Your Hart

T he town of Gin Harbour rose out of the fog like the back-
drop of a horror movie, the peaked roofs of the tall wooden
houses floating on a hazy cushion of white. Ava had never seen
anything like it. In her world, the *real, actual* world, the houses
were all below the clouds.

"I don't like it here," Eden whispered, leaning forward from
the third-row seat in the van as they rolled slowly through the
town in eerie silence.

"I don't like it either, Edie," Ava whispered back. "It feels like
a ghost town."

"There's people all over the place," Antonio said, catching
Ava's eye in the rear-view mirror. Since Bryce had stayed behind
in New York for a few days and David was already at the B&B,
Antonio and Javier had been the ones to pick the Hart kids up at
the airport. And even though Ava had known about this plan in
advance, she still couldn't hide her disappointment at seeing their
faces when she stepped off the plane.

"See?" he said, pointing at an elderly couple walking arm in arm up a hill that was so steep it had steps built into the sidewalk. It was the third elderly couple they had seen, hair as white and wispy as the fog they were driving through. Ava was beginning to think there wasn't a single person in Gin Harbour under the age of ninety-four.

Ava pulled her feet up under her on the seat and glared at Antonio. "I mean, like, a literal *ghost town*. Like the town is a literal ghost."

"Whoa, a literal ghost?" Antonio said. "Like a ghost that doesn't understand figures of speech?"

"You're not even funny in any way," she said.

"A town can't be a ghost, can it?" Eden asked, her voice trembling. "How can a town be a ghost if a town doesn't have a soul?"

"Oh my god you guys, it's just fog," Val said dully, still facing out the window, his dark hair falling over his forehead and into his eyes, hiding what Ava knew was an incredibly well-practised eye roll. "Don't act like you've never seen fog before."

"This isn't fog," Ava said, kicking him. "It's the cold, creeping breath of all the people who have died here from complete boredom."

Antonio had agreed to no filming during the drive, but a few minutes before they arrived at the house, Javier switched on his camera. Ava sighed. She had been practising her reaction the entire way in from the airport, vacillating between wanting to give an over-the-top, obviously fake performance of excitement and enthusiasm, and giving nothing at all. She had decided on nothing at all.

Hart's Desire, or Mariner's Inn, as it had previously been known, sat on top of a steep hill at the end of a road called Cherry Tree Lane. As the van chugged up the incline, Ava gazed at the trees and wondered if any of them were actual cherry trees—not that she knew what a cherry tree looked like. When she glanced back down the road, she realized the fog, which had settled low into the harbour, was now below them, and she could see the roofs of the houses peeking out of the mist all the way down to what she imagined must be the edge of the ocean, although she had yet to lay eyes on it. She wondered if it was like this all the time, if the locals went on faith that the water was really there.

When the house finally revealed itself through the trees, Ava shuddered with revulsion. It was even more disgustingly quaint than in the photos she'd seen, with its ghost-story dormer windows, the wrought-iron gate with ornate points in the shape of tridents, the sagging porch with peeling pink and cream paint, the scalloped entranceway with the words *Hart's Desire* etched in gold on the fanlight window above the transom. The inside was probably one giant doily. To most people, the house was surely a dream, gorgeous and historical and full of charm and mystery. But to Ava it was grotesque, the perfect setting for the future true-crime documentary that her life was surely about to become.

As the van pulled in front of the house, David appeared on the porch. He had already become more country—his beard a little scruffier, his hair unkempt, his cheeks rounder. He was even wearing a fisherman's sweater. He spread his arms wide. "Welcome home!" he called as they peered out the windows, the van crawling to a halt.

"Home," Ava said, sliding back in her seat. "What do you know, it *is* where the Hart is."

She had meant it to sound sarcastic, but Antonio grinned, and she immediately wished she could take it back.

"Hey," he said. "That's really good. With some music and editing, we could use that for the promo. I'm going to back down the driveway so we can get it again."

Ava bit her lip so hard she could taste blood. She thought about Javier, standing with the camera in the hallway outside of their apartment as they left it forever, telling them to *just go back in and come out one more time*—and then one more time, and one more time, every take like a finger in the wound. "We can't have one moment to ourselves, can we? Not one moment."

"It won't take long," Antonio said.

"I'm not saying it again," she said. "Use what you have or don't. I don't care."

Antonio threw the van into reverse, unfazed. "Fine, we'll get Eden to say it," he said as they backed down the driveway. "Our focus group really responded to her in the pilot."

"What's a focus group?" Eden whispered, the words bumping out of her mouth around the knotted hill of her thumb.

"It's a group of people who think they actually know what they're talking about." Ava stared out the window, trying to ignore the low hum crescendoing in her brain. "Don't say it, Edie."

"Eden," Antonio said, parking the van at the bottom of the driveway before turning around in his seat. "This is really important, okay? Remember what your dads said about saying your lines?"

"They're not *lines!*" Ava yanked Eden's thumb out of her mouth. "Edie, stop it!"

"Why am I in trouble? I didn't even do anything."

"Tell her to say the line, Ava," Val said. "I just want to get out of this goddamn van."

"Then get out!" Ava said. "You know what? I'll get out too." She turned to Antonio. "Make her say whatever you want. I don't care." She opened the van door and grabbed her backpack. She stopped before closing the door, glaring at Val.

"Ugh, fine," said Val, climbing over the seat.

As she closed the door, she heard Antonio call "Rolling." Their backpacks slung over their shoulders, Ava and Val trudged up the driveway, past the cherry trees that were maybe not cherry trees, up to the big ugly gingerbread house that was apparently their new home.

The first thing Ava learned about the house was that they weren't allowed to leave it. "At least not for the first few days, until the pilot airs," Antonio said as they sat around the kitchen table that first night, rain pounding against the windows. They had apparently arrived in Gin Harbour on the cusp of tourist season, when the souvenir stores were still shuttered and the local diner was the only restaurant open during the week. Soon, Antonio told them, the harbour would start to fill with superyachts owned by reclusive American millionaires, and the waterfront would be overrun with retirees with fold-out maps and sensible shoes hunting for cheap lobster dinners. Once the tourist season hit, they would be a drop in the ocean. But for now, the town was closed up tight, its solitude a curtain around it, and anyone new would stand out— especially the Harts. "We want to keep people from getting too curious. We don't want people leaking spoilers."

"As long as this *roof* doesn't leak, we'll be fine," David said, pulling Eden up on his lap.

"Are these the kinds of jokes we all have to make now?" Ava asked. "Like, now that we're all small-town we can't even be funny?"

"If you think you're going to get a rise out of me today, you are dead wrong, child." He rested his chin on Eden's head. "I mean, look at this place. It's beautiful. It's just what we needed. Some space, some breathing room. I feel more relaxed already." He took in a deep breath. "Smell that salt air."

"All I can smell is hundreds of strangers' BO all mixed together," Val said.

"That's not BO. That is the stench of desperation."

David tipped his head back, gazing skyward with a mock pleading expression. "Lord, how did I, your devoted and compassionate son, raise such nasty, smart-mouthed children?" Eden made a sound of protest, and he cupped his hand over her mouth. "Smart. Mouthed. Children."

"Those smart-mouthed children are going to make this show a hit," Antonio said.

For the next few days, while they were trapped in the house, Ava passed the time reading old waterlogged paperbacks she found in the attic, and playing board games with Val and Eden— Battleship, Clue, Chinese checkers, old games that the previous owners had set out for the guests. But mostly she sat in the window seat in the front room, staring down Cherry Tree Lane toward the harbour, wondering what was out there. What were Gin Harbour girls like? What did they wear, what did they do for fun? Did they just spend all their time on boats? Surely there was at least one girl in town who liked art, or music. One girl who had always felt out of place, who wished she could run off to the big city. One girl who had dreams of escaping the fog.

One afternoon, Ava lay on her stomach on Val's bed, reading about Gin Harbour on her laptop while he unpacked all his *Star Wars* Lego. She had Wikipedia open in one tab, and the Barnes and Noble website open in another—she had seen pictures of the Gin Harbour library and she was pretty sure they didn't even have a poetry section, that it was all books about knitting or nautical terms. There wasn't even a *café*.

"It says here there are two thousand people in Gin Harbour. That's barely more than our *old school*."

"How does a town even function with only two thousand people?" Val asked. "Is that even enough people to do every job?"

"Well, considering at least half of those people are probably fishermen, I'm guessing not."

Val took an X-Acto knife to the top of a new box, holding his hair out of his face with the back of his hand so he could see. "Maybe everyone does double duty," he said, pulling the flaps back.

"Like the vet clinic is also the hospital. Or the garbage collector is also the police chief."

"Great," said Ava, scrolling past picture after picture of boats in the harbour. "We'll figure out when garbage day is and go rob a bank. Oh my god." She rolled over onto her back and threw her arm over her face. "Their gallery is full of *folk art*."

"What's folk art?" asked Eden, appearing in the doorway.

"Beat it," Val said. He tossed a wad of rolled-up packing tape at her, but it landed just short.

Eden kicked it back. "No," she said. "I want to know what you guys are talking about."

With one arm still across her eyes, Ava motioned to Eden. "Come here, Eedle-Beetle," she said. "I'll tell you a harrowing story about art made by peasants."

"Like the bird?" Eden climbed onto the bed and curled up next to Ava, sticking her thumb in her mouth.

"No, not like the bird. Like a poor person."

Val shook his head. "You're such an elitist."

"And you're a hypocrite." Ava propped herself up, bringing Eden with her. "Edie, take that out of your mouth. You know what Dr. Rosen said." Eden popped it out sheepishly and tucked her hand under her arm, wiping off her saliva.

Val heaved the box onto its side and an avalanche of Lego tumbled to the floor. "You know, I can't wait for the world to find out what a snob you are," he said as the last brick landed on the pile.

"You're just jealous because you know that television viewers are going to like me better."

Eden lifted her head. "Do you think television viewers are going to like me?" she asked.

"Keep saying things like that and they will for sure. You'll be the star of the show and Val will be stuck sitting in his room all day brushing his hair and writing sad songs about fishermen's daughters while you travel the world visiting with your adoring public."

"Now who's the hypocrite?" asked Val. "What happened to your whole 'I would rather sleep in a bathtub full of ferrets than be some airheaded attention whore.'"

Eden's thumb hovered just outside her mouth. "I don't want to be an attention whore," she said. "That sounds bad."

"It is bad," Ava said. "But it doesn't have to be that way. This could be fun, like a game. Every day is a game of pretending."

Eden stared at her, eyes wide. "What are we pretending to be?" she asked.

"Reality television stars," Ava said.

Later that night, Ava lay in her new bed under a musty antique quilt that David promised they would replace as soon as they could go into town and thought about the show. Even to her, it seemed doomed to fail, with its hokey name and cheesy premise that so obviously pandered to the lowest common denominator, the very bottom of the barrel of American taste. She wondered if Antonio felt the same way. Was this part of his life's plan? Had he ever had any kind of artistic integrity? Or had he always been a pathetic sellout? Either way, he clearly had no idea what he was doing.

"Ava?"

She turned to find Eden standing in the doorway. "What's the matter?" she asked, sitting up and flicking on the light.

"I know you said we were only pretending." She paused, her thumb twitching beside her. "But I'm scared. What if everyone hates me?"

Ava reached an arm out. "Come here." Eden padded across the room and climbed onto the bed. From somewhere deep within the bones of the house, there was a repetitive clanging that quickly sped up to a vibration before fading away, leaving nothing but a hollow, horrifying silence.

"What was that?" Eden asked.

"Just the house. Old houses make noise." Even though it was June, the house was cold, and she adjusted the quilt over her feet. "New houses too, probably. In New York there was so much other noise we didn't hear them."

"Remember the guy with the stereo on his bike who rode by every morning singing 'I Wanna Dance With Somebody'?"

"Of course. That's how I knew it was time to leave for school." Ava tilted her head back and started singing the chorus. Eden joined in at the end, belting out "with somebody who loves me!" When they stopped, the room echoed with the absence of their voices. Outside, a dog howled.

"I miss New York," Eden whispered.

"Me too, Edie."

Eden's eyes were wide in the dark. "Tell me the California story."

Ava smiled. "Okay. But then you have to go to bed." She pulled Eden into her, and her sister lay her head on Ava's shoulder. "You probably don't remember this, but when we were very little, we lived in a rusty orange van on the side of the highway in California. All the people who lived in the town knew us as 'the kids in the van,' and in the mornings they would bring us things on their way to town."

"What kind of things?" Eden asked, the way she always did.

"Things like mittens, or leftover Easter candy, or flowers they'd picked at the side of the road. Sometimes during the day we'd walk along the edge of the highway and collect the garbage that people threw out of their car windows. The people driving by would throw their garbage right at us, which actually made it easier. We filled bags of garbage and took them to the gas station at the turn-off, where the man who pumped the gas would give us sandwiches in exchange for picking up the garbage. The sandwiches were good but usually smelled like gas, like the man's hands."

"Why didn't we stay there?"

"The mayor thought it was bad for the town to have kids living in a van by the side of the road, and one night they towed the van over to the next town while we were all asleep. But that town's mayor didn't want us either, so he towed us to the next town. This went on for months, with all the mayors towing us to the next town in the middle of the night, all the way across the country, until one morning we woke up and we were in New York City, in front of Dad and Papa's apartment.

"And what did Dad and Papa do?" Eden whispered.

"They came outside and Dad said, 'It's just like in my dream,' and Papa said, 'These children belong to us now, these are our children.'"

"Avalon and Valhalla and Eden," Eden said, closing her eyes. "Our little piece of paradise. No matter where we are."

"No matter where we are." Ava felt Eden's body relax into sleep against her. She closed her eyes, but she knew sleep was not going to come, so she lay there listening to the house creak and groan until the sun rose in the east to once again lose its battle with the fog.

The next day, Antonio set up the camera in Ava's room for her first Gin Harbour confessional. She sat cross-legged on her bed, the camera in front of her on a tripod, while Antonio positioned himself off to the side on a folding chair, prompting her, although all his questions would be cut out in post-production. The whole thing made Ava cringe—the deception of her being alone, of divulging her deepest secrets. She couldn't even talk to her old friends anymore. What made him think she was going to talk to all of America?

Antonio sat with legs spread wide in the chair. "What do you like about Gin Harbour?" he asked, leaning forward, hands clasped between his knees, a priest preparing to absolve her.

"My favourite thing about Gin Harbour is all the vampires," Ava said, staring directly into the camera. "And, like, how they're not trying to be all attractive like those fake *Twilight* vampires, you know? They're not ashamed of their bloody fangs and pale skin and having to bite people and stuff. They don't want to be normal. They just, like, own it."

"Okay, Ava," Antonio said, sighing as he leaned back. "Have you made any friends yet?"

"I don't really know *how* to make friends with a vampire. I mean, what movies do vampires even watch, you know? Do they like horror films? Or is that offensive? What if you're a vampire and everyone thinks you want to watch horror movies, when in reality you want to watch, like, *High School Musical* or something?" Ava cupped her hand to her mouth. "I'm actually thinking about becoming a vampire," she said in a loud whisper.

Antonio reached over and switched the camera off. He studied her face. "Is this really what you want to say, Ava?" he asked. "Is this really what you want the world to think you are?"

"I don't care," she said, pulling on a loose thread in her quilt. "Besides, how do you think I'm going to make friends anyway? I'm not even allowed to leave the house."

"You know, we can replace you," Antonio said as he began dismantling the camera. "We could have your character go off to tend to a sick aunt or something. Or maybe boarding school. Then we could hire someone more camera-friendly to play you."

She raised an eyebrow at him. "Seriously? Is that an option? Because sign me up."

"Sorry, kiddo. For some reason, you're the only actress the network wants in the role."

"The role. Ha." The thread grew longer as she pulled, and she imagined the entire quilt unravelling beneath her, along with the bed, the floorboards, the house. Maybe if she pulled on it long enough, there would be nothing left of the world but a pile of thread.

"Sure, it's a role. You're an actress, and you're playing the part of Avalon Hart." He zipped up the camera bag and slung it over his shoulder, grabbing the tripod in his other hand. "Ava, I've been doing this a long time. Trust me when I say, if you think about it that way, things are going to be a lot easier for you."

"What, that I'm an actress named Avalon Hart playing the role of Avalon Hart?"

"It's the part you were born to play." He gave her a mock salute and left the room.

The thread ripped off in her hand.

Finally, on day five, the sun came out. "Oh, you miraculous wonder!" Ava yelled from her bed. "You big, beautiful ball of plasma! Bestow your light and heat upon us!" She raced down the stairs, sliding to a halt in front of the door, where David stood, drinking a cup of coffee.

"Hello, young miss," he said, smiling at her. "And where do you think you are going?"

"Outside," Ava said, hoping that if she said it confidently enough he'd just let her go.

No such luck. "You most certainly are not."

Ava groaned loudly. "I can't even go on the deck?" She was aware of how whiny her voice sounded, but she didn't care. "I'm dying of vitamin D deficiency!"

David shrugged and took another sip of his coffee. "There's a screened-in porch off the kitchen, you'll probably get some sun there."

"This is torture!" David patted her on the shoulder but didn't say anything. "Seriously, I'm pretty sure this violates the Geneva Convention!" She could see David's head shaking as he retreated into the dining room. "I hope this is getting filmed! I hope the world finds out that you're keeping your children prisoner!"

For the next hour Ava paced around the house like a caged lion, restless and annoyed. She went into the porch and pressed her face against the screen, trying to breathe in the fresh air, feeling the mesh digging into her skin. She felt so out of place here. She was sure she would never get used to the noises, the odd angles of the hallways, the slope of the walls. Every night she dreamed of their old apartment, and would wake with a start, wondering where she was, her body heavy with the ache of *missing*—her home, her city, her friends, her life. She would murder someone for one more minute in Central Park. She would die for a strawberry basil gelato.

Behind her, a local girl named Lynn or Lindsay or Lucy was loading dishes into the industrial-sized dishwasher, leaving three plates and two forks for Bryce to add in later—anything B&B-related done onscreen was also done off-screen by someone who actually knew how to do it. And even though they hadn't started officially filming, Javier was walking around trying to capture some candid moments. Ava had become adept at avoiding him, hiding in all the shadowy corners of the B&B, making sure there wasn't any footage of her. She knew she couldn't hide forever, but she was going to damn well try.

"Hey," Ava said to Laura or Lauren or Lola, who turned to her, wide-eyed and startled. "Where can you get gelato around here?"

"You mean . . . like ice cream?" the girl asked. "There's some in the freezer. Vanilla, I think, or maybe Neapolitan." She paused. "Do you want me to get you some?"

"No. Thanks, but that's not what I want." She didn't know what she wanted. Except that no matter how hard she tried, it would never be this.

Just then, Bryce walked into the kitchen, his arms full of clothes. "Hey," Ava said brightly. "Want to go get a gelato?"

"Honey, we're in crisis mode here," Bryce said, dumping the clothes on the table. He stared down at the pile, his lips pinched into a thin line. "My blue jacket is ripped and it's going to completely throw off the continuity. This is a disaster."

"Come on," Ava said. "We've been trapped in this house for days. Did you know we've been in Gin Harbour for almost a week and we haven't even seen the ocean yet?"

"The ocean is overrated." He opened the back door. "Antonio, I need you, sweetheart! Where are you?"

Ava picked up the blue jacket and examined it. "It looks okay to me," she said.

"That's my *other* blue jacket. I'm hoping it's similar enough. Where's Antonio? Antonio!"

"Antonio's dead," Ava said somberly. "I killed him and buried his body in the backyard. Don't worry, I set his camera up next to it to catch any animals that try to dig him up. I'm hoping to pitch a new reality show called *Who Stole Antonio's Femur.*"

Bryce snatched the jacket out of her hands. His face was tight, as tight as she had ever seen it. Apparently, all the space and salt air were doing nothing for him. "Ava, I appreciate this Wednesday Addams vibe you've got going on here, but didn't you hear me?" He shook the jacket in front of her face. "I am trying to avert disaster here."

She swatted his hand away, sending the jacket flying across the room. "And I am trying to maintain my sanity!" she yelled.

Silence filled the kitchen, and regret started a long, slow crawl up Ava's limbs. But Bryce put his hand on her shoulder. "Okay," he said. "You know what? You're right."

"I am?" Ava slumped into him, and he wrapped an arm around her. "I mean, I am."

"What is all this yelling?" David asked, coming in through the doorway, followed by Val and Eden. "Ava, are you trying to swindle Papa into letting you go outside?"

"David," Bryce said quietly. "We have to let them go outside. This is crazy."

Ava blinked up at him, her head still pressed up against Bryce's side. She felt an understanding pass between her dads. Finally, David sighed. "To the outside!" he proclaimed, sweeping his arm out and bowing deeply. Eden squealed in delight, and she and Val ran for the door. Ava heard Bryce's heart beat quicker in his chest, his muscles tensing through his shirt. She tilted her head upward to face him.

"Thank you," she mouthed.

They took the van, David driving, with Bryce in the front seat next to him, the three kids in the back. None of them knew where they were going, but they followed the coastline until Bryce spotted a sign that said BEACH and then they turned off, bumping along gravel until the road ended near a tiny strip of sand abutted by a tumble of jagged rocks. It wasn't the kind of beach Ava was expecting, but the three of them scrambled out of the van like prisoners into the light and raced for the edge of the water, their skin prickling from the salty air, still chilly even though it was June.

They all stopped short as their toes hit the water, which sent them scrambling back up the sandy embankment, Val falling backward onto his hands, Eden shrieking.

"What was that?" Ava squeaked, the pain still radiating up her toes. "What the hell is with this water?"

Behind them, David was doubled over, bellowing with laughter. Even Bryce was grinning. "That, my darling daughter, is the Atlantic Ocean," he said. "And what you are feeling is the sting of about sixty degrees Fahrenheit."

"People swim in this?" Val asked, still sitting in the sand, rubbing his hands over his toes.

"Who knew I raised such soft children?" He held on to Bryce's shoulder as he slipped out of his own shoes, then gestured to Bryce, who cocked an eyebrow.

"Most certainly not," he said.

David shook his head, bending over and rolling up the bottoms of his pants. He walked to the edge of the water and ploughed into it up to his knees, turning back to them and raising his arms. "You are all a huge disappointment to me!" he shouted, the water lapping against his shins.

"And you're a complete freak!" Ava shouted back.

"It's really too bad," David said, reaching into the satchel hanging over his shoulder. "I guess I'm going to have to eat this tub of Finelli's Gelato by myself."

"Finelli's!" squealed Ava. "Where did you get that?"

He smiled, then reached back into his bag and pulled out three plastic spoons. "I have my ways."

She looked at Val, who shrugged. "Okay, let's do this. Come on, Edie," Ava said. She hoisted her sister onto her back and the three of them ran back to the edge of the water, shrieking and giggling as they picked their way tentatively out to David, while Bryce watched from the shore, the sun keeping the fog bank at bay long enough for them to have this moment, here on the beach—this moment only for them.

In early July, the pilot premiered. They all watched it together, the Harts and Javier and Antonio and a few other members of the crew, all nervously bunched up in their tiny living room, spare and modern and far removed from the kitschy seafaring nostalgia of the rest of the B&B. Antonio had his Bluetooth in his ear, and was muttering softly to Bob and Tess, the network execs, as they waited for the show to start. If this didn't go well—well, Ava didn't know what would happen. She had hoped it would fail, had been praying for it every night, but now she felt doubt creeping in. If the show tanked, would they really get to go back to New York? Or would they have to stay in Gin Harbour and actually run a B&B to make a living? And what would happen to her dads? She thought about Bryce in the car in New York, about the worry on his face, the way his eyes fell when he said the word *wasted*. She had wanted the show to fail so badly, she had forgotten that she didn't want *him* to fail.

"Home. What do you know, it *is* where the heart is," she heard Eden's voice say through the television screen, as melancholy string music began to swell.

"Oh my god," said Val

"That's me!" said Eden.

Ava said nothing. She sat with her knees pulled up to her chest and watched as a girl who vaguely resembled her sat in a vaguely familiar restaurant and learned that she was going to be on television. She barely even recognized herself—were those her hunched shoulders, her pursed, thin lips, her lifeless eyes? Who was this girl with her hair falling limply, the baby fat of her chin doubling under her scowl? As she watched, something went soft in her stomach, expanding and mutating until she felt as though her body was pressing into all four corners of the room, an amorphous mountain of flesh suffocating everything and everyone around her.

At the next commercial break, she stood up. "I can't watch," she said. "It's too weird. I can't do this."

"Oh, come on," said Val, grabbing her hand and pulling her back down to the couch. "Don't be an idiot. Just watch the stupid show." But he didn't let go, and Ava felt the vibrations from the nail flicking on his other hand travelling all the way up one arm and down the other.

Off to the side, in her peripheral vision, a camera whirred quietly, the red light blinking as it watched her watching herself. Without even thinking about it, she felt her body react: her back straighten, her chin tilt upward, her eyes widen. That light she was sure would haunt her for the rest of her life, whether it was actually there or not—just outside of her vision, glowing steady and bright, an unblinking red eye following her every move. Reminding her that everyone was watching. She closed her eyes and prayed for the feeling to fade.

"What the hell is with this water?" said a voice that was both strange and familiar.

Her eyes flew open. Onscreen, she saw the five of them. At the beach. David rolling up his pants, wading out into the surf. Ava with Eden on her back, following him in. Their shrieks and laughter. The sun through the fog.

Ava jumped to her feet and turned to Antonio, who was standing by the door, phone in hand. "You *followed* us?"

Antonio pressed a button on his headset. "What are you talking about?"

"That was supposed to be for us," she said. She could feel the tears coming, but she bit her lip. She was not going to cry. Not in front of *him*. "That was supposed to be our day. And you *followed* us."

"Ava," David said. He stood and came over to her and scooped her up as easily as a stone from the ground. "Antonio didn't follow us. There's a dashboard camera in the van."

"There's . . ." She turned to Bryce, who averted his eyes. "There's a camera in the van? And you knew?"

"All access," David said softly. "Remember?"

A tiny explosion went off in her head. "I don't want this," she said, as the tears finally began to fall. "I don't want this," she sobbed into David's shoulder over and over again, her body shaking against his as the credits rolled.

Halston Market Research Group
Focus Group Discussion Transcript and Analysis – *Home Is Where the Hart Is* Pilot **Re-Shoot**
LifeStyle Network, 2009

Total participant time required: 43 minutes + 15 minutes
Total number of participants: 6 (new)
Moderator: Jensen Lee

SECTION FOUR: CHARACTERS

Moderator: Let's talk about the characters on the show. Which one of the Harts did you think was most relatable?

A: Oh my gosh, Eden.

C: She's such a sweetheart. With the thumb-sucking and the lisp . . .

D: So adorable. And Val! Those eyes . . .

B: My thirteen-year-old daughter is going to love him! I can see him becoming a real star.

Moderator: And what did you think about Ava?

B: Mmmm . . .

E: A bit over the top?

F: Like she was trying too hard to make people like her.

E: Yeah! Definitely trying too hard. Too excited about everything. Like, calm down, girl.

[Laughter]

A: Right, like in that scene at the beach, carrying Eden out into the water on her back like that? Who does she think she is, Mother freaking Teresa?

Mags

May 2009

———◇———

"The First Time"

A n hour before the band's first gig, Mags watched while Sam
and Becca shared a fifth of vodka in a gravelly, garbage-
strewn downtown parking lot. They passed the bottle back and
forth, Becca sipping and squirming with her gum stuck to the end
of her index finger, Sam licking drops from the rim before tilting
his head back. Becca giggled, then stuck the gum back in her
mouth while she waited for her turn.

They were sitting on the ground between two parked cars: a
Ford Taurus and a Jeep. The Jeep had a bumper sticker on the back
that said *Jesus is Coming . . . Look Busy*. Becca thought this was
hilarious. She was leaning against the fence, bare legs stretched
out in front of her, ankles laced into shiny, brand-new Doc Martens.
Sam sat beside her in his holey jeans and T-shirt, knees pulled up
to his chest. Mags was standing, because like she was going to get
gravel stuck in her ass. Besides, she couldn't sit still, the gravel
crunching under her feet as she paced back and forth. Above them,
a single star glowed in the sky, and she stared at it until it faded to

a tiny spark, thinking, *God give me strength not to knock her goddamn teeth in* and *if she touches my boyfriend one more fucking time I swear I will throw her over this fence.*

"Are you sure you don't want some?" Becca asked Mags, all pouting lips and hopeful, batting eyelashes. When Mags didn't answer, she shrugged. "Fine. More for me."

"No way," said Sam. "I get her share."

"Awesome," said Mags. "Another night that ends with your head in the toilet." Actually, two heads—Becca was definitely one of those girls who got drunk fast, tried to stick her tongue down your throat, then started to cry and passed out in the bathroom, face streaked with mascara. It was so boring. Oh, boohoo, you're a screwed-up sixteen-year-old. Big deal. Who wasn't.

"Whatever," said Becca, dismissing Mags with a wave of her hand, the momentum knocking her over onto her elbow. Somewhere out in the street, a car honked. Becca jumped, and vodka sloshed out of the bottle and over her arm. Sam took her wrist and ran his tongue over it. "Gross," said Becca, wiping her wrist on her shirt.

But she looked up at Mags and there was light in her eyes. Mags stared back until Becca became a blur, fading away like a star.

At first, living with Sam had been so stressful it was almost unbearable, Mags's breath hitching every time she heard voices above her or footsteps at the top of the stairs. But Sam was right: his parents were rarely home, and even when they were they never came downstairs. The basement even had its own entrance so she could go in and out unnoticed, sneaking down the alley and hopping the fence a few minutes before Sam, and then meeting him on the corner to walk to school together. Sam only went upstairs himself to grab food from the kitchen; if the Coles noticed an increase in their grocery bill, they never said anything. Nights were spent tangled up together in Sam's single bed, falling asleep to sad songs about trucks and birds and car accidents and dead wives that gave Mags strange, melancholy dreams. When she woke in the middle of the night in a panic—startled by a car door closing or a toilet flushing or a garbage can knocked over by a raccoon—Sam would put his hand on her back until her pulse slowed and she started to relax, allowing herself to breathe this air she had believed she had no right to breathe.

She never heard from Frankie.

In the afternoons, Mags usually followed Sam to band practice. She had always imagined that one of the best perks of having a boyfriend in a band was behind-the-scenes access, being able to see how the lyrics were hammered out, how the melodies took shape. The reality was sitting on a mildew-covered couch in Zac's garage while Paul and Sam tuned their instruments for half an hour, then played half a cover song before Zac's mom came running out to the garage to tell them to turn it down. "The whole neighbourhood can hear you!" she hollered through the door one afternoon. "No one needs to hear an off-beat cover of 'Comfortably Numb.'"

"God, Mom! It's not off-beat!" said Zac, throwing a drumstick across the room, narrowly missing Mags's head.

"Watch it!" Mags said, irritated. "I still need that eye."

Zac shrugged. He was all muscles and hormones in a ripped tank top, a tiny, taut ball of ADHD drumming on everything, compelled by a constant, driving inner rhythm. "It's the rock and roll lifestyle. You signed up for this."

"Oh, yeah. *Super* rock and roll. *God, Mom*," she whined. "*Stop embarrassing me in front of my friends. And can you bring us some juice boxes?*"

Zac turned to Sam. "Couldn't you find us some better groupies?"

"I would, but I can't get rid of this one. She literally moved into my basement."

Mags threw the drumstick back across the room at Zac. "Go back to playing your Fleetwood Mac covers and leave me alone."

"I *hate* Fleetwood Mac," Paul muttered, head bent over his guitar. Mags was sure she'd only ever seen the top of Paul's head—since she'd been coming to practices, she couldn't recall a time when he *hadn't* been bent down over his guitar. At first, she thought he was scared of her, but then she realized he didn't even think of her at all. Paul knew more about music theory than any of them—she imagined him seeing music as mathematical equations to solve. And that, from Mags's point of view, was why the band didn't have any songs of their own. Paul didn't care about lyrics. To him they were just an overlay, something to make smart music interesting for dumb people.

Mags knew Sam was completely in awe of Paul—he would never push back. Maybe that was why Mags felt like she had to. "You know, you guys are never going to play a real show until you have some songs," she said. "Unless you want to play weird experimental jazz in coffee shops until you're, like, forty."

"Don't worry, we've got it covered," Paul said. "Our new singer is going to write us some."

"What new singer?" Mags glanced at Sam, who began fiddling with his bass strap, not meeting her eyes. "Who is he? Do I know him?"

Paul crouched down, fiddling with his amp. "*She.* Becca Stigler. She goes to your school."

"Becca Stigler?" Mags laughed. "You're joking, right?" No one said anything. "Becca Stigler? Sailing champ Becca Stigler? Junior prom queen Becca Stigler? *Dating John Jacobs* Becca Stigler?"

"Not anymore," Sam said. "They broke up three weeks ago. He's dating Carly Theriault now."

"Since when do you care about the dating drama of our school's elite?"

"Since Becca Stigler broke up with John Jacobs three weeks ago and asked if our band needed a singer."

Mags blinked her eyes slowly. "She just . . . asked?"

"Yeah."

Mags leaned back on the couch, dread now fully bloomed in her chest, as a vague memory came into focus: Mags sitting on the front steps of their school a few weeks earlier, leather jacket slung through the strap of her backpack, Sam's bass in its case on the ground in front of her while he ran to his locker to get his math book, and Becca Stigler saying, "That's so cool your boyfriend's a guitarist"—the first words she had ever spoken to her even though they had two classes together.

"This is going to end badly," Mags said, but none of the boys were listening to her. She didn't fully understand what she was feeling—this tiny, sharp grinding in the pit of her stomach—but she knew she wanted to make it stop. To make *this* stop.

But Becca Stigler was like a train, barrelling forward. At band practice the next day, she showed up with her hair in pigtails, wearing a beat-up Sex Pistols T-shirt she had clearly bought, pre-distressed, at the mall. She was so transparent that Mags couldn't believe Paul and Zac had fallen for it. And she *really* couldn't believe Sam had fallen for it.

"This is going to be *so fun!*" she said, squeezing Mags's arm before Mags snatched it away. "What do you want me to sing? I know all of Taylor Swift's stuff by heart."

"Here," said Sam, handing her a piece of paper.

"tlhiH boch parHa' jul? What the hell is that?"

"It's Klingon," Paul said, suddenly intensely interested in scraping off a piece of duct tape stuck to one of his cords.

"It means 'you shine like the sun,'" Sam said. Becca beamed. Mags stuck her tongue out in a mock gagging motion.

Zac slammed his drumsticks down on the snare. "Can we please just play already?"

"This whole rebellious-little-rich-girl thing is so dumb," Mags said later, as they were walking home. "It's so obvious. I almost feel sorry for her. Up until a week ago, she was on the fucking cheer-leading squad."

"She was an ironic cheerleader," Sam said. "You know, like the ones in the 'Smells Like Teen Spirit' video."

"They weren't ironic," Mags said, shifting her backpack. "They were anarchists."

"Is this because of the time we went to Wendy's?" Sam asked. "I told you I was sorry about that. I know it was a dick move." There had been a group of them—Sam and Becca and the posse of flannel-wearing, brain-dead stoners she had traded in her preppy pageant-queen friends for. They all shared a small Frosty and then got kicked out for posting pictures of the kid with Down's syndrome who cleaned the trays. Mags had been livid. That wasn't Sam. Sam was a music nerd. Sam collected vinyl. Sam went *bird-watching*. Sam did not get kicked out of restaurants.

"Yes." Mags started to walk faster. "That is reason four hundred and seventy thousand why I don't like her." Of course that was it. None of it had anything to do with the fact that Becca was prettier than Mags, or had nicer clothes, or that she did this annoying thing where she said a person's name ten million times in a conversation—"Hey, Sam, what did you get on that history test, Sam? Oh god, Sam, I think I totally failed it, Sam, Sam, Sam." None of it had anything to do with the fact that she thought she could come into Mags's world and own it.

A few days later, when Sam, Mags, and Becca arrived at the garage, Zac pounced on them as they walked in the door. "We have a gig," Zac said, grabbing Sam and shaking him. "We have a *mother-fucking gig!*"

"We don't *have* a gig," Paul said. "We were offered a gig. We can't take it."

"It's an opening slot with Deer Carcass!" Zac said, shaking Sam harder. "Deer Carcass, Sam!"

Mags dropped her backpack on the couch. "Whoa. That's huge." Deer Carcass were a band from Moncton who had just been signed to a big American label and were now obviously the new favourite band of every single person at their school.

"Oh my god," squealed Becca. "I love Deer Carcass."

Zac let go of Sam, who wobbled backward from the momentum. "Of course you do!" he shouted. "Everyone does. It's *Deer Carcass!*"

"Zac!" his mother bellowed from inside the house. "Stop shouting. The whole city can hear you!"

"It's *fucking Deer Carcass*, Mom!" he shouted back, putting Becca in a headlock, sending her into a fit of giggles.

"Zac, shut up. We're not doing it," Paul said. Zac let go of Becca, who straightened up, flushed. "We can't. We're not ready."

"Paul's right," Sam said. "We've never performed in front of anyone. We can't just go out there and perform for a club full of Deer Carcass fans."

"Why not? We have to start somewhere."

"We don't even have any songs."

"Yes, you do," Mags said. Everyone looked at her, and she felt her mouth go dry. In the past few weeks, she had filled her note-book with lyrics, carrying it around with her while waiting for the right moment to share them with Sam. Well, this was the moment, wasn't it? *Say it*, her voice screamed in her head. *Tell them!* But seeing them all stare at her expectantly, she knew they would never want something she wrote. Why would they? She was just the bassist's girlfriend, a groupie. She was nothing. "I mean, Sam does. Sam wrote lyrics."

Everyone was silent. "Are they any good?" Paul asked. Mags nodded, avoiding Sam's eyes, and pulled the notebook out of her backpack. She handed it to Paul, who flipped through it. "Okay," he said. "We can try it. Here." He handed the notebook to Becca. "Let's figure out some melodies."

What had she expected to happen? Becca was the singer, she would need to see the songs. But as she watched Becca take the notebook from Paul's hand, she felt as though she were actually taking Mags's heart directly out of her chest—digging into the flesh, cracking the ribs, ripping it from its aorta as Mags stood there, defenceless. Then the four bandmates got into position, oblivious to the gaping hole in Mags's sternum, black and bottomless and pulsing with fury as she sat back down on the couch where she belonged.

—◇—

Now it was the night of the show, and they were meeting the rest of the band at the bar. On the way, they stopped at the Paperchase for chocolate. Mags and Sam got Wunderbars, because that was what they always got. Becca got Junior Mints.

"I like your hair," the guy behind the counter said to Becca, pointing to the pink streak that had appeared amidst the blonde a couple of days earlier.

"Thanks," said Becca. "I did it with a Magic Marker." She stood on her tiptoes and leaned over the counter. "Feel it! It doesn't even come off."

The counter guy tentatively fingered the strand. "Cool." Becca's knee bumped against a box of Aero bars and they fell to the floor.

Mags moved past the racks of magazines toward the door. "Are we going to have to wait for her to blow him?" she asked Sam.

Sam shook his head and took a bite of his Wunderbar. "You're such a bitch," he said. It came out sounding like *Mmmmphummmmp*, but Mags knew what he was saying.

Once they were outside, Becca skipped ahead and linked her arm with Sam's. "Hurry up," she said to Mags over her shoulder, heavy-lidded and flushed. "I don't want to miss the opening act." She turned back to Sam. "Wait, who's the opening act?"

"We're the opening act," said Sam. Then he leaned over and pretended to bite her shoulder.

Something snapped in Mags's brain. She had spent weeks listening to Becca mangle her lyrics, singing in the breathy baby-voice that all the indie girls seemed to use, breaking all her vowels and emphasizing all the wrong words. And in all those weeks, what had Mags done? Sat on the couch in Zac's garage, where she didn't belong. Slept in Sam's bed, under Sam's roof, where she didn't belong. She had let her guard down, given Becca an opening. Becca had already taken her words. If she took Sam too, Mags would have nothing left.

"Hey!" she yelled. Becca and Sam both stopped and turned, gazing at her questioningly. Mags clenched her fist and swung. She knew it should be Becca she was punching, Becca and her stupid poser face. But it was Sam's face her anger was directed at, Sam for being such an idiot, for being so easily manipulated, and most of all for thinking like the bassist in a band when he should have been thinking like her boyfriend.

"What the hell?" He seemed more confused than angry, touching his cheek where her fist had made contact as though he didn't quite believe it had happened.

"No!" yelled Mags, her extremities going numb, her vision starting to blur, voices fading in and out—that old feeling she thought she'd contained, the fire in the depths of her. "You do not do this to me, Sam."

"Do what?!" Sam yelled back. "What is wrong with you?"

"Nothing! There is *nothing* wrong with me!"

"Okay, okay." Sam's face changed suddenly, softening. He reached out an arm for her, pulling her into him, into the spot where she fit, her body rigid under his arm.

"There is nothing wrong with me," she said again, softer.

"I know." Sam laced his fingers through her hair. "Christ," he said, bringing his other hand up to his nose. "Great, now I'm bleeding."

"Oh my god," said Becca, her eyes glued to Sam's bloody nose, her face draining of colour. She doubled over and vomited on the ground.

"Dammit," said Sam.

"Oh, awesome," said Mags, shaking her head. But the tension was draining out of her, the fire fizzling out, the universe back on course.

"It's okay," said Becca, wiping her mouth with the back of her hand, raising her head, her face blotchy, ruined. Then she vomited again, half-chewed Junior Mints spraying across the sidewalk. On the other side of the street, a group of kids started cheering. Becca hiccupped. Then she started to cry.

I hate to be right about these things, Mags thought. But really, she didn't.

When they got to the bar, Paul and Zac were already there. They tried to clean Becca up as best they could, talking Mags into taking her into the washroom to try to fix her makeup.

"We can reapply it, but I'm not sure it's going to help," she said to Becca as she sat on the edge of the counter, tears streaming down her face.

"You hate me," she wailed. "Why do you hate me?"

Mags sighed. "I don't hate you, Becca. I just don't know you."

Becca wiped at her face, but it only made it worse, eyeliner smudging out to her hairline. She swayed a little on the counter as she stared at Mags. "We go to school together, remember? We're in Mr. Whatshisface's math class."

Mags half-heartedly rubbed at the eyeliner. "I mean, I don't know who you really are. Seriously, *this*? This isn't you. This is just something you've tried on."

"Are you talking about this dress?" Becca asked. "I got it at a thrift store. I thought it was cool."

"Never mind," Mags said.

Becca started sobbing again. Mags turned away from her and started fixing her own makeup instead, darkening her lids with the same slate grey shadow that was currently running down Becca's cheeks.

"She can't do this," Paul said, after Mags dragged Becca back to the green room, still splotchy and mascara-streaked, a dribble of vomit down the front of her dress. "This is a disaster."

"Well, that's it," Zac said, throwing his drumsticks on the ratty couch. "Our one shot and we fucking blew it."

Mags sucked in a breath. It had never occurred to her to ask for what she wanted. But thinking about the way that Becca decided who she wanted to be and became that person—why couldn't Mags do that? Why couldn't she just be the person she wanted to be?

"I can do it," Mags blurted out. "I can sing."

The three boys turned their faces to her. "You?" said Sam, staring at her as if she were a stranger. She glared at him. *Yes, me*, she thought. *Why not me?*

Paul shook his head. "You don't even know the songs."

"I can figure them out."

"This isn't the time or place for *figuring stuff out*, Mags. This is a real show, in front of a real audience, opening for a real band, and you don't know the songs, you haven't rehearsed with us once. Hell, I don't even know if you can actually sing! Do you have any musical talent at all?"

"I *do*," Mags said, feeling her confidence waiver. "I mean, I think I do." But suddenly she wasn't so sure. Anyone could sound good singing in front of the bathroom mirror, or belting out along with the radio in the car. But Mags had never tried to sing with a band before. She had never even held a mic in her hand.

The four of them stood in a tableau, Zac with his head in his hands, Paul with his guitar hanging limply around his neck, Sam staring hard at Mags, working something out.

"She does," Sam said suddenly. "She can sing. I've heard her. And she knows all the lyrics. She wrote them."

"I thought you wrote them," Zac said.

"Nope. She did." Sam kept his eyes fixed on Mags. "She was being modest. But I should have told you the truth from the beginning."

Everyone was silent. Paul and Zac exchanged a glance. Mags felt her heart speed up in her chest, so full of love for Sam in that moment she thought it might explode.

"Okay," Paul said finally, shrugging. "We've got nothing to lose."

It wasn't the enthusiastic response that Mags had been hoping for, but she would take it.

The boys went out first, and Mags followed. The stage lights were so blinding that she momentarily stumbled, then regained her footing as she stepped up to the mic stand and wrapped her hands around it. The band kicked in with the opening bars of "White Lies"—one of the first songs she had written, one that she knew like she knew the contours of Sam's face. She stood there, liquefying. She felt everything soften: her limbs, her thoughts, her field of vision. She knew before she even opened her mouth to sing: this was where she was meant to be.

And then she sang.

The quietness surprised her. The inward calm, the way it settled the chaos inside her, the music a protective layer between the disharmony of the outside world and the stillness of her thoughts. Nothing could disturb her, nothing could touch her—in this room full of strangers she was free, and in that freedom she felt buoyant, as though she had never felt free in her life before. She could have been a different person, standing there in the middle of the stage. She didn't have to be Mags—lonely, scared, angry Mags. Mags who couldn't say the things she needed to say. Mags without a voice. She could be anybody.

And then it was over. It was over. Nietzsche's Watering Can was leaving the stage and Mags couldn't remember a single moment of the show, couldn't even remember the time passing, could only remember the calm. And people were talking to her and she was talking back: an outer persona had somehow manifested itself, taking care of the mundane details of navigating real life, while inside she floated languidly in an endless galaxy of stars, oblivious.

In the green room, the boys were jubilant. Sam picked her up and swung her around, but all she could think about was the next time, about when she'd get to do it again.

"So, you're going to stay in the band then?" Paul asked.

"Yeah," Mags said. "But Jesus Christ, guys. We have to come up with another name."

"What, then?" Zac asked.

Mags tilted her head back. "Align Above," she said, the words coming from deep within that universe inside her.

Deer Carcass

May 27 at 11:24 AM

Thanks for the magic last night Halifax! We had a blast. And huge shout out to Nietzsche's Watering Can for warming up the crowd!

Terra McLeod You guys rule! Please come back soon!

Like • Reply • 4h

Megan Marie Anyone know anything about the opening act? They KILLED IT!

Like • Reply • 3h

> **Hailey Hsai** They're called Nietzsche's Watering Can! The guitarist and the drummer go to my school!! They rock so hard.
>
> Like • Reply • 3h
>
> **Joshua Crabtree** The singer chick was hot.
>
> Like • Reply • 3h
>
> **Keegan Cowie** Yaaa nice ass
>
> Like • Reply • 3h
>
> **Jenelle Yacuba** I thought she kind of looked like a dog. Like what are those dogs with the weird long faces
>
> Like • Reply • 2h
>
> **Joshua Crabtree** Greyhound lol
>
> Like • Reply • 2h
>
> **Jenelle Yacuba** Yesssss she's a greyhound.
>
> Like • Reply • 2h
>
> **Keegan Cowie** Nice ass tho
>
> Like • Reply • 2h
>
> **Paul Van Ness** Hello Megan, thanks so much for your interest in our band. Just to let you know, we are now called Align Above, and you can find all our info on our MySpace page. Hope you check it out!
>
> Like • Reply • 2h

LIFESTYLE NETWORK
Your Life. Your Style. Your LifeStyle.

Memorandum

To: LifeStyle Network Executive Producers   Date: Monday, June 7, 2010

From: Bob and Tess Axelrod   Extension: 00676

Re: **Cancellation—Home Is Where the Hart Is**

As you are likely aware, *Home Is Where the Hart Is* has been averaging a 0.4 rating among adults 18–49 in the first half of its second season. Even after the shifted focus, the show continues to disappoint in key demographics. Following this week's episode, which sunk to a 0.12 rating, we have decided to put the show's production on hiatus. The fifth and final episode, which is wrapping production in two weeks, will air on July 8 as planned, but no more episodes will be produced at this time. We will be meeting with Jane later this week to discuss recouping our advertising revenue and any of our assets still tied up in the show.

It is imperative that you not discuss this with any member of the Hart family without first speaking to Jane. We have heard through our channels that David Hart may have already retained legal counsel, and we therefore request a moratorium on communication with him without our lawyers present.

Please direct any media requests to Maria.

Bob Axelrod, President and CEO   Tess Axelrod, CFO
LifeStyle Network   LifeStyle Network

cc: Maria Nunes, Jane Burton-Brown, Antonio Rivera

Ava

June 2010

———◇———

HIWTHI S02E05:
Change of Hart

"**H**er name is Julia, okay?" Antonio said from the front seat of the van. "*Julia*. Can you remember that?"

Ava rolled her eyes and rested her head against the window in the backseat as they inched down the main street in downtown Gin Harbour. The same trundling middle-aged couple had passed them three times as they waited in the world's dumbest traffic jam, caused by a gaggle of Canada geese wandering down the centre of the road.

"Ava?" Antonio said, catching her eye in the rear-view mirror.

"Brooklin, I got it," said Ava, smiling sweetly at him.

"*Julia*." He exhaled slowly. "Jesus Christ, Ava, you're going to send me to an early grave."

They were on their way to a shoot at Gin Harbour Junior-Senior High. Of course, Ava didn't actually *go* to GHJSH—all of the Hart kids were home-schooled by a rotating roster of teachers flown in from New York. Still, the premise of this episode was that Ava was trying to convince David and Bryce to let her go to a friend's cottage for the weekend. But first they had to convince the viewing public that Ava *had* a friend. They were filming at the school on a Saturday, with some actors they'd brought in from Toronto, kids with dumb names like Brooklin and Jax that the network had to change to something less dumb for the scene. Ava had been pretending to forget that, just to rile Antonio up. Riling him up had become her one little way of feeling in control during the times she wasn't. Like when she was literally being taken somewhere against her will.

The first season of *Home Is Where the Hart Is* had been a slowly unravelling mess, with a long line of unlikeable guests and dropped storylines, including David fighting a city bylaw infraction (fake), a storm that took off part of the roof (completely fake), and Bryce's awkward friendship with a semi-bigoted neighbour (mostly fake). The show had *failed to capture the hearts and minds of viewers*, according to Bob and Tess. The show had *not engaged the key demographics*, according to the market research. The show *sucked all the air out of the room like a gaping black hole*, according to a random commenter on the show's Facebook page. No one had thought the show would be renewed for a second season, but it was, if unenthusiastically. Now, the network planned to focus more on the family, and for the first time ever, Ava was going to have her own episode. Bob and Tess had finally put their foot down, telling her (or telling Antonio to tell her) that she either did the episode or they would do it for her, lacing together candid footage to make it appear that she was doing what they wanted. So Ava capitulated, resigning herself to this episode with all the stoic grace of an early Christian martyr being burned at the stake.

Antonio pulled into the empty school parking lot and switched off the van. When Ava got out, she saw a group of kids around her age hanging out on the bleachers by the soccer field, two boys and a girl, dressed mostly in black even in the heat. For a tiny, glorious second, Ava imagined herself going over to them, saying something cool and inscrutable, and tumbling wildly into one of those quick, bright summer friendships that she read about in novels, all tanned, salty skin and breathless secrets. But then she watched them for a few minutes—laughing, smoking, pushing each other, drinking Slurpees that were probably mixed with stolen liquor—and she realized that would never happen.

"Yo," one of them called over to her, a boy with long, stringy hair wearing a Slipknot T-shirt. "What's going on? You guys making a movie?"

"Something like that," she said, leaning against the side of the van.

He narrowed his eyes at her. "You're on that reality show, right? The one with the two gays?"

"*American Idol?*" the other boy asked.

The girl pushed him. "There's no gays on *American Idol.*"

"Fuck there isn't. What about that British guy?"

"Not all British people are gay, dickwad."

"It's not *American Idol*, Derry, you piece of shit," the first guy said. He grinned at her, jumping down off the bleachers. "There's a bunch of them and they all live up at the old Mariner's Inn. She's got an *adowable widdle* sister and a Chinese brother. She's supposed to be the hot one, I guess, though I can't really see it."

"He's not Chinese, he's Cambodian," Ava said, anger pulsing in her chest. "Also, fuck you."

"Here that, Bo?" the girl said. "She wants to fuck you."

"Yeah, she does." He moved closer. "On second thought, maybe she is *kind* of hot."

The door to the back of the van slammed shut and Antonio appeared, with Javier behind him holding the video camera. "How you boys doing?" he asked.

"Hey, is that thing on?" Bo asked.

Antonio smiled. "Yep, and we're sending all this footage to your mom."

The kids all turned and ran, scampering across the soccer field like deer being chased by a dog.

"My hero," said Ava, keeping her head down so Antonio couldn't see her reddening cheeks.

"You see why we don't want you mixing with the locals now? Why we hired actors to play your friends?"

"Yeah, heaven forbid we strive for any level of authenticity," she fired back, pretending not to feel the sting of the words he'd strung together: *hired* and *friends*.

Antonio raised an eyebrow at her. "I can call Bo and Derry back if you'd like." Ava walked away, pretending not to hear him. She just wanted to get this over with so she could go back to staying under the radar, hiding away from the cameras until the show finally crashed and burned.

———◇———

Ava had locked herself in her room after the pilot aired, having discovered that she could pull the doorknob out on the inside, which made it impossible for anyone to come in. Thirty-six hours later, David came at the door with a screwdriver, taking it off its hinges and replacing it with a shower curtain, declaring her door privileges officially and permanently revoked.

The following week, they all gathered in the family room to watch the second episode—David in his recliner with his tablet and clipboard, Antonio pacing the room behind them, Bryce with his hands folded in his lap, the three kids on the floor.

"You'll like this," Bryce said to her as she sat down, her back rigid against the coffee table, only there under threat of having all her devices confiscated indefinitely. "I hear they're starting with you."

"Fantastic," Ava said. But as the opening sequence started playing, Ava felt her insides squirming, a mixture of anxiety and a perverse kind of pleasure. She was only human, after all. And this was national television.

The episode started and Ava saw herself standing at the kitchen sink, washing dishes, her back turned to the camera. *When did this happen?* she thought. *I don't remember this at all.*

"Have you made any friends in Gin Harbour?" an off-camera voice asked.

"I don't really know *how* to make friends," Ava heard her own voice say, on screen.

"*With vampires,*" Ava said, leaning forward on the floor, the words sticking in the back of her throat. "I said 'with vampires.' And I wasn't washing dishes, I was in my room!"

"I mean, what movies do people even watch, you know? Do they like *Twilight* or *High School Musical?*"

Ava jumped to her feet, gesturing wildly at the television. "I didn't say any of that!"

Val grinned. "It sure sounded like you did."

"I mean, I did, but not like that. I said the words, but they changed them all around."

"Ava, honey, it's okay," said David. "I'm sure you just forgot that you said it. It was a few weeks ago already, and we're all under a lot of pressure."

"I didn't forget! I *never* would have said any of that." She spun around to glare at Antonio. "You did this!"

Antonio raised his hands. "Don't look at me," he said. "I just shoot it and send it in. Take it up with Bob and Tess."

"I *will*! I *will* take it up with Bob and Tess!" She crossed the room and yanked the electrical cord out of the wall, the television screen flickering out to a chorus of protests. "They want to mess with my words? Fine. Have fun messing with nothing." She kicked the television stand for good measure, then stormed off to her room, her family's laughter following her up the stairs. When she got to her room, she tried slamming her shower curtain, but it only fluttered with an unsatisfying plastic *whoosh*.

For the next few months, whenever someone asked her a direct question on camera, Ava was silent. Not only was she silent, but she would find ways to disrupt the shoot—turning the lights off when she walked into a room, holding up her cell phone flashlight when the camera was on her, wearing too much branded clothing for them to blur out. Occasionally, something she said or did slipped through and made it onto the show, but for the most part she was invisible. After a while, her invisibility started to feel like a costume she now wore permanently—in her mind she had become the mysterious, enigmatic Hart sister, gliding quietly and elegantly across the screen, appearing only in the corner of your eye so you weren't even sure you had actually seen her at all.

Staying off camera gave Ava the freedom to do what she wanted, but it also meant she had a lot of time on her hands. She started going for long bike rides, which she was allowed to do only on the weekends, only in the afternoons, and only if she didn't stop anywhere or talk to anyone. That was perfectly fine with Ava—she didn't *want* to talk to anyone, although sometimes she did stop at the beach and sit on a rock and watch the ocean. The water was grey and cold, the rocky beaches covered in rotting seaweed and seagull shit, broken mussel shells so sharp they sliced into the bottoms of your feet like tiny steel blades. But even still, she supposed the North Atlantic was kind of beautiful.

At night, she would prop herself up in bed with her laptop, obsessively scrolling though the show's social media accounts, searching for the worst reviews, the darkest comments, the most horrifying posts. She told herself it kept her going, seeing how much everyone hated the show, but deep down she knew she liked the exhilaration it stoked in her, that sizzling spike of adrenaline. It was oddly thrilling to watch the show's failure to launch, even though occasionally she would come across a comment about David and Bryce or Val and Eden—about how desperate they were, how pathetic, how disgusting, or worse—and become overwhelmed with the desire to throw her laptop across the room. But the few comments that were about her didn't even register—it was as if they were talking about some other Ava Hart with a double chin, with an annoying laugh, with a stupid, ugly face.

Secretly, she liked to think the show was tanking because she wasn't on it, although she would never say that to anyone. She just sat back and waited for it all to implode.

—◇—

Inside the school, Ava leaned against a locker next to Julia (née Brooklin). Wardrobe had put her in a short denim skirt that seemed to ride up every time she moved, so she tried to keep herself in one position as she said her lines. "I really want to come, but my parents are kind of strict," she said, resisting the urge to reach down and yank on the hem of the skirt.

"My parents can talk to them. I mean, we'll be at a cabin in the woods. What kind of trouble can we get into?" They both smiled at each other. Ava knew it was pretend, she *knew* it, but still she reacted—how could she not? It had been so long since she had talked to another girl her age. And Brooklin's smile seemed genuine. It really did feel like they had connected.

"Cut," said Antonio. Javier lowered the camera. "Great, that's great. Hang on." He reached into his pocket and pulled out his phone. "Hello?"

"God, I hope we're done. This takes forever," Ava said to Brooklin, who wasn't listening, her back turned to Ava as she texted on an impossibly tiny flip phone. "Have you done a lot of reality shows before?"

"What?" said Brooklin, her eyes still on her phone.

90

"I just asked if you had done a lot of reality shows before. It seems like a weird gig, pretending to be a real person."

"Uh, *yeah*," Brooklin said, her fingers furious on the phone's keypad. "It's called *acting*."

Right. Ava paused, then tried again. "I'm going to go to the vending machine. Want anything?" When Brooklin didn't answer, Ava sighed and wandered down the hall in the direction of the cafeteria.

As she stood there in front of the vending machine counting change from her pocket, she heard Antonio's voice coming through the door to the kitchen. "No, it's going really well. The actress is great." A long pause. "No, Bob, I didn't get the memo. You really want to cancel it in the middle of the season?" He paused again. "Give me two more weeks, Bob. I promise you. If it doesn't work out, I'll bring them all back to New York myself."

Had she heard correctly? Could it finally be over? Ava allowed the idea to settle on her like flakes of snow. She was there, she was right there—standing in front of a window, the New York skyline stretching out in front of her, the sounds of people yelling, cars honking, the smell of hotdogs and exhausts, the electric charge of a place that was *alive.*

The kitchen door opened, and Antonio came striding out. He stopped when he saw Ava, who turned quickly to the vending machine. "Just getting a Snickers," she said. "You don't want to let the talent get hungry now, do you?"

"Talent?" said Antonio, making a big show of looking around. "I don't see any talent." His lips pulled up in a half-hearted grin, but the worry remained in his eyes.

As the Snickers bar fell from its wiry perch and spilled into the cavity at the bottom, Ava pursed her lips together to keep from smiling. She reached in and grabbed the bar. "So," she said, unable to help herself. "We're getting cancelled."

Antonio turned to her sharply. "Where'd you hear that?"

"Just now. You. On the phone." She tore off the top of the wrapper and bit off the end. "You made a convincing case, though."

Antonio's shoulders, usually so infuriatingly rigid, now slumped down as if God himself were pushing down on them. "Yeah, well, there's a lot riding on this show." His eyes flicked toward Ava, and then away again. "For you guys, I mean. You've sacrificed a lot for this."

"Hey, I'm nothing if not self-sacrificing," Ava said. "But I suppose, if the show *had* to be cancelled, I would *somehow* find a way to carry on."

"How heroic of you. Truly noble." Antonio leaned back against the vending machine. "I know *you'll* be fine, Ava. You're young and beautiful and smart. You'll have plenty of chances to make your mark. But some of us . . ." He paused, rubbing his fingers against his palm the way he did when he was anxious about something. "Some of us are out of chances."

Ava felt a spark of pity. So Antonio did have a stake in this, after all. "Hey, I clearly know nothing about anything. But it seems to me that *Home Is Where the Hart Is* is a pretty shitty way to make your mark on the world, anyway."

"You're probably right."

Silence passed between them. Finally, Ava held out her Snickers bar. "Want some?"

Antonio took the bar from her, shoving the rest of it in his mouth. When he'd finished chewing, he tossed the empty wrapper at her and grinned, his teeth coated in chocolate.

"Give me an inch," he said. "It's part of the job. I would have thought you'd know that by now."

Ava shoved the wrapper into her pocket. *Maybe I do*, she thought.

——◇——

Ava didn't tell anyone about what she'd heard. She didn't have to. A slow, creeping feeling of doom spread over the house, skulking along the baseboards and up the walls, hiding in the corners ready to spring out at any moment. As they tended to do when they were anxious, David got louder and messier, and Bryce got smaller and neater, the two of them cancelling each other out as the tension grew and grew. No one ever said the word *cancellation*, but the air was thick with it. Her dads acted as though there was a wrecking ball pulled back into position, ready to crash through the walls of their lives, leaving nothing behind but a pile of useless rubble.

Ava almost felt bad about it.

The two weeks of production on Episode 5 passed quickly, with the network not even bothering to send any scripts beyond that. The final script centred around a couple from Idaho who were in town to compete in an oyster-shucking competition.

"People underestimate us," the woman had told Ava that morning while she drank her coffee in the kitchen. "Being from a land-locked state and all. But you can get oysters anywhere these days. It's amazing."

"It *sounds* amazing," said Ava, feeling her heart swell with goodwill. She loved this woman, this Idahoan oyster shucker, with her big, poufy blonde hair and Tasmanian Devil tattoo on her bicep. This woman was special. She was magical. She was the last guest ever at Hart's Desire.

That afternoon, while the Idaho couple practised in the kitchen under the watchful eye of the HIWTHI cameras, Ava and Val and Eden held their B&B Olympics in her room, which mostly involved events like seeing who could hold their breath the longest (Val) or drink a litre of Coke the fastest (Ava) or walk the entire length of the room on their hands (Eden). Then, high on sugar, a lack of oxygen, and a blood rush to the head, they sang karaoke with the beat-up machine Val had brought with him from New York—old classic rock songs like "Welcome to the Jungle" and "Bohemian

93

Rhapsody," Val and Ava belting out song after song, until their voices rasped and their foreheads were slick with sweat.

"When can I go?" Eden asked, bouncing up and down on the edge of the bed.

"Wait, wait, I've got one," Val shouted, his eyes wild with the Coke rush, cueing up "Born in the U.S.A." Ava and Eden jumped on the bed, laughing and out of breath as Val fell to his knees, unzipped his hoodie, and ripped it open, head thrown back. Ava was jubilant, practically trembling with joy. She felt as though she were coming out of a long, dark tunnel, stumbling and grateful and hungry for beauty and light.

"What do we do now?" Val asked when the song was over, slumping into Ava's desk chair and propping his feet up on the windowsill.

"I don't know," said Ava. "Maybe they're done downstairs. I don't hear any oysters being shucked." She knocked Val's feet away with her hands. "Wanna go check?"

Ava and Val went to the door that separated their private rooms from the main B&B and opened it a crack. Ava shrugged at Val, and they crept down the hall on the other side of the door toward the stairs, then peered over the banister.

"You don't have to creep." They both turned around to see Javier, the camera mounted on his shoulder. "I was just coming to find you. We're done with the oysters and Antonio wants a scene where you all try eating them."

"Uh, that is so not happening," said Val.

Javier shrugged. "Not my call," he said. Suddenly, they heard music coming from down the hallway. "What's that?" he asked.

"We must have left the karaoke machine on," Ava said.

The three of them went back down the hall, and that's when they saw Eden standing on Ava's bed. The karaoke machine was on, the mic in her hand, as she belted out the chorus of "I Wanna Dance With Somebody."

"Oh god," said Ava.

"Shhh," said Javier as his camera started filming.

Eden tipped her head back and belted out the final *meeeeeee* in a shimmering vibrato, as delicate as spun sugar but still as earthy as rain. But it wasn't her voice that stopped Ava's breath in her throat. It was the way Eden's face scrunched up when she sang, the bob of her head, the sway of her hips, even the way her hand fluttered on the mic—it all radiated pure joy.

Ava saw it in her mind as clearly as if she were watching it through the viewfinder. That New York skyline view disappearing, the buildings crumbling, the sounds and smells fading, everything blanketed in grey, everything muted by fog.

It was inevitable, but Ava still cried when she heard the news.

"Look how happy she is!" David exclaimed, kissing the top of her head. "I know, baby, we were worried too." She turned her head and tried to catch Bryce's eye, but he had his head lowered, and was straightening and re-straightening his tie. At least he had the decency not to pretend to think she was happy. At least he had the decency to look away.

As soon as Antonio had seen the clip, he disappeared with the footage back to his hotel. A few hours later, the clip was uploaded to YouTube; within two hours it had over 20,000 views. When they woke up the next morning, it was up over 250,000 views and had already been shown on three late-night talk shows, including *Late Night with Zoe Conrad*. By noon, it was official. Not only was the show not being cancelled, it was being renewed for two more seasons.

"Isn't it amazing?" David continued. "Our own little Eden, saving us from the brink of destruction!" He lifted Eden in his arms and danced with her across the kitchen, then set her down on the counter with a slightly stunned expression on her face.

"I don't understand what's going on," she said, her thumb travelling toward her mouth. "We were on the brink of destruction?"

"For goodness' sake, David, stop being so dramatic." Bryce crossed the kitchen and lifted Eden off the counter. "We were on the brink of no such thing, sweetheart. It just means that people like watching you, and because of that, we can keep making the show a little while longer."

"And that's a good thing, right?" She turned toward Ava, her thumb now buried in her mouth up to the pad, her index finger hooked over the top of her nose, her forehead creased over her deep brown eyes, which gazed questioningly at her big sister. It was all too much for Ava to take. She turned away from Eden and buried her head in her hands.

"Ava's just relieved that we're not going to be homeless," David said. "Now, you've got to go upstairs and pack, honey. You and I are going to New York in the morning to be on *The Cynthia Show*!"

If Ava could have smashed her head straight through the table in that moment, she would have. "Excuse me," she whispered, and ran upstairs to her room.

That night, after everyone was asleep, Ava slipped out of the house. Screw "only in the afternoon." Screw "not stopping." Screw *everything*. She grabbed one of the guest bikes out of the shed and pedalled down Cherry Tree Lane in the direction of the water, pulled there by some kind of force. Or maybe it was because everything in Gin Harbour sloped toward the ocean. Either way, she was moving away, and that was all that mattered. Away from the house. Away from her family. Away from whomever it was she had become while she was there—someone she was suddenly aware was not the person she thought she was. She wasn't elegant and mysterious, an enigmatic shadow who everyone was dying to know more about. She was a loser, an outcast, skulking in the corners of the television screen. She was *like that weird creepy kid you catch watching you sleep at summer camp*, the one they kept off-screen *so the cameras won't break*, the one that *even a dog wouldn't hump*.

All this time, she had thought she was in control—staying silent, keeping hidden, protecting herself. But she had given them exactly what they wanted. An Ava who shut up. An Ava without a voice.

Eventually, she found the beach. She stripped down to her underwear and picked her way over the rocks and through the seagull shit, moving tentatively under the light of the nearly full moon. But it didn't matter how dark it was, how cold, how the rocks stabbed at the bottoms of her feet. She needed to do something. When she reached the water, she stuck out her big toe and held it there, waiting for the ebb of the wave lapping against the shore to reach it. Then she took a deep breath and stepped into the water, cringing through the sting of cold until the initial pain subsided. She moved forward that way, incrementally, waiting for each inch of flesh to react and then adjust, until she was completely submerged, the water swirling around her body like thick black oil, silently lapping against her skin. She thought about that first day at the beach with her family last year, how she had believed everything might actually turn out okay. How stupid she had been. How overwhelmingly naïve. She understood now— no one had her best interests at heart. Certainly not her dads. She couldn't even trust her brother and sister anymore. She only had herself.

She lifted her feet from the bottom and felt herself become weightless, the salt buoying her up even as it stung her lips and made her cough as she inhaled. Kicking her legs gently, she swam out beyond the pier and lay on her back, staring up at the stars until she could feel her feet going numb. She turned her head, gazing out across the black water, and realized she had only ever swum in pools before—in chemically blue cement structures, water captured and tamed like an animal in the circus. She had never been in wild water before. It felt freeing. But somehow it also felt sad.

I should go back, she thought, as she felt her eyelids grow heavy. *This isn't good. I should go back.*

When she opened her eyes again, she suddenly realized she couldn't see the shore. Panicked, she spun around, but everywhere she turned was ocean, and her limbs were suddenly dead weights hanging from her torso, pulling her down. Black water filled her eyes, her ears, her nose. She breathed out, sending a trail of bubbles behind her as she kept swimming, down or up she couldn't tell, it was all just darkness.

She flipped over onto her back again and peered up through the ripples of the ocean. She knew she should be frightened, but all she felt was an eerie calm. There was a bright light over her head that she realized was the moon, but instead of swimming for the surface she went down further, the water growing colder and colder and blacker, until she couldn't see anything but her hands in front of her. She moved slowly, her lungs burning, her heart thundering in her ears. And then, everything stopped. Nothing moved, nothing hurt, and everything was quiet—a silence deeper than anything she had ever known, as though sound had never existed at all. *I am where I am supposed to be,* she thought. *I am home.*

She would have stayed there forever. But suddenly her body jolted into action and she realized her legs were already kicking reflexively toward the light of the moon, compelled by a basic survival instinct she was too exhausted to fight. She burst to the surface, heaving herself into the air and gasping for breath. The salt water was everywhere, but in the distance, she could see the headlights from a car on the highway, curving around the cove. She followed them until they were directly across from her, and then she pushed her heavy limbs through the water, swimming toward them, splashing and flailing until she could feel her feet touch rock.

Stumbling onto the shore, she lay on her back for a moment, feeling the earth hard against her spine, aching with desire to go back, to let the sea cradle her, to feel that nothingness once more. But instead, she crawled on her hands and knees back to her bike, pulled on her clothes over her sticky, still-wet skin, and headed for home.

Later that night, as she lay in bed, she heard Eden come into her room, like she had a thousand nights before that, her footsteps soft as she crept across the floor.

"Ava?" she whispered. Ava kept her eyes shut, letting her chest rise and fall under the blankets, feigning sleep. "Ava, I'm scared." Eden moved closer. "Please don't be mad at me. I don't know what to do."

Through one cracked eyelid, Ava saw Eden crouch down next to her bed.

"Will you tell me the California story? Please?"

But Ava only squeezed her eyes shut even tighter, waiting until she heard Eden's breath grow quieter, her footsteps retreating in the dark.

"I Wanna Dance With Somebody" – Eden Hart Karaoke

1,176,683 views

👍 85K   👎 1.3K   SHARE

LifeStyle   SUBSCRIBE 3.2M
Published on June 18, 2010

#EdenHartSings

Watch *Home Is Where the Hart Is* star Eden Hart channelling the great Whitney Houston in this exclusive video clip. And catch full episodes Thursday nights at 8 pm EST, only on LifeStyle!

750 Comments

Coolin 2 min ago
SO CUTE! <3 LOVE

JimPica724 2 min ago
you can tell she's going to be hot when she grows up
View all 18 replies

Yoolie 3 min ago
TFW a 11 yr old sings better than Whitney
View all 2 replies

Maddie Deene 4 min ago
Idk she sounds pitchy to me. Love the attitude tho, keep it up girl!
View all 6 replies

WickedWitch54321 4 min ago
Annoying mini-pop can't even come close to Whitney, she is a legend and
a queen!!!!!!!!!!!!!!!

Dizzydelia 5 min ago
OMG ADORABLE can't wait to see her on Cynthia next week!

Pichudo 6 min ago
Trash

SalO 6 min ago
I love her!!!!!!!

Hadley Freeze 7 min ago
She is ugly lol how is she on tv.

Mags

August 2010

––––◇––––

"Love Infinite"

The deer was on the hood before any of them saw it. It had come flying out of the dark and jumped straight into the path of the van. Mags let out a scream as it thumped against the windshield, shattering the glass into a starburst, one inky black, bewildered eye staring at her through the centre. Next to her, in the driver's seat, Paul cranked the wheel, a delayed knee-jerk avoidance response, and the van careened across the centre line and stopped with the front bumper inches from a guard rail, that thin piece of metal separating the road from the sheer drop into what Mags could only assume was Lake Superior, although from where she sat it looked more like the edge of the earth.

When Paul had first brought up the suggestion of an Align Above tour, Mags had been excited. After months of playing gigs relentlessly in Halifax, the band had picked up a good-sized following, and she pictured adoring fans, autograph sessions, meeting other bands. She had not pictured all their shit piled in the back of Paul's mom's minivan and driving on endless roads through tiny towns they had never heard of, playing to audiences who had never heard of *them*, giving their all onstage in front of five people, including the bartender, or to locals scattered around the room trying to play pool or watch the game or shout conversations over the songs they had just poured their goddamn souls into. They got robbed in Edmundston (a bunch of punks making off with two mics and one of their amps), and their van was vandalized over-night in Rivière-du-Loup (PUSSIES carved into the side door with some sharp object). They all got the flu in Kingston and got kicked out of their motel in Sudbury because Zac mouthed off to the housekeeper. After gas, food, and lodgings, they were firmly in the red, even with the sales of their homemade EP and the T-shirts Zac had designed himself and had screen-printed for free at his cousin's shop.

And now they had murdered a deer. Mags was sure of it. The eye on the windshield was blank, unblinking.

"What the hell was that?" Zac yelled from the backseat. "Did we just hit someone?"

"No, we hit a deer," Paul replied, the calmness in his tone belied by his face, which had gone so pale it glowed in the moon. He cut the engine, and silence filled the van. Then, as quietly and gracefully as a dancer gliding across a stage, the deer began to slide down the sloped hood, hovering for a moment at the brink in the spotlight of the van's headlamps before disappearing soundlessly over the guard rail and into the yawning jaw of the lake.

The four of them scrambled out of the van and rushed to the rail, peering down over the edge. The hood of the van was smeared with blood, and there was a dent in the centre that, in Mags's mind, was the exact imprint of a deer spine cracked in half. Below them was a great, gaping abyss, a long, sheer cliff face that plunged into the depths of Lake Superior. The deer was nowhere to be seen.

"Poor buddy," Mags murmured, trying to focus in the dark.

None of them could take their eyes away from the drop. Sam put his arm around her, pulling her into him. "At least we've given him a burial at sea. Or lake, I guess."

"Yeah," she said. "It seems fitting somehow." She could smell the thick deodorant he'd caked on in a failed attempt to mask the layers of body odour that had accumulated since his last shower, which was days ago. She surreptitiously sniffed her own armpit, knowing she smelled just as bad.

"Maybe he wanted this," Zac said. "Maybe he was tired of life as a deer. Maybe he ran out in front of us on purpose."

"Animals can't be suicidal," Mags said.

"Sure they can." Zac put his hands in his pockets and took a step back from the railing, his eyes still transfixed on the lake. It was strange to see him so calm, so focused. It was as if after the chaos of the collision everything was now muted, tamped down, still. "I read an article about a bridge in Scotland that dogs keep jumping off and no one knows why. It's totally metal," he added, almost as an afterthought, making sad little devil horns with his fingers.

Mags leaned in closer to Sam, feeling a chill creep through her body. "It's totally *disturbing*."

"If animals can commit suicide, can they also get insurance?" Paul asked. "If not, I might as well jump in there after him, because my mom is going to kill me anyway."

"It's been nice knowing you, then," Zac said.

The four of them continued to stare down into the lake. Mags watched strange shadows floating in front of her eyes, shapes made from the fluctuating light of the moon behind the clouds. She wondered whether the deer had died on impact, or whether it was still alive when it slipped over the edge, plummeting past grey slate rocks and disappearing into the icy lake. Whether it had risen back to the surface then, or whether it had merely sunk, settling somewhere among the shipwrecks resting in the murky depths.

There was no cell service in the particular dip in the road they found themselves in, so Paul and Zac had started walking down the side of the highway—cell phones in the air, searching for bars—leaving Sam and Mags behind to watch the van. It was cold, but neither of them wanted to get back in the van, so Sam went to dig a blanket out of the back while Mags rummaged around in the front seat for the bag of Cheetos she'd bought at the gas station before leaving Wawa. She wasn't particularly hungry, but she needed something to occupy her hands, her mind. When she closed her eyes, the deer stared back at her from the inside of her lids, helpless and accusatory.

"Here," said Sam, emerging from behind the van. He wrapped the blanket around her shoulders. "We'd better cut the lights. If the battery dies I think Paul might die too."

He climbed across the passenger seat and turned the key, and suddenly they were plunged into a darkness deeper than Mags had ever known. She felt a lick of primal fear, cold against her spine. "I can't see you," she said, trying to keep the panic out of her voice.

"Give it a second," Sam said. As her eyes adjusted, his face emerged out of the moonlight, his mouth wide open. "Please feed me."

Mags ripped open the bag of Cheetos and put one in Sam's mouth. "You're lucky I like you."

"I *am* lucky," Sam said, reaching into the bag. "You're the one with the Cheetos."

They stood there in silence for a few minutes. It was the first time they had been alone together in weeks. Since the tour began, they had shared every space and moment with Paul and Zac. Was it all in her head, or did it feel a bit awkward now, being alone with him after all this time?

"This feels weird," Sam said, as though he could read her mind. He took a handful of Cheetos and stuffed them in his mouth. "I don't even know what to do without those two around," he added, in between crunches.

"I know," said Mags. "Sometimes it's like I'm dating the three of you."

Sam licked the Cheeto dust from his fingers thoughtfully. "Do you think we have time to do it in the van before they get back?"

"Doubt it. Besides, it feels wrong. It would be like having sex at a crime scene." Mags leaned against the side of the van, feeling it rock gently under her weight. "What do you think is going to happen now?"

"We get the van fixed," he said, shrugging. "Then we carry on with the rest of the tour, become rich and famous, live happily ever after."

"Or the van is a write-off and we have to go home, and your parents kick us out of the house, and Paul and Zac kick us out of the band, and we end up living in a box under the MacKay Bridge for the rest of our lives."

Leaning against the van beside her, Sam interlaced his fingers, still wet with his saliva, with hers. "I guess the reality is probably something in between those," he said. "Anyway, my parents won't kick us out. We'll always have the basement."

Mags squeezed his hand. "I don't know if I can do it anymore, Sam." Those words, kept so long inside, felt heavy in her mouth. "The sneaking around. It's exhausting. I'm exhausted."

"Okay." Sam put his arm around her. "We'll get our own place, then."

"You know we can't afford that." Since dropping out of high school the year before, Mags had been fired from a dozen jobs, including a movie theatre, a dollar store, two pizza places, an ice

106

cream stand, and a tanning parlour/laundromat combination called the Tan 'n' Spin. She wasn't a bad employee, but the music always came first, and if a gig came up that conflicted with a shift, the gig won out every time. But the idea of her and Sam having their own place drove her to keep trudging around the city, wrinkled resumé in hand, trying to convince another harried old business owner that her shoddy work history was a testimony to the state of the economy, and not to her inability to show up for work. But even if she could hang on to a job, she knew she'd barely be able to cover groceries. "We'd have to eat cereal and hot dogs for the rest of our lives," she said.

"Those are my two favourite food groups," he said. Mags smiled. She appreciated what he was trying to do, but she could feel herself coiling back into herself, the need to survive blocking out all other thoughts. She was back on that tightrope, the ground falling away from her as her feet gripped the cord, and she told herself to focus only on placing one foot in front of the other. *Don't look down. And don't you dare look ahead.*

Mags could feel Sam shivering next to her, so she adjusted the blanket to cover his shoulders as well. Beyond the guard rail, the lake shimmered in the moonlight in a way she found both familiar and strange, as though she had seen it in a painting once, or read about it in a book. It almost made her feel homesick, but for something she'd never had. "I know you said the reality is in between," she said. "But neither of us are very good at in between."

"That's why we work," said Sam. "We make each other meet in the middle."

She knew what he meant, but Mags still couldn't help but wonder if even the middle was too far out of reach.

By the time the tow truck arrived, it was after one in the morning. They got towed to a garage in Thunder Bay, where they left the van in the lot and walked half an hour down a busy expressway until they found a crappy motel that they could afford—the parking lot humming with June bugs, the neon sign fizzling at the top of its rusty pole, missing letters transforming *Lakeshore Inn* to *Lake hor n*. As soon as they got to the room, Mags double-checked all the windows to see if any of them were broken, then stripped the sheets to examine the two mattresses for bedbugs. Even Paul, who had worried about leaving all their gear in the van at the glass shop, admitted that it was probably better off there.

The next morning, Paul went to check on the van while Mags, Sam, and Zac waited in the motel restaurant, nursing terrible, acrid coffees. When he got back, he had bad news. "It's going to take at least a week to fix everything," he said, sliding into the booth next to Sam. He shook his head. "That stupid deer."

"What does that mean, then?"

"It means the tour is over. And we're going to be stuck in Thunder Bay for a week before we can drive home."

"Jesus fucking Christ." Zac slammed his hands on the table, knocking over the sugar canister, which spit out a pile of white granules. "We're stuck in this shithole for a week?"

Mags caught Sam's eye, as if to say *I told you so*, but Sam shook his head. "Why does it have to be over?" he asked. "Why can't we just get the van fixed and then keep touring? It's the same amount of driving from here to either coast."

"Because, Sam, we have no money left. And after van repairs, we will have *less than* no money. I've already had to get my mom to pay for this stupid room with her credit card for the next week." Paul picked up Sam's coffee and took a sip, then made a face and put it back down. "You're all welcome, by the way. We won't have to sleep at the bus terminal."

"Or under a bridge," Mags muttered.

Sam kicked her under the table. "At least we can play our

show here tomorrow night," he said. "Maybe something good will happen there."

"Nothing good ever happens," Paul said. "You know this."

"No, I don't know this," Sam said. But he didn't argue further. They all just stared down at the table, searching for answers in the depths of their coffee cups.

Mags probably stared the hardest, but she came up with nothing.

—◇—

That afternoon, Mags went down to the waterfront with the old guitar Paul begrudgingly let her borrow, and sat on a bench next to the marina building with the case open in front of her. Over the past few months she had taught herself some chords and learned to play some covers, putting together a set of songs that she loved and were simple enough—mostly quiet, acoustic versions of '80s power ballads and '90s grunge anthems. She had been busking in every town they stopped in, making just enough to pitch in for food, and when there weren't a lot of people around, she used the time to write her own songs.

Lyrics had been coming easily to her, but composing music was turning out to be a struggle. She was still in awe every time she plucked at the strings, feeling the sound leave her fingers and reverberate around the room. Although she would never say it out loud to anyone, to her it felt like magic. She wanted to harness that magic, to tame and connect it to her lyrics. She just didn't know how.

She had only been there an hour when the sky suddenly opened up and it started to pour. She ran for the nearest shelter, which happened to be a covered bandshell in the middle of a field. She gazed out at the lake, watching the raindrops hit the surface, and then saw something near the edge of the water. Leaving the guitar safe in its case under the shelter, she pulled up her hood and ran to the shore, propelled forward by panic. Was it a person? It couldn't be a person. It was probably just some driftwood, a tree or a piece of pier that had become dislodged in the storm.

But it wasn't a log, and it wasn't a person. She climbed over the rocks and came face to face with an eye. A familiar eye. The eye of a deer. A very alive deer, standing on the shore in the rain, watching her.

Surprised, she felt herself lose her footing on the slippery rock and tumble to the ground. When she looked up again, the deer turned abruptly and galloped away.

"You don't know it was the same deer," Sam said later, as they sat drinking cheap beer on the floor of the motel room while the rain lashed the windows outside. "You couldn't have *recognized* it."

"I did, though. I recognized her. I *knew* her." Because she knew, in that moment, it had to be her. "It was the eye. I will never forget that eye."

"I think you *want* to think it was the same deer."

Mags exhaled slowly, trying to stay calm. "It was the same deer."

"Mags." He laughed. "Come on."

"Sam!" She clenched the beer can tightly, and it buckled under her fingers. "Why can't you just believe me? Or at least pretend to believe me. I mean, what does it matter to you if it was the same deer or not? Why is it so hard for you to go along with me on this?"

He laughed again, more bewildered this time than amused. "Because it's not realistic?"

Mags jumped to her feet. "*You* are talking to *me* about realistic? You, the same guy who thinks we can keep living in his parents' basement for the next ten years without them knowing? The same guy who thinks that we're going to have our big break in *Thunder Bay*? I just wanted to believe we didn't kill that deer. I was just trying to meet you in the fucking *middle*." She grabbed the guitar and stormed out of the motel room, leaving Sam sitting there on the floor, mouth gaping slightly.

Outside, it was still raining, but there was an awning over the door, and she sat down in the little plastic deck chair and tried to let it go. She knew it was stupid for her to get so angry. Stupid for her to believe that it could have been the same deer. But, for once, she had just wanted something to work out.

Her fingers found the strings. She didn't know what she was playing until her left hand began moving on the fretboard, and she realized it was a melody that she hadn't played before. That no one had played before. Eventually, the words came to her too. She opened her mouth and started to sing.

Later, she came back into the motel room to find Sam already in bed, his face lit up by the glow of his phone. "What was that you were playing?" he asked. "I couldn't really hear it clearly, but it sounded good."

"Nothing." Mags sat down on the edge of the bed. "I'm sorry," she said.

Sam propped himself up. "No, I'm sorry. Look, I've been going through apartment listings." He turned his phone around to show her.

"Sam . . ."

"No, listen. I want to take care of you, okay? I have savings, and I can work. There's no point in me going to university anyway, since we're going to have our big break soon and become rich and famous." He put his phone down on the bed. "Don't worry, I'm kidding."

"Who knows, right? It might happen." Mags lay down next to him, curling herself against his body. "And I don't need you to take care of me. I'll get another job. It'll be tough, but we'll make it work." She almost believed it. And she supposed that was a start.

———◇———

The next night was their show in Thunder Bay. They half-heartedly worked their way through their set list to a pub full of people who hadn't realized a band was going to be playing and were just trying to enjoy their food. About three-quarters of the way through, after an older man near the front of the stage eating dinner with his wife had asked them if they could "turn it down a bit," Zac put down his drumsticks.

"Well, fuck this. I'm going to get a beer," he said.

Paul, Sam, and Mags stood there for a minute, unsure of what to do. In the silence they left behind, the room filled with chatter, with forks and knives clinking on plates, chairs being pushed back from tables.

Sam slid his bass strap up and over his head. "Well, I mean, it's not like we're going to have our big break in Thunder Bay," he said, looking at Mags. "We might as well go home."

Home. That word again. Mags motioned to Paul's acoustic, which was sitting on its stand. "Can I borrow that? I have something I want to play."

Paul raised an eyebrow. "You want to play guitar?"

"Yeah. I kind of wrote something." When Paul still hesitated, she added, "Come on, it's not like anyone's paying attention."

"Of course you can," Sam said, picking up Paul's guitar and handing it to her. He glared at Paul. "At least someone is putting in the effort to make things happen around here."

Paul rolled his eyes. "Fine," he said. "I guess you can't mess things up more than they already are."

They left the stage and Mags put the guitar strap over her head, stepping toward the mic. She placed her fingers awkwardly on the fretboard and strummed, feeling the strings buzz unpleasantly against her nail, ripping it halfway off. She paused. Maybe this was a bad idea. But then she glanced toward the bar and saw Sam watching her, his face glowing, and she realized he had never seen her like this, from the audience. He had never seen what she was able to do. So she stuck her nail in her mouth and ripped the rest of it off, repositioned her fingers, and started to play the song she had written the day before.

It felt different, being up there without anyone else. The stage seemed so huge, like it was engulfing her, like there wasn't enough of her, alone, to fill it. But as soon as she started playing—something that she had completely written herself, something that was entirely hers—everything changed. She could feel herself growing, expanding, her voice filling the stage, the pub, the city, the world. It was like she was nowhere and everywhere all at once. Her eyes were open, but all she could see was light and stars.

Then the song was over, and she came back swiftly into her body, the last note echoing across the pub. No one moved. No one spoke. Not a single fork clanged against a plate. All eyes were fixated on the stage, on her, but the only ones she could see were Sam's, shining with pride as he stood by the bar, beer bottle clutched between white knuckles.

He put down his beer and started clapping, breaking the spell. Everyone else in the room began clapping too. And in that moment, Mags knew. Nothing had really changed, but somehow everything had. This was their moment. This was what they had been waiting for.

Mags was home.

Form Submission – New Form – Thunder bay show at the Forge

Squarespace <no-reply@squarespace.com>
to <alignabove@eurekamail.com>

Name: Tom Baker
Email Address: tombaker@eurekamail.com
Subject: Thunder bay show at the Forge
Message: Dear Miss Kovach,

I am nearly quite embarrassed to be writing these words, as I don't normally do this kind of thing, but I happened to be out dining with some friends on the night of June 21, expecting simply a quiet, ordinary evening of sorts at one of our humble local establishments when I was struck by the most Beautiful, Angelic voice I had ever had the most amazing opportunity to hear. Even more in awe was I when I looked up to Behold this heavenly voice was as yet attached to an incredibly gorgeous and sexy face and body on the stage as though on a cloud descending from heaven directly into my Heart. I apologize for my extreme language but there is really no other way to describe the attracted feeling I had upon seeing you, this stunning creature on stage in front of me as if God had put you there just for me. I am also an artist so I understand the deep connection and passionate you have toward your art and your calling, you can see some of my work at www.thomasjohbaker.angelfire.com/artwork, if you tell me which one is your favourite I will send it to you free of change. I would like to honour you with a drawing of yourself as well if you are ever back in our city, or perhaps from a photograph if you could send me one, preferably wearing something black (lace or spandex) and not covering too much skin. Not for sex of course but for drawing, as it is preferable.

Your devoted servant,
Tom
(Sent via Align Above)

114

edenmariehart **Follow**

edenmariehart Thank you guys so much for all the bday love!!! This has been the most exciting, exhilarating, uplifting year of my life, and none of it would be possible without all of you. I have the best fans in the business, and I can't wait to party with you on my birthday special. We will sing some songs, eat some cake, and celebrate the joy that is this precious life we are blessed with. And don't forget to send in all your beautiful artwork! I love you all!! XO Eden

Load more comments

mylittlebownie EDEN YOU ARE BEAUTIFUL 🌈🌈🌈🌈 🗡🌹🗡

greeneyegirl65 Flawless 😍

_tytyly_69 люблю тебя 😍 красотулька

mylittlebownie LOVE YOU EDEN ✨🧡✨🧡🌙🦋🌈 Ω🌹🖤🍉🌹🗡

mylittlebownie I'M YOUR BIGGEST FAN EDEN 🖤🖤🖤

mylittlebownie MY LOVEEEEEEEEE Ω🍉🖤🦄

mylittlebownie AWESOME 🍉🌙🍉🌹🗡🧡✨🍒Ω

mylittlebownie MY BABY HART I LOVE YOU 😊😊😊😊🗡 🌈🌈🌈🌈🗡

tania_schreiber12 Happy B-Day 🎉 We all support and love you 🍒😌

edenator_sg.cc Te amooo

peachimika follow for follow

mylittlebownie FOLLOW ME EDEN Ω🗡🍉🖤🦄

mylittlebownie EDEN WHY ARE YOU NOT REPLYING TO ME 🌹🌹
🔪🌹🌹👩👩👩

herbal_detox_system Happy birthday, Eden! Keep it up!

mylittlebownie REPLY EDEN 🔪

mylittlebownie REPLY EDEN 🔪

mylittlebownie REPLY EDEN 🔪

mylittlebownie REPLY EDEN 🔪

mylittlebownie REPLY EDEN 🔪

mylittlebownie REPLY EDEN 🔪

Ava

January 2012

———◇———

*Y**ou are beautiful*, the banner said. Unrolled, it measured at least six feet in length, the words painted on with poster paint, pink and blue and yellow, edged with glitter that fluttered to the floor like ash as Ava spread it out across the kitchen table, letting the ends drape over the sides. *re beauti*, it said now. Ava liked it better that way. It could be an experimental poetry collection, or an article in some pretentious design magazine. *Re: Beauty. Re-beauty.*

"*You are beautiful* is so last month," she said to Val, who was wrestling with a bubble-wrapped envelope full of what turned out to be two-dimensional paper flowers, cut from construction paper and painted with more glitter. "This should say *Survivor*. At least it would be shorter."

"Why do they all have to use glitter?" Val asked, brushing a large swath of it off his sweater and onto the floor. "I find it everywhere. I found some in my cereal this morning."

"What's the matter, Val, don't you want to *sparkle*?" Ava said, before blowing the glitter off her hand into the air, a shimmering

117

cloud hovering in the space between them. "Besides, little girls love glitter."

Val grimaced, stuffing the last of the paper flowers back in the envelope and making a mark on the clipboard in front of him. "This is not from a little girl," he said. "Unless you know any little girls named Jim who currently reside in Terre Haute Federal Correctional Complex."

"Ew. Get rid of those." Ava sat back in her chair, examining the banner. "This is filling me with existential dread. What was it Keats wrote? 'Of the wide world I stand alone, and think, till Love and Fame to nothingness do sink.'"

"Or, in the immortal words of Britney Spears, 'I'm Miss American Dream since I was seventeen.'"

Just then David came in, an armful of mail clutched to his chest, leaving a trail of loose envelopes behind him like Hansel and Gretel's breadcrumbs. "Ooh," he said, dropping the pile on the ground. "I like that banner. We'll put it up over the window here. It'll look great." Ava and Val said nothing. "Oh, come on, you guys. Cheer up. Eden is going to love this. It's going to be the best birthday party ever."

"Uh-huh," said Ava. "Nothing says 'best birthday party ever' like a bunch of decorations made by crazy people."

Because Eden was famous now, she had fans to make her birthday decorations. On the show blog, the network had asked people to mail in their best creations for the chance to have their handiwork featured on *Home Is Where the Hart Is Winter Special: Happy 13th Birthday, Eden!* For the past three weeks, Ava and Val had been opening envelopes, cataloguing all the crafts, and throwing out the obviously terrible ones. How they got saddled with that job, Ava couldn't quite remember, except that it was pretty obvious to everyone that the two of them had nothing better to do. Neither of them had had a storyline all season that lasted more than one episode. Thanks to Eden, they had basically become background actors in their own lives.

David lifted the banner reverently, stretching it open to its full, *You are beautiful* glory. It was long enough to take up his entire wingspan and still sag in the middle. "Gorgeous!" he proclaimed, letting the banner drop again, glitter puffing out around him as it landed. "Absolutely gorgeous."

"Sure." Ava opened another envelope, this one containing a piece of white Bristol board that unfolded into the shape of a unicorn, with a picture of Eden's face pasted on its head. She immediately flattened it out and placed it on top of the banner.

"Eden and Bryce's flight lands at three p.m. today," David continued. "I'm going to go into the city to pick them up, so we should try to have all the decorations ready before then." He wrinkled his nose, picking up the unicorn. "Well, this is just creepy."

"Can I come?" Ava asked. It had been so long since she'd been out of Gin Harbour she was beginning to forget what the real world looked like. Weren't all houses a hundred years old, with giant, lumbering porches and stained glass embedded in the doors? Weren't all towns eerily silent all winter, save for the clacking of ice chunks against one another as the waves pushed them toward the shore, the constant howl of the wind banging against your front door? Weren't all streets muted under a blanket of snow, and lined with shuttered craft stores and empty bistros, with signs proclaiming they serve the *World's Best Fish Chowder?* Ava wouldn't know. She had been stuck in this old-timey sea shanty for all of eternity.

But David shook his head at what she could only assume was partially the unicorn and partially her. "I need you two here to wait for the event planners."

Ava groaned. Because Eden was famous now, she got to do publicity tours while her brother and sister got to open her fan mail. Because Eden was famous now, she got to be gushed over by

119

Ellen and Kelly and Whoopi while her brother and sister got to *wait for the event planners*. Because Eden was famous now, her thirteenth birthday was going to be a huge, on-air celebration, while her sister's fifteenth birthday had passed quietly, with a Dairy Queen ice cream cake and a trip into Halifax to go see a movie, where afterward a trio of hockey moms had cornered her in the bathroom and forced her to take a selfie with them, even though she had spent the past hour and a half crying her eyes out at *The Tree of Life*.

Because Eden was famous now, her brother and sister had a little taste of fame. To Ava it tasted a lot like strong whiskey, or dark chocolate. It was bitter, but she could see how someone could like it. She could see how it could become addictive.

As soon as David left, Ava went into the front room, lugging a large plastic tub of decorations behind her. When she got there, she found Val dressed in his parka and pulling on his winter boots. "Where the hell are you going?" she asked.

"Out," he said.

"Out where?"

"None of your business."

Ava grabbed his boot out of his hand. "You're kidding me. There is no way you're leaving me here by myself."

"I assure you, I am," He snatched the boot back. "Don't worry. I'll be back before anyone even notices," he said with a grin.

Ava and Val's confinement order had slackened over the past year, mostly because no one cared where they went. They had even enrolled at GHJSH the previous fall—Ava in eleventh grade, Val in tenth—and although they were expected to be available for filming, if the call sheet didn't have their names on it, they actually had to go to class.

Now, Ava sat down on the stairs dejectedly, watching Val wrap the world's longest scarf around his neck. "Can I come with *you?*" she asked, knowing the answer.

He laughed. "And destroy this whole air-of-mystery thing I've so carefully cultivated? Where's the fun in that?" He heaved the door open against the bitter January wind and gave her a little wave before closing it behind him.

"Ahh! This is bullshit," Ava yelled. She picked up the top of the plastic bin and hurled it at the closed door. "Why does everyone have a life except me?" But she *knew* why. Television viewers liked Eden best. The local kids liked Val best. David and Bryce liked being on television best. And who liked Ava best? No one.

She was on her way to the kitchen when the phone rang— possibly the last landline in all the wide world. "Hello, Hart's Desire, where all your nightmares come true."

"This is Beth from Beth's Event Planning. I'm confirming the address for the Hart party today. We just arrived in Halifax, and we only have the refrigerated vans for the ice sculptures for another three hours. Will that be enough time? We still need to assemble the chocolate fountains too."

Ava squeezed the receiver so hard she thought it might crumble in her hand. Ice sculptures? A chocolate fountain? There was only one person in this house who got everything. And that was Eden.

"Oh no," said Ava. "Didn't Cindy call you? Cindy!" Ava pretended to yell out into the kitchen. "Did you forget to call Beth from Beth's Event Planning and tell her the party was cancelled?"

"It's *cancelled*? But we came all the way from New York. We were speaking with a . . ." She paused, and Ava could hear pages rustling. "Bob and Tess? At LifeStyle?"

"The cancellation order *came* from Bob and Tess. Cindy was supposed to call you. But *Cindy can't seem to do her job right*!" Ava yelled out the last part into the kitchen.

"But I've already sent two of my assistants to pick up the horses for the parade, and the fireworks are being delivered as we speak!"

"I don't know what to tell you, Beth."

121

"We had a contract!" Beth sputtered. "You're going to have to pay the full amount, as well as reimburse us for our travel and time."

"Well, *someone* is. Right, Cindy?" But Beth had hung up. Ava smiled to herself. *Let her eat Dairy Queen cake, then,* she thought. *See how she likes being treated like the rest of us.*

When David, Bryce, and Eden got back from the airport at 4 p.m., Ava was sitting in the front room, reading. "What happened?" David asked her, looking around the room in shock. "Where are the event planners?"

"I have no idea," Ava said. She kept her eyes focused on her book, an Alice Munro short story collection from the library with plastic on the cover that crackled when she opened it.

"Why didn't you call them?"

Ava shrugged. Without even lifting her eyes she could tell that David was on the verge of spitting rage. She'd thought all this success would have made him more relaxed, but as the show climbed higher and higher in the ratings, David's fuse grew shorter and shorter.

"This is a disaster," he said.

"Leave her alone, David," Bryce said. "It's not her job to keep tabs on these kinds of things." He walked over to her and kissed her on the top of her head, which made her flinch involuntarily. He straightened up awkwardly, adjusting the button on his shirtsleeve. "Anyway. We'll figure it out. I'll go check on the crew and see if they're ready."

Ava didn't know why she was always doing that. Wanting to be touched, but physically recoiling whenever someone tried. No wonder everyone liked Eden better. When she looked up from her book, her sister was standing in the door, New York still glowing off her—the electric charge in the backs of her eyes, the imprint of the pavement in the soles of her feet, the smell of exhaust on her clothes. Their eyes met.

"Hi, Ava."

"What do you want?" Ava asked sharply.

"Nothing." Eden brought her thumb to her mouth and began gnawing on her cuticle, in what Ava assumed must be the latest evolution of her oral fixation. For a moment, she thought Eden was going to cry. Well, what did she expect? A parade? This wasn't New York or L.A.; no one was going to kiss her ass here. Ava had seen the comments on Eden's heavily curated Instagram posts, and she scrolled through every single one of the hundreds that appeared every time Eden posted anything—*Eden I love you Eden follow me Eden you are a perfect please be my friend*. Everyone seemed to think there was something magical about her because she had that thousand-watt smile and scrunched up her face when she was embarrassed and said things like "Who's George Clooney?" when interviewers asked if she'd rather meet him or Brad Pitt. But Ava knew she was just a regular kid—a thumb-sucking, Harry Potter–loving, horse-obsessed, annoying, bratty little kid. There was nothing special about her. There was nothing special about any of them.

Of course, Ava only assumed Eden was still all those things. She hadn't actually spoken to her in months, other than when she was scripted to. Off camera, Ava deleted her texts and stayed out of the house as much as she could when Eden was home. Ava would never admit it, but what had started as anger toward Eden for the part she had played in the show's renewal had hardened into a deeper resentment. Ava knew it was unfair, but she didn't care. Eden had everything now. She would be fine without Ava.

David pulled out his phone. "Go upstairs and unpack," he said to Eden. "We'll find out what's going on, okay? Eden?"

"Okay." Eden picked up her bag and headed for the stairs. "Ava, do you want to come see the new sneakers I got?"

"No thanks," said Ava. She flipped the page of her book, the shape of the paragraphs on the page shifting slightly. If she flipped the pages fast enough, would they gallop like ponies, thick wedges of words racing toward an invisible finish line? She flipped another page, then another.

"Stop that," David snapped, snatching the book from her hand.

The hairs on the back of her neck bristled. She grabbed the book back and clutched it to her chest. "Why are you mad at me? Val's not even *home*."

"I'll deal with your brother when he gets back." He glared at her, taking in her holey sweatpants, her Spider-Man T-shirt. "At least change your clothes. We want the world to think you care about your sister." He pulled the phone away from his ear. "Why aren't you answering? Aren't you running a business?"

Ava stretched her legs out, resting them on the plastic tub of decorations, which was on the floor in front of her. "I thought how unpleasant it is to be locked out; and I thought how it is worse, perhaps, to be locked in," she said under her breath.

David swatted her feet off the tub, and they hit the ground with a loud thump. "Go upstairs with your sister. And stop quoting Virginia Woolf to me. I played Archduke Harry for an entire summer at the Forestburgh, I'll have you know." He glanced down and sighed. "Don't worry, I'll hang these up too, since I'm the only one who cares about this party, apparently."

Ava followed Eden upstairs. "They're Nike Zooms," Eden said over her shoulder. "They gave me two pairs, do you want the other?"

"Your feet are, like, three sizes bigger than mine," Ava said.

"Oh." At the top of the stairs, Eden paused. "I have some sunglasses too, if you want to see them."

"Eden, I don't want any of your stupid free garbage," Ava said, pushing past her sister and heading for her own room. "Tell David to call me when they need me. I have homework."

124

"Wait!" Eden called after her. Ava stopped in the doorway to her room, rolling her eyes. "I . . . I wanted to ask you something." She pulled out her phone. "I know I'm not supposed to be on Facebook, but I was so bored when I was at the hotel." She fumbled with it for a minute, then turned the screen toward Ava. "What does this mean? I know what some of the words are, but they don't all make sense together."

Ava took the phone from her. It was a screencap of a comment from the show's Facebook page in response to one of Eden's videos. Ava read the first two lines, then deleted the photo. "You shouldn't be reading this," she said, handing the phone back to Eden even though part of her wanted to smash it on the floor right there in front of her. "Social media is a cesspool of human garbage. These people are literal trash."

"But Dad said it was important. Dad said it's where the real people are. He said I should go on my Instagram and talk to people, the way Taylor Swift does, and it'll make people like me more. But I don't even know the password." She held her phone in her hand like it was a weight dragging her down. "I don't want to talk to literal trash people."

"Dad doesn't know anything. Don't listen to him." Ava crossed the room and sat down on her bed. Despite herself, she was starting to feel bad for Eden. "Don't you have other people to help you with this stuff? Handlers or publicists or, I don't know, personal life coaches or something?"

Eden frowned. "I don't think so."

"Well, you should. Because it can't just be Dad."

"Maybe *you* could help me."

Ava rubbed her temple. *Don't let her con you,* she thought. *Don't let her play this poor little famous girl card on you. She is the reason your life is this daily gauntlet of nonstop humiliations.* But still, Eden *was* her sister. "I can't," Ava said. "I don't know anything about being famous. You're the expert, you figure it out."

She saw the hurt in Eden's eyes, and she felt her resolve crumbling. It was easy to forget, watching Eden mostly through the lens of the camera as she did, that she was still a kid. "Okay," she said, reaching her hand out. "Let me see . . ."

"Ava!" David's voice was a hailstorm thundering up the stairs. "Get down here."

Shit. Ava dropped her hand and gripped the sides of her bed, trying to stay upright as the force of David's anger pushed her backward.

She could tell that Eden felt it too. "What happened?" she whispered.

"Nothing," Ava said.

She waited, feeling the seconds that passed like a heartbeat in the room, *duh-dum, duh-dum* vibrating the air slightly as she held her breath. Then, footsteps, growing nearer, louder. The shower curtain was ripped down from her doorway as David exploded into her room.

"What did you do?" he said, grabbing her roughly by the shoulders, her skin yielding like soft fruit under his fingers. "What did you do?"

"Let go of me," she shrieked, trying to twist out of his grip.

"David!" Bryce yelled from the doorway. David let go of her shoulders and she crumpled to the bed. "What the hell are you doing?"

"Do you want to tell him, or should I?"

"I don't know what you're talking about."

David glared down at Ava, who made a show of rubbing her shoulders as she scowled up at him. They held each other's eyes for what seemed like minutes. She could hear his breath rasping through his lungs and she knew he was trying to regain control of himself, to keep from lashing out at her again. She hadn't been frightened—she knew he would never actually hurt her. But the intensity of his anger had surprised her. It was just a stupid party. What did it matter?

When he finally spoke, his voice was calm. "Ava cancelled the event planners. You know, the ones that Bob and Tess flew in from New York. We have no chocolate fountain. No fireworks, no ponies, no parade."

Bryce turned to her sharply. "What?"

"No, I didn't," she said, her cheeks growing hot.

"Oh, you didn't? Then who answered when they called, pretending to be someone named Cindy?"

"I didn't pretend to *be* Cindy," Ava said under her breath. "I pretended to *yell at* Cindy."

"Either way, Beth from Beth's Event Planning is on her way back to New York as we speak."

"Who cares?" Ava retorted. "Why don't you just get her a Dairy Queen cake? Or is that not good enough for your precious little princess?"

David laughed, but there was no joy in it. "Ava, my darling. I am sorry if you didn't like your birthday. I am sorry if you're unhappy with your sister's success. But let me be clear. This is not some little family get-together. This is supposed to be a *television extravaganza*. We have no event planner, which means we have no party. Which means no shoot."

Ava wrapped her arms around her knees, sinking back against her pillow. She had only wanted to ruin the party a little, to take away Eden's stupid chocolate fountain. She had only wanted the party to suck. She hadn't meant to ruin everything. "Why can't you have the party without all that stuff? Why do you have to cancel everything?"

"The whole point of the party was *all that stuff*, Avalon. Now we're going to have to fly Beth and her team back on another day, bring back the crew, the actors, everything. How do you think Bob and Tess are going to feel about paying all these people to come back, Ava?"

"I didn't think—"

"No, you didn't."

Ava could see the anger building in David's face once more. She turned to Bryce, looking for backup, but he had his eyes closed, as though he were praying for a beam of light to transport him to the next realm.

"Do you think this is a game, Ava? This is our livelihood here. This is our *life*."

"No, I don't think it's a game," she said. "I don't. I'm sorry, okay? I'm sorry."

"She's sorry, David," Bryce said. "Let's forget about it and concentrate on getting things back on track." He looked so tired, so defeated. *Did I do this?* Ava wondered. *Am I the reason my dads are both so miserable?*

David spun around to face Bryce. "You're always defending her," he spat. "You never let her take responsibility for her own actions."

"Well, *one of us* has to watch out for her," Bryce said. "*One of us* has to act like a father."

"If you figure out who, let me know," Ava said.

"Get out," David said, his voice low, face dark. "I don't want to see you for the rest of the day."

"But this is my room."

"This room is the network's room, actually. Everything here belongs to the network. Do you understand what I'm saying? Nothing is yours, Ava. You have nothing."

Ava stood up, her legs shaking, her eyes coming to rest on Eden, who she had forgotten was there.

"It's okay, Ava," Eden whispered, her thumb at her mouth, ripping at her cuticle. "I didn't even want a chocolate fountain. I didn't want any of this."

"Go to hell," Ava said, running past her down the stairs and out the door.

———◇———

She walked for what seemed like hours along the side of the road, wearing only her sneakers in the frozen winter wasteland, her toes growing numb as the sun set and the temperature dipped. It was after six when the van pulled up ahead of her. She felt a flutter of hope that David had come to get her, and they could have a moment alone so she could tell him how sorry she was. Because she *was* sorry, regret etching deeper into her heart with every step she took away from the B&B.

But as she approached the van, she saw Antonio was at the wheel. He leaned over and opened the passenger door. She thought about walking away, but the pull of the van's heat was too strong. "What are you doing here?" she asked. "Aren't you freaking out about this party too?"

Antonio shrugged. "I was more worried about losing one of my key actors to frostbite."

"I probably deserve it." She got in the van and pushed her frozen hands against the vent, feeling them start to thaw. She glanced at him. "Shouldn't you be turning around?"

Antonio shrugged. "I don't know. Do you want me to?"

"Not really."

"Me either."

Antonio drove out of Gin Harbour and onto the secondary highway that curved along the edge of the ocean. While they drove, Ava kept her legs tucked under her, feeling the headlights of the oncoming cars track across her body while she watched the ocean breathe in and out from the shoreline and timed her own breath to the waves. They drove until they reached the neighbour-ing town of Mahone Bay. To Ava it might as well have been the same town as Gin Harbour—it had the same candy-coloured houses and harbour full of boats, their masts gently clanging in the breeze. Antonio parked the van behind a tall building and Ava followed him up a set of stairs to a pub on the second floor.

"Javier says he comes here sometimes when he gets tired of drinking in the one good pub in Gin Harbour," Antonio said as he held the door open.

Ava hesitated. "What if someone recognizes us?" she asked.

Antonio pulled his baseball cap off his head and put it on Ava's. It was far too big for her, and fell low over her eyes. "There," he said. "You're like a totally different person now."

Like the B&B, everything inside the pub was decorated with a nautical theme—on every surface there was an anchor or rope or sail. At one end of the bar a band was playing, several men with guitars and fiddles singing the kind of jig-and-reel, pseudo-Irish crap that Ava had come to understand was the only music people ever seemed to play in Nova Scotia. Behind them was a female backup singer, all fiery red hair and in a kilt, looking as if she would prefer to be anywhere else but there. Ava didn't blame her. She couldn't imagine what it would be like to have to play this music, night after night. In front of the band, a few older couples were dancing, moving awkwardly together and apart and then together again, their feet moving too slowly to keep up with the music.

Ava sat at a table in the corner while Antonio went to the bar to get them drinks. "If you ever tell anyone about this, I'll kill you," he said as he put two pints of beer down.

"That's okay, because my dads would kill *you*, and then we'd both be dead," said Ava, taking a sip. "We'll have so much fun together in the afterlife."

"There are no cameras in the afterlife, at least."

"Well, not in heaven, anyway."

"I don't believe in heaven."

130

"Neither do I." She stuck her finger in the foam at the top of her beer and swirled it around. "Why are you being nice to me? I've been kind of an asshole."

Antonio laughed. "You really have." His eyes dropped down to his beer. "But I get it. I understand why."

"You do?"

"Sure." He took a sip of beer. "I'm the enemy. It's kind of my job."

"Right now, you're actually the only friend I have. I mean, my dads hate me right now." Her stomach twisted as she thought of the exhaustion on their faces, the disappointment.

"Don't worry. They'll get over it."

"Yeah right. They'll probably never talk to me again. It doesn't matter anyway, it's not like I'm ever on camera."

Antonio raised an eyebrow. "I would have thought you'd be happy about that," he said. "Wasn't that what you always wanted? To not be on camera?"

"Yeah, but that was when it was my choice." Ava sat back abruptly, surprised at her own words. *It was supposed to be me*, she thought. Despite all her derision, the games she played, she had assumed that the world would fall in love with her. "Anyway, it's dumb. All of it is dumb."

"If you say so."

They sat in silence in the warmth of the pub, listening to the band singing something about how they wished they were in Sherbrooke now—a song Ava had heard a hundred thousand times since she'd arrived in Nova Scotia, a song that everyone in the province seemed to know, word for word.

"I hate fiddles," Antonio said after a while. "And I hate boats. And I *really* hate fish."

Ava toyed with the coaster on the table in front of her. "If you hate all that stuff, why are you here, then?"

"It's a job."

131

"There's lots of jobs," said Ava. "I'm sure you could have found one closer to home."

Antonio gave a half-smile. "I guess maybe that was part of it," he said. "I thought it would be an adventure. I didn't know it would be so hard to be away. Or that it would go on for so long." That half-smile again. He pulled out his wallet and flipped it open. Inside was a picture of a blonde, chubby woman with an equally blonde, chubby toddler. The kid, which Ava couldn't tell was a boy or a girl, was all its mother, had none of Antonio's dark good looks. "Molly and Micah," he said. "My wife and kid."

"Are you sure? That picture didn't come with the wallet?"

Antonio flipped the picture over. On the other side was a wedding photo: Antonio and Molly, outside in a park, autumn leaves artfully arranged in piles at their feet. "As far as I can remember, it's real," he said. "Five years now."

Ava flipped the picture back over and stared at it for a few minutes. "They seem nice," she said, feeling the back of her throat close over. She pictured their weekends together, at the park, Antonio holding each of them by a plump mittened hand. They probably all slept in the same bed sometimes, made couch forts, watched silly movies, went grocery shopping together, Antonio running the cart down the aisle like a race car. They probably made pancakes on Sunday mornings, adding in random things from the cupboard or the fridge in different combinations to see what they tasted like. "They live in New York?"

"Yeah." He closed his wallet and shoved it back into his pocket. "You know, I'd never even been out of the state before this."

"Me either," said Ava. "I love New York. I don't understand why anyone would ever want to leave."

"I didn't love it." Antonio took a long drink of beer, and then wiped his mouth as he put the glass back down. "I just got stuck there."

132

Ava didn't ask how he got stuck. She was pretty sure she already knew the answer. "I hate it here a lot," she said. "But you know what? I think I hate everything right now."

"You'll change, Ava," Antonio said. "You're young. You'll change a million times before you become who you are. And even then, you might still change again."

Ava thought about this. "But how do I know if I'm becoming who I'm supposed to be or who everyone wants me to be?"

Antonio finished the rest of his beer. "I don't know, Ava," he said. "Let me know when you figure it out."

Of course he didn't know. No one did. *Well, screw it,* she thought. Ava finished her beer too, slamming the empty pint glass down on the table. "I'm sick of thinking about myself," she said. "Let's dance."

Antonio looked at her. "You sure you want to give up your dark corner?" he asked.

Grabbing the brim of her hat, Ava pulled it down further over her eyes. "I'm like a totally different person, remember?" Maybe it was the beer talking, but she *felt* like a totally different person.

As they moved toward the dance floor, the bouncy jig gave way to the strains of a ballad, and the backup singer stepped forward to the mic. Ava paused, unsure of what to do, but Antonio took her hand and put his other hand awkwardly on her waist. She couldn't remember ever being held by someone who wasn't part of her family, and she tensed up, then relaxed as the woman began to sing, her melancholic voice snaking its way under Ava's skin as she leaned into Antonio's chest.

Next to them, a couple was kissing, both blonde and pale and glowing in the dim bar lights, the woman's lips lightly tripping across the man's lips, his cheek, his neck. Antonio's hand pressed against Ava's back, warm and gentle, an expanding wave of pleasure radiating out from under it. She felt weighted, solid, *real*, as though her body was finally taking up space in the world. For the first time in years, she was more than just an image on a screen, a character in a script, an extra in the story of someone else's life. Up until that moment, how could she have known that she wasn't a figment of someone's imagination? How could she have known she was really there?

That night as she lay in bed, Ava made herself come for the first time ever, her fingers furious under her sheets, her thoughts a hazy jumble of bodies and movement and heat and music—the sound of the singer's voice, her hair a fiery halo around her head, the violin bow stroking across the strings, the blonde woman's lips on her lover's neck, Antonio's hand on her back, her dad's anger, her humiliation. Then finally a feeling so raw and feral that she bit her own lip as it ripped through her, the heat in her body and the taste of her blood in her mouth, tinny and brackish, her muscles stretching and contracting, her skin sparking, alive.

I am here, she thought. *I am here. I am here.*

TMI Online
News — Sports — Celebs — Watch — Connect

Feud Alert! Hart vs. Hart
By Sadie Jackson

January 23, 2012 8:57 am

Sibling rivalry or just bad blood? If you are a regular viewer of the popular reality television program *Home Is Where the Hart Is,* you might have
noticed someone was missing from star Eden Hart's birthday special,
which aired last week on LifeStyle. That someone is her sister, Ava Hart,
who has been a regular on the show since it first aired in 2009.

So why wasn't Ava there to help her sister celebrate her 13th birthday?
As an insider source at LifeStyle told TMI Online in an exclusive interview, the two appear to have had a falling out. "Ava has always been jealous of her younger sister's fame," the source reported. "She throws
temper tantrums whenever Eden is around, and even tried to sabotage
Eden's birthday party by tipping over the giant chocolate fountain they
had brought in for the party! There was chocolate everywhere!"

According to the same source, dapper dad David Hart stepped in to save
the day, finding an alternate location for the party (along with an alternate chocolate source, we hope!). Although a LifeStyle rep denies there
is any conflict between the two, Eden and Ava didn't appear together
onscreen at all last season, and with this upcoming season focusing on
Eden's burgeoning modelling career, we can't picture them reuniting any
time soon.

As always, TMI Online wants to know: Are you #TeamEden or #TeamAva?

10 Comments

PinkBoots 22 min ago
#TeamEden

Yabbo 37 min ago
#TeamEden

Delia Lee 38 min ago
#TeamEden obvs

SallyO 54 min ago
Who would be anything but #TeamEden????

Homer J. Simpson 1 hour ago
#TeamEden

Gill Purcell 1 hour ago
Idk who Ava is but I hate Eden so #TeamAva I guess lol

Mandabobanda 1 hour ago
#TeamEden

Peter Smyk 2 hours ago
#TeamEden

JuicyG 2 hours ago
You suck TMI

Voula 2 hours ago
#TeamEden

Mags

January 2012

———◇———

"Fare Thee Well Love"

"Hey. I was just wondering. Are you wearing that kilt the traditional way?"

The voice was coming from behind the stage. Mags didn't even glance up from the mic stand she was assembling. "One hundred and seventeen."

"Excuse me?"

Mags turned around to find a man in his fifties in a ball cap and a navy windbreaker standing behind her, a pint of beer in his hand. "You are the one hundred and seventeenth person to think he's the first one to ask me that question."

The man's face fell, but only briefly before he rallied again. "Come on, honey, don't be like that," he said, winking over at a table of other ball-cap-and-navy-windbreaker-wearing men of varying paunchiness. Their hats all had the same gold lettering on them— Mags guessed either curling club or union, but she didn't care enough to think about it further than that. "Maybe I'll hang out back here and see if I can find out the old-fashioned way."

Mags clicked the final piece into place, then slammed the mic stand onto the ground. "If you don't go back to your seat I'm going to shove this mic stand up your ass."

From across the room came a chorus of jeers and snorting laughter. Annoyance flickered on the man's face, or maybe a hint of something darker. Then it was gone, replaced by a grin, gap-toothed and menacing. "Love me them feisty redheads," she heard him say as he walked back over to his table.

Later, as she stood onstage, surveying the crowd, Mags thought about how she hated the middle-aged men the most. The bros she could handle, with their short-sleeved plaid shirts and cargo shorts, their Canadian flag tattoos, a sea of baby faces and beer breath hopping up and down in front of the stage yell-singing along to "Home for a Rest" as they sloshed their drinks into the cleavages of their tank-topped, ombré-haired girlfriends. They were harmless, parodies of themselves, and would inevitably wind up getting caught pissing on the side of a Starbucks and thrown in the drunk tank or passing out in the back of a cab while their girlfriends made out with each other. And the old drunks, the ones with the wet eyes and the gin blossoms bursting on their noses, white spittle congealing in the corners of their mouths, so pickled and rotten they could barely even speak—they didn't even register on her radar. If one of them tried to touch her, she was sure they would disintegrate into dust at first contact.

No, it was the middle-aged men you had to watch out for. Unhappy with their jobs, left by their wives, with their thinning hair dyed and their belts pulled tight to try to hide their widening middles, their clothes a little too trendy and their laughs a little too forced. They drank too many rum and cokes and wanted you to think they were chill dudes, up for anything—while underneath they raged and simmered, their belief that the world *owed* *them* a bile brewing in their fat bellies. They came to the Pint and Parrel on Friday nights and waited for her after the Brigatines got offstage. Offered her shots of Liquid Cocaine, asked her if she wanted to come back to their place and smoke a little weed. Called her a cunt when she turned them down, their fun-guy veneer as thin and easily swept aside as a cobweb by a breath of air. Their inability to live up to their potential, to achieve what they felt they deserved in the world—it was not *their* fault, but somehow *yours*. Mags had seen it in their beady, weaselly little eyes. Pure hatred.

Like this one now, dancing with a girl young enough to be his daughter, his sleazy hand sneaking under her shirt and up her back as she clung to him. He wasn't quite old enough or pathetic enough to be one of the paunchy, lecherous fools crowding around Mags after her set, but the youth and beauty of the girl in his arms made him seem one of them just the same. The couple slowly disappeared into the throng of people crowding the dancefloor, swaying gently, oblivious to the shouts of the crowd around them, the beer glasses raised in salute, the flailing dancing.

Watching the two of them, Mags somehow felt responsible—it was *her* voice that had brought their bodies together. She could barely make it through the rest of the song without choking. When it was over, she stepped back out of the spotlight, waiting for the band to fire up another singalong rendition of "Mary Mack," one of the crowd favourites at the Pint and Parrel.

"Do a high kick!" she heard one of the ball cap guys call from their table. The Brigatines' fiddle player, a sixty-year-old Cape Bretoner named Juanita who had short, spiky, pink and purple dyed hair and towered over all of the men in the band, shot her a look of pity.

"It gets easier, love," she whispered. "Another forty years and they'll stop even paying attention."

If I'm still doing this in another forty years, you might as well shoot me now, Mags thought.

—◇—

"You shouldn't even be playing with that shitty old-man band," Sam had said to her earlier that day, as she was ironing her shirt in the kitchen while he ate dinner. "It's making you bitter. Plus, you hate all that Celtic music crap."

"Right," said Mags. "And what am I supposed to do, work at McDonald's?"

Their first EP, which they had released the previous fall, had done well, but not retire-to-the-French-Riviera well—not even pay-the-rent well. And for the past six months they had been working on new material for a full-length album—one that there had been little to no label interest in—and barely playing any live shows at all. Mags had started sitting in with the Brigatines right after Align Above got back from their last cross-Canada tour, as well as with a wedding band called Small Fry. Sam hated it. But then, Sam had rich parents. Mags took in the plate of toast in front of him, the mug of fair-trade coffee, the bowl of raspberries, and wondered if he even knew how much any of it cost. If he ever had to think about adding it all up in his head as he watched it getting rung through at the grocery store, calculating it down to the last penny. No, he never had to worry about what would happen if he couldn't afford grocer-ies or the rent for this shithole apartment they shared with Paul and Zac, because his parents would cover him. Mags didn't have that option. She either paid her rent, or she was out on the street.

Sam popped a raspberry into his mouth. "You'd be cute in a McDonald's uniform," he said. He grinned, blood red berry stain-ing his teeth.

"I would last two days at McDonald's," she said. "And you would get sick of the smell of French fries." She had only ever been good at one thing—her string of failed employment from the past few years was testimony to that. Everything else in the world was crowded out by music. There was no room for anything else. So she sang "Barrett's Privateers" on Friday nights at the Pint and Parrel for all those leering, middle-aged creeps, and "Walking on Sunshine" at the boat club on Saturday nights for all the polyester brides before they tossed their bouquets to their squad of drunken bridesmaids, and she counted herself lucky that she was still able to sing—even if it had to be on someone else's terms.

As she was finishing up the ironing, Paul came down the hall, his phone in his hand. "I just had a call from Danny at X-Wing. Their headliner for the harbour cleanup fundraiser thing tonight fell through and they want us to play it."

"Oh, sweet!" said Sam, grabbing another handful of raspberries. "They've sold out Alderney Landing for that. That's, like, eight thousand people."

"Yeah, and Holster are co-headlining. They just signed with Barry Hill at Ignatius Records."

Mags took in a slow breath. "How much does it pay?"

"It's a charity gig, Mags," Paul said, drawing up to her and squaring his thin shoulders as he tossed his phone from hand to hand. "It doesn't pay. But think of the exposure."

Trying to contain her anger, Mags carefully peeled her shirt back from the ironing board. "I can't do it. I have a Brigatines gig tonight."

Paul's jaw hardened. "Shit," he muttered. Mags waited. "I guess we know where your priorities are."

"Yeah, paying my *rent*. Unless our landlord has magically started taking *exposure* as payment, I'm sorry, but I can't." She could feel Sam trying to catch her eye, but she avoided his gaze. She knew what he was going to say, and she wasn't going to give him the chance to say it.

But Paul wasn't going to be put off that easily. "You're really going to do this? You're really going to make us miss this?"

Mags stuffed the ironing board in the cupboard and closed the door. "No, Paul. I'm not going to make you miss this. Please feel free to play without me. It's what you want anyway, isn't it?"

"Mags!" Sam said. "Stop it."

Paul laughed. "Oh, now you think I want you out of the band?"

"What, then? You're getting weird and power-trippy with me about playing a last-minute gig for *exposure*?"

"If I'm getting weird and power-trippy, it's because I want what's best for the band." He leaned in close as he spoke, and Mags could see the sweat on his forehead, the little red marks his glasses left on the bridge of his nose. He spoke evenly, but there was a sharp edge to his voice. "And I want to work with people who also want what's best for the band."

"If by 'best for the band' you mean 'someone who does whatever you want,' you should find another fucking lead singer," she hissed. "I'm out." She grabbed the rest of her Brigatines uniform off the table and stormed out of the kitchen.

In the room she shared with Sam, she sat down on the bed and put her head in her hands, trying to slow her breathing. She had to calm down—the rest of the Brigatines would be there to pick her up in the van any minute. When she finally dropped her hands and opened her eyes, she saw Sam standing in the doorway.

"Tell me you didn't mean that."

"Of course I didn't mean it." she said. "But I still have to go play this gig."

"Is it just because of the rent? Because I could—"

Her eyes darkened. "Don't," she said, her voice low.

He threw up his hands. "Fine. I get it. But I have to do something. What would change your mind about this?"

"I don't know, Sam." She stood up and began fumbling with the button of her jeans. "For some big producer to fall out of the sky and give us a record deal?"

He gave a weak smile. "That sounds like it would be painful for someone."

She pulled off her jeans and flung them across the room. "Good joke. You're super funny."

"Come on." He crossed the room and touched her cheek. "Talk to me."

Mags sighed. Wrapping her arms around his waist, she leaned her forehead against his, her rage gradually dissipating. She wasn't angry at him. She wasn't even really angry at Paul. Her anger was old, simmering, the same feeling that had been there for months— a slow boil of frustration and fear that bubbled up to the surface of her mind as self-doubt. *Why don't we have a record deal? Why was this other band more successful? What was the point of any of this?*

"The whole big-producer-falling-out-of-the-sky thing?" she said quietly. "You know it's never going to happen, right?"

"We've just got to keep going, Mags. Something is about to happen, I can feel it." Sam pressed his forehead harder against hers, his eyes overlapping into one at the bridge of his nose.

Mags stared into his one eye and wished she could feel the optimism he was feeling. It had been there, early on. But after so many bad shows in so many small towns, so many skeevy promoters and creepy fans and condescending music journalists and other asshole bands—what did it get them, in the end?

"We're building our fan base," Sam said, as if he could read her thoughts. "I mean, we put out an EP, how many people can say that?"

Getting exposure. Building a fan base. What did that even mean? She pulled away from Sam. "What we did before doesn't matter. We have an album's worth of material that no one wants. We're right back where we started." She lay her kilt on the bed and picked up the pin. "Did you know the last producer I sent our record to sent me back a note asking if we had ever listened to Arcade Fire? We're an indie band from Canada and he thinks we've never heard of Arcade Fire?" She jabbed the pin through the kilt and directly into her thumb. "Ahhh! Fuck this stupid thing." She stuck her finger in her mouth.

Sam gently pulled her thumb from her mouth. "It's okay."

"But what if it's not?" she whispered. "What if we don't make it? What if this is it?"

Sam was silent for a moment. Then he said, "I don't know." She could feel his body tense, and she realized he was scared too. And if they kept talking this way, they would drag each other down into a pit of doubt.

Reluctantly, Mags pulled herself away from Sam and picked her kilt up off the bed, fingering the heavy material as she thought about what to say next. "Okay," she said eventually. "I believe you. If you feel it, you feel it." It was a lie, of course. But it would make everything okay, for the moment. "I still have to go to Mahone Bay tonight. But I'll make sure I don't miss any more Align Above shows."

"That's a relief," Sam said. "I was beginning to think we'd made a mistake trading Becca for you." Mags rolled her eyes and threw her kilt at his face.

———◇———

When the Brigatines' set was over, Mags bolted from the stage to the bar, ordered a shot of whiskey and a beer chaser, and stood there pounding it back while daring someone—anyone—to approach her, to touch her arm, to call her "sweetie."

When she looked down the bar, she saw the man from the dance floor standing next to her, his head in his hands while he waited for the bartender to finish pouring his draft. Close up, Mags had to admit he was attractive, possibly even younger than he first appeared. Somehow it made it worse, that he was leading on this young girl when he most certainly could have any woman he wanted. Mags finished off her beer, wiped her mouth, and narrowed her eyes at him.

"Where's your child bride?" She hadn't meant it to come out. Or maybe she had.

The man raised his head. "Excuse me, what did you say?"

"Nothing," Mags said. On the other side of the room, a table full of older couples burst into raucous laughter. She tilted her head back and studied the ceiling, all dark wooden beams and wrought-iron fixtures, a line of nautical signal flags strung up along one side. *What am I doing here?* Mags thought, a faint thrum of panic growing in her chest. *This isn't where I'm supposed to be.*

When the bartender put the man's draft down on the bar, Mags snatched it up immediately and took a long drink.

"What the fuck are you doing?" the man asked.

Mags paused. "This is payment," she said. "For having to watch you grope that little girl on the dance floor." She brought the beer back up to her lips, staring him down. He stared back at her, trying to comprehend what she had said. *Come at me*, Mags dared him with her eyes. But he just got up from the bar and walked away. Mags finished the beer, put down the glass, and signalled to the bartender. It was only 8 p.m. The Alderney show would be about to kick off. "Can you call me a cab?"

"Sure," he said. "Where are you going?"

"Halifax." The bartender raised his eyebrows but didn't say anything, only picked up the phone. Mags glanced over at the stage, to where the rest of the Brigatines were getting ready for their next set. She felt a twinge of guilt, but it was fleeting, a muscular flick that pulsed once then melted away.

As she stood outside and waited for the cab to come, the cab that was going to cost her more than she'd have made if she stayed, she thought about that night in Thunder Bay. Standing up there on the stage, feeling the energy around her—for the briefest of moments, she knew, beyond a shadow of a doubt, that they were going to make it. And even in her darkest hours, that feeling was still there—even though it was buried beneath the piles of bills and unanswered phone calls and torn-up pages of song lyrics and overflowing ashtrays and catcalls from the audience, even though it was buried under all the bullshit of her ordinary days, it was still there, an ember burning quietly beneath the ash.

The Brigatines would survive without her. And maybe Align Above would survive without her too, but she would not survive without them.

The Shore
A Website for Halifax

Music>>Reviews
Show review: HarbourFest II at Alderney Landing

By Henry Cullen

If you've ever had your morning jog along the beach at Point Pleasant ruined by a used condom stuck to your shoe, you know that Halifax Harbour, despite a certain mayor's delusions, is not going to clean itself. And for the past two years, local bands have wanted you to know that they, too, care about the raw sewage being pumped into our biggest local attraction. This year's HarbourFest lineup included some local favourites as well as some newcomers, who managed to hold a rowdy crowd's attention for a combined three and a half hours. Openers Halo and Shark Church kicked out high-energy sets that place the bar high, and hometown heroes Holster—in one of their last local gigs before relocating to the Big Smoke—kept the party going with a set list that included a number of back-catalogue favourites as well as newer material. But it was last-minute addition Align Above who really stole the show, working the already-primed audience into a frenzy with their combination of searing guitar, driving bassline, and the powerhouse vocals of Mags Kovach tying that big sound all together with an emotional and sensual performance that will surely be talked about for years. Align Above might not have been household names before, but at least for the 8,000 people stuffed into Alderney Landing last night, they certainly are now.

PART
TWO

Sally O'Grady

@ograderz

Heads up, Gardeners! Eden is going to be filming Zoe Conrad tomorrow at 2 pm. Meetup will be at the side entrance of the March Theatre at 9 am. See you there! Also: a reminder you have 36 hours left to fill out our latest Facebook poll, If Eden Were My Daughter! #gardenofeden #edenhart #hartsdonyc

11:23 pm – 20 March 2013

103 Retweets 2,854 Likes

Melvin Walton @melvinwalton524 15 min

Replying to @ograderz

I'd take her to Disneyland and Instagram photos of her riding the teacups! #gardenofeden #iloveyoueden #wherethehartis #hartsdonyc

Todd Kim's Grandmother @kim_t0dd 14 min

Replying to @melvinwalton524 @ograderz

I'd build her a treehouse in the backyard where she could have sleepovers with her friends and play Truth or Dare! #gardenofeden

Sally O'Grady @ograderz 14 min

Replying to @kim_t0dd @melvinwalton524

Those are great ones! Make sure to add them on Facebook! #gardenofeden

Wherever you go @bee_reality 13 min

Replying to @ograderz @kim_t0dd @melvinwalton524

Just heard all the Harts are outside their old apartment! Can anyone in the Upper East Side confirm?????? #gardenofeden

Sally O'Grady @ograderz 13 min

Replying @bee_reality @kim_t0dd @melvinwalton524

Omg heading over there right now!! Will report back! #gardenofeden

151

Todd Kim's Grandmother @kim_t0dd 12 min
Replying to @ograderz @bee_reality @melvinwalton524
Meet you there! #gardenofeden

Ava

March 2013

———◇———

HIWTHI S05E01:
Hart to Hart

T he following spring, the network decided it was time to
bring the entire Hart clan back to New York for a week, to
hit the talk show circuit and do a photo shoot for *Celebrity* magazine, as well as film scenes for their Season Five premiere. It was
the Harts' first publicity tour as a family. As if any of them mattered except Eden.

"I don't see why I have to go," Val complained as they waited
in the airport lounge. Ava and Val were being chaperoned by
Antonio during the flight to New York, where they would meet
up with Bryce and David and Eden, who were already there. As if
they even needed a chaperone. Ava was sixteen—in the olden
days, she would have already been married with three kids.

"I thought you missed New York, bud," Antonio said.

"I'll save my thoughts for the confessional."

Ava had felt the same way as Val. This wasn't at all how she
had imagined returning to New York—briefly, as part of her
younger sister's entourage. But still, as the day approached, she

found herself getting excited at the prospect of going home. Not that she was going to let Antonio know that—especially after he presented them with the world's hokiest script, loaded with New York clichés and big-city banalities. "I hope you talk about being glad to be *back in the hustle and bustle*," she said. "And how much you missed the bagels."

"*Hustle and bustle* might be the stupidest phrase in the universe," Val said, glaring at Antonio.

Antonio leaned back in his seat. "What's bugging him?" he asked Ava, who dropped her eyes back down to her book.

"He doesn't want to leave Christie," she said.

"Who's Christie?"

"No one," Val mumbled.

"His new girlfriend. He doesn't want you to know about her because he doesn't want her on camera. You know, in case Carmella sees it."

"Who's Carmella?"

"His old girlfriend."

Val slid down in his seat, flicking his hair over his face to cover his eyes. "And thank you for that, Ava," he said, glaring at her as he popped in his earbuds.

She and Val were supposed to sit together on the plane, but Antonio slipped into the seat beside her, shoving his bag under the seat. "Your brother's mad at you," he said.

"What else is new."

"Well, you're reading a book. That's something I haven't seen before."

"Are you kidding me?" Ava closed the book quickly and stuffed it into the seat pocket in front of her. "You obviously haven't been paying attention."

Antonio was silent for a moment. "You're right," he said finally. He pulled out his phone and held it toward her. "Tell me something I don't know about you, Avalon Hart."

Her hand flew up to her face, but then she splayed her fingers and peeked through. "Are you filming this? God, don't you ever stop?"

"This isn't for the show. It's for me." He shifted in his seat, grinning at her. "Tell me your deepest, darkest secrets."

"No!" She was trying to be indignant, but a smile crept onto her face. "I mean, I don't have any secrets. And if I did, you'd probably already know about them. You're like Father Confessor over here, getting everyone's most private thoughts all the time."

"Oh, come on," he said. "We all know those aren't real. Give me something. Something just for me."

"Okay, I do have a secret," she said, levelling her gaze at him. Maybe it was because New York was waiting on the other end of the flight, but she felt bolder and more at ease with herself than she had in a long while. "But I can't tell you what it is."

"What about if we play Twenty Questions?" He switched the camera to front-facing. "This is Antonio Rivera, reporting live from seat 17D, where we're about to play What's Avalon Hart's Big Secret?"

Hearing him say her full name sent a shock through her body, and she was suddenly hyper aware of everything around her—the scratchy airplane seat upholstery against her skin, the vibration of the plane's engine, the air from the vent above caressing her face. She felt it all. "You can try," she said, closing her eyes. "But you're never going to guess it."

"Does it involve another person?"

"Yes."

"Does it involve a family member?"

"No."

"Someone at school?"

"No." Ava shifted in her seat, opening her eyes and staring at him. She lifted one eyebrow, something she had practised in the mirror after watching Vivien Leigh do it in *Gone with the Wind*. "I don't think you really want to know this."

He lowered his phone. Held her gaze. "Maybe I do," he said.

"Would either of you like a drink?"

Antonio turned from her abruptly, flashed a winning smile at the flight attendant. "I'll have a rum and Coke, please and thank you."

"Me too," said Ava.

"Hold the rum in hers."

Ava rolled her eyes. "No fair."

When the flight attendant left, Antonio picked up his phone again, but he didn't turn the camera on. "Don't wish it all away, Ava," he said, twirling the phone in his hands, watching it spin.

"Don't wish what away?"

"Your youth. It'll be gone before you know it and then you're going to wish you had it back." He raised his eyes to meet hers. "You're going to wish it so hard that it almost kills you."

Ava took a sip of her Coke, feeling it crackle on her tongue. The fizz expanded in her gut, prickling through her entire body, building up in all the corners of her—the crooks of her elbows, the backs of her knees, between her legs. She turned her face away to stare out the window, watching the plane's wing shuddering under its own velocity, thinking that she knew how it must feel.

—◇—

New York in March, slate grey and damp, was nothing like Ava remembered it. She felt as though she were on a movie set made to look like New York, everything flimsy and fake and too much of itself, like someone's idea of what New York should look like. The people were all just extras in a movie, the street signs made of Styrofoam, the buildings like two-dimensional cut-outs that she could knock over with a brush of her hand. She missed it, of course she did. But maybe the New York she missed no longer existed anywhere but in her own mind.

They drove from one old haunt to another—the park, their school, David's favourite deli, the used bookstore Bryce used to take them to on Sunday afternoons—the camera following them, always following them.

"Oh, the koi are all still here!" Eden said as they stood in front of their old apartment building. "There's Charlie, and Marvin, and Bubbles . . ."

Ava blinked at her sister, the sound of the traffic and the stench of the sewage making her eyes water after so many years away from it, a city girl no longer. "You're making that up," she said. "Those fish never had any names."

"They did!" She turned to David. "They did, right? You told me they did."

David shrugged. Bryce next to him burrowed down into his coat. The city seemed to shrink him. Maybe it was shrinking them all. Except Eden, who in the past couple of years had transformed from an adorable, anxious child into a beautiful, neurotic preteen, long and lithe and taller than everyone in her family, everything about her getting stretched, exaggerated, over the weeks and months. Instead of sucking her thumb, she now toyed with her hair, curling the ends around her finger and pulling on them to varying degrees, depending on how upset she was. Now, Ava could see the tip of her finger protruding from the tangle, purple and engorged with blood as she stood there staring at Ava expectantly.

Ava peered into the pond. "Those probably aren't even the same fish."

"He told me they had names," Eden said softly, letting her hand dip into the water.

A crowd of people stood watching them from behind a row of large men in black jackets. Private security, Antonio had told them, just in case. Ava tried to picture the worst-case scenario: the crowd moving toward them, morphing into one entity, a limbless amoeba with a thousand sets of crazy eyes, a thousand protruding arms waving a thousand flashing cell phones, a thousand wet mouths screaming *I love you I love you I love you* as it swallowed them whole. Was this what Eden had to deal with every day? Ava felt a flash of pity for her sister, but it disappeared just as quickly as she watched Eden raise a mittened hand to the crowd, beaming at them from behind her protective detail.

"Can we go now?" Ava asked, crossing her arms over her chest. "It's freezing out here. Plus, those people are creeping me out."

"Imagine," David boomed, not paying any attention to her, as usual. "Up there, fourteen storeys in the sky, is the place where you all were raised, where you took your first steps, where we laughed and played and learned to be a family."

"Oh god," said Ava.

"Don't call him that," said Val. "One of these days he's going to start believing it."

"Right here, on this very sidewalk where we now stand, is where you all learned to ride your bikes . . ."

"I didn't," said Val.

"You're making this up," said Ava. She narrowed her eyes and it felt as though her family was fading away from her, in and out, in and out. It seemed like it had been years since they'd all been together like this, and now they were like old friends at a high school reunion, awkward and strange, without anything to talk about except remember-whens.

"I fell and skinned my knee!" said Eden, skipping across the path. "Right here, in front of this fountain. I cried and you told me that I had to get back up and try again, because that's what life was about—getting back up and trying again." She turned to David, suddenly skeptical. "That's what you told me."

"Right, honey," David said, without meeting her eyes.

"I think we have enough now," Antonio said. They all shoved their hands into their pockets and turned away from the pond, blocking out the crowd that had been steadily growing around them, as they wordlessly made their way out to the street.

Next to the car, Antonio's wife, Molly, waited with Micah. "I think that's very sweet, what you said about getting back up and trying again," she said to David, hiking Micah up higher on her hip and giving Antonio a kiss on the cheek. "Tony, you should tell our baby that, when the time comes. Tony? Will you tell him?"

Ava rolled her eyes so hard she thought she was going to pass out. Ava had learned everything she needed to know about Molly the second she came rushing toward them at LaGuardia, dirty toddler in tow, exclaiming *we'll be best friends, I know it* as she enveloped Ava in a vanilla-scented hug. Molly had probably worked at a bank or in an insurance office until Micah was born, then stayed home after her maternity leave. She wrote a mommy blog about finding yourself after your baby or getting your body back after baby or pursuing your passion after baby or something like that. She ordered printed photo books off the internet. She knew how to roast a chicken, and she was proud of it.

"Yeah, *Tony*," Ava said. "You should definitely tell him."

Antonio took Micah out of Molly's arms. "I won't need to tell him," he said, peppering his face with kisses. "He's going to be the best bike rider there ever was in the whole world."

"He'll be good at everything. Just like his daddy," Molly said, now wrapping her arms around both of them.

Ava turned to Val and pretended to stick her finger down her throat. But inside, she felt like crying. What must it be like, to be with someone who loves you that much? To be a part of a family like that?

"Should we get some lunch?" David asked as he opened the car door. "We could do a really great scene at Costa's. The owner loves me. We used to go there all the time, remember, you guys? The place with the old-fashioned scale in the foyer?"

"I remember," said Ava. "Good to know you're not *completely* reinventing our past."

"Ava."

"Can I go back to the hotel room?"

"*Ava!*"

"What? It's not like you're going to need me for the scene anyway. It's just going to all be Eden." David glared at her. "Fine." She climbed into the car. "But I'm going to get the biggest pizza there is and I'm going to eat the whole thing."

"No pizza for us," Molly said, climbing in next to them. "We're strictly paleo these days, right, Tony?"

While they drove, Ava stared out the window, wondering how Molly had become the ordinary, boring person she was. Maybe her secret dream as a kid had been to be a pilot, or play an instrument, or go to Paris, but she had given up on it before she had even graduated high school, knowing dreams were for people who didn't understand the real world. In university, she had probably thought it was romantic that Antonio was a filmmaker, but now she hated the lifestyle, and wanted him to come back to Hoboken or wherever it was they lived and maybe work at the local television station, or in advertising, something nine-to-five, so he could be home on weekends to coach Micah's soccer team. And now, this was her life. Making holiday centrepieces as a hobby, or collecting things with penguins or rabbits on them, knick-knacks on a mantel, plates hanging on walls. A glass of wine with dinner and maybe a martini on girls' night, never losing control. Never letting Antonio touch her except on the weekends, and even then she often had a headache, or she was too tired, or Micah needed one more story. It made Ava want to lash out at her, for reasons she couldn't quite understand. She was mad at Molly for wasting her life. But she was also mad at herself, for wanting a life she'd never thought she should want.

When they got to the restaurant, Ava ordered a whole pizza, eating it in large, greasy bites as Molly picked at her salad.

"You're so lucky, Avalon," Molly said. "I remember when I was your age and I could eat anything I wanted."

"You still can," Ava said. She picked a piece of pepperoni off her plate and studied it, her fingers glistening with grease. "Or is there a law I don't know about?"

"No law." Molly laughed, revealing teeth teeming with masticated bits of kale. "Just don't want to get fat."

She leaned across the table toward Molly. "What do you mean 'get'?"

No one said anything. Molly sat back in her chair, her face a deep scarlet.

"Ava," Antonio said quietly. "What are you doing?"

"Nothing," said Ava. Everyone kept staring at her, and she felt a fault line crack open somewhere deep inside herself. She jumped up from the table and ran out of the restaurant. Outside, it had started to rain, but she kept running anyway, down the block and around the corner, as far as she could get from the restaurant without getting lost, needing to get away, away. She pulled herself into the doorway of a boarded-up bodega before letting the tears come, hot and unrelenting, as she held on to the brick wall with one hand and doubled over, trying to breathe through the sobs.

How had this happened? She was so angry all the time, so mean, so sad. She had become a vibrating mass of restless energy, a seething ball of need. Some days it seemed like all she did was eat and masturbate, one hand in a chip bowl and the other snaked down the front of her underwear in some kind of fever dream, desperately trying to make it all stop. But no matter how many cupcakes she shoved in her mouth, no matter how many furtive orgasms she gave herself under the covers at night, it was still there, this violent ache in the deepest part of her. Every waking minute full of wanting. And the problem was, she didn't even know *what* she wanted. Except that it was everything. She wanted everything.

"You okay?"

Ava looked up to see Eden standing in the doorway, a polka dot umbrella held over her head. "Not really," she said. She straightened, and was surprised to discover that she and Eden were the same height, even though she was standing on a step. "Why'd they send you?"

"They didn't. I just left. I'm pretty sure David's having a heart attack right now. He really wanted to have a scene with me and the owner of Costa's." She reached into the pocket of her military jacket, pulled out a tube of lip gloss, and ran it over her lips. "You know, that Molly chick is a pure bitch. She drives me crazy every time I'm here, like trying to pretend to be my mom or something. One time she actually referred to herself as my 'positive female role model.'"

Ava shrugged. "I *did* call her fat."

"She *is* fat."

"No, she's not. And even if she was, I still shouldn't have said it. That's not me." She pulled her hands into her sleeves, realizing she had no coat. "Anyway, when did you go all Mean Girl?"

"I'm not mean, I'm honest."

"Yeah, right." Ava shook her head. She didn't want to be having this conversation with Eden. She didn't want to know how Eden felt about Molly. She didn't want to know how Eden felt about *anything*. "You should go back. Just leave me alone."

"No."

"Eden, just go, okay? I don't want you here."

"Oh my god!"

They turned to see a woman standing on the sidewalk a few feet away, holding her phone up in the air.

"Eden! Eden Hart! It's me, Sally!"

Ava turned to Eden. "Do you know that woman?"

Eden shook her head. "We'd better go." When Ava didn't move, her sister grabbed her hand and dragged her down the sidewalk.

Over her shoulder, Ava saw the woman running toward them, so they began to run too, their feet splashing through puddles as they made their way back toward the restaurant.

"Hey, wait! Eden, it's me! From your fan club!"

A small crowd of people had stopped on the street, watching the woman as she huffed after Ava and Eden, trying to figure out what the spectacle was. A few of them had joined in, and as a group they seemed to move faster, like a rock picking up momentum as it rolled down a hill.

In a low voice, Eden said, "Ignore them. Talk to me about something else."

"Uh, did you hear about Tammy, the day cook from the B&B? She got fired. Apparently she was stealing booze."

"Oh no. I liked Tammy."

The crowd running after them had grown to at least a dozen people now. Ava could feel her heart speed up in her chest. "Well, you steal booze, you have to face the consequences, I guess."

"Ava, did you steal something?" someone called out from the crowd. "Is that going to happen next season?"

"Relax," Eden said, but all Ava could see was a wall of phones being held up in her face, a loud din of voices calling out their names. A woman put her arm around Ava's shoulders and pressed her sweaty cheek against hers, snapping a selfie while Ava raised her arm like a battering ram, trying to get through the crowd. Then there was a tug on her sweater from behind, and she fell to the ground.

"Please," Ava said. "Just let me get up." But when she tried to push herself up off the wet concrete, a large shoe came down on her hand, grinding her fingers into the ground. She screamed and fell forward onto her knees, but then she felt another shoe in her side as someone stumbled over her, a hailstorm of obscenities showering down on her from above. A hand reached down and yanked her to her feet, pulling her close as a phone hovered in front of her for another selfie, her own terrified face staring back at her from the screen. She squirmed free and whirled around to face another camera, then another, and another—bodies crushing against her, faces coming in too close, damp cheeks pressed to her skin, sour breath filling her lungs, hair in her mouth, an elbow in her stomach—and everything started to go black.

"Hey," she heard Eden say from somewhere in the distance. "Back off!"

Suddenly there was coughing and sputtering, and as the crowd dispersed, Ava's eyes began to burn, so she squeezed them shut. When she opened her mouth to breathe, she realized she couldn't.

"Come on," Eden said, her voice muffled. Ava could feel Eden's hand on her arm, dragging her forward once again. "We need to get out of here." Ava forced her eyes open a crack but everything was still blurry, so she let Eden lead her down the street until she couldn't hear the crowd anymore. "Sit here," Eden commanded, and Ava let her knees collapse, her back finding cold brick.

"I can't see," said Ava, jamming her fists desperately into her eyes.

"Jesus, don't rub it," said Eden. Ava felt cold water splashing on her face and the pain started to dissolve. "You've gotta shut your eyes when someone fires off bear spray," she said. "These are basic survival skills, Ava."

She blinked until her vision began to clear. Eden's eyes were rimmed with red and she had her scarf tied around the lower half of her face, her chin jutting forward in a way that made her seem so much older, so hardened, a world-weary soldier rather than a carefree fourteen-year-old. In one hand, she held an empty plastic water bottle. *Who is this girl?* thought Ava, wiping away the tears running down her cheeks. *Where is the meek little mouse I was with earlier today?*

"How was I supposed to know you had bear spray? What are you, like, some kind of super spy or something?"

164

"I don't trust those security lunkheads to protect me." Eden picked up her umbrella, which was overturned in a puddle, still open, and started shaking it. Then she capped the empty water bottle and tucked it back in her bag. "Did you know that when I was in L.A. last year someone tried to attack me with scissors? I swear to you, Ava, this guy just came at me, screaming something about wanting a piece of me. A literal piece of me. And security was nowhere."

"What did you do?"

"I kicked him in the balls. Then I jammed the heel of my hand into his nose. Like this." She reached out and touched Ava's nose with her palm. "I learned it on YouTube."

Ava pulled the sleeves of her sweater down over her hands and started wiping at her eyes. "It's like I don't even know you anymore." She said it as a joke, but suddenly it didn't feel like one. None of them knew each other anymore. "So that little sweetie-pie act back at the apartment building—that was just for the cameras, I guess, right? Playing it up for the YouTube clicks?"

"It's Child Star 101." Eden's eyes were flat, emotionless. "We're not supposed to grow up, until we *are* grown-up. No in-between stages, no awkward phases, no figuring shit out. It's either sticker books or sex tapes." She pulled in the spokes of the umbrella, wrapping the Velcro back around it. "I'm not ready for sex tapes yet."

"That's really messed up." Ava paused. "Why do you let them do this to you?"

"It's what I signed up for."

"Did you?" Ava thought back to that day in the kitchen when the news about the show's renewal broke. At the time, it didn't seem like Eden had wanted any of this. Ava knew she should feel some sort of sisterly compassion for her, but the memory of that day just enraged her all over again. Back then, Eden had let everyone steamroll over her because she didn't know any better. But now she was playing along, and somehow that made it so much worse. "It doesn't really matter. I guess this is what you do now. Put on this perfect-little-princess act so you can stay famous."

"I guess it is," Eden said lightly. "I mean, it's better than being stuck in Gin Harbour."

Ava gritted her teeth. "At least we can agree on that."

They sat side by side on the ground with their backs against the wall, watching the rain pour off the roof of the building across from them. Neither of them said anything, because there was nothing more to say.

———◇———

Fade in.

THE HART FAMILY is sitting on a couch next to late-night personality ZOE CONRAD. They laugh at a joke that CONRAD has just told, a lame attempt at a pun featuring their name. They look happy, peaceful, like a fun-loving family, one that you would want to invite over for Sunday dinner.

CONRAD

So, it must be really great for you all to be back in New York. How does it feel? Ava, let's start with you.

AVA

(Looking directly at the camera) It's been amazing. I'm so glad to be back. I really missed the bagels.

EXCLUSIVE VIDEO: Nuclear Meltdown! Eden Hart allegedly pepper-sprays fans, gets arrested in NYC
By Sadie Jackson

March 22, 2013 8:32 am

Last night in the Big Apple, reality TV's reigning sweetHART got into an argument with some fans outside Costa's Pizzeria, then allegedly fired off some pepper-spray into the crowd, TMI has learned.

Fourteen-year-old Eden Hart was outside the famous pizza joint with an unnamed friend when a crowd started to form. Without warning, the pretty preteen whipped out a canister and was spraying everyone— including several members of Garden of Eden, her unofficial fan club, who had been following her on her publicity tour through NYC.

"People were coughing, choking . . . one woman had to be taken to hospital," an unnamed source and a high-ranking GoE member told us. "I used to love her so much. I thought of her as my daughter. But now I feel like she's going down a bad path. I'm probably going to have to join a new fan club. Who's that little one who sang that song on *Ellen*? Maybe her, I don't know."

NYPD sources confirm that the police were called and multiple statements taken, but we're told no charges have been filed.

LifeStyle Network representatives have yet to issue any comment on the incident, or on rumours that Hart may have been on a drinking binge the night of the incident.

Word has it that Hart has now fled the country, and is hiding out in Gin Harbour, Canada, where her show, *Home Is Where the Hart Is*, is currently based.

An anonymous source close to the production tells us that although Hart may appear sweet as pie on the show, "she can be a real diva on set, making outrageous demands, and treating her manager/dad David like crap!"

TMI Online wants to know: Do you think Eden Hart is a sweetie or a spoiled brat?

9 Comments

> Clandy 1 min ago
> **Brat**
>
> Sarahhhhhh 1 min ago
> **brat**
>
> x_ilo_x 1 min ago
> **such a brat**
>
> SallyO 1 min ago
> This is bull. Seriously, you guys should be ashamed of yourselves, making up stories about poor, little, innocent girls. Eden deserves better than this, and all you haters can go screw yourselves because Eden doesn't need you, she is better than all of you.
>
> Ron Swanson 2 min ago
> **brat**
>
> Jen McLeod 2 min ago
> **Brat**
>
> JuicyG 3 min ago
> **You suck TMI**

xela 3 min ago
brat

Peter Smyk 3 min ago
brat

alignaboveofficial   **Follow**

---

alignaboveofficial Halifax, it's been a hell of a ride. We'll miss you! Come out to the Octopus tonight to say goodbye! #halifaxbands #halifax4life

Load more comments

kathkrammer we are so sad to see you go!

megamona678 I remember the first time I saw you guys, at that all ages club on Gottingen. I knew then that you were going to be huge. I feel honoured to have been able to see you so many times over the years. You will kill it in Toronto! 😍

jackfrancis018 can't wait for the show!

stivanypie Halifax loves you!

xohamburgerxo sellouts

sarah_hannah767 @xohamburgerxo seriously? You think they should stay in Halifax and play at the Octopus for the rest of their lives?

xohamburgerxo @sarah_hannah767 They don't have to go to Toronto. Toronto sucks.

Mags

July 2013

———◇———

"Not Dead Yet"

*A*lign *Above "Goodbye Halifax" Shows* was what the posters said, but the closer the dates of their final hometown concerts came, the more Mags was having doubts. There was an old, familiar fear welling up inside her, and she moved through her days with it sitting like a lead weight in her chest.

"You know, maybe we shouldn't leave," she said, as they were finishing their soundcheck for the first of their three sold-out shows at the Octopus. "The scene here is just getting started."

They all stared at her incredulously. "The scene here is *over*," Paul said.

"You don't know that." She ran her fingers lightly over the mic stand. "We could leave and it could explode, like it did in the early '90s. And then we'd be the idiots who missed it."

Shaking his head, Paul unplugged his guitar from his amp and began winding up the cord. "Or, we could be the idiots who stayed and waited, thinking that the anomaly that was the Halifax music scene in the early '90s is going to somehow repeat itself."

"It *won't* repeat itself if all the good bands leave."

"Jesus Christ, Mags. You were the one who suggested the move in the first place," Paul said. He threw the cord in his equipment box a little too forcefully. "*We've outgrown this city*, you said. *We need to move forward*, you said. Well, the only way forward is Toronto."

Mags knew Paul was right. They had played in Toronto before, of course, but it was always in and out—they needed to stay. No more stopping there between shows in Kingston and Sudbury, no more watching the city where they were destined to make their mark receding in the rear-view mirror. Over the past year, they had had minor successes, enough to keep them going after Mags quit the Brigatines, enough to stave off the desperation and despair—a live EP release, an East Coast Music Award, a North by Northeast showcase, a small write-up in *Canadian Music*. They had even received some major label interest. So where had this feeling of dread come from? Why did she suddenly feel as through Toronto was going to ruin them?

"I just don't think it's the right time," she said.

"I hear what you're saying," Sam said carefully, trying to tread water in the space between Mags and Paul, the way he always did. "Halifax has been good to us, but you know as well as the rest of us that Halifax is too small to break us."

"Being a Halifax band is part of our identity," she said. "If we don't have that, what do we have?"

Paul picked up the equipment box. "How about a *future*?"

"Who says we can't have that here?"

Paul's phone dinged, and he pulled it out of his pocket. Mags sucked in her breath. Recently, Paul had become obsessed with media coverage of the band, and had set up a Google Alert on his phone. That dinging sound had started to make Mags sick. "Listen to this. 'Align Above could do great things, but they have started to stagnate in Halifax, their newer songs practically indistinguishable from their old songs.' And that's from Henry Cullen at *The Shore*, who loves us."

"Pretentious dirtbag," Mags said. "Our new stuff sounds *nothing* like our old stuff."

"Fuck this," said Zac, getting up and grabbing his jacket off the back of his chair. "I don't give a fuck if the scene here explodes or not. I'm sick of seeing the same stupid faces at Canada Day at Alderney Landing and New Year's Eve at the Marquee and at the Pop Explosion or any of the millions of shows we've played here." He shoved his drumsticks into his bag. "It's always the same sweaty cans of Schooner, the same drunken walk home across the Commons, the same greasy Gina's breakfast, the same crappy write-up in the paper. I am done with this city, and if you guys don't move, I'm moving without you."

—◇—

"You know, there's things I'm going to miss about Halifax too," Sam said. "Our rent here is so affordable. And from what I hear there are no donairs in Toronto."

It was the morning before their final show, and by this point the lead weight in Mags's chest had grown into a boulder, pinning her to the bed. She looked around the room—the first room that had been really, truly hers—with its sloped floors and tea-coloured walls, a chipped windowsill just big enough for a little potted cactus. Mags had never owned a plant before, had never owned anything except four shirts and two pairs of pants. When they were packing up to leave, she had dropped the cactus, the pot shattering on the floor. Mags wasn't superstitious, but how could she not take that as an omen?

"Don't patronize me. You hate donairs."

"I don't hate them." Sam propped himself up on one elbow, leaning his head against his hand. "They give me heartburn. That could change. Or I could take a Tums."

"Forget donairs, okay?" Mags ran her fingers along his bicep, wiry and pale and run through with bluish veins that pulsed delicately beneath the skin. In the wake of her touch she saw goose pimples rise on his arm. "I just don't know what there is for us in Toronto."

"Uh, a recording contract, for starters. Paul says there's a lot of interest there."

"We can always sign with someone in Toronto and then fly back and forth. Lots of people do it. It wouldn't have to change anything."

Sam pushed back the covers and swung his legs over the side of the bed. "That's really what you want?" he asked, picking his jeans up off the floor and pulling them on over his boxers. "You want to live in Halifax and fly back and forth to Toronto to record?"

Mags buried herself deeper into the bed. "Why not? I mean, it's such a cliché. Another Maritime band fleeing the province at the first sign of success."

"Are you going to tell me what the hell is really going on?" He gazed down at her, his hands on his hips, shirtless, jeans unbuttoned. "I thought this was a done deal. Paul and Zac already signed a lease. We have a place lined up. We have gigs that *you* scheduled. And we've already played two sold-out shows at the Octopus full of people who think we're leaving."

"I know." Mags rolled over, pressing her face into the pillow. "And you're being so nice and I'm being so unreasonable and it's driving me crazy." Lifting her head slightly, she peeked up at Sam. "I feel like it's too soon. It's too fast. I need more time to think."

"You don't get it," he said. He sat back down on the bed and caressed the side of her face. "We're going to do this show tonight, and then we're going to move to Toronto and we're going to sign with a major label and we're going to be famous and make music forever and be happy together for the rest of our lives. And that's an order."

Mags exhaled slowly. She knew it wasn't only the thought of leaving the apartment behind that scared her—there was something else, something she couldn't name that was stoking her fear. But she also knew you didn't get anywhere in life if you let the fear take over. One foot in front of the other. "I'll be fine. I just need . . ." She stopped, unsure of how to finish the sentence. What *did* she need?

"I know there's things you're going to miss . . ."

She laughed. "Like what? All my friends are in the band. All my favourite places have closed or moved to Dartmouth or become a Pizza Hut. All the other bands I like have left. There is literally nothing left here for me."

The tip of Sam's tongue protruded from between his lips, a thought vibrating on it. "What about Frankie?"

Mags bolted upright in bed. "I told you never to say her name to me."

"I know. But—"

"There is no *but*. This has nothing to do with her." Blindly, Mags fumbled for clothing on the floor. "I can't believe you would even think that."

Sam crawled across to her side of the bed, reaching for her, trying to get her to slow down. "Mags, I know you . . ."

But she was already dressed. "Really? Because it doesn't sound like you do," she said. She grabbed her purse and stormed out of the room. She knew how to make a quick exit.

Mags spent the rest of the afternoon at the Octopus, where she sat in the green room drinking beers with a couple of the tech guys until she realized it was an hour before they were scheduled to go on and Sam still hadn't shown up.

"I don't get it," she said to Zac backstage as she listened to Sam's voicemail pick up for the third time. "We had a bit of a fight this morning, but it's not like him to be late for something. He wouldn't jeopardize a show just because he thought I was being kind of a bitch."

Zac took a sip of beer and leaned precariously back in his chair "Were you?" he asked. Mags glared at him.

Finally, with forty-five minutes left to spare, she raced back to their apartment in their Civic, worried and angry. Maybe he had left a note, she thought, or maybe he had taken a nap, forgotten to set an alarm. At least it was a start, a place to look. At least it kept her from catastrophizing, picturing gangs of knife-wielding teenagers jumping him in Victoria Park, desperate suicidal plunges from the MacDonald Bridge, buses skidding through stop signs and smashing his body to pieces. Most likely, he had lost track of time. Lost his phone. Lost his sense of direction. Lost *something*.

When she got back to the apartment, she ran up to their second-floor entrance, taking the steps two at a time. The door was unlocked but Sam was nowhere to be found. She dashed from room to room, but the moment she walked in she could feel his absence in the house like a phantom limb. She was about to leave when she noticed the back door was ajar. She peered through the dim light down the narrow back stairs. When her eyes adjusted, she saw Sam lying in the foyer at the bottom, a garbage bag split open next to him. His body was splayed across the floor and up one wall at an odd angle, his legs folded in on themselves in the constricted space.

Mags flew down the stairs and knelt on the bottom step next to him, suspended in a sea of plastic meat trays and coffee filters full of used-up grounds, the smell making her stomach heave. "Sam, what happened? Are you hurt?"

His eyes fluttered open, and he blinked up at her in confusion.

"I must have fallen down the stairs when I was taking out the garbage." He tried to shift his weight toward her, then winced and rolled back."

"It's okay, it's okay." Mags stood up, her heart racing, as she tried to think of what to do. What did people do in these kinds of situations? "A hospital. We need to get you to a hospital."

"No!" Sam shifted, and a wad of tinfoil rolled off his leg. "Just help me up. Please. We have to do the show."

"Are you kidding me? You can't do the show."

"I have to." He attempted a smile. "I don't want anyone thinking I threw myself down here to avoid our last hometown performance."

But Mags was too upset to laugh. "How long have you been lying here?" she demanded, sweeping his hair away from his eyes and staring into them. Why were they so glassy? Did his pupils seem dilated? She couldn't tell. Why couldn't she tell?

"I'm not sure," Sam said. "I think I might have been unconscious for a bit of it."

"Oh my god." Mags brushed some old coffee grounds off her jeans. Her knees were soaked through with garbage juice, and there was a piece of last night's sushi stuck to her arm, but she didn't care. "I'm calling 911."

Sam grabbed her leg. "Mags! Just help me up, okay? I'll be fine. I think I cracked a rib or something. I can move my legs and my arms. I'm not paralyzed."

"Okay," Mags said. Trying to take deep breaths. Remembering what they said on television about concussions. "Tell me what today's date is?"

"It's Saturday, July 13, 2013. My name is Sam Cole and your name is Magdalena Kovach. We live at 2238 South Park Street. The prime minister of Canada, unfortunately, is Stephen Harper." He turned his head to look at her. "Are you happy now?"

"No, I'm not happy!" A thin trickle of blood streamed from one of his nostrils, and Mags pulled her hand in her sleeve and wiped it away gently. "You're bleeding," she said softly.

Sam reached up and touched his face. "Just get me to the show," he said. "Please."

Mags exhaled slowly, then nodded. If this was what Sam wanted, then this was what she was going to do. She stooped over and slid her arm underneath him, bringing him to his feet with almost no effort at all. A chill ran through her body from the soles of her feet to the back of her neck. Sam had always been thin, but now he felt positively weightless. Had he been losing weight? How had she not noticed? "How does that feel?" she asked, trying to keep the tremor out of her voice.

"Not too bad." But he was clearly in pain. He put a foot up on the step and grimaced. Mags repositioned her arm under his armpit and pulled him up the first step, and then the second, and the third. "See? I can do it. I told you, I'm fine. I just need to get to the show and everything will be good."

"Sure," said Mags.

She knew she was supporting his entire weight, but the expression on his face was so hopeful that she didn't dare say anything. She couldn't. She couldn't bring herself to tell him he couldn't do it on his own.

She got Sam to the Octopus with zero minutes to spare, and laid him on the couch in the green room while she went to search for Paul and Zac. She found them in the wings with the stage manager, talking in a tight circle.

"Jesus Christ, you're here," said Paul when he saw her, rubbing his hand over his face. "Where the fuck have you been? Where's Sam?"

"In the green room. He . . . well, he fell. At our apartment.

I think he might have cracked a rib or something." Paul and Zac and the stage manager all murmured exclamations of surprise and concern, but Mags knew they all only had one thing on their mind. "He says he can play. He wants to play. Give us, like, fifteen minutes," she said, hoping they would protest, that they would offer to talk some sense into him, that they would act like human beings for once.

"Yeah, yeah, of course," Paul said. He turned to the stage manager. "We'll let the crew know." The three of them disappeared quietly, avoiding any further talk on the subject. *He's your friend*, Mags wanted to scream. *He's not just your bassist, he's your fucking friend. At least pretend to care.*

Back in the green room, Mags changed her pants and fixed her makeup with a shaking hand, keeping an eye on Sam on the couch. "You look like you put on that eyeliner while riding a roller coaster," Sam joked feebly as she helped him to his feet.

"Don't worry, I'm a trendsetter. In a few weeks everyone will be doing their eyeliner like this."

They walked together in the dark to the stage, where Paul and Zac were already waiting. Then Mags strapped Sam's bass over his shoulder and sat him on a chair. "I can stand," he whispered, but she could feel the tension release when he sat down, and he didn't fight her.

She stood at the mic and squinted her eyes at the crowd, unable to hear them over the pounding of her heart in her ears. Everything felt terrible, wrong. For the first time ever onstage, there was no rush of adrenaline, no flush of joy, nothing. Just a numbness. As the lights came on, she saw a speck of blood on her scarf. Suddenly, she felt as though she was choking on the air in the room. She peeled the scarf off and flung it away, not even caring where it went, as long as she didn't have to see that speck of blood, as long as she didn't have to acknowledge the buzz of worry it activated in her gut. It was as if she were standing on a high cliff, the audience in a ravine far below her. She couldn't see, couldn't hear anything.

Still, she stepped to the mic to sing. It was the only thing she knew how to do. And when Mags turned and saw Sam, sitting in his chair with his bass resting on his lap, his head bent in concentration, she knew it was the same for him.

After the show, Mags took Sam home.

"I told you, I'm fine," he said unconvincingly as she put him into bed, his face caved in with exhaustion. "'It's just a flesh wound.'"

"You dork," she said, pulling the blanket up over him. "You're going to have to cut out all that nerdy shit when we get to Toronto." As she moved toward the door, she paused and turned around. "'Now go away or I will taunt you a second time,'" she said softly, in a terrible British accent. But Sam was already asleep.

In the kitchen, she sat with a cigarette and a glass of wine and stared at her phone. It had been over four years since she had last spoken to Frankie, four years since her sister threw her out on the street. When Mags had left that night, she had been sure Frankie wanted her out of her life forever. But what if she was wrong? What if she had burned that bridge behind her while Frankie was standing on the opposite side, reaching out her hand?

It seemed impossible. But as soon as Sam had said Frankie's name, she knew he was right. And she had been so mad at him for seeing right through her like that, seeing the parts of her that she couldn't—or maybe didn't want—to see. But where had that anger gotten them? Sam was lying in bed, broken. And Mags was here, phone in hand, unable to sleep.

Mags knew it was late, but she also knew Frankie. It wasn't a big deal, really. It would only take a flick of her finger. A muscle twitch. The slightest caress.

Frankie answered on the seventh ring. "Hello?" she rasped over the loud music in the background, some kind of strobing EDM with a heavy bass drum and a fast breakbeat. "Who is this?"

"Frankie. It's Mags."

There was a long pause. In the background, Mags could hear

people talking, shouting, screaming. A party, or a club. She had imagined Frankie at home, stoned on the couch watching *Friends* reruns, or alone in her dark bedroom, woken from sleep. She should have known she'd find Frankie lit up like New Year's Eve fireworks at some warehouse rave in Burnside, trying to figure out whose dick she was going to have to suck to get more MDMA.

Mags was about to hang up the phone when Frankie finally spoke. "Who the fuck is Mags?" she said, then she laughed, stilt-edly, as though she were copying the way she thought people were supposed to laugh.

"Frankie . . ."

"Yeah, I know, I know. She's the big rock star. Living large down by the Arm with her rich-ass boyfriend and leaving poor Frankie rotting up in the Towers with the roaches."

"What? How did you know that?"

"What, you think I didn't keep tabs on you, little sister?" The music muted considerably, and now Mags pictured Frankie locked in a bathroom stall, platform sneakers pressed up against the door to keep it closed. "I know all about you and your little band. You've made quite a name for yourself in the city."

Mags took a deep drink of her wine, realizing she had lost all ability to read her sister. Or maybe she'd never had it in the first place. Finally, she put her glass down and picked up her cigarette with a shaking hand. "How come you never called, then?"

"Oh, I'm sure you've been much too busy to talk to me." There was a loud bang in the background. "Hey! I'm fucking using this stall!" Frankie yelled. Mags couldn't hear the person's response, but she did hear Frankie's: a stream of expletives ending with the phone going momentarily dead.

"Frankie? Frankie, I'm moving to Toronto. I thought you should know."

"Fine, get the fuck out of here!" Mags didn't know if Frankie was talking to her or the other person. "Can I borrow fifty bucks before you go?" she asked, this time definitely to Mags. "I'm a little short on rent this month." A pause. Then: "I'm coming out there and you can say that shit to my face!"

Mags hung up the phone. She stared at the blank screen for a long time, trying to recall one good memory of her sister. There must have been some, from before Karolina died—watching Saturday-morning cartoons, walking to school in the winter when the snow-banks were piled higher than both their heads, crawling into bed together when Karolina had to work a night shift and talking under the covers until they both fell asleep. But Mags knew these were fantasies. For as far back as she could remember, she had watched cartoons alone, walked to school alone, fallen asleep alone. She and Frankie had been two strangers living under the same roof, each locked in their own private battle, each siloed by their own wild rage.

Maybe they could have broken out of their isolation, if one of them had tried. Maybe Mags's phone call had been too late. But as she stared at her phone, still hot in her hand, she knew that at least it had accomplished one thing.

She was ready to go.

—◇—

They arrived in Toronto the next Saturday, Sam and Mags in their car trying to keep up with Paul and Zac in a U-Haul as they zig-zagged between traffic on the 401, the truck swaying ominously. Mags drove the entire way, while Sam slept in the passenger seat beside her. In the week since his fall, sleeping seemed to be all he could do. Even though he told Mags he wasn't in pain, he still sometimes cringed when he laughed, holding his arm across his torso. Mags knew it had been a mistake not to take him to the hospital, but Sam had been adamant.

"What would they have done, anyway?" he'd asked when she brought it up again in the car.

"Uh, fix you?" Mags said as she pulled out into the passing lane, trying to keep her eye on the juddering U-Haul in front of them. "Or at least give you some dope painkillers to dull the pain while your body fixes itself."

"Painkillers are placebos. A modern conspiracy by pharmaceutical companies to steal money from sick people. You might as well give me a jellybean."

Ahead of her, Mags watched the U-Haul weave around a bus. She tried to signal to change lanes, but a steady stream of bumper-to-bumper cars was determined not to let her in. "Will a jellybean shut you up about conspiracies?" she said. "'Cause I have a whole bag of them in the back."

"Yeah, it might," said Sam, turning around in his seat and rummaging through their stuff in the backseat. "But you have to pick out all the green ones." He procured the plastic bag from under an avalanche of pillows and blankets and empty Tim Hortons cups, all the usual road trip detritus, and Mags pretended not to notice the grimace on his face when he turned forward in his seat again. She hadn't told him about Frankie yet, but she would. She didn't want to add to his pain.

"You know, for a guy who's all about the rock and roll lifestyle, you sure are weird about candy," she said, focusing on the road in front of her instead of watching him squirm in his seat, trying to find a comfortable way to sit.

"Dibs on Weird About Candy for my next band name," he said. "You know, when I get sick of you losers and launch my pretentious side project."

"Not The Rock and Roll Lifestyle? Because that would make more sense for a bass-driven side project."

"Oh no. I'm moving into an experimental electronic phase. I might even bring in a keytar." Sam dug into the bag of jellybeans. "You already took out the green ones."

"Don't ever say I don't do anything for you," Mags said. She finally pulled out around the bus, which was wrapped in an ad for that television show Sam liked, *Home Is Where the Hart Is*. Beneath the windows was a picture of the family standing in front of a house—two men and a boy and a girl, looking up at a third girl, barely a teenager, with huge brown eyes that spread across three windows, and a smile that traversed the wheel well. How weird it would be, Mags thought, to have your giant face on the side of a bus.

"Do you think they're standing outside because of the deer?" Sam asked.

"What deer?"

"The one in the home." Sam shot her a sideways glance. "Or did my joke get ruined because you don't know what a hart is?"

"Your joke didn't get ruined," Mags said. "It wasn't funny in the first place." She pulled in behind the U-Haul, safely past the cluster of traffic. Ahead on the road, a sign said *Toronto: 132*. Almost there. Almost home free.

"I love that show," Sam said. "Remember that episode where they went back to New York, and then Eden got in trouble for pepper-spraying a bunch of people? That was amazing."

"Oh, right, sure, I remember." Mags glanced over at him. "Eden's the deer, right?"

Sam settled back against his seat, spreading his legs wide, and folded his hands over his chest. He closed his eyes and smiled. "You weirdo," he said. "I love you."

"I love you too," Mags said, but Sam was already asleep.

June 15, 2014

5 Things E-Hart Did This Week That Will Make You Say WTF
ICYMI (JK we know you didn't)

By Stella Stewart

Most of the world (and probably other worlds too) have been on 24/7 EdenWatch this past week, ever since the 15-year-old television star's drunken fight with model Bebe Romano sparked a spree of increasingly bizarre behaviour that has been as entertaining to watch as it is baffling. But just in case you've been vacationing on the outer rings of Zeguma (where we hear there's no WiFi), here's a rundown of the five craziest things she did in the past seven days.

1. Showed up at a New York Style Week after-party wearing a garbage bag that had YOU ARE ALL TRASH painted on it: She said later it was intended for the paparazzi, but we're sure Bebe and her crew took it to heart. AS DID WE ALL, EDEN.

2. Posted a photo on Instagram of herself eating a hamburger: Sure, this one doesn't seem so weird, until you consider that Hart is a strict vegetarian, and has appeared in ads for the vegan fast food pioneers SoyBoy over the past year. Reps for the California-based chain were quick to publicly cut ties with Hart, calling her actions "barbaric" and "basically as bad as Hitler." Come on, Eden, eat your shame in private like the rest of us.

3. Sprayed ketchup all over LifeStyle Network president Bob Axelrod's car: Maybe she was still hungry after eating that hamburger.

4. Picked a Twitter fight with Cher: And Cher stans were NOT. HAVING. IT.

5. Fired her manager, then rehired him the next day: We all knew that dad-ager David wasn't going anywhere, but wasn't it secretly kind of fun to watch her giving it to him outside the Ivy?

Ava

June 2014

———◇———

HIWTHI S06E08:
Break Your Hart: Part One

"**I** don't understand how Delia lost her underwear in Art History in the first place." Ava sat with a pickle jar tucked into the curve of her arm, curled up in the armchair where David liked to sit on show nights, his glass of brandy in one hand and his phone in the other, scrolling through the show's social media feeds. "I'm pretty sure that sexy violinist she screwed was looking for books on Ravel, not Rodin."

"You are the only person in the whole world who would notice something like that," said Val, who was sitting on the couch, his feet propped up on the coffee table without Bryce there to tell him to move them.

Ava and Val were watching *Librarians of Florida*, a TV show about young, hot librarians working and partying in the Sunshine State. As their own reality show continued on largely without them, they had become fans of several other reality shows. Ava liked *Devon's World*, about a single mom of septuplets who goes back to school to become a pastry chef, while Val preferred *Cats and Cons*, about a cat rescue group run by a group of ex-convicts. But LOF was their favourite, the one that they watched religiously every Tuesday night. It had everything Ava and Val loved to hate in a reality TV show—trashy leads, ridiculous manufactured drama, and a lot of sex against bookshelves.

"I just can't believe they had Isobel find them," Val continued, reaching over to take the pickle jar. "That whole woman-finding-her-lover's-underwear-shelved-in-with-the-post-Impressionists trope is so *done*."

"Oh, yeah. Like the whole famous-person-tries-to-live-like-regular-folks thing is so fresh and innovative," Ava said. "Prepare to be inoffensively charmed by these two glamorous but hilariously helpless big-city dads, their adorable, precocious youngest child, their brooding, sarcastic middle child . . ."

"And their pain-in-the-ass oldest child." Ava threw a pillow at him. "What?" Val said with a shrug. "You are."

"Maybe our next storyline will be about me finally snapping and murdering you."

"Doubt it." Val stuck a pickle in his mouth and crunched. "We don't get storylines, remember?"

Ava shifted in her chair, sinking deeper into its David-shaped dent. "They're missing out. I mean, who wouldn't want to watch us sitting here in our own filth, ripping apart other reality TV shows?"

"'Our own filth'?"

Ava gestured to the floor in front of her, which was littered with junk food, takeout containers, dirty clothes—the detritus of teenagers left unattended. These days they often both slept in the living room, each spread out on one of the couches, lying under quilts slightly damp from the fog seeping through the cracks in the windows, the light of the television flickering on the backs of their eyelids.

Val shrugged. "Yeah, okay. That's fair."

After five years of never being alone, it was strange to suddenly *always* be alone. The B&B, which in mid-June should have been bustling with people, sat eerily empty. Eden was off somewhere on her Instagram-filtered adventures and everyone else had been pulled along in her wake, filming the show that was now simply referred to as *Where the Hart Is.* "Home" might still be where *some* of the Harts were—namely, Ava and Val—but it wasn't where *the* Hart who mattered was. Ava glanced to her left, where a row of decommissioned cameras sat against the wall, unable to fulfill their purpose but still always there. Sometimes she imagined them turning themselves on of their own free will, lenses slowly unfurling, cameras twisting on their stands to follow Ava as she walked into the kitchen to get a glass of water, or as she went upstairs to bed.

"Do you ever feel like you're being watched? I mean, now. Like, all the time."

"So you're saying *now*, when there's no one here and no cameras running, *now* you feel like someone is watching you?" Ava nodded, biting her thumbnail. "I think you're suffering from Stockholm Syndrome."

"Of course I am. You are too."

"Maybe we should go and audition for other reality shows. We could be on, like, *Celebrity Big Brother* or something."

"No way. I'm setting my sights on *LOF*."

"Shhh," Val said. "Look at this."

LOF was over and now a tabloid television show was airing its intro. "Tonight, on *Hollywood Weekly* . . . Eden Hart: From Television Treasure to Total Trainwreck? We have the exclusive, never-before-seen footage of her Style Week meltdown earlier this week."

"Eden had a meltdown?" Val asked.

"They're exaggerating. She got in an argument with a Victoria's Secret model. She called her a few things she probably shouldn't have and got kicked out of a club. I saw this 'exclusive footage' on

ChatterFuel two days ago." Val stared at her. "What? I read it for the quizzes."

Onscreen, they flashed to a shot of David yelling at a group of paparazzi, Bryce standing behind him, forever his shadow. After the pepper spray incident, both of them now travelled with Eden, to keep her in line and to stop her from slipping up again—or maybe, Ava imagined, half hoping she would. If wholesome, apple-cheeked Eden had been compelling television, hot mess Eden had become a national obsession. So far, all of her acting out had been relatively harmless, aside from the fight with Bebe Romano. But her misbehaviour was building toward something, Ava could feel it. And it would appear that everyone else could feel it too.

"David, David!" the *Hollywood Weekly* reporter called out as her dad pushed past him. "Is there any truth to the rumour that Eden is in a relationship with a member of Boys Will B Boys?"

"No comment," David said, pushing Bryce ahead of him into the backseat of a car before climbing in himself.

"Jesus Christ," Val said. "That piece-of-shit band? What is going on?"

"I'm telling you, it's all made up. David thinks this stuff will get her more Instagram followers or whatever." Currently, Eden had 2.6 million followers, not that Ava was counting. Not that Ava cared.

"How do you know all this? You guys aren't even talking."

It was true. Other than a few perfunctory texts, Ava hadn't spoken to Eden in months. But she read the gossip blogs and tabloid sites with increasing ferocity, scouring social media daily for any information about Eden. She didn't know why she did it. Maybe it was for the same reason everyone else did—to see her fall.

"Can you please change the channel?" she asked. "I think *Underwater Welders* is on now."

But Val was glued to *Hollywood Weekly*. "You need to see this, Ave."

190

Ava reluctantly turned her attention back to the television, where one of the anchors stood on sky-high heels in a brightly lit studio, a picture of Eden frozen with her arm over her eyes hovering above her right shoulder. "Sources from within the show's production team report that after several on-the-road specials following Eden Hart, the show will be returning to Gin Harbour, Nova Scotia, for the remainder of the season, where the Harts will presumably go back to doing what they are known for—running a bed and breakfast."

And that was how Ava and Val learned their family was coming home.

---◇---

"I'm bored," Eden said the minute she got home, wandering around the B&B like she'd never been there before. She had two friends in tow, both named Kayla. Ava knew one was the daughter of a film producer and the other was a model, but she didn't know which was which. They followed Eden around everywhere she went, all tanned skin and perfect mouths, blonde hair swinging behind them.

With her family and the full production crew back at the B&B, there was activity day and night, and more people around than Ava ever remembered there being—people jostling through the narrow halls, taking way too long in the bathroom, leaving their equipment all over the house. It had been easy for Ava to avoid Eden in the first few days, with so much going on in the house, but now, as they got back into the rhythm of daily shoots, it was getting harder. Eden and the Kaylas seemed to be everywhere, their long limbs and phone chargers draped over every piece of furniture.

By the fourth day, even their dads had had enough. "Why don't you watch television," Bryce said as he untangled a giant knot of extension cords that the crew had left on the breakfast room table while Eden stalked through the house, tension radiating off her like soundwaves. "Or better yet, read a book. I'm sure Ava has some you could borrow."

From her seat in the front window, Ava glared at him. But her gaze softened as she took in his hunched shoulders, his face twisted in concentration. The more chaotic things became, Ava had noticed, the worse his compulsive cleaning tendencies seemed to get. *What happened to you?* Ava wondered. *How did you let yourself fade away like this?*

"You can go in my room and look if you want," she said. Was Eden old enough for Toni Morrison? Or maybe she would like Jane Austen? It would be nice to have someone she could talk to about some of her favourites.

"No thanks," Eden said breezily, picking up the end of one of the cords and looping it around her neck. "I think I'd rather kill myself with this extension cord."

Right. How stupid of me. "You'd rather kill yourself than read a book?" Ava kept her eyes down on her own book. "Of course, you might learn something. You know, other than how to shape your eyebrows or whatever."

"That's not in *your* book?" Eden asked, peering at Ava from across the room. "Oh, obviously not."

"It's funny how you never really read any great literature about makeup," Ava said, flipping her book over and squinting at the back cover. "Nope, not a single poem in here about lipstick. Not one measly line about contouring and highlighting. It's almost as if, I don't know, writers want to spend their time writing about things that *actually matter.*"

"I never, like, *got* poetry," one of the Kaylas said, all sharp angles and taut terracotta flesh curving against the chair she was perched on, a fashion magazine draped over her knees. "I mean, why not just write the words in actual sentences like a regular person?"

192

"Ava loves poetry," said Eden, dropping the cord and crossing the room to rest her chin on the top of Kayla's head. "It's all she ever reads. She's very, *very* smart."

"The only kind of poetry I like is Drake lyrics," said Kayla.

"That makes so much sense to me," said Ava.

"Are you calling her stupid?" Eden straightened up, her eyes wide. "You're going to sit there and talk shit about my friends in front of me?"

"Eden," Bryce said, but his voice was hollow and far away, and the tangle of cords never left his hands.

Ava rolled her eyes, closing her book and tucking it beside her on the window seat. "We're not at a club, Eden. There are no paparazzi here. You don't have to act all tough."

"Who says I'm acting?"

"Eden, Jesus, it's fine." Kayla flipped a page in her magazine, shaking her head. "Who cares what she thinks, she's nobody."

"She thinks she's somebody," Eden said. "She thinks she's somebody who can say shit like that to me and get away with it."

"I can say whatever I want," Ava said. "I'm not the one who's acting like an idiot in front of the cameras just to get more sponsors or higher ratings or whatever it is you think you're going to get from all this ridiculousness. I'm not the *attention whore.*"

Eden flinched, and for an instant Ava felt a twinge of regret. Then Eden stormed across the room to stand over Ava, her fists clenched in fury. "You don't know what the hell you're talking about," she said. "You don't know anything about me."

"You want to come at me?" Ava stood up from her seat, suddenly aware that she was at least half a foot shorter than her sister. "Fine, come at me. Punch me in the face. Prove my point, Eden, go ahead, just do it."

"Why do you even care about any of this, anyway? This is all just a *game*, remember, Ava?"

"Stop it, both of you!" Bryce yelled, throwing the cords down on the table. Both Ava and Eden turned to him in surprise. "I've had enough of this. You two apologize to each other right now."

"Sorry," Eden mumbled.

"Sorry," Ava repeated.

For a moment, Ava thought she saw a brief flicker in Eden's eyes of the sweet, funny kid she used to know. But had she ever really known her? Eden had been playing a role for so long it was impossible to know which parts of her were real and which parts were put on, constructed, carefully arranged. Ava doubted if even Eden knew. And it sickened her to realize that she had been the one to tell Eden that this was just a game. She had been the one to tell her that being Eden Hart was just a role she had to play.

Back then, Ava had thought she knew Eden so well. But standing there, watching her sister's back receding up the stairs, she was struck with the sudden realization that no one can ever know anyone at all.

—◇—

That night, as Ava was falling asleep, her phone went off. A Facetime call from Eden. *Yeah, right*, Ava thought, lying back down on her pillow, imagining Eden and the Kaylas in the room next door, drunk off the bottle of David's brandy she saw them steal earlier in the night, and accidentally calling her while they posed for selfies. She didn't need to see that. She didn't need to see anything Eden had to show her.

But her phone kept buzzing, and eventually her curiosity got the better of her. When she answered, she was surprised to see the background was dark, and Eden appeared to be outside.

"Ava!" she cried as the connection locked in, her voice pitched high, her eyes bright and manic as she swayed in the frame. "Guys, guys, Ava will know this!" She gestured to someone off-screen, and a face Ava didn't recognize appeared over her shoulder. "Ava, listen, I have a question. Lobsters live in salt water, right?"

"Yes, of course." The phone shuffled, and Eden's face was replaced by one of the Kaylas. Squinting at the screen, Ava realized they were standing by water, a large boat stretching out along the dock behind them. "Wait, where are you guys?"

Kayla's eyes narrowed, her lids slackened under the weight of some kind of intoxicant, her mouth gaping. "We were, um, partying? On this boat? With, um, some guy?"

The other Kayla appeared. "Oh, hey, it's Poems," she said, moving her face closer to the screen, and Ava could practically smell her breath, thick and sour. She took a drag of a cigarette and blew it at the camera. "That's what we call you now. Poems."

Somewhere off-screen, there was a loud crash.

"Where's Eden? What are you guys doing?"

"We are about to undertake a fucking *rescue mission*," the second Kayla said. She stuck out her tongue and then flipped the camera around, panning it across the lamplit waterfront. She stopped in front of a restaurant called The Fish Hook. Glass was scattered across the boardwalk, and as Kayla raised the phone, Ava could see the front window had been smashed out completely, the shriek of an alarm skipping through the darkness across the water. Several people were standing on the boardwalk peering through the opening, but no one was doing anything. Suddenly there was a loud crash from inside the restaurant, and a moment later Eden and another girl appeared in the window, their arms full of live lobsters.

"Be free!" Eden screamed, throwing her armload onto the boardwalk, a pile of green shells and antennae, spider-like legs entwined as they made their way, en masse, down the pier.

"Kayla," Ava shouted. "Kayla!"

"Oh my god," Kayla drawled as she turned her gaze back to the phone. "It's still you? I thought we were filming this for TMI."

Taking in the crowd that was forming behind them, cameras in the air, Ava sighed. "Well, I'm sure someone is."

Kayla turned around. "Sweet."

"Can you please stop her? She's going to get in huge trouble."

"Oh my god," Kayla said again, flicking her cigarette somewhere off the dock. "Go read some poems, Poems." Then the screen went blank.

"Dammit," Ava said, throwing her phone across the room. She thought about who in the house she could get to deal with this. Not David and Bryce, who would clearly die of heart attacks. Not Val, who wasn't even home. Definitely not Antonio, who would film it all and package it up for a Very Special Episode of *Where the Hart Is*.

"Dammit," she said again, and began digging around under her bed for her shoes.

By the time Ava reached The Fish Hook, the crowd had grown to about fifty people, all with their cell phones out. They formed a wide circle on the boardwalk in front of the restaurant, where the alarm was still sounding, a surreal background score to the silent liberation of what seemed like hundreds of lobsters, all scuttling toward the pier, pushing the onlookers back with their elasticked claws raised.

As Ava pushed her way into the circle, Eden appeared in the broken window, her arms laden with more lobsters. She skipped over to the pier and tossed the armful over the side into the water. "Swim, little babies. Swim for freedom." Then she made her way back across the boardwalk and began trying to usher the rest of the lobsters to the edge. Several onlookers joined in, but others were scooping up lobsters for themselves.

"Eden," said Ava, picking her way through the rippling pod of upturned claws. "What the hell? This is thousands of dollars' worth of lobsters."

196

"Ava!" Eden turned and hugged her. Her shirt was damp against Ava's chest and when she peeled away, she left a lingering stench of fish on her sweater. "I'm so glad you're here. Help me free these beautiful slimy weirdos."

"You're not freeing them, you're sending them to their death. Their claws have elastics on them, for Christ's sake. Do you even know anything about lobsters?"

"I know that they don't deserve a life packed into a tank, waiting to become someone's *meal*."

"Eden, if you think this is going to get you back in with SoyBoy, you're wrong. They're not going to want a criminal as a spokeswoman." She put her hand on Eden's arm. "We need to leave before the cops show up."

Eden shook her hand off. "No," she said, staring at Ava as though she didn't even recognize her. "We're on a *mission*." Her eyes focused in. "Go home, *Poems*."

"Do you really think that name is a burn? That's like me calling you . . ." She tried to think of something Eden liked, but she was coming up blank. "That's like me calling you . . ."

"Hey," Eden yelled, pointing at a woman in a cowboy hat and cut-offs with a lobster in each hand. "Put those down."

"Eden! You're going to get arrested."

Eden whirled around to face her. "What do you even fucking care?" she screamed. "You haven't said more than two words to me in months. You don't answer my texts, you don't like my Instas, you don't even watch the show."

"You have like five trillion Instagram followers! Millions of people watch your stupid show!"

"You're the only one who matters!" Tears wobbled on the edge of Eden's eyes, but she blinked them back. "I said, put those down," she yelled, turning back to the woman. "Those are my babies!"

"No, those are my dinner." The woman shoved the lobsters in her purse, their claws sticking out the top, elastic bands growing taut as they struggled. The rest of the lobsters, their claws still bound by elastics, kept making their way over the edge of the pier like lemmings. Ava vaguely wondered if they could sense the water on the other side of the ledge, or if it was a coincidence.

"Eden," Ava said gently. "I'm sorry. Come on." Then, in desperation, she added, "Let me tell you the California story."

Eden's face softened. She cast her eyes down at her hands, red and raw from the lobster shells, and for a moment Ava thought she was going to bring her thumb to her mouth. But she dropped her hands to her sides, her features hardening again. "That story was such *bullshit*. That mayor would have been arrested, you know. I looked it up."

Ava stared at her, confused. "It . . . it wasn't real, Eden. It was just a story I made up for you. You knew that."

"Of course I knew that." Eden pressed her lips together, then clenched her fists as though she were trying to hold something in. Her eyes met Ava's for a brief second, before they flicked away. "You stupid bitch," she said suddenly. "Give them back!"

"What?"

Eden pushed past Ava, and Ava turned in time to see her sister knock the lobster-stealing woman to the ground. As the two of them struggled on the boardwalk, a few guys in the crowd began to cheer. The Kaylas joined in, both their phones high in the air. The woman's purse overturned and the lobsters climbed all over each other, trying to get out.

"Eden!" Ava grabbed her sister by the hair, pulling her off the woman. To her surprise, when she let go, Eden whipped around and slapped her across the face.

"Leave me alone, Ava!" Eden snarled. "Why are you even here?"

"You called me!"

"Since when do you come when I need you?"

"I've always been here, Eden. I'm always right here. You're the one who's never here."

"Because I'm out there! Doing what everyone else wants me to do!" She was yelling now, her voice harmonizing with the alarm. "Everyone wants to tell me how to act, what to do, who to be. *Just be like this and we'll love you, Eden.* But you're my sister. You should be the one person who loves me no matter who I am."

"I do love you for who you are!" But even Ava could hear how hollow her words were.

"You promised me it would never change, that we would always be Ava and Val and Eden. And then suddenly it was me."

"Eden . . ."

"You were supposed to protect me!" She lunged at Ava, her eyes wild, pushing her hard in the chest.

Ava stumbled backward under the force of the blow, feeling her foot catch on something behind her. She let a small "oh" escape from her mouth as she started tipping backward. The last thing she saw was Eden's face, fixed with a mixture of anger and fear, and something else, something she couldn't quite put her finger on— and then she was falling. And her skull split open with light and sound and then there was water everywhere.

As she sunk through the depths, her consciousness blinking slowly on and off, like a dying battery, she was surrounded by dozens of lobsters, all of them silently and gracefully drifting down to the bottom of the ocean. She stared up at the sky, trying to find the moon, a star, the headlights of a passing car. Some kind of light to guide her. But, just as she always suspected, there was nothing.

EXCLUSIVE VIDEO: Ava Hart's Assault, Dramatic Rescue Off the Coast of Nova Scotia

By Sadie Jackson

June 23, 2014 7:13 am

TMI has received exclusive video of *Where the Hart Is* star Ava Hart's dramatic ocean rescue last night, after allegedly being assaulted by her co-star and sister, Eden Hart.

The video, shot by Ava's close friend, model Kayla Rhys, shows three bystanders diving into the frigid North Atlantic Ocean to retrieve the unconscious starlet. According to Rhys, Hart was knocked out and then pushed into the ocean by her sister during a vicious attack.

"Eden was on a rampage, and Ava tried to stop her," Rhys said. "She was just trying to be a good sister, but then Eden snapped and started beating on her. Once she'd knocked Ava out, she dumped her in the water. I thought she was coming for me next. I was so terrified!"

Police confirm that a 17-year-old female was transported by air ambulance from Gin Harbour to Halifax with non-life-threatening injuries, although they have so far refused to release any names. No charges have been laid against 15-year-old Eden Hart, but a source close to the show reports that she has already been admitted to rehab.

Our thoughts and prayers are with the Hart family during this difficult time.

TMI Online wants to know: What's your get-well message for Ava Hart?

9 Comments

MellieMellieMellie 31 min ago
We love you Ava get well soon!

Alison Church 33 min ago
XOXO Be strong Ava!

huing_ 33 min ago
WE'VE GOT YOUR BACK AVA! #teamava

SallyO 36 min ago
You guys are all so quick to judge but you don't know the real
story. Ava Hart is a liar and a whore and this is a publicity stunt to
discredit her sister and get attention DON'T BELIEVE THE HYPE
Eden Hart is the victim here and all you haters can go to hell

Abraham J. Simpson 37 min ago
Love u Ava!!!!

Mariana Diaz 40 min ago
¡Mejórate pronto!

JuicyG 44 min ago
You suck TMI

Nosidam 45 min ago
XOXOXXOXOXO LOVE YOU AVA XOXOXOXOXOXO

Peter Smyk 45 min ago
Stay strong Ava!

LIFESTYLE NETWORK
Your Life. Your Style. Your LifeStyle.

Memorandum

To: LifeStyle Network Executive Producers   Date: Monday, June 23, 2014

From: Bob and Tess Axelrod   Extension: 00676

Re: **Cancellation—Where the Hart Is**

In light of recent events, we have decided to cancel *Where the Hart Is*. We realize this comes at an inopportune time based on the increasing amount of public interest in the show, but taking into consideration Eden Hart's age and the suspected involvement of alcohol in yesterday's incident, specifically, Jane has advised this to be the best course of action given the optics.

We will be meeting with series producer Antonio Rivera in the coming days to discuss possible opportunities for monetizing the incident going forward.

Please direct any media requests to Maria.

Bob Axelrod, President and CEO   Tess Axelrod, CFO
LifeStyle Network   LifeStyle Network

cc: Maria Nunes, Jane Burton-Brown, Antonio Rivera

Mags

February 2014

———◇———

"Bright Outlines"

They wanted Mags front and centre in the shot.
"Let's mess her hair up a little, like she just got out of bed,"
the photographer said. "And let's lose the sweater. What does your
bra look like, sweetie? Oh good. Black. I like it. Let's go with that."

Suddenly there were hands all over her. She shivered as they
took off her top, put their fingers in her hair, arranged her arms
over her head in various positions. She glanced sideways at Sam,
trying to catch his eye, but he was with Paul and Zac, crowded
around the television propped up on a shelf in the corner of the
studio. The three of them relaxed and fully clothed and probably
high, waiting to step into the shot at the last minute without any
kind of makeup or wardrobe or coaching on facial expressions.
They were serious musicians. They were fine as they were.

The photoshoot was for their first magazine cover, promoting
Align Above's major label debut. Slated for a summer release, the
album was almost finished and buzz was already growing—word
had been spreading about the intensity of their live shows, and one

of Mags's favourite artists, Wylie Daniels, had given them a shout-out in a *Rolling Stone* interview. But Mags had been finding the publicity difficult to navigate. She had written most of the songs, but not one person had mentioned that fact during the interviews. Not the journalists, not Paul and Zac. Not even Sam. The only thing anyone ever wanted to talk to her about was her clothes, or her hair, or her stage presence, or what it was like to be the only girl in a band full of guys. They barely even mentioned her singing. Sometimes she felt as though she were another instrument, another stage prop to pack up in the van with everything else at the end of the night. And still she smiled, answered all the questions, giggled at the jokes. Partly she was intimidated, yes. But also she knew she needed to play the game. Whatever it took. She just wanted to sing.

In the corner of the studio their new manager, Emiko, was standing by the door, her ear glued to her cell phone. Emiko managed a few Toronto bands, including their old friends Holster, who said she was the best around. All Mags knew about her by this point was that she was always on her phone—Mags was certain she had never seen her without it. What did that ear even look like? Mags wondered. She pictured it deformed, a knobbed edge on an otherwise delicate shell.

"Emiko," Mags called across the room. Without turning her head, Emiko held up a finger signalling for Mags to wait, then wandered out of the room. *I'm here for you*, Emiko had said when they first hired her, but so far it seemed like she was only here for herself. Or whoever was on the other end of that phone. At one point, Mags had hoped she and Emiko could be friends, share a beer at the end of the night, talk about something other than music, other than the band, other than the boys. But friends had each other's backs. They didn't leave each other to flail in the wind, to become nothing but a body, cross-armed in a lacy bra under harsh studio lights, the bright outlines where skin meets air in sharp relief against a night-black curtain.

Emiko didn't even drink beer, Mags discovered one night, a sweaty bottle of Clancy's clenched in each hand as she waited for her to get off the phone. "I only drink clear liquids," Emiko said, gazing impassively at Mags's meagre offering, and so Mags drank them both, sitting backstage waiting for the boys to finish playing pinball with the crew so they could go home. More and more, it seemed, all she wanted to do at the end of the night was go home.

"Okay, great, let's get started," the photographer said, waving his hand through the air to round up his assistants.

Mags glanced around desperately, but no one was paying attention to her.

"You see," Sam was saying, pointing to the television, where the image of a giant candy-coloured house appeared onscreen, "the family's last name is Hart, and the B&B is called Hart's Desire."

"That can't be their real name," Paul said, scratching his head, his unwashed hair forming a stiff cowlick where his hand passed through. Of course, no one would brush it down, just like no one would trim Zac's nose hair or put concealer on the dark circles under Sam's eyes. They would say it was cool, it was rock and roll. Never wash your hair again, they'd say. Stop showering and let everything grow out and fester and smell. It doesn't matter. You're a man. You're supposed to be a little dirty, a little rough around the edges. You're supposed to be human.

Mags tapped the photographer on the shoulder. He turned around, but he stared right through her. "If you don't like the sweater, I have another shirt in my bag," she said.

"Shhh," the photographer said. "Don't move."

"Okay," Mags said. "Sorry." She tried to smile at the photographer, but he waved his hand at her dismissively.

"No smiling," he said. "Think sexy thoughts. We need you to smoulder." He rubbed her shoulder. "Don't worry, sweetie. My assistants will tell you what to do."

Mags shrugged his hand off her shoulder. "I *know* what to do," she said. "This isn't my first photo shoot." *And don't touch me*, she thought but didn't say out loud. How was it that it had been so easy for her to handle the skeeves at the bar when she was playing with the Brigatines, but now, when it came to one pretentious photographer, she had forgotten how to stand up for herself?

The photographer sighed. "Just do what they tell you."

He was gone before Mags could protest further. It wouldn't matter anyway, she knew. So she did what they said, moved the way they told her to, let her body be arranged into the shapes they wanted. And then the boys moved in beside Mags and *snap, snap, snap*, it was done. She hadn't even had time to check her hair, talk to Sam, or peek down to see if her nipples were showing. When it was over, someone handed back her sweater and she slipped it on, wrapping her arms around herself, pulling herself in. Sam gave her a wink as he shook the photographer's hand, and Mags resisted the urge to jab her finger right through his eye.

Later that night, they played a gig opening up for an American band that Mags had never heard of. Right before they went onstage, she and Sam had a massive fight in the green room, so loud that the venue manager had to come in and tell them to keep it down, the bar patrons could hear them over the music.

"I can't believe you didn't stand up for me!" she yelled as she angrily rummaged through her makeup bag. "That photographer could have had me *naked* and you wouldn't have noticed."

"I thought you were fine with it!" Sam said, waving his arms in the air, his right hand gripping the neck of a beer bottle. "Why didn't you say anything?"

"I tried!"

"You didn't say anything to me."

"I didn't think I had to!" She pulled out a powder brush and some powder and began violently applying it to her cheeks in the mirror, the bristles bending awkwardly under the force.

She didn't want to be mad at Sam—he'd seemed so fragile since they moved to Toronto that sometimes she was afraid she might break him. It had taken months for his body to heal after his fall in Halifax, and Mags was convinced he still hadn't, not fully— that he had only learned to live with the pain. So she kept all her frustration inside, or tried to channel it into her music. And it had worked, for a while. But this was something she couldn't channel away. "You're supposed to have my back, Sam. You're supposed to watch out for me."

"And you're supposed to be an independent woman who can take care of herself."

"Oh, that's such a cop-out. Saying you don't want to help me because you think it's important for me to help myself."

"Isn't it?"

Mags exchanged the powder brush for some mascara and went in on her eye. "Of course it is. But it's just as important for me to know you're on my side."

"Well, how am I supposed to know that, Mags?" He took a drink of his beer and then wiped his mouth with the back of his hand. "How am I supposed to know when I'm supposed to rescue you and when I'm supposed to let you take care of yourself? When one guy touches your ass I'm supposed to stand back and let you handle it, but when another guy makes you take your shirt off I'm supposed to act like a man and punch him out? Should I write all this down? Is there some kind of cheat sheet for this, Mags? Or am I supposed to read your fucking mind?"

"That's not fair," Mags said, throwing the mascara wand onto the table in front of her. She caught Sam's eye in the mirror. "You knew I had that under control, you knew it, but you stepped in anyway." It had been the promoter for one of their early shows in Toronto, before they had moved here. Just came up behind her out of nowhere in the dressing room and squeezed. Mags had been in the process of telling him what she was going to do with his hand if he touched her again when Sam came charging at him, shoving him up against the wall, holding his arm up against the guy's throat until his eyes started to roll back in his head. The promoter had refused to book them ever since. "Besides," Mags continued, "things are different now."

"Please," Sam said, sitting down on one of the couches and spreading his arms wide. "Enlighten me."

She leaned back against the counter, staring him down. "No one listens to me, Sam. It's like I'm fucking invisible."

He laughed bitterly. "Don't let Paul and Zac hear you say that," he said. "They might remind you of all the times we've been referred to as the backup musicians for Mags Kovach."

"At least people call them musicians!"

"Let's not get started on that again." Sam drew in a deep breath, and Mags could see him preparing to capitulate. *Don't you dare*, she thought. *Don't you dare patronize me.* "Listen. I know this is hard. But you need to take care of yourself. I'm not always going to be here to save you."

Fury lashed like a laser beam behind her eyes. "Oh, really? Because as far as I can tell, you are *never* here anymore. Where are you, Sam? The world could be caving in around you and you wouldn't even notice."

"Guys!" Paul stood in the doorway, guitar in one hand and a beer in the other. Even from across the room, she could smell the reek of weed. "Quiet the fuck down." He turned to Sam. "Wanna . . . ?" He made a puffing gesture with his hand.

"Sure," Sam said. Then, seeing the expression on her face, he shook his head. "Actually, nah, go ahead. I'm fine."

"What about me?" she asked, glaring at Paul. "Why didn't you ask me?"

"You've got to get your shit together, Mags. We're on in ten minutes, and you've only got makeup on half your face."

"Maybe I did that on purpose!" Mags yelled as he walked away. She turned back to Sam. "You guys should try having to spend an hour getting ready to go onstage instead of just pulling on a T-shirt that doesn't smell and going out back to get baked."

"I didn't even go!" His face flashed with a brief moment of pain—whether it was mental or physical, Mags couldn't tell. Likely both. It was as though the closer the band got to their dream, the more life it took from him. Mags sometimes wondered if he had made some kind of crossroads deal with the devil, and success was quietly eating away at his soul. Here they were, on the cusp of greatness, and everything felt so, so wrong.

"Jesus Christ, Sam, just go, I know you want to." She stared at him. When he didn't move, she threw her makeup bag at him, scattering tubes of lipstick and bottles of foundation across the floor. "Go!"

Sam slammed his beer bottle down on the table and left the room without a word. Mags bent over and picked up her favourite lipstick, which had shattered on the floor, and started to cry. She wiped at her face, and when she brought her hand away it was smeared with black. Great. Now she would have to start all over. Because as much as she wished it were possible, she couldn't just go out there and sing. She couldn't just be Mags Kovach, person with a job. She had to play a part. And her reward was the singing, it was true. But for the first time, she wondered if that was going to be enough.

Fights in relationships never really end, they get dog-eared, a folded-down corner of a page to remind you of where you left off for when you're ready to return to it, notes in the margins to remind you of what you were angry about in the first place. Mags and Sam dog-eared their fight and went out on stage and played as though

God himself were in the audience, God or Rick Rubin, whoever. Then, as was their post-show tradition, they fucked in the backstage bathroom, Mags's ass resting on the sink, her dress hiked up around her waist, her heels pressed against the doorframe.

"I'm . . . still . . . mad at you . . ." she said as Sam thrusted up against her, his face red, his blue eyes like slits in the flickering bathroom light. "This . . . doesn't change . . . anything. Oh god," she moaned as he bit down on her neck. "Do that again."

Sam brought his mouth to her ear. "You don't get to be mad at me," he breathed. "And I'm not doing that again until you apologize."

"That's not fair."

"Not fair at all." He snaked his tongue over her neck, and she dug her fingers into his shoulder, arching her back. "Say you're sorry."

"No."

"Say it."

"No."

"*Say it.*"

"*No!*"

Sam grabbed Mags's hips and pulled her forcefully toward him, holding her suspended over the sink, his fingers digging into her flesh as he shuddered against her. Mags wrapped her legs around his waist, but she couldn't hold on, her body slipping from his grasp as his fingers loosened. Her ass hit the edge of the sink, which separated from the wall with a loud crack, Mags screaming as the two of them tumbled to the ground in an avalanche of plaster and drywall, landing hard on top of the sink, their limbs in a tangle, water spurting freely from a pipe jutting out of the wall, spraying across the tiny bathroom.

Mags scrambled over the slippery floor and pushed herself up against the wall while Sam grabbed on to the toilet, hauling himself to his knees, his now flaccid penis still hanging free, his bare white ass in the air. Water ran down his face in rivulets as the pipe gushed above his head. Mags looked down and saw her dress was ripped all down the front, her breasts already starting to prune from the moisture.

Their eyes met, and they burst into laughter.

"Holy shit," Sam said, shaking his head like a dog as the gush slowed to a trickle. "We are supremely screwed."

"Yup," said Mags. "We're dead." She reached out and took his arm, which had been slashed by a jagged edge of porcelain, blood welling from the centre of an aggressively blooming bruise. "And you're bleeding."

"It's fine," he said. "Just a flesh wound."

His mantra, now. She traced her finger gently over his arm, along the widening gash. He cringed but didn't stop her. Both of them were starting to shiver, but they didn't move. "I don't know how to do this, Sam," she said eventually, keeping her eyes down, watching the blood mingle with the water and run off onto the floor.

"Do what?" he asked, wiping his other hand across his face, in a futile attempt to dry it.

"Be tough. Be vulnerable. Be a singer. Be your girlfriend. Be a fucking *grown-up*. Be everything everyone wants me to be."

Sam pulled her in with his uninjured arm. She could feel his heart racing under the thin, wet material of his shirt. "You don't have to be anything but yourself," Sam said, pressing his lips to her dripping hair. "You don't have to be anyone but Mags. Okay? Whatever happens, remember that. You are Mags."

Wordlessly, she nodded. She knew it wasn't as easy as that, of course, the same way she knew their fight wasn't over, it was dog-eared at a later chapter. But in that moment, sitting on the floor in the flooded bathroom with her dress half off and her underwear still around one ankle while the venue staff and the rest of their band banged on the door outside, it was enough. For now, it would have to be enough.

"Did you finish?" Sam asked, cupping one of her puckered breasts in his hand.

"No," she said, and he peeled back the wet edge of her dress and slid his fingers between her legs, his other arm clasped around her neck, his legs pinning her legs to the ground. She pressed back against him, feeling the puddle ripple underneath her, cool water and warm skin, his lips hovering beside her ear as she rose on the tide of his breathing, in and out, in and out, breath, breath, breath.

—◇—

The next few months, Mags thought about that moment every day. About how in that tiny pocket of time, it seemed like everything was going to be okay.

It didn't matter that by the next morning it was clear that Sam's arm was broken, or that they ended up at Toronto Western Hospital, where the X-rays showed a broken rib that had never healed from his fall. Or that after a whole three-ring circus of tests the cancer showed up. It didn't matter that they had to schedule the rest of their recording sessions around chemotherapy, or that Sam had to stay seated for every performance because he was too weak to stand, or that she knew Paul and Zac had conversations, behind closed doors, about whether they should find a new bassist. It didn't matter. It didn't matter that her heart broke a little every time she stepped onstage, knowing that Sam had vomited everything up moments before the show, that he had spent the previous three days in bed, unable to move, but that he still insisted on playing, on recording, on travelling, on pulling his weight. That night, none of it mattered except the two of them.

"You will pry this bass from my cold dead hands," Sam had

said one day when she tried to help him load the van on the way to the studio. "And I am not dead yet."

"Maybe that should be our album title," Mags said. Preserving the jokes, because that was what they did with each other. That was their normal. That was how she could still do normal.

He put on his best radio-announcer voice: "This week's number-one album is *Not Dead Yet* by Align Above." He grinned at her. "I like it." He closed the back doors of the van, and then sat on the bumper, catching his breath. "Hey, remember that time we hit the deer? On our drive to Toronto?"

Mags sat next to him. She wished she had a cigarette, but she had stopped smoking in front of Sam. "That was in Thunder Bay," she said gently. The chemo had made his mind fuzzy, and he was incredibly self-conscious about it. "Like four years ago. We didn't hit anything while we were driving here."

Sam furrowed his brow, running his hand over the peach fuzz of his head. "I swear to you there was a deer on our drive to Toronto," he said. "On the 401 somewhere."

"That stupid show." Mags leaned forward, her hands on her knees. Her hair fell over her face, but she didn't push it back. She knew Sam liked to do it. "That Hart show. You made a joke about a deer in the house."

"Right." Sam reached out and took a lock of her hair between his fingers, tucking it behind her ears. "We should get married," he said.

Mags smiled. "I know," she said.

He knew, Mags thought. When he fell down the stairs, he must have known. That there was something very wrong. That the moment he walked into a hospital, it would become real. And that's why he resisted. And even though there was a part of her that wished she had pushed him to go to the hospital that day in Halifax, knowing that they would have caught it seven months

213

earlier, and he would have had seven more months of treatment, she wasn't sure she would have traded this time together. Because even though deep down they had both known something was wrong, for those seven months Sam's illness was just a feeling, a grey cloud of doubt growing between them, something that hadn't yet been broken by a final pronouncement, a diagnosis. And a cloud can lift, give you some relief. Reality never does.

Shout Out – Canada's Music Scene

Coming into Alignment Continued from page 4

just doesn't feel like a relevant question," Van Ness responds. "We do the music we do, and we don't like to compare ourselves to others. I mean, of course I have influences, everything from Fugazi to Yo La Tengo to early Neil Young. Mark Knopfler is obviously a huge idol of mine. And I really love the new Schoolboy Q. It's so raw and authentic. I really enjoy music from every genre, as long as it's honest."

I turn my attention to Kovach, who has been fairly silent during the interview, leaning back in her chair, surveying us with those sultry eyes. "So what's it like being in a band full of guys?" I ask.

She leans forward across the table. "What an interesting question," she says. "I've never been asked that before." She bites her lip. "I guess I'd have to say it's . . . a barrel of fun."

Ava

June 2014

———◇———

HIWTHI S06E09:
Break Your Hart: Part Two

Ava knew before she opened her eyes that she was in a hospital. Even though she had never been in one before, she had seen enough medical dramas to recognize the soft beeping, the antiseptic smell, the feel of the starched sheets. As consciousness crept in, she kept her eyes closed for as long as she could, shielding herself against the reality that she knew awaited her: she was alone.

Finally, she opened her eyes and sat up slowly, fighting off dizziness. There was a tube clipped into her nose and several wires attached to her chest, and she pulled them all out except for the IV in her hand, too scared to look at the needle piercing her skin. She kept her eyes open, because to close them was to go back there, to the darkness, the weight of the water heavy on her chest. The back of her head throbbed gently, but otherwise she felt physically fine. She could still feel the ocean inside her, rocking her gently back and forth as she lay there, staring at the ceiling.

The room was white and bare, save for a bouquet of flowers on the nightstand. Maybe they were from David and Bryce, maybe they were just downstairs, getting snacks, or talking to the doctor. Maybe it had been Val's turn to sit with her, and he'd stepped out because he couldn't get any reception on his phone, or Eden and the Kaylas had gone outside to smoke. She had no idea how long she'd been out—her family could have been there for days, vigilant by her bedside. But even as the thought came to her, she knew it wasn't true. Someone had brought her cosmetic bag and a pair of her pajamas, which lay folded on the side table, but otherwise, there was no evidence that anyone had ever been there. No imprint of a body in the chair beside the bed, no empty coffee cups in the garbage, no book splayed open on the windowsill. Still. There had to be a reason. They wouldn't just leave her here. Someone had to come for her.

She got up and pushed her IV stand into the bathroom, where she splashed water on her face and rinsed out her mouth, but everything still tasted salty, her body brined by the sea. She filled the sink and began scrubbing herself with a paper towel and hot pink soap from the dispenser, the sickly sweet peppermint smell of it making her retch as the paper towel disintegrated on her skin. When she got back to her bed, she repositioned the IV stand and sat down on the edge of the mattress, her legs and arms still streaked with pink, and tried to breathe. Then she leaned forward and dropped her head between her knees, the heavy weight of her hair, caked with salt and knotted together into ropey dreadlocks, tumbling over her shoulders and draping around her face. She took a clump between her fingers and felt the salt tingling on her skin, flaky crystals of it shimmering down to the ground as she shook her head.

Suddenly, the memory came back to her, piercing her like the sharp taste of the brine on her tongue. The pier, the fall. The lobsters floating beside her, seraphim gently leading her to heaven. Eden's words peppering her heart like buckshot: *You were supposed to protect me.*

A shiver of revulsion ran through her body. She grabbed her makeup bag and dumped out its contents on the bed, excavating a comb from the pile, but when she tried to rake it through her hair, it got stuck almost immediately. She pulled with increasing desperation until finally she gave up, falling back against the bed with the comb still stuck in her hair. She could feel the tears coming, but she held them back. She couldn't handle any more salt on her skin.

She sat back up and poked listlessly at the pile on the bed, searching for something that might help. She picked up a pair of nail scissors, testing them out between her fingers, feeling their stiffness yield as she hinged them open and shut. Then she began cutting her hair—slowly at first, and then, as the knots began to fall, hacking at her hair violently, trying to get through it all before the scissors began to rust from the salt.

"Hey," she heard a voice say. "Be careful, you're going to cut yourself."

When she glanced up, there was a man standing in the doorway. A boy, really—he couldn't have been much older than her, but it was hard to tell from the layers of exhaustion on his face, bones protruding sharply through delicate, wilting skin. He was wearing a pair of black jeans under his hospital gown, and his head was shaved bald, although patchy hair still protruded on his chin beneath startlingly red lips. Her first instinct was to tell him to leave her alone—the last thing she wanted was to talk to a stranger, someone who could have any number of distressing motives. But there was kindness in his eyes, and as he leaned against the doorway, watching her with an expression of mild amusement mixed with concern, she felt the weight of what had happened with Eden crash in on her and she dropped the scissors to the floor, where they landed soundlessly in a pile of hair as light as straw.

"I messed it up," she said. "I messed it all up."

"No, no you didn't." He glanced down the hallway, then back at her. "Can I come in?" Ava nodded. He came into the room and sat on the bed next to her, then leaned over and picked up the scissors off the floor. "You just have a spot here . . . May I?" Ava nodded again, and he ran his hand gently over her head before making careful snips along the edge of her hairline. Ava kept her eyes downcast, feeling the warmth of his hand and the cold metal against her skin. "There," he said when he finished. "It looks great."

She stared down at the nest of hair at her feet. She did feel lighter, but instead of making her feel better, it only made her feel worse. As though now she had nothing to anchor her at all. As though at any moment she might rise up and float away. She didn't want the hair back. But she didn't want it to be gone, either. She wanted there to be a third option, something entirely outside both of those things. But, of course, there couldn't be.

"What do I do with it all?" she asked.

The man chewed his lip, studying the little pile. The hair on his chin moved up and his mouth worked, and Ava wondered why he didn't shave that too. "Well," he said. "You could probably donate it."

"To who? A tree planter?"

The man laughed. "Maybe the lead singer of a '90s ska band."

"An Ayurvedic healer."

"Hey, don't make fun of one of the world's oldest holistic healing systems." Ava widened her eyes incredulously. "I'm kidding," he said. He smiled, and his face transformed, the creases softening, the lightness in his eyes lifting all the dark corners. "That stuff is garbage."

Ava smiled too. It had been a while since she'd talked to someone about something other than the show, other than Eden. If this man recognized her, he didn't let on, and it felt good to have an ordinary conversation, even if it was under extraordinary circumstances. "Does it really look good?"

He leaned back and studied her. "It looks . . . like a guy in the hospital with Stage Four cancer cut it for you with nail scissors," he confessed. "But *you* look great. You can totally pull it off."

"Thanks." She fiddled with the tie on her hospital gown. "Do you really have Stage Four cancer?"

The man nodded. "I'm sorry to say that's true too."

"That's . . ."

"The bad stage, yeah."

Ava paused, fiddling with the tape holding the IV tube in place on the back of her hand. "What does it feel like?" she asked eventually.

"It feels like I'm on the edge of panicking. All the time." He smiled sadly. "I spent my whole life looking to the future. Moving forward, onto the next thing and the next thing. Now, there is no future. I don't know what to do with that." He picked up a piece of Ava's hair from the ground and balled it up in his fist. "My wife says I have to live in the present, put one foot in front of the other, like on a tightrope. But I don't really know how."

You seem so young to have a wife, Ava wanted to say. "How long have you been married?" she asked instead.

"Four days." He brought his right hand to his left, twisting the ring on his finger. "Looking to the future, you know? It's stupid. To go all *'til death do us part* when death is right there, standing over you."

"It's not stupid." Ava swung her legs beneath her, feeling the sea still churning just below the surface of her skin. "It's romantic."

"Maybe on TV. But not in real life." He paused. "We've been dating since we were fifteen. We've grown up together. Sometimes I worry that we've become so dependent on each other that things will fall apart if one of us is gone. If I'm gone."

Ava considered this. "But maybe they won't," she said. "I bet she's stronger than you think."

He laughed shortly. "I bet you're right." He raised an eyebrow. "So what're you in for?"

"My sister tried to drown me." As she said the words, she

realized how ridiculous they sounded. "I mean, it's fine. I probably deserved it."

"And I probably deserved the cancer." He stood up. "You know, the longer I look at your hair, the more I think I like it."

Ava reached up and touched the back of her head, so unfamiliar to her now. She felt exposed, vulnerable, but also somehow free. "Thank you," she whispered. And then: "Can you . . ." She gestured to the pile on the floor.

"Sure." The man leaned over and picked up the hair. "My Tibetan drumming circle leader is going to be so thrilled." He left the room without turning around.

Ava leaned back on the bed, letting the ebb and flow of the ocean in her body lull her back to sleep.

—◇—

Later—it could have been a few minutes or a few hours—a nurse came in. "Oh, you're awake," he said. "I'll let the doctor know." His eyes rested on the wires and tubes she had extracted from her body. "You're really supposed to keep those on."

"Sorry," Ava said. "I panicked."

The nurse picked up her wrist, feeling for a pulse. "Well, you're still alive, so I guess they weren't that important," he said, winking.

"How long have I been here?"

"They brought you in last night." The nurse dropped her wrist, made a note on a chart. "Your dad's outside, by the way. He's been waiting for you to wake up. Should I tell him to come in?"

"Of course," said Ava, relief surging through her body.

She propped herself up in bed, running her hand over her shorn head. She wondered which one of her dads had come for her, and which one had gotten stuck with . . . everything else.

But when the door opened again a moment later, she blinked in confusion, something igniting under her skin. It wasn't David or Bryce who came into the room. It was Antonio.

"Hey," Antonio said, a little too brightly. "How are you feeling?"

How am I feeling? Ava wanted to scream. *How am I feeling? How would* you *fucking feel?*

"Fine," she said instead, turning away from him as he crossed the room to stand beside her bed. There was no point in screaming at Antonio. He was here, after all. He was the only one who was ever here.

"Your dads . . . they wanted to come," he said.

"Sure they did."

"Ava . . ." Antonio touched her shoulder, but she shrugged him off, curling herself up. "They had to take Eden to rehab. In California."

At the mention of Eden's name, Ava felt her stomach churn. "I don't care."

The bed shifted under Antonio's weight as he sat down on the edge. "The restaurant promised not to press charges if she got help. It was a really quick decision, but your dads thought it would be best if they took her right away, got her settled. They all left this morning."

And they both had to go? Eden gets two parents and I get none? She didn't say it out loud, but the thought hung in the air between them. "Where's Val?" she asked.

"They didn't want him staying at the B&B alone, so he went to Christie's. Or Charisma's, I'm not sure. He'll be there for a few days. We didn't know how long you'd be in here."

"I guess you'll be going too?" she said into her pillow. "With the rest of the crew, I mean. I can't wait to see A Very Special Episode of *Where the Hart Is: Rehab Edition.*"

"No. I wouldn't . . . Anyway, the network has put the show on hiatus for now." He paused. "But I wouldn't do that. Even if they wanted me to."

Ava knew he was telling the truth. She rolled back over to face him but kept her gaze in the middle distance, trying not to make eye contact, fearing that if she did he would see all the things she was thinking, all the ways she was hurting. "Can we not talk about this anymore?"

"Okay, sure." He paused, narrowing his eyes at her. "Is that . . . Did they have to cut your hair?"

Ava raised her hand up to her head again, feeling at the haphazard strands. "No. That was me."

"It looks good," he said. She raised an eyebrow at him. "Okay, fine. It looks like you took a hacksaw to it. But you're making it work."

Ava laughed. "You're the second person who's told me that."

"Well, it's true. It's very Edie Sedgwick."

"Who?"

"Never mind." They were both silent for a moment. "She's really sorry, Ava. I've spent a lot of time with Eden over the past couple of years, and I have never seen her so upset."

Ava breathed in slowly. "When can I go?"

"Now, if you want."

She nodded. "I just want to go home." But the words sounded empty, and she realized she didn't know where home was. She thought about the story she used to tell Eden when she couldn't sleep, the one about where they had come from. She had been surprised that Eden had believed it, but then again, maybe Ava had believed it too, or at least wanted to. But there was no van, no California, no burning-hot sun. There was just a family that had been cobbled together by different bits of secret tragedy. There was just a family who didn't know how to be a family at all.

She shut her eyes again and this time she saw Eden's face, looking down on her as she fell from the pier, and suddenly she realized what it was she had seen. The expression on Eden's face, the one she couldn't put her finger on.

Relief. It was relief.

She dressed in the clothes Antonio had brought from the B&B— a bizarre combination of plaid flannel shorts, Val's Death from Above 1979 T-shirt, and a holey grey cardigan she had found in the attic. Someone had washed the clothes she had been wearing when she was brought in, but she couldn't bring herself to put them on. She had no idea where her shoes were, so she left her feet bare. Antonio carried her cosmetic bag and the flowers, which were from the network executives. *Get well soon*, the card read. *From Bob and Tess and everyone at LifeStyle.*

Get well soon. As though she had had her tonsils out. As though they weren't the ones responsible for all of this.

"I've got the van, so if you want to sleep in the back or anything, you can," he said, adjusting the vase under his arm.

"I've been sleeping for like twenty-four straight hours," Ava said. "I think I'm okay." She pulled the sleeves of the cardigan down over her hands, probing for the holes in the cuffs she had stretched open with her thumbs over the years.

Antonio watched her, amused. "I brought you weird clothes. I'm sorry."

Ava poked one thumb through a hole, then another. "This is actually my favourite sweater," she said, wiggling her thumbs at him. "I've ruined it just to my liking."

Antonio smiled at her, and she smiled back. The elevator made a dinging sound, and then the doors opened to the lobby.

There was an overwhelming light, so dazzling it momentarily blinded her. It was as if she were walking into the nucleus of a very bright star. *How long have I been in darkness?* was all she could think as her vision adjusted, and she began to make out the shapes in front of her. *How long has it been since I've seen the sun?*

"Ava!" voices yelled from across the washed-out space. "Ava, over here!"

She blinked again, shielding her eyes with her hand. She wasn't outside, she was still in the hospital, and it wasn't the sun that was blinding her, but the flash of what seemed like a thousand cameras, maybe millions. She wrapped her sweater tightly around her body, hunching down, instinctively trying to fold herself in, to make herself as small as possible. To hide all the vulnerable parts of herself.

"What is this?" she croaked out. "What's happening?"

"I don't know," said Antonio, moving closer to her as they stood in front of the crowd. "I didn't know they were here. I'm sorry, Ava."

"Where's Eden?" another voice yelled. "Ava, do you know? Have you spoken to her?"

"Ava, did Eden try to drown you on purpose?"

"Please," Ava said, lowering her head. "Please, stop."

The crowd was closing in, and she imagined them like the tide, advancing on her, rising over her as she was stuck there in the sand, her body rocking back and forth with the waves. Instinctively, she leaned into Antonio, clinging to him as if he were a buoy in the harbour.

"Ava!" a different voice yelled. "I love your hair!"

"Okay, that's enough," said Antonio. He lifted her up in his arms like she weighed nothing and carried her away from the crowd, down a hall, and into the parking garage stairwell. He put her down on the ground as the door shut behind them, then he grabbed the handle, gripping it tightly. "They probably won't follow us, but you never know."

Ava leaned back against the wall. The concrete felt too hard, too close beneath her feet. Even though she had only been a few

225

feet off the ground, Ava felt as though she had been dropped from such a great height. "Where did they all come from? How did they know I was here?"

"I don't know, Ava. I swear to you I don't."

As they walked toward the van, she thought about that night when she and Antonio drove to Mahone Bay, how stupid she had been to think she could keep any moments to herself. All her moments were public property. They always would be. Those people in the lobby, with their phones and their cameras and their questions—they were a reminder that everything about her belonged to the world. And the world could take it all from her whenever it wanted.

When they got back to the B&B, the lights were all off. Antonio offered to stay, but Ava told him to leave. She would be fine being alone. She was always fine being alone.

All she wanted to do was sleep, but whenever she shut her eyes she saw crowds of people grabbing at her, pulling at her clothes, her hair, her skin, until she was nothing but meat and bones stumbling along. So she got up and went downstairs to make some tea.

When she walked into the kitchen, there was someone already there. Antonio, sitting at the kitchen table with his head in his hands, reams of call sheets spread out on the table in front of him.

He raised his head when Ava came in. "I'm sorry," he said. "I couldn't do it. I couldn't leave you alone."

Slowly, Ava moved toward him. Among the papers she saw a picture of her dads, standing on the porch of the B&B, waving to some unseen guest coming up the driveway. She pushed everything aside and climbed up and over the kitchen table, propelled forward by some momentum she didn't understand or know how to stop. Her foot kicked over the salt shaker, and as she pressed her mouth against Antonio's, she heard every grain as loud as a firework as they showered down onto the floor.

Everything disappeared, silence radiating out from a single point of stillness. There were no thoughts in her head. There was no salt on the floor under their feet, no call sheets, no kitchen table, no room around them, no sad old B&B, no cameras.

There was nothing except the kiss.

Then Antonio pulled away, and instantly everything came flooding back—the thoughts, the room, all of it—and Ava buckled under its weight.

"Ava," said Antonio, finally.

"I'm not sorry," she said, at the same time. She had paper stuck to her knees, grains of salt embedded between her toes. It was as if everything were breaking all around her.

"Ava," Antonio said again. And then again, and again, like he was trying to learn how to say it. *Ava, Ava, Ava* until she worried her head might explode with all the *Avas* she was trying to keep hold of.

"Shh," she said, but he kept on repeating her name. They weren't touching, but their bodies were so close together that she could feel the vibrations of his diaphragm as he breathed in and out. *Antonio*, she thought, but couldn't say, couldn't connect the name with any sort of meaning, and instead she wondered, vaguely, if she was going to throw up.

"Ava. Ava. Ava."

She kissed him again just to shut him up.

This time, his hands found the space between her shoulder blades and her hands found the back of his neck and his hands found the low hill of her belly and her hands found the length of his thighs, and then a flurry of belt buckles and bra straps and buttons and zippers and cotton and denim and skin, and then they were on the table and he was inside her and it wasn't beautiful or tender or passionate or anything that she ever imagined it would be. It was sad and desperate and brutal and catastrophic. And she never wanted it to end.

"Everything's going to be okay," Antonio said when it was over, smoothing her hair and brushing crumbs off her bare clavicle. "It's going to be okay." But he looked like he was staring down the barrel of a gun.

Ava didn't believe him. Not for a second.

ChatterFuel
Style

July 3, 2014

4 Reasons You Want Ava Hart's Hair
The Television Star's New Cropped Do is the Look of the Summer

By Stella Stewart

1. It's Super Cute: Ava might just have been coming off a near-drowning when those pics that broke the internet were snapped, but daaaaaaamn girl.

2. It's Low Maintenance: The struggle is real! We all think we're rocking beachy waves when in reality what we have is more like a bird's nest. With short hair, you can swim all you want and still come out looking surfer-girl chic.

3. It's Easy to DIY: No doubt Ava had a team of stylists strategically designing her signature haphazard look. But you can get the same effect with a pair of kitchen shears for a fraction of the cost!

4. Everyone's Doing It: You don't want to be the only girl at the club who's still tying her hair back in that tired old messy bun, do you?

Mags

July 2014

◇

"Downtown"

How to make tea in a palliative care ward: fill the kettle with water from the plastic jugs on the counter, because the tap water is undrinkable. Legionnaires' disease, they tell you. Don't ask what that is—you don't want to know. Search the cupboard for the one teapot he likes, with the cherry blossoms and the crack along the side. If it's dirty, wash it. It is the only teapot in the ward he would drink from, before. Drop in two teabags. Take the milk from the fridge and pour it into the little milk pitcher. Think about his voice. Think about it so hard your brain hurts with the force of it. Think about it so hard that you never, ever forget it.

Make up a tray with teacups, teapot, milk pitcher, and sugar bowl: all chipped. Wait for the water to boil. Listen to Petula Clark singing "Downtown" on the radio and try to remember if he ever sang it to you, sitting on the dirty rug at midnight, candles and incense burning on the windowsill behind him. Know that he never did—that wasn't the kind of song he would have sung—but try to remember it anyway. Don't cry. Look out the window instead, at the little people walking around on the sidewalk seven storeys below, the sun on their bare arms. Downtown, where all the lights are bright. Remember that it is summer, even though the ward is cold. Remember that you haven't been outside in four days. Remember that he hasn't been outside in twenty-three.

When the kettle boils, pour the water into the teapot. Lift the tray gently and carry it down the hall, slowly. One foot in front of the other. Elbows at your sides to control the shaking. Be careful to keep your eyes focused straight ahead, away from any of the other rooms, from any other faces. Pour tea for yourself. Drink one cup, two cups, four cups. Fill every grieving hole with tea. Pour tea for him. Make sure to put the milk in first. Take a swab from the jar, the swab meant to moisten his mouth, that he will suck on reflexively like an infant sucking on a nipple. Dip the swab in the tea and blow on it, taking care it is not too hot, then run the tip gently across his gums. Watch his cracked mouth moving, watch the way the stubble on his upper lip bends as his skin crinkles up and down, up and down. Remember that this is the only thing you have left of him: the slow trickle of saliva, the faintest shadow of life.

Mags and Sam were married on a Thursday night, on the harbour-facing patio of a seafood restaurant called The Fish Hook, on the Gin Harbour waterfront. Even though it was June it was still cold, as it always was on the coast, and the guests all shivered under propane heaters, waiting for Mags to make her entrance.

They had been living in Toronto for almost a year but decided to get married in Nova Scotia. "It's where all our memories are," he said, and Mags didn't argue, even though the last thing she cared about was the past. She wanted to be in the moment, she wanted the present. She wanted *now*. Of course, what she really wanted was the future, but by then she knew they weren't going to get it.

"No one gets married on a Thursday," Emiko said. But she came anyway, placing a white fur stole that had belonged to her own mother around Mags's shoulders, and watched from inside the restaurant as Paul and Zac walked Mags across the patio. Sam's parents were in Borneo, so they didn't even bother to tell them about the wedding. There were other people there—old friends from high school, maybe one or two people from the record label. But Mags couldn't remember any of that. All she remembered was Sam, bald from the chemo and red-cheeked and awkward, standing at the end of the patio, the lights from the boats in the harbour sparkling on the rippled surface of the water, a gentle rain drizzling down from the sky.

Later, they ate figs wrapped in prosciutto, slurped cold oysters right from the shell, drank champagne. Mags danced with Paul and then Zac, and Emiko made a speech about how Mags had told her on the first day they met that she was going to marry Sam, which made Mags cry even though she knew it wasn't true. It was all perfect, easy, relaxed. Mags wondered what she had been afraid of.

But deep down, she knew. Four days later, instead of sitting on a plane to San Francisco for their honeymoon, she was sitting in the emergency waiting room at the hospital. Waiting, because that's what you did in waiting rooms. Waiting for your turn, for news, for answers. Waiting to see if you are going to be okay. In those rooms you were healthy and not healthy at the same time, illness and wellness existing inside you simultaneously. Plus, the coffee was terrible. Back in Toronto, Mags always brought her own to the hospital, in a travel mug that said *Oshawa Public Library* on it. She had no idea where the mug came from. She didn't even know anyone who lived in Oshawa. But here in Halifax, she had been unprepared. She had thought that maybe, just maybe, she could leave her hospital mug at home.

She tried to make a joke of it to the woman sitting next to her, tiny and blurry-edged, her eyes on the television mounted on the wall playing *Frozen* on repeat. "Tastes like it was made with harbour water," Mags said, swirling the coffee in the paper cup. "I'm surprised there's not a used tampon floating in it."

The woman turned to her. "Did you say something?" she said.

"The coffee," said Mags. She threw back the last gulp, trying to swallow it down without tasting it. "Never mind."

Mags had come to understand that people in hospital waiting rooms either didn't want to talk about the reason they were there, or it was all they wanted to talk about. The people who wanted to talk, Mags thought of as dilettantes, dabblers in the world of tragedy. People for whom the whole journey from triage to discharge was just a story to tell later over dinner and drinks. She'd smile and listen to them talk about how they sprained their ankle chasing their dog, or how their wife got food poisoning at a company picnic because someone left the mayo out of the cooler, or how their kid got a concussion jumping off the couch pretending to be Superman, and she wished she had a similar story to tell. Wished for earaches, wished for urinary tract infections, wished for fingers slammed in car doors.

And then there were the people like her. The ones who brought their own travel mugs full of coffee. The ones who always had extra phone chargers and granola bars tucked in their purses. The ones who knew exactly which door to walk through, which nurse to talk to, how much change they would need to pay for parking. They didn't ask you how you got there or who you were waiting for. Instead, they showed you cute dog memes on their phones and recapped their favourite television shows, went on long diatribes about how terrible the mayor was, got into lengthy debates about fashion trends. There was no talk of vacation plans or upcoming birthdays or photos of kids or grandkids or puppies. There was often no past and there was certainly no future. There was just this room, this chair, this person you would never see again, two people scrabbling against each other for some tiny fragment of humanity.

When the nurse finally called her into the room, she found Sam and the doctor locked in an argument. "We need to admit him," the doctor said as she walked in.

"No," Sam said. "We're going home."

"You're not well enough to travel."

"I don't care."

Mags knew she should stay out of it. She gazed out the window at the parking lot below, trying to block out the voices by letting herself be mesmerized by the cars circling around and around, the lift and fall of the gate at the entrance, the doctor and Sam a mere low drone in the background. It wasn't until the droning stopped that she snapped out of it, blinking her eyes in confusion at the doctor standing at the foot of the bed, eyes on his clipboard, Sam nowhere to be seen.

"It's a side effect of the drugs," the doctor said without looking up. "Another reason he shouldn't be travelling." Mags stared at him uncomprehendingly. The doctor sighed. "You'd have to strap him into a diaper. Aren't you even paying attention?"

From behind the closed bathroom door, Mags heard Sam moan. She shut her eyes and briefly, ever so briefly, wished for another life. She could be a cage fighter, maybe, or a nun. She could rescue sea turtles in South America. She could work at the bank and marry a man named Todd who took great pride in his lawn. Anyone other than this woman, sitting in a hospital room, listening to her husband of four days noisily evacuating his bowels three feet away from her while a condescending medical resident wearing a Wu-Tang T-shirt under his white coat glared at her judgmentally.

"It's his call," Mags said, rubbing her tired eyes. "If he wants to leave, we leave."

"I want to leave," she heard Sam call feebly from behind the bathroom door.

The doctor sighed again and scrawled out a prescription. "Loperamide. It'll slow it down. And for god's sake, tell him to see his oncologist when he gets back to Toronto." He dropped the paper on the bed and walked out, shaking his head.

A few minutes later, Sam emerged, pale and sweaty in his hoodie and jeans. "Thanks. I was running out of steam."

"Don't think this means I'm on your side about this, because I'm not." Mags picked up the prescription and folded it, matching the edges up precisely. "But I took this vow, for better or for worse or whatever, and so here we are." She put the paper in her pocket. "Just know, though, that this is definitely the 'worse' part."

"Jesus," he said. He sat down on the edge of the bed, pulling the sleeves of his hoodie down over his hands. "You think I wanted this to happen? You think I'm happy about being stuck here when we're supposed to be driving down the California coastline in our rented convertible?"

"Obviously not."

"Well, what then?"

"Why can't you just do what the doctors tell you? Why can't you rest and take care of yourself? Why do you have to be so stubborn?"

"I don't know, okay? I really don't know." They sat in silence for a moment. "I met a famous person," he said eventually. "She's in the next room. I helped her cut her hair."

"I guess you can cross that off your bucket list."

Sam pulled his knees up to his chest, revealing the outlines of his bony ankles through his fraying white sports socks. She was suddenly overcome with the desire to cradle those delicate bones in her hands, to protect them—and at the same time, she wanted to break them, to snap them between her fingers. She was angry at their delicacy, at their quivering fragility, at their inability to do their job. These bones that had given up on being bones.

She cleared her throat. "What do you want to do now?"

As if he could read her thoughts, Sam cupped his hands around his ankles. "Be better," he said. "I just want to be better."

After they left the hospital they drove around through the darkest hours of the night, not talking, not wanting to go back to their hotel, but not having anywhere else to go. Eventually, they ended up at Lawrencetown Beach, where Mags parked next to the stairs to the boardwalk.

The beach was deserted, a brisk offshore wind keeping the early morning surfers at home in bed. Sam walked to the edge of the water and was gazing out to the east, where the light had turned a deep crimson, the glow of the sunrise bleeding away from the horizon and up into the night sky. It made Mags think of the sunrises of her childhood, when Karolina would have to get up while it was still dark out to catch the bus to work. She always tried to be quiet, but Mags would wake up anyway, sitting on the edge of the bed, watching her brush her long hair, wrapping it around and around itself in a long rope and knotting it at the back of her head. Mags remembered how happy she felt on those mornings, being too young to understand how difficult their life was. There was only her mother's hair and the sunrise, everything so beautiful and happy and idyllic.

This sunrise felt nothing like that. Mags stared out at the red morning sky and she could see only fire, everywhere fire.

She took a few steps forward into the break, the frigid, foamy water circling her ankles. Then she turned around and pulled Sam's face to hers, trying to drag him back into the present, back from the edge of whatever black hole he was staring into. As he looked into her eyes, his face brightened.

"Remember when we came here after the Marquee show?" he asked.

"Of course." It hadn't been how she imagined losing her virginity. The cold, the wind, the sand everywhere. Racing the sunrise for the last few moments of darkness. One eye on the lookout for an early morning dog-walker, or a fisherman offshore with a good pair of binoculars. What she had imagined: the weight of Sam's body on hers, belonging to her, only her. What it felt like to have someone inside her beyond a few curious straying fingers, pushing her open, tearing his way in, breaking her. The pain, sure. The things she already knew, the softness of his lips, the shape of his hipbones, the way she had to angle her body to keep them from hurting her. The pressure of his fingertips on her shoulders. The smell of his breath. The way he held her after he came, stroking her back, saying her name. The peace she felt, then.

The sadness, though, that was unexpected, like a slow burn through to the deepest layer of her skin. Because it was over. Because it could never be everything she wanted it to be.

She had thought that sadness would go away, would dissipate through all the nights they spent together, the talking and the touching, fighting and fucking, crying and laughing and tearing at each other's skin. But it never really did. It was as though the more you got to know someone, the more you realized you could never know them at all.

But still. You had to keep trying. She took Sam's hand and led him away from the shore toward the dunes, pulling him down into the sand.

———◇———

They had only been back in Toronto for three days before Sam was hospitalized again. Even as she drove him there, Mags knew this time it would be for good.

At first, people had come to see him: Paul and Zac, a distant cousin on his father's side, the owner of a club where Align Above frequently played. They brought cards and flowers and beamed healthy smiles, they smelled of the outside and brightness and life. His parents called every day from Rome or Caracas or Ubud or wherever in the world they happened to be, but they didn't come home. Once every few days, Emiko would bring food for Mags and they'd eat in the family lounge—a room with couches and a television and an ancient ping-pong table, a room designed to be comforting but that only reminded you that you were in a hospital, with its outdated magazines, the bottles of hand sani, the fake flowers. And then Emiko would leave without even so much as a glance toward Sam's room. But after Sam started slipping in and out of lucidity, after they induced the morphine coma and the business of dying began for real, people stopped coming. The nurses made a cot for Mags next to Sam's bed, although most nights she fell asleep in front of the television in the family lounge, not registering what she was watching, aware only of the flickering light.

It was strange, waiting for death to come. Mags had always assumed it came swiftly, taking you by surprise. When the doctors had told Sam the cancer had spread and he wasn't a candidate for another round of chemo, Mags had supposed that one day she would wake up and walk into his room with his morning tea and discover him gone, peacefully reclined against the pillows, a wispy soul fluttering to heaven on angel wings or some stupid thing. But the reality had been weeks of slow disintegration in palliative care, waiting as parts of Sam shut down one by one: his liver, his kidneys, his brain, until there was nothing left but skin and bones, a faint heartbeat. And even still, death would not fucking come.

Mags didn't want Sam to die. She wanted him to live, to be alive, to get back up on stage and play, to do all the things that he said he was going to do but never did, all the things he promised Mags. He promised. He promised. But this—this was not living. This was a kind of horrible limbo she didn't understand. His heart was still beating, his skin was still warm. But his eyes, when she lifted his lids, were empty.

One day a nurse told her that there might be a reason Sam kept hanging on the way he did. She had seen it before. They all had. That maybe he was waiting for something to happen. Or not happen.

238

"I'm the one who's holding him here," Mags said to Emiko, sitting in the hospital Tim Hortons, trying not to stare at the old men with IVs in their arms and their gowns hanging open. Emiko had come to see her on her lunch break, in a suit and heels. Mags was in her pajamas. They both drank coffee. An open box of twenty assorted Timbits sat on the table between them, untouched. "I can't let him go."

"I don't know what to tell you, babe," Emiko said, fiddling impatiently with the tab on the lid of her cup, sneaking glances at her phone. It was hard to believe that life still went on. "There's no road map for this kind of thing."

Mags lowered her eyes down into her coffee. Emiko stopped her fiddling.

"This is not my life," Mags said.

"But, babe, it is. And you're going to have to get used to it." Emiko stood up and air-kissed Mags's cheek. "I have to go. I'll see you at the studio later?"

"Don't leave," Mags said, her eyes pleading. "Stay a little longer."

Emiko gave her a pitying look. "I'll be at the office if you need me," she said, squeezing Mags's shoulder before walking toward the door.

At Emiko's touch, all of Mags's composure shattered. "Come back here!" she yelled. She grabbed a Timbit, one of the jam-filled ones, and hurled it at the back of Emiko's head. Emiko hesitated but didn't turn around. "What are we even paying you for? Isn't it your fucking *job* to be here for me?"

Mags picked up another Timbit and threw it, and another, and another, pelting the back of Emiko's head with donut holes, then— after Emiko had disappeared into the hospital hall—the door, until she felt a hand on her shoulder and she collapsed onto the table, the ridiculousness of it all completely overwhelming her: the garishly lit hospital coffee shop, the nightgown-clad onlookers, Emiko's hair powdered with icing sugar like a sloppily decorated chocolate cake, the two tiny apple fritters Mags continued to hold on to, even as they crumbled to pieces in her fists.

—◇—

That night, when most of the families had gone home and the graveyard shift of nurses and orderlies were just coming on, Mags slipped into Sam's room. His eyes were closed, his eyelids fluttering softly, as they had done for days now. With every breath he took, phlegm rattled in his lungs, shaking his now tiny body, making Mags involuntarily clear her own throat. A soft red light flashed steadily on the digital output screen of his IV, saline and morphine and whatever else. For one alarming moment, Mags wondered if maybe Sam was still in there, if maybe he was not dying after all, and inside his brain he was screaming for freedom. Maybe all he needed was a sandwich and a strong cup of tea, and then he would open his eyes and sit up and tell her he had a new lick for that song he had been struggling with.

But Mags knew this wasn't true. She didn't even hope it was true. But it made her sick to think that she would never know for sure.

She leaned over. "Baby," she said. "I love you."

Sam's mouth moved, his lips sliding over his gums.

"I'm going to be fine." She paused, her eyes focusing on the fraying edge of Sam's hospital gown. "I don't need you anymore." She sat back down on the unmade cot and thought about how much it hurt, in the midst of everything, to think that Emiko was probably right. And the second she admitted that to herself, it meant she was totally, completely alone.

"Anyway," she said, straightening up. "That's it. You can go now, okay? Go now. Go." She turned and walked out of the room, every inch of her body blistering with grief, but her eyes stubbornly dry.

At five in the morning the nurse woke her. A rerun of *I Love Lucy* was playing, muted, on the television. Someone had covered her with a blanket. "It's time," he said. Mags pushed the blanket off with her feet. She wondered what kind of television station still played *I Love Lucy*, and who they expected to be watching it at five in the morning. This is what she was thinking about all the way to Sam's room. She thought about it as she curled up next to Sam on the bed, her face pressed up against his, listening to his breath, his horrible, wheezing, rattling breath, the time lapsing between each gasp growing longer and longer. She thought about it as she waited, waited, waited.

Maybe old people got up that early. Maybe they watched the reruns with their breakfast, and remembered when they were young and happy and in love.

At five thirty, the pulse had completely faded from Sam's wrist.

At five forty-five, it was gone from his neck.

At six, there was no trace of a pulse, but still a breath, a terrible, heartbreaking breath, every thirty seconds.

Every forty seconds.

Every minute.

His breath in her ear.

. . . breath.

. . . breath.

. . .

Greywolf Artist Management Inc.

For Immediate Release

Toronto, Ontario – July 22, 2014

It is with great sadness that we announce the death of one of our family. Sam Cole, bassist for the Toronto-based indie rock band Align Above, passed away peacefully in his sleep on July 22, after a short battle with cancer. He was 21 years old.

Originally from Halifax, Nova Scotia, Cole dedicated his life to his band, and to his wife, Align Above singer Mags Kovach.

"We are devastated at this terrible loss," said Paul Van Ness, guitarist for the band. "Our commitment now is to honour the work that meant so much to him, and continue to stay true to the music Sam wanted to make. And to make sure to be here for Mags, of course."

The band was in the process of recording their full-length debut album when Cole was first diagnosed, but he was able to complete work on the majority of the tracks before his death. The album will be released later this fall on KBI, with a portion of proceeds from the initial sales going to the Canadian Cancer Society.

PART
THREE

Reality Check
Reality TV Writing for Reality TV Fans

Absence Makes the Hart Grow Fonder ensures viewers get their fix of Hart drama (and heart puns)

Kelly Gibson, staff writer
11/21/14 9:00 am Filed to REVIEW

Unless you've been living under a rock, you've heard of Eden Hart, the YouTube star we watched transform from a peaches-and-cream preteen to a hot-mess-in-hot-pants on her LifeStyle reality television show, *Where the Hart Is*. (It's only the real superfans who remember the show in its original, feel-good, family-friendly form, *Home Is Where the Hart Is*, which featured a whole slew of Harts trying to run a B&B in the picturesque fishing town of Gin Harbour, Nova Scotia.)

Now that the teenage trainwreck is, predictably, in rehab, it's her older siblings' time to test out the spotlight. *Absence Makes the Hart Grow Fonder* follows Avalon and Valhalla Hart (yes, those *are* their real names) as they return to their native New York City and try to make it as, well, reality stars, we can only assume. The show, which premiered a mere four months after the cancellation of *Where the Hart Is*, is now five episodes into its first season, snapping up the coveted 9 pm slot on Thursdays.

Ava (18) and Val (17) (as they prefer to be called) are likeable enough— Val has both the eyelashes and the disaffect to become a real teenage heartthrob, and Ava is still riding high on her 15 minutes, garnered when Eden pushed her sister off a pier during her epic breakdown this spring (we'll never look at lobsters the same way again). But neither has the infectious charm of their younger sister. And while that might just be a matter of the two young stars getting used to living under the constant

245

gaze of the camera, the real problem with *Absence* is that it doesn't know what it wants to be.

In the first few episodes, Ava and Val don't do much more than make ham-handed attempts to rehash old family drama in a painfully obvious bid to remind viewers of their more famous sibling. In the fourth episode, for instance, Val and Ava discuss where to go for dinner, and somehow Eden's name comes up no fewer than 37 times (we counted). The rest of the show is as aimless as its two stars, neither of whom seem to have any interests outside of fixing their (now-famous) hair or staring moodily out of windows.

We would never want to speak ill of the struggling C-lister, so let's chalk this one up to bad timing. After all, maybe the LifeStyle execs should have taken their own advice and let us feel the absence of one Hart before trying to shove two more down our throats.

Ava

November 2014

———◇———

AMTHGF S01E05:
Cross My Hart

"I don't know a single person here!" Ava yelled to Val over the music, an annoying remix of whatever Rihanna/Drake song was popular that week, hacked up by a DJ who thought being able to press some buttons on his MacBook made him a real musician. Ava hated people who thought they were good at things. At least she knew she wasn't good at anything. Except maybe getting guys to buy her drinks, of which she now had two, one in each hand, the first a Grey Goose martini bought for her by some walking Calvin Klein ad who claimed to be one of Justin Bieber's backup dancers, and the second a can of PBR bought by a smarmy nineteen-year-old internet startup millionaire. Ava didn't care, she'd take them both.

"You mean nobody knows *you*," said Val.

"I'm just fulfilling my contractual obligation," Ava said. One of the stipulations in the contract for their new spinoff show—ludicrously, but predictably, titled *Absence Makes the Hart Grow Fonder*—was that she and Val had to be photographed at least once a week at a hot New York nightclub. And there was no way in hell she was going out again this week if it wasn't happening tonight.

Val shook his head. "That's why you came out tonight? For your weekly photo op? I thought you were actually interested in something other than yourself."

Ava shrugged, then handed Val the can of PBR. "I need to keep up appearances."

"Don't let them eat your soul, Ave." Val drained the can of beer and then tossed it onto the nearest table. "Now, which one of your fuckboys is going to buy me another?"

Ava ignored him, sipping her martini as the music stopped and a couple of techs came onstage, the room filling with the anticipatory cacophony of instruments being tuned. "What is this band, anyway?" she asked, feeling her blood heat up as the vodka hit it.

"Align Above. Remember, I told you about them? They're from Nova Scotia," Val said. "They're going to be huge." When Ava turned away, he grabbed her shoulders and pulled her back around. "Sometimes it can just be about experiencing something great, Ave. Sometimes it can just be about the music."

"Whatever," said Ava, although she kept facing the stage. Her stomach heaved, but she downed the Grey Goose martini anyway, hoping that the drunkenness would overtake the nausea. She wasn't sure if she was sick from the drink, or just sick, but she suspected it was the latter. The truth was that she hadn't come for the band *or* the photo op. She had come to get out-of-her-mind drunk and forget for one tiny second the shitshow that was her life.

"Oh my god, it's Ava," someone said, her name piercing the register above the tuning instruments. She allowed herself a brief eye roll before plastering on a smile, swallowing everything else down as a pack of wild girls descended on her from the other side of the room, all lip gloss and wet mouths ready to carry a piece of her home in their chemically whitened teeth. "Oh my god, can we *please* take a selfie?"

248

"Fuck yeah," said Ava, letting her words rasp across her throat like sandpaper. She leaned back and pursed her lips, flashing a peace sign. The girls shuffled in around her, one of them holding her phone up. In the phone's screen, all she could see was a sea of shiny, platinum pixie heads, identical to hers, each one of them wearing their hair like a disguise. And Ava was no different. She might have been the most disguised of all.

—◇—

They had been filming a fight scene earlier that day, in which Val was trying to convince Ava they should go back to Gin Harbour to visit Bryce and David. It was fake, of course—David was in Japan shooting a vodka commercial, and Bryce was on vacation with some friends in Cabo. Ever since *Home Is Where the Hart Is* ended, unceremoniously, after that night at the pier, the two of them had been travelling separately, and Ava wondered vaguely if they would get a divorce. Not that it mattered to her—even if they had been at the B&B, she wouldn't have gone to see them. Within a week of her release from the hospital, Ava and Val had signed the contract for their spinoff, and she had left for New York before David and Bryce got back from California. As far as Ava was concerned, they had made their choice—and that choice was Eden and the cameras that followed her. It wasn't Ava's fault that after Eden had been in rehab for a few weeks, the cameras had turned elsewhere, leaving David and Bryce in the unseemly position of having their devotion to their troubled daughter go completely undocumented.

The set-up for the scene might have been fake, but the argument with Val was not. "They want to see you," Val told her as he sipped his coffee. It was a warm afternoon for late November, and they were sitting out on the terrace, where they were eating breakfast in their pajamas, stretched out on lounge chairs.

"They know where we are," said Ava, tossing a piece of her muffin to a pigeon perched on the parapet. The pigeon only had one full leg—the other one a pink stub jutting out of the silvery grey feathers, flopping erratically as it descended on the crumb. She was about to throw another piece when Val pushed her arm down to stop her.

"Jesus Christ, Ave, can you stop? It'll never leave."

Ava shrugged Val's hand off and threw it anyway. She knew he was right, about the pigeon and their dads. But she didn't care. Secretly, she thought the pigeon was beautiful, with all those sleek, iridescent feathers, those silvers and purples threaded together, changing colour in the sun. It's just that no one ever paid attention, that's all. No one else ever bothered to look.

"She flew all the way up here," Ava said. "She deserves a reward."

"Bryce said he's been calling you, texting you every day. You haven't responded to anything. They don't want to show up here without you saying it's okay."

"It's *not* okay." Ava tossed another piece of her muffin. "You know if they came it would just be to get back on television."

"That's not true."

"Oh yeah? Why do you think they went to California in the first place? It's not because they gave a shit about Eden. They placed their bets on the wrong fucking daughter and now they're trying to backtrack."

"Cut," said Antonio. "Ava, can you do that line again? This time without the swearing?"

Ava sat up, startled. She had forgotten they were filming. "Can't you bleep it out?"

"We'd rather not." He motioned to Javier, who set the camera up for a second take. "Just from 'They placed their bets on the wrong daughter.'"

Ava shivered as she heard her words repeated back to her. "No," she said. She jumped to her feet, and the pigeon flew off. "I don't want to do this."

"Ava," Antonio said.

"Don't you dare say my name like that. Who the hell do you think you are?"

She felt her cheeks flush as Antonio stared at her from across the balcony. "Guys, can we have a minute, please?" he asked.

Javier wordlessly switched the camera off and went inside. Val stayed put, turning to Ava with a raised eyebrow. It was impossible to tell how much Val knew, but she suspected it was more than he let on. She gave an almost imperceptible nod, and he got up. "I guess I'll go get more coffee and muffins for the stupid pigeons," he said.

"I thought we had a deal," Antonio said, once Val had disappeared back inside. "We could do the scene about your dads if we didn't bring up Eden anymore."

"Well, the deal's off then, because you just did."

"Actually, *you* did. It's always you."

"So what?" she snapped. Antonio didn't say anything. She turned and leaned against the parapet, gazing out at the Manhattan skyline. Ever since she'd returned, she had been trying to remember what it was she'd missed so much about this city. Nothing seemed to move her anymore. "Why are we even here?" she asked.

"Don't get like that." Finally, Antonio crossed the balcony and stood beside her, putting his arm around her. "This is a really great opportunity for you. You just have to let people in a little more."

"A really great opportunity," Ava repeated, her words getting lost in the soft flannel of Antonio's shirt. There was only one reason she had signed that contract for the spinoff, and it had nothing to do with opportunity. It had nothing to do with her anger, either, although it was easy for her to pretend it did. It had only been about Antonio. She tipped her head back, studying his face, as she had so many times in the past five months, trying to figure out what he was thinking. But she never could.

"Don't worry," he said, stroking her chin with his index finger. "We can pick this all up tomorrow. I'm sorry I pushed you, okay?"

Panic spread through Ava's chest, the way it always did when Antonio was about to leave. Because leaving only ever meant one thing. "Val's going out tonight," she said. "You should stay, we could get some dinner."

"I wish I could." Antonio kissed the top of her head and let her go. Then he walked back across the balcony and started packing up his gear.

"But we'll have the place to ourselves."

"Come on. You know I have to go home."

Home. Ava hated hearing that word come from his mouth, because the words *to Molly* always hung in the air after them, unsaid. Ava pulled her phone out of her pocket and instinctively opened the front-facing camera. She saw her own face, puffy and pale, and frowned. She flipped it around, and when she did, she saw Antonio put down his gear and stare at her. She gave it another try. "I was thinking we could order in from that new Thai place down the street, maybe watch some Netflix?"

"A second ago you were ready to pull down the sun to burn me with it. Now you want to watch movies?"

"Well, yeah," said Ava. "I mean, I thought maybe we should have a talk about our future."

"Our future?" Antonio slung his bag over his shoulder. "Ava, what are you talking about?"

Once, back at the B&B, Ava had walked into the kitchen while Antonio was on the phone with Molly, talking about Micah. They weren't arguing, exactly, but Antonio's tone wasn't warm, either. "Tell him not to worry about it," he said, sounding annoyed, as if the last thing he wanted was to be having this conversation. As if he was realizing right then that he had made a huge mistake in

252

marrying her, in tying himself to this ordinary woman who only wanted to talk to him about ordinary things. That his life could have been so much more. His life could be so much more.

At least, that's what Ava had thought at the time. Now, she knew otherwise.

"Never mind, just leave," she said, storming into the apartment, where she went straight to her room and slammed her door, half hoping he would follow her, but knowing that he never would.

Later, after she heard him leave, she sat on the edge of her bathtub, waiting for it to fill, and ran her fingers over the twenty-three tiny notches carved into the top of her feet, one for each time Ava and Antonio had slept together over the course of five months. She didn't know why she did it. Looking at them most days made her feel sick.

"Everything is going to be okay," he'd said after that first time, and she'd wanted to believe him. She'd imagined the two of them back in Manhattan together after he left Molly, a cute little loft apartment, strolls in Central Park, coffee and croissants in quiet cafés, pizza on the floor in the light of a raucously pink sunset. Maybe Micah would visit on weekends, and they would take him ice skating, or to the zoo. She had her whole life scripted into a Nora Ephron movie when she'd put her pen to paper and signed herself up for another round of the circus of humiliation that was reality television.

But Antonio's version of "okay" had been something altogether different. And even though Val had slipped back into city life as if he had never left—establishing his position as the New York music scene's number-one fanboy and the guy at the show who always had weed—since they'd been back, Ava didn't know what to do with herself or how to keep from spiralling out of control. She didn't have any interesting obsessions, any idiosyncratic hobbies, any adorable neuroses. Alone in the loft after the camera crew went home, she would wander aimlessly from room to room, pick things up and put them down again, sit on the balcony and stare out at the sky. She hadn't even really been out of the apartment except to pose for her weekly publicity shot at whatever place was hot that week, walking in, doing a single circuit of the club, and then leaving without even getting a drink. After years of dreaming about coming back to New York so her life could begin again, now she just sat at home and waited for something to happen.

And it was in those moments that she wondered: Was Antonio the real reason she had come back to New York? Or was it because of those cameras lined up against the wall? Was she afraid that without script editing and colour correcting, without the gleam of the key light softening her features and the boom mic capturing the slightest nuance of her voice, she would discover she didn't really exist at all?

Well, screw it, she thought, letting her foot fall into the scalding-hot water. She wasn't going to stick herself up on a shelf for the night like a prop. She was done with sitting around and waiting. She switched off the taps and pulled out her phone, texting Val.

Where are you going tonight?

Show at Davenport. Y?

I'm coming with you.

She slid into the water, letting her phone fall to the floor.

———◇———

When the pack of wild girls had all left, she found Val again, near the front of the stage. "That was gross," she said. "I'm so sick of being surrounded by a thousand me's."

"Sometimes I'm sick of being surrounded by *one* you," Val said, but his heart wasn't in it. His face was shining in the purple and blue stage lights, making him seem like a rapt disciple waiting to be blessed. Val was an aspiring musician, because of course he was—his secret no longer such a secret, sheet music and records littering the floor of their apartment, lyrics tacked to walls. He had a guitar strapped to his body as he made toast or brushed his teeth, his fingers diving down to the strings at every free moment, tripping over some exorbitantly irritating riff that he would play and replay, over and over until, Ava assumed, either he got it right or she went crazy and killed herself. He also knew all the latest New York bands, following them around from gig to gig, fixated as a groupie. She had to remind herself that Val was only seventeen, just a kid. For all his posturing, for him the world was still a place where beautiful things were made by passionate, dedicated people, a place where anyone could be anything and art was all that mattered. Somehow, amidst all the cameras and celebrity, Val had managed to keep this essential part of himself protected. Ava didn't know how. Her own shell had cracked long, long ago.

This band, Align Above—for Val, they were the pinnacle of all the beautiful things, mostly because he had seen them play once in Halifax, hitchhiking into the city from Gin Harbour and sneaking into the bar even though he was only fifteen. And even though back then he'd never told her about anything he did, that night he had come home buzzing with an excitement that was so tender it was painful to watch, full of bold proclamations about them becoming the Next Big Thing. And then, they did. And, Ava knew, some tiny part of Val wanted to take ownership of that, like a sports fan wearing their hat at just the right angle takes ownership of their team winning—that somehow his belief directly contributed to their success. In some corner of his brain, he belonged to the band now. Or they belonged to him.

From the tension in the room as the band warmed up, Ava knew that he wasn't the only one. The crowd seemed to hum with a low buzz of energy that was slowly but steadily beginning to build. Ava wondered if the band did it on purpose, standing there and teasing the crowd with their instruments, stroking them just enough to get them fired up, and then pulling back, making their heads spin with craziness as they waited, waited.

"Avalon," she heard someone say behind her.

"No," she said, without turning around.

"Avalon," the voice said louder. Ava looked at Val, but his eyes were transfixed on the shadowy figures with their shadowy instruments. She took a sip from her martini and then slowly turned around to face Antonio.

"What are you doing here?" she asked.

"You know very well what I'm doing here. You go to a club, I have to follow you. It's part of the contract."

"I won't tell if you don't."

"Val already told them. But I feel like you knew that already." Antonio sighed the deep, heavy sigh of someone who sighed for a living, or someone who wanted you to *know* they sighed for a living. "What kind of game are you playing here?" he asked.

"I'm not *playing* anything. I only wanted a night out with my brother."

"Right. You, who never goes out." He ran his hands through his hair, exasperated. He glanced furtively around the club to see if anyone was watching, then leaned into her ear. "Is this because I wouldn't stay with you tonight?" he whispered angrily. "You decided to go out and force me to stay with you?"

"No one's *forcing* you to do anything. Go home if you want."

"Some people have *jobs*, you know," he said. "I need to do my *job*."

"Well then, maybe you need a vacation," Ava said. "You know, a nice week on a beach somewhere with your beautiful *wife*."

"Ava . . ."

"No, you're right, that would be horrible. I think you probably need a night off. Here, let me get you a drink." She waved at Justin Bieber's backup dancer, blew him a little kiss. He smiled, made a drink motion with his hand. She nodded.

"I don't want a drink," Antonio said, and Ava could see his jaw muscles working like rotors under his skin. "I want you to go

256

to the bouncer and tell him to let Javi in with the camera so I can film your ridiculous shenanigans and then go home and get some sleep." She couldn't remember a time she had ever seen Antonio angry, even when she was at her worst-behaved. It thrilled her, in a way she couldn't explain. It made her want more.

"Fuck you, Antonio," she said, downing the rest of her martini before letting her glass fall from her hand. It hit the ground with a smash, shards of glass flying everywhere.

Antonio reached out and grabbed her arm, twisting it, hard. "No, fuck *you*, Avalon."

For a moment, Ava thought he was going to hit her. But instead, he switched his grip on her arm and dragged her across the dance floor to the back of the club, down a long hallway toward the bathrooms and out a back door into the alleyway. The door slammed behind him as he let go of her arm, swinging her toward a wall next to an overflowing dumpster.

"Too bad Javi didn't catch *that* on camera," Ava said, rubbing her arm. "Did no one see that?" she yelled toward the door. "What is wrong with everyone?"

"What is wrong with *you*?" Antonio said. "You've been acting crazy for weeks."

"You're mad at me for being crazy?" Ava swung at him wildly with her fist but only managed to graze the sleeve of his jacket. She swung again, this time connecting with his upper arm. "*You* are the reason I'm crazy, Antonio. You. *You are the reason.*"

Antonio drew back his shoulders, and Ava retreated against the wall, bracing herself for whatever came next. But all the anger had deflated out of him, and he dropped his head, sinking in on himself.

"I know," he said. "I know. I'm so sorry."

"Dammit," Ava muttered. She pulled his head into her chest. "Stop it, okay?" She cupped her hand under his chin and lifted his head, kissing his mouth. "Just stop it."

Within seconds he had her skirt up and was pushing her against the wall. Ava wrapped her legs around him and pressed her forehead into his shoulder, letting her mind empty. For one glorious, shining moment she could feel it all drain away—all the stress and the pressure, the show and Val and Molly and everything—gone in a flash of heat and adrenaline. But just as quickly, it was over, and the world came roaring back in. She kept her legs locked around Antonio's waist, feeling him still hard inside her, her breath coming in heaving gasps as she raised her head and rested her chin on his shoulder.

"Are you going to leave Molly?" she whispered, her mouth inches from his ear.

He pressed his forehead against the wall behind her. "I don't know," he said.

"Right," said Ava. She untangled herself from him and pulled her skirt back down, walking back into the club without turning around.

"Wait," said Antonio, grabbing her arm.

As she opened the door, a wall of sound hit her. No, not a wall, a giant wave—a great breaker crashing down over her as she tried to swim out of the wake, limbs thrashing, lungs sputtering for air. Antonio still had a grip on her arm, but he was far away, drifting, suddenly irrelevant as Ava surfaced and moved through the crowd.

There were four musicians on the stage: a guitarist, a drummer, a bassist, and, standing in the middle of them all, a woman with a red spotlight setting her hair on fire. The wave of sound built again, growing louder and more insistent. But this time as it reached its apex, instead of breaking, the singer stepped to the mic, wrapped her hands around the stand, and opened her mouth.

For a moment, the sound of her voice hung in the room, suspended. Then Ava felt it rip through her, propelled by an engine of vodka and adrenaline, pulsing against her temples as if it were

258

trying to push itself out through her skin. Any other time—sober, without the imprints of Antonio's hands still on her back, without the screams of the wild girls still ringing in her ears—she might have stood outside of it, might have walked out of that bar as though nothing had ever happened. But now she found herself riveted in place as that voice split her open, exposing everything she had ever tried to hide, the darkest, most terrifying, desperate parts of herself spilling out as she stood there drowning in the sound, swaying almost imperceptibly to the beat of the drums like seaweed in a current.

"Avalon," Antonio said, but his voice was far away, and Ava knew that soon he would be too. He would give up and go outside to find Javier, and they would report everything back to Bob and Tess from LifeStyle, and maybe it would be the last time, maybe it would finally be the end of things for Ava and Val. Or maybe they would give them another chance, and Ava would fuck up again and *that* would be the last time. Either way, Ava could feel everything rushing away from her, as though she were standing on a beach, watching as her life drifted further and further out to sea, every moment thinking, *I can still get it back, I can still save it,* but still not moving, not doing anything, until finally it was too far gone.

Instead, she let herself be pulled toward the front of the stage by the music, and watched the band play through the rest of their set. When they finished, the singer turned abruptly and walked off the stage, and Ava felt herself plummet back to the earth.

"I thought I'd lost you," the backup dancer said behind her. "Are you okay?"

But Ava kept staring at the spot on the stage where the singer had been. Her vision pulsating in and out, fading then clearing, riding the crest of her heartbeat.

—◇—

Ava woke up the next morning in a haze of smoke and headache. The last thing she fully remembered was doing shots at the bar with a man who said he was a baseball player, although she couldn't remember what he looked like or what team he played for. Everything else came in brief flashes—falling down in the bathroom, losing her earring, a cab ride. Snippets of a conversation with a woman on their balcony, could that be right? She grabbed her phone and checked her social media, but she hadn't posted any photos, nothing to give her any ideas as to where the rest of the night had gone. She supposed it was probably for the best. LifeStyle hated it when she posted her own photos. Everything on her social media had to be carefully curated, planned, and styled, though posed to seem as natural as possible. A drunken selfie with a man who, let's face it, was probably lying about being a baseball player didn't exactly fit the bill.

Ava tried to sit up on the couch and was instantly sent back down with a searing pain through her shoulder. It must have been the fall in the bathroom, she thought. She pushed herself up again, gingerly, and made her way to the kitchen. Maybe Val was up and could give her some insight on what happened last night. Even though she had no memory of him after the band stopped playing, that didn't mean he wasn't there. He always kept an eye on her. He was a good brother.

When she got to the kitchen, she was surprised to find a red-headed woman, in a long, black T-shirt and bare feet, carefully and quietly rummaging through one of the drawers. "That drawer is mostly takeout chopsticks and packets of soy sauce," Ava said.

"Shhh," the woman said, without turning around. "Your brother's still asleep."

"He'll sleep through anything," Ava said. She opened a different drawer and pulled out a spoon. "Is this what you're looking for?"

The woman smiled. "Thanks." She seemed familiar, but Ava couldn't quite place her.

Ava opened a cabinet and took down a mug. Scrolling through her hazy memory until, suddenly, she stopped on an image. "You're the singer from that band."

The woman raised an eyebrow. "Yes," she said. "I am."

Leaning against the counter, Ava rotated the mug around in her hand, trying to make her brain kick into gear. There was only one reason the woman would be here, in their kitchen, making coffee. "You slept with Val," she said.

The corners of the woman's mouth twitched into a fleeting smile. "Yes, that's still true." She picked up the coffee pot and motioned it toward Ava.

Ava held her mug out and the woman poured. It smelled strong, the way Ava liked it. "That's great," she said. "He seriously loves you."

"So I hear." The woman poured some coffee for herself and brought the mug to her lips, watching Ava. "You don't remember me, do you?" she asked eventually.

"Of course I do," Ava said. "I was at the show too."

"Right." The woman sipped her coffee thoughtfully. "My name's Mags."

"Ava."

"I know." She smiled. "What I mean is, do you remember anything about what happened last night?"

Ava took in a sharp breath. "Did I do something stupid?"

"No, you didn't." Mags paused for a long time. "No," she repeated eventually. "You really didn't."

"I don't know if I believe you," Ava said. She stared down into her coffee cup, trying to see her reflection. But the liquid was flat, black, lifeless.

"You did tell me my boobs looked smaller in person."

Ava's eyes flicked up to Mags's chest, and then her face. "They do," she said. "It's a camera trick. Like how they always take my photo with my head tilted to the right, because studies show left-cheek poses are supposed to make you seem emotional and expressive. Apparently, this is something I need help with." She took a drink of her coffee. "Me and the *Mona Lisa,* I guess."

Mags put her mug down. "Let's see." She moved to Ava's left side, then her right. "Oh, I see it now," she said. "It's like you're a completely different person. Sweet, kind, vulnerable." She moved back to the right. "Stone-cold bitch."

Ava moved her right cheek forward. "I guess I'll have to walk into rooms like this from now on."

"I know I, for one, would feel better if you did." Mags picked up her mug again, peering at Ava over the rim. "This might sound weird for me to ask you, but . . . are you okay?"

"Yeah, of course," Ava responded automatically. Then she paused, feeling her face flush. How long had it been since someone had sincerely asked her that? Mags at least deserved a real answer. "I mean, no. Probably not. But I'm not going to kill myself or anything."

"I hope that's true, Ava." Mags drained her coffee and put the mug down on the counter. "Tell your brother I had to leave, okay? And you know what? Tilt your head whatever way you want." She touched Ava's cheek, briefly, before walking away down the hall, and for the rest of the morning Ava felt the delicate line her finger had traced hot on her skin, like a brand.

Flash: Good morning, Cincinnati, I'm Johnny Flash, and this is the *Morning Mashup* on CKBV, 102.3 on your FM dial. It is currently 8:15 am on February 12, for those of you who are keeping track, and this morning I'm here with Mags Kovach and Paul Van Ness from the band Align Above. Currently in the middle of a massive North American tour, the band is in town playing a sold-out show at the Harley tonight. Mags, Paul, welcome to CKBV.

Van Ness: Thanks for having us.

Kovach: Yeah, great to be here.

Flash: How's the tour been going?

Van Ness: It's been great. We've had such an amazing response around the country since our very first show in New York. It's hard to believe it's almost over.

Flash: And you're headed to Europe next?

Van Ness: Yes, we wrap up this leg back home in Toronto next week, and then we head out again a few days later. It's been such a whirlwind, it's hard to even wrap our heads around it.

Flash: I bet it has. Your album *Nothingview* was released last November to almost instant critical and commercial success. How surprising was that for you?

Van Ness: Completely surprising. I mean, we believe in what we do, of course. But you never know how people will respond.

Flash: Well, you have definitely tapped into some key demographics. I know my wife bought a copy the day it dropped, and she hasn't bought a

CD in years. And my daughter has been playing it non-stop for the past three months.

Van Ness: That's nice. Tell them thank you.

Flash: There's obviously something in your music that people are really connecting with. Any idea what that might be, Mags?

Kovach: I guess . . . I mean, we love what we do. People can hear that, maybe. In the music.

Flash: Your voice has been described as a force of nature, and your live performances are . . . well, *emotional* isn't even a strong enough word. What drives you?

Kovach: I think we just covered that, Jimmy.

Flash: It's Johnny.

Kovach: Oh.

Flash: I know this is tough to talk about, but you recently lost your husband and bass player, Sam Cole, to cancer. That must be hard for you all, to perform without him.

Van Ness: Yes, of course. Sam was instrumental in putting this album together. All the bass tracks are his. We hear him in every song we play.

Kovach: You do?

Van Ness: Of course.

Flash: And no doubt this contributes to the emotional quality of your performance, Mags.

Kovach: No doubt.

Flash: It's probably what people are responding to. That grief.

264

Kovach: People are buying the album and coming to the shows because they want to hear me be sad?

Flash: [laughs] It's kind of our natural instinct, isn't it? As humans? To seek out that raw emotion to remind us that we're all human, that we're all connected by something larger . . .

Kovach: To stare at a train wreck, you mean.

Van Ness: That's not—

Flash: I'm just saying, it probably hasn't hurt your ticket sales . . .

Kovach: Fuck you, Jimmy. This interview is over.

Mags

February 2015

———◇———

"The Worst Place to Be"

"**F**ive minutes," Emiko said, sticking her head in the door of
Mags's dressing room.

"Okay," Mags said without looking at her.

She was sitting in front of the mirror, watching the edges of
her face wobble under the light, her features fading and then re-
appearing as if the mirror were a giant Etch A Sketch that someone
kept shaking and then redrawing. It was probably that pill Paul had
given her an hour earlier, or the one that Emiko had given her, or
maybe a cumulative high from all the pills she had been taking since
starting the tour, all the alcohol she had pumped into her system.
Trying to find the perfect balance. This one keeps you up, this one
brings you down. This one helps you remember all the things you
need to remember. This one helps you forget all the things you want
to forget.

Three months into their North American tour, and they were
in Boston or Pittsburgh or Baltimore—hell, they could have been in
Cleveland for all Mags knew—about to play another sold-out show,

266

the eighteenth or twentieth or twenty-fifth in a row. The same face-less mass night after night, the same non-descript green rooms, the same lights blinding her as she stepped out onto the stage. She had started drinking that morning before the sun had even come up, sunk down in a seat in the back of their tour bus with a six-pack of Old Milwaukee, watching the world outside change from deepest night to the orangey glow of dawn before switching from beer to bourbon. She had even done a few lines of coke in the bathroom right before their call, procured from a squirrely looking guy she found backstage who she assumed worked for the venue but could just as easily have been trying to steal their equipment.

But she still felt like the balance was off tonight. She swam through the halls of the venue to wait in the wings, unable to feel the tips of her fingers, unable to focus on the faces of the people around her. She wondered what the temperature was outside. What night of the week it was. Whether Valentine's Day had happened yet. Whether this haze she was in was from all the drugs, or something else. Whether it even mattered. Whether any of this mattered.

Next to her was Josh, the kid who Paul and Zac and Emiko had hired to replace Sam as their bassist. They had auditioned him without Mags because she hadn't wanted any part of it. Also, she'd been drunk and had forgotten it was happening. He had avoided her for most of the tour. He was, after all, replacing her husband.

"Sounds like a good crowd out there tonight," she said, a feeble attempt at small talk, her tongue thick in her mouth. "Looks like it's at capacity."

"Yeah," said Josh nervously. "It's sold out."

She pulled back the curtain and peered out at the audience, but it was all a blur, eyes glowing from inside an amorphous black fog. "That's bonkers. Who knew they liked us so much in . . . where are we, anyway?"

Josh looked at her like she had three heads. "Toronto. We've got two shows here, tonight and tomorrow night."

The word smashed into her gut like a cannonball, momentarily stealing her breath. They were in Toronto. She was home.

"Let's go," Paul said, coming up behind her.

"We're in Toronto!" she said, an edge of desperation in her voice that she hadn't expected. "Paul, we're in Toronto."

"I know," he said, not unkindly. But still, he gave her a little shove. "And they're waiting for us."

She stepped out onto the stage. Immediately she felt that power surging through her, that electric shock of adrenaline that hit her like a taser at the beginning of every show, building up from the soles of her feet to the crown of her head. She walked up to the mic, each step sending reverberations through her body, her hand connecting with the mic stand, her palm curling around the familiar cold metal as if it were being called home. Even though the lights were off, she could feel the energy coming off the crowd, the tension rippling against her skin.

She took a deep breath. The noise grew to a deafening roar. *I am not going to cry. I am not going to cry. I am not going to cry.*

The lights hit her. And she burst into tears.

The first time it happened was in Boston, the second show of the tour, following the kickoff in New York. Mags had felt a strange ache in her body, one that at the time she attributed to the abuse she had been putting herself through, all the sleepless nights, the intoxicants, the general heaviness of her bones. But ever since that night on the balcony with Ava, she could feel something inside her coming apart, as though the threads that held her together had been slowly and quietly undone by the sight of this other woman's grief.

When she stepped onstage in Boston, her voice broke almost immediately, a lump forming in the back of her throat that she didn't recognize until she opened her mouth again and a sob came out. She reached up and touched her face and was surprised to find that her cheeks were wet with tears. She was standing onstage in front of three thousand screaming fans and she was crying.

She managed to get through the song, then whispered to Paul that she needed a break, they should do an instrumental. He stared at her strangely—they never played instrumentals this early in the set—but nodded. Backstage, she ran to the bathroom, splashed water on her face, looked at herself in the mirror—her bloodshot eyes, her swollen skin. It was a sad song, she thought, a song about Sam, although she had sung it plenty of times before without any incident.

"It's normal," Emiko said afterward, when their regular set was over and Mags collapsed in the dressing room, her face red and swollen, listening as the crowd outside chanted for an encore. She had barely made it through, her voice breaking during every second song, the tears flowing freely as she stood onstage, going through the motions of performing. "Your husband just died. You're going to cry sometimes."

"This . . . I don't know. It was different." She hadn't cried much in the months after Sam's death, but when she did, it was like a passing thunderstorm, furious and sudden, abating just as quickly. Still, she had been holding it together. She had been *functioning*. And aside from that one night in New York, she hadn't done anything she regretted. At least, not yet. But trying to sing with a broken heart was like trying to run with a broken leg. It wasn't that she felt sad so much as she felt a physical pain. "It comes on like an explosion, and I don't know how to make it stop."

"It's been a rough few months. And now everything is happening quickly for you and the band. It's natural for you to feel overwhelmed, after everything."

A rough few months. Mags wanted to rip the perfect sleek ponytail off Emiko's perfectly oval head. Instead, she gritted her teeth and said, "I just want to make it stop."

"We'll find you something." Emiko rummaged through her purse, pulling out bottles and plastic bags and dumping them all out on the table in front of her. "Pick one."

Mags poked a baggie with her finger. "I don't know what any of these are."

"It doesn't matter. Any of them will work." When Mags continued to hesitate, Emiko snatched a bottle, shaking out two pills and handing them to Mags. "Come on now, eat up. You've got to get back out there for the encore."

"I hate you," Mags said, picking the pills out of Emiko's palm and swallowing them. "I hate you and this band and everything to do with this stupid industry. The only thing I don't hate about it is me."

Emiko smiled. "And that's why people love you."

And so Mags went back out, and she performed better than she ever had before. She was wild, passionate, wailing, spilling her whole heart onto the stage and then leaving it there as if she had a never-ending supply. And even in her inebriated state she could tell the audience was eating it up, laughing as she swung the mic stand like a sword, cheering as she gave the finger to the security guard who stopped her when she tried to stage-dive into the crowd. But Mags knew it was an act. It was just Mags pretending to be Mags, putting on a mask, going through the motions.

Minutes later, Mags stumbled back into the wings. She closed her eyes, letting the noise of the crowd wash over her, reminding herself that this was the only thing she'd ever wanted.

Except she had wanted Sam too. And what did one matter, without the other?

After that night, the tears didn't stop. For the rest of the tour, Emiko kept feeding her pills—enough to keep her floating above her grief, the pain present but bearable, the tears a permanent salty slick on her cheeks. And afterward, when she came down from the pills, she would start to drink. She told herself it was to help her sleep, to eradicate those dreams that woke her in a panic every morning—where was she? what was she doing? where was Sam?—the alcohol instantly dissolving those walls in her head that kept things organized, grief leaking out everywhere, messy and beautiful and strange. She'd wake in the afternoon dry-mouthed and embarrassed, more determined than ever to move forward, live her life, make things happen. But that would only last until she had to talk to someone, until she had to be Mags Kovach, and then the whole cycle would start all over again. Eventually, Mags had retreated so far into herself that she felt like she was looking at the world from the bottom of a deep, dark hole.

"Maybe I should take some time off," she'd said to Emiko, after a particularly brutal show in Philadelphia, where she had fallen off the stage and kicked one of the security guys in the shin when he tried to help her back up. "Cancel the rest of the tour dates. We can do that, can't we?"

"Oh, honey, no," Emiko said. "If we hold off now, that's it, the band's finished. Do you think that's what Sam would have wanted? Do you think he'd want everything he worked so hard for to just disintegrate because he was gone? I know you're tired, but don't you want to do this for him?"

Maybe she was right, but Mags was in no shape to argue. So they stayed on the road, and she kept doing everything she could to forget that she was alone. She was no longer the Mags who needed to be in charge. So much easier to let the pills be in charge.

But when the radio host in Cincinnati had suggested that people were coming to her shows just to see the mess she'd become, she had responded by walking out of the room, locking herself in the bathroom and chugging back whiskey from her flask as Emiko banged on the door. And when, right before their show in Chicago, Emiko had sent her a link to a story on a popular online music site titled "Music and Love Aligning: The Heartbreak of Mags Kovach," she had trashed the green room, pushing over the catering table and dumping piles of cut fruit and vegetables onto the floor. She told herself it didn't matter what she did. But then she'd see her tear-streaked face on the front page of a paper or splashed all over the internet, and Mags would remember that people were watching her now, waiting to see what she'd do next. She was setting herself on fire and everyone was just watching, cameras out, waiting to see how hot she would burn.

———◇———

Home. Her key in the door, fitting with such a familiar scrape that it was almost like being transported back in time. As though she would open the door and Sam would be there, sprawled out on the couch watching a movie or coming out of the bathroom wearing a towel or saying "Hey baby, I'm in here" from whatever room he was in. She pulled the key out, stared at it for a minute. Considered turning around, walking back down the hall, getting in a cab, and never coming back.

Eventually, though, she went inside.

It had been three months since she'd been home, and the apartment was cold. As she crossed the room to turn up the thermostat, she had the sense of something being disturbed, some quiet rest the room had been undertaking in her absence, the walls exhaling with the almost indecipherable sigh of a peaceful moment coming to an end. *Too bad,* Mags thought. *You don't get off the hook that easy. He was a part of you too.*

She opened the fridge, but there was nothing in it except a bottle of vinegar, a long-expired carton of milk, and a lump of something rotten that she realized was the remnants of an Asian pear Emiko had bought for her, back in the early days after Sam died, when Mags wasn't capable of feeding herself. She'd kept herself holed up in the apartment for weeks, watching and rewatching all those '70s gangster movies that Sam loved so much—*Mean*

Streets, Get Carter, The Long Goodbye—and sitting out on the fire escape, smoking, crying to Johnny Cash, Kris Kristofferson, all Sam's favourite music. Unable to deal with the silence, with the ghosts in the shadows.

"You need to move," Emiko had said, dropping off a bag of groceries—a strange assortment of rare fruit, dried pasta, and candy bars that made Mags question if Emiko had ever bought groceries before in her life. Mags knew she was right, but the thought of going to see apartments by herself, signing a new lease by herself, moving all her things to a new place by herself—it was too overwhelming, too exhausting. And then they left on the tour, and she didn't have to think about her apartment, or think about all the memories of Sam contained within these four walls. Until now.

She sat down at the table, letting the deep silence settle around her. From the other room, she could hear the ticking of the clock that Sam had bought at a flea market that time they rented a car and drove out to Prince Edward County to see what all the fuss was about. Sam with his bare feet on the dashboard, pointing out each cow he saw, making her pull over at every antique store, every fruit stand. At first, she tried to push the memory away, the pain almost unbearable. But then she realized: she wanted it. She wanted the grief back. Not the tight, steel ball of grief, teeth-grinding and nauseating, that the pills compacted her pain into, but the hot, sticky, uninhibited grief that came with the drinking. She wanted to swim in her grief. She wanted to crack her grief against the wall and watch it trickle down to the floor, she wanted it to flood the entire world, she wanted it to swallow her whole.

And so she began steadily drinking her way through the liquor cupboard.

Later she remembered some parts: singing all her favourite songs at the top of her lungs, standing on the fire escape smoking cigarette after cigarette, asking a passerby if they could get her some coke, throwing snowballs at the bus when it stopped at the corner to let passengers out. She put on her best dress. She fell in the bathroom and thought she might have chipped her tooth. Then she was up on her feet again, and maybe she was even dancing. She was pressed up against the window, kissing it, the glass cold and metallic against her tongue. She was on the bed, jumping. She knocked over a lamp, then challenged it to a pillow fight. She finally cried when she ripped her best dress while trying to take it off, ripped it all the way down the side. She sat naked on the floor and wailed, cradling the dress in her arms before throwing it across the room. She punched the floor and her hand was numb, maybe even broken. She was going to find a bar, and she was going to start a fight. She was going to find someone and fuck their brains out, she was going to find a perfect marriage to rip apart. She was going down swinging. She was raging, she was raging.

The only way she was going to make it through . . .

The only way she was going to make it through this night . . .

The only way she was going to make it through this night was to . . .

She was not going to make it through this night.

—◇—

She felt something moving underneath her. At first, because she was dreaming of a forest, dark green and misty, she thought it was a wild animal burying itself beneath her. But then consciousness broke through in jumbled bursts, and she was vaguely aware that she was not in a forest and that the thing moving underneath her was someone's hands, and then those hands were pulling her, dragging her someplace. In a moment of sheer feral panic, Mags began to thrash, some bare resemblance to instinct kicking in and making her fight. But her legs were entirely limp and her arms felt like dead weights, and when she tried to speak she found that her mouth was somehow cemented shut. It was so much easier to stop fighting, to let those hands pull her to wherever they wanted. It didn't matter anyway, because she didn't know where she was. Her eyes tried to focus, and as she moved through the liquid space, objects drifting in and out of her fuzzy vision, she began to recognize things: her shoes in the closet, her couch, her giant living room window with the old-fashioned sash, the warp and woof of her hardwood floor. Everything was upside down, but in a way that made sense to her, as if it should have been overturned all along.

She cracked apart her lips and forced her gluey mouth to open, her parched tongue limp against the inside of her cheek. She managed to croak out one word—"Sam"—and then everything began to fade away. She tried to wiggle her fingers and toes, struggling for consciousness, but she was too tired to fight. The darkness won.

Shannon Duncan
@shann0ndee
I am happy to report that Align Above are as incredible live as everyone says. If you can get tix for tomorrow night's show, Toronto, DO IT #alignaboveatmercerhall
11:54 PM – 19 Feb 2015
22 Retweets 113 Likes

Talisha @teebot45 47 min
Replying to @shann0ndee
Such a great show! I was kinda bummed Mags didn't throw an amp into the crowd or anything, tho

Shannon Duncan @shann0ndee 23 min
Replying to @teebot45
She WAS bawling by the end

Talisha @teebot45 21 min
Replying to @shann0ndee
She does that every night! I was hoping for something more dramatic lol

Alba Noe @superkittyxx 17 min
Replying to @teebot45 @shann0ndee
Did you catch when Zac had to pick her up off the floor behind the drum kit after "Serendipity"? She just dropped, wouldn't get back up #alignaboveatmercerhall

Talisha @teebot45 21 min
Replying to @superkittyxx @shann0ndee
Damn I missed that!!!! I hope someone got pics

Ava

February 2015

—◇—

AMTHGF S01:
Hiatus

When Ava was little, she thought that "morning sickness" was "mourning sickness." To her, there was something funereal about being pregnant, and it seemed appropriate that a woman's body would mourn for the days when it had been free of parasitic life forms. As she got older and understood that the sickness happened in the morning, she secretly still thought of it as grief—albeit the kind that manifested itself in hourly visits to the ladies' room to ralph in the toilet.

Now, as Ava sat on the edge of the bathtub, a garbage can between her knees, a thin thread of vomit unspooling over her lip as she stared at the little plus sign on the pee stick, she still wasn't convinced her first instinct was wrong.

When that plus sign first appeared, she had tried to break the stick in half. But the plastic stick, rigid and pee-slick, had instead flown out of her hands and across the room, landing behind the radiator. She got down on her hands and knees and probed the cobwebby depths, trying to retrieve it, wondering why no one had ever created an easily snappable pregnancy test for women who didn't want to be pregnant. Surely there was a market for it. Surely there were other women out there for whom snapping that stick would be, if not wholly satisfying, a nice diversion from having to think about the mess they were in.

But even covered in dirt and dust, the plus sign was still there. In her head she counted backward—it had been six weeks since she had last been with Antonio. After filming for the first season of AMTHGF had ended, he and Molly and Micah had gone to Acapulco for a holiday while Ava stayed home obsessively checking Molly's Instagram feed and working her way through the crate of gelato he had given her as a Christmas present. "You know, I can get gelato now any time I want," she said when he gave it to her, and he'd looked so crushed that she'd fucked him right there on the living room couch, even though Val was due home any minute. She regretted it later, as she scrolled past picture after picture of his lean, beautiful, tanned body stretched out across white sand, or his charmingly gap-toothed smile squished up next to Molly's gummy one in a selfie in front of the ocean. Remembering how she had promised herself, after that night in the alley, that she wouldn't let it happen again. And, of course, she *really* regretted it now, as her stomach heaved one more time, the last of the gelato forcing itself up her esophagus.

"Ava?" Val's voice came through the door. "Are you okay?"

Ava lifted her head. "Go away."

But she hadn't locked the door. He made a face as soon as he saw her, before backing away from the smell. "The toilet is *right there*."

"Too far." Ava shifted over on the edge of the tub, using one butt cheek to cover the pregnancy test.

"What did you even get up to last night?" Ava didn't answer. "I thought you only went out for the cameras. We're not even filming right now."

"Maybe I'm learning to like the celebrity lifestyle." She pulled the garbage can to her chest. "Don't I look glamorous?"

"Like the next cover of *Vogue*." He paused, then pulled out his vape from his pocket. "Want some of this? It might make you feel better."

Ava's stomach lurched. "No, thank you."

Val shrugged, bringing the vape to his lips. "Fine, more for me," he said.

Ava watched him from over the rim of the garbage can, wondering when he had become such a pothead. She couldn't remember him ever smoking before they came to New York. But there was a lot she hadn't known about her brother back then. The hard edge he had now, hidden behind his bloodshot eyes—had it always been there? Was it just the closeness of the cameras now that made it easier to see?

Exhaling, Val pulled his shirt up over the lower half of his face. "Seriously, what died in there?"

"Only my dignity." She spat into the can, trying to avoid his eyes. She could tell he didn't believe her. For a brief moment, she considered telling him everything. But the thought of how far back she would have to go, all the explanations she would have to give him, all the questions he would inevitably ask—it was too much. She just wanted to be left alone with her garbage can and her pee stick. Her stomach came to her rescue, hurling up a stream of what at this point could only be pure bile.

"Okay, I'm out," said Val, closing the door. "Text me if you need anything," he added from the other side.

"Will do," Ava said weakly. But unless he had a time machine, there was no way he could help her.

—◇—

Ava knew she was lucky not to have the cameras on her as she floated through her days in a confused stupor. But she also hadn't seen Antonio since he'd come back from Acapulco, and they had to talk about this.

She convinced him to meet her at a ramen place she liked in SoHo, dim and random enough that she could usually get away with not being recognized. Still, she wore the blonde wig, the one that reminded her of the hair she had before. Part of her hoped it would remind Antonio too—of a time when things were easy between them, when the two of them would joke and flirt, when everything was pure possibility.

"I've forgotten how to eat soup with long hair," she joked as loose strands trailed in the broth, then immediately regretted it as Antonio sighed, twirling his chopsticks in the noodles. She felt stupid, pathetic, desperate. It hadn't even been that long since she'd seen him, but something had changed. She didn't know how to be around him anymore.

All this will change, she thought. *When we have a family.*

But Antonio was nervous, vigilant. He couldn't keep from looking around the room. "Why are we here?" he asked. "We shouldn't be seen in public together."

"Don't worry, it's fine. Producers have dinner with their stars all the time. No one knows about . . ." She trailed off, not knowing how to finish the sentence. "I missed you," she said instead.

Antonio speared a piece of pork with one chopstick. "I missed you too," he said before putting it in his mouth.

Watching him chew, Ava's stomach churned, but she ladled a spoonful of broth anyway. "It's funny, I'm actually kind of looking forward to doing the show again. It's been strange without all the cameras around. Like I don't know what to do with myself." She brought the spoon to her lips and sipped delicately, hoping the soup would stay down.

"Yeah, it will be good." Antonio put down his chopsticks,

shifting uncomfortably in his seat. "Listen, Ava, assuming the show gets renewed, I've asked Bob and Tess for a more supervisory role going forward. Javier's ready to take over some of the more hands-on stuff."

"But you *love* the hands-on stuff." Ava's heart fluttered. "What are you going to do instead?"

"I need to spend more time with my family. I just . . ."

My family. "This is because of Molly, isn't it?" Ava could hear her voice getting louder, but she didn't know how to contain it. *My family.* "She's making you do this. She's trying to control you, control your life."

"Shhh." He briefly touched her hand, then pulled away quickly, sighing once more. "This is why I didn't want to do this in public."

"But we never do anything in public! We never do anything like a normal couple."

"We are not a couple!" He leaned forward, forcing her to meet his gaze. "It wasn't Molly's idea, okay? It was mine. It has to stop. This," he motioned between the two of them, "has to stop."

All the blood in Ava's body rushed to her ears, a giant wave breaking over her head. She let it crash over her, then sat back in her seat, feeling winded. She had known it was coming. Of course she had known. She suddenly felt so sorry for that girl of five minutes ago who thought she could change things. And yet, even now, all she could think about was what she could say to make him stay.

She straightened her napkin, adjusted her bowl, then folded her hands in her lap.

Staring at him—those deep brown eyes, those dark eyebrows ridging his heavy brow—she suddenly realized how easily, in that moment, she could completely ruin his life. But that wasn't what she wanted. What she wanted, she knew, was impossible—the words *my family* dissolving any image she might have had in her head of *their family.*

She took a deep breath, closed her eyes, and proceeded to vomit all over the table.

Before they stepped out of the restaurant—Ava pale as a ghost, Antonio possibly even paler—she knew the paparazzi were there, like they were every time she didn't want them to be.

"Ava!"

"Are you sick, Ava?"

"Did you get food poisoning?"

Antonio walked ahead of her, pushing through the cameras to get to the cab waiting by the curb, but he didn't touch her, didn't help her. Ava felt a twinge of sadness, thinking back to that night at the hospital, how he had carried her in his arms through the crowd. Everything was still ahead of them, then, the two of them hovering on the precipice of so many possible outcomes.

She climbed into the backseat of the cab, the cameras trying to reach in the door as Antonio climbed in after her.

"Got a hangover, Ava?"

"Ava, are you pregnant?"

As the cab sped off, Antonio turned to her. "You're not, are you?"

Ava let her head fall against the window. So many possible outcomes. And yet, really, there had only ever been one.

"Of course not," she said.

That night, she sat in her room watching old *Home* footage on her laptop. Her in the kitchen of Hart's Desire, describing the process of making boxed macaroni and cheese as though she were on a cooking show. "I'm using two litres of locally sourced Gin Harbour tap water here, to enhance the delicacy of the dry pasta," she said as she stirred the macaroni in the pot. "And I've seasoned it with a pinch of authentic Windsor table salt, mined in the ancient salt quarries of Windsor Table." She pronounced the last part with a fake French accent, *weendsoor tahblay.*

"Seriously?" she heard Antonio say off-screen.

"It's in the Salt District of Southern France."

It was the only televised conversation they'd ever had. When the footage first aired, Ava had been upset—the scene was so ridiculous that she hadn't even bothered with any of her usual sabotage tricks, thinking it would never air. But now, watching herself on the screen, she wished there was more. She wished she had let him follow her with the camera everywhere, so she could see herself the way he saw her, through the lens—the way he lingered on her hands as she stirred the pasta in the pot, the way he caught her smile in the sunbeam of light coming in through the kitchen window. It was so intimate it was almost unbearable. No one had ever seen her the way Antonio had seen her.

As she closed her laptop, loneliness engulfed her. Val was asleep in the next room, but it wasn't Val she wanted. She pulled out her phone and typed a text, her face glowing in the light of the screen.

Papa. I need you.

She stared at the words for a long time. Then she deleted them.

It was another three days before she could get an appointment. Luckily for her, it was snowing that Monday and there were no paparazzi outside the building, no fans rushing up to her outside the clinic to tell her how much they loved her. Still, she wore the brown wig this time, tied back under the hood of her plain black parka, a scarf pulled up around her nose.

Afterward, they gave her cookies and a juice box, sat her in a chair facing the Home and Garden Network. There were two other women in the room, but neither of them were paying attention to her, lost in their own thoughts, their own impatience or anxiety or relief. She would have crossed a desert for a shot of vodka—something she hadn't been able to stomach with her mourning sickness—but she supposed that wasn't on the menu. "You guys must keep some alcohol around here somewhere," she said, half-jokingly, to the volunteer who brought her the cookies and juice. The volunteer looked at her sadly, shaking her head, and Ava sipped her juice box through the tiny straw, feeling she had let the volunteer down in some fundamental way. The room was filled with sunshiny artwork, bright colours, positive quotations on posters, a cadre of women's studies undergrads non-judgmentally distributing snacks, but make one little joke about wanting a drink and suddenly you were unworthy of it all.

When it was time for her to leave, Ava put her regular clothes back on, bundling herself back up in her parka and her scarf. A different volunteer brought her out into the waiting area in a wheelchair.

"Who's taking you home?" the volunteer asked.

"Uh, no one," said Ava, pushing herself out of the chair. "I'll take a cab. I'm okay."

The volunteer gently but firmly pushed Ava back down. "I'm sorry, we can't let you do that," she said. "We're required to send you home with a responsible caretaker."

Ava laughed, maybe a bit too long for someone who was trying to convince the world that she was capable of taking care of herself. "That's not going to happen," she said. "Just let me go, I won't tell anyone."

The volunteer picked up the phone at the reception desk. "I can call someone for you if you give me a number," she said.

"I don't have anyone!" Ava stared at the volunteer, clenching her jaw. The volunteer stared back. Ava realized this was not something that she was going to be able to argue her way out of. Biting her lip, she sat back down in the wheelchair. "Okay, fine," she said. The volunteer cradled the phone against her ear. "The number is . . ." The minute the volunteer turned her back, Ava jumped to her feet. Immediately, she felt the blood drain from her head and her vision start to blur. Still, she continued to stumble forward. The volunteer hung up the phone and ran toward her, but it was too late—by the time she reached her, Ava had already crumpled to the floor.

When Ava opened her eyes again, the volunteer was standing over her, along with several other people who had been in the waiting room when she fainted, all dressed in the same open-backed hospital gowns. They all looked at each other anxiously as she struggled to sit up, and Ava knew they were watching her and seeing their own future—or, at least, their future if they didn't have loving partners or friends or family or whatever, someone in their life who they could lean on, someone who made them feel a little less alone. She pulled her hood back up over her head, straightening her scarf, daring them all to say something. But they just shuffled back to their seats, clutching their gowns, adjusting their hospital bracelets. Ava hoped she had made them all feel better about themselves. She really hoped that her pathetic, lonely life had cheered them up some.

A nurse came over and helped her back into the wheelchair, instructing her to put her head between her knees. She still felt dizzy, and she was pretty sure that if she moved she was going to throw up. The volunteer put her hand on Ava's shoulder.

"So?" she asked.

"I guess there is someone you can call."

It took Antonio an hour to get to the clinic from Long Island, during which time Ava sat in the wheelchair, sweating in her parka, staring straight ahead. When he walked in, all the women in the room turned to look at him, to see for themselves the person she had been so reluctant to call. He wheeled Ava out in the wheelchair without saying a word.

She hated having to call for him like she was a helpless child. But even though she told herself he was the only one she could call, she knew it wasn't true. She could have called Val. She could have even called someone from the network. No, she had wanted him to know. She wanted him to face the consequences of his actions. Why should he be let off the hook? Why should he get to stay at home with his family while she was here, suffering, alone? He was the one who should have known better. He was the one who'd fucked up.

He didn't say anything as they left the clinic, as they crossed the parking lot, as they got in the van, as he backed out of his parking space and pulled out into the road.

"There's a subway stop a few blocks away," Ava said, finally. "You can drop me there."

"You can't take the subway," Antonio said, his hands white on the steering wheel. "You heard what they said."

"They said I had to leave with someone. I left with someone." She leaned forward as he rounded the corner. "Just drop me here."

"No," Antonio said, pulling over to the side of the road and putting the van in park. He turned to face her. "When were you planning on telling me about this? Or were you going to keep it a secret forever?"

"I don't know," Ava said. "I didn't think a teenage pregnancy would be a good fit for the storyline of Season Two, you know?" She glanced around in an exaggerated way. "Where is Javier, anyway? I figured he'd be in the backseat with the camera rolling."

"Ava," Antonio said. "Stop. Stop it."

"Oh, I see how it works," said Ava. "It's fine to air our dirty laundry all over the television screen. But when it's yours, it's off limits."

"Jesus Christ. How many times do I have to say it? This is my job. My job is to document the Hart family. And trust me, it's the most fucked-up job in the world." .

"Well, sorry we ruined your life."

Sighing, Antonio leaned against the steering wheel. "Are you okay? Does it hurt?"

"No," said Ava. "It feels like nothing." She stared out the window, knowing that to see his face, the expression of benign concern there, would make her cry. And she had promised herself that she would never, ever let him see her cry again.

"Ava," Antonio said. He reached over and cupped her face, gently guiding her eyes toward his. "I miss you."

He leaned forward and kissed her, and she thought about all the times she had dreamed about this exact moment, how she craved his kiss like air, how she had convinced herself she needed it to live. Now, it sent knots folding up in her stomach.

With their lips still touching, she asked, "Are you going to leave Molly?"

He was silent for a long time, his breath warm on her mouth. "No," he said finally.

"Okay," she said. "That's it, then. That's enough." As she opened the car door, she paused, gazing down at her feet touching the sidewalk. "Goodbye, Antonio."

She got out of the van and walked along the snowy street toward the subway. She still felt woozy, but she knew this time she wasn't going to pass out. She could feel Antonio's eyes on her, but he didn't follow her, and she willed herself not to look back. *Don't look back. Don't look back.*

———◇———

For the next few days, she kept herself locked in her room, telling Val she had a migraine. As lonely as she was, she was good at being alone. She tried to read, listen to music, but mostly she just slept. She had no idea where her phone was, but she didn't care—she didn't want to know if Antonio had called, and she *really* didn't want to know if he hadn't. It was so much better to stay in her cocoon, marking the time by watching the sun crawling across her bedroom floor.

It was Thursday night when curiosity finally overtook her, and she emerged from her room, bleary-eyed, to look for her phone. Walking out into the main room, she saw Val sitting on the couch in the dark, his face lit up by a video game on the television screen. Beside him was a girl in a crop top and a baseball cap who Ava didn't recognize.

"Hey," Val said, his eyes flicking to her, then back to the game. "You look like shit."

"Thanks," said Ava. "I'm actually feeling better." She narrowed her eyes at the girl, who had her fingers in her mouth as she stared intensely at Ava. "Have we met?"

"OMG," the girl said, through a tangle of moist fingers. "You're Ava." She reached up and took off her baseball cap to reveal a head of short, platinum blonde hair. "I fucking love you."

Ava felt her body sag under an invisible weight. "Seriously?" she said, ignoring the girl and glaring hard at Val. "One of my doppelgangers in my own living room?"

Val shrugged. "I don't control the universe."

"You control who you let into our apartment!"

"Christ, chill already." Val jammed his index finger repeatedly against the controller. "It's not like I slept with her. She just sold me some weed."

"I could give you some if you want," the girl said eagerly, leaning forward like a puppy straining at its leash. "Maybe it could be, like, a part of your show or something?" Her eyes darted toward the row of cameras against the wall, and she began fluffing up her hair. "Like, are they recording right now?"

Ava shook her head in disbelief. "Are you brain-dead? You're a drug dealer." Val and the girl both started giggling. Ava shook her head again and shuffled toward the kitchen.

"Oh, hey," Val called after her. "Your phone's been blowing up like crazy. I think it only stopped because it died."

Ava turned around. "Is there something going on? Something with the show?"

"Unless it happened in *Grand Theft Auto,* I've got nothing on the past twelve hours," Val said over the din of gunfire exploding from the screen.

In the kitchen, she found her parka on the floor where she had thrown it when she got home from the clinic. She rooted through the pockets until she found her phone. Val was right—dead. She found a cord and plugged it in, sitting and staring at it for what seemed like hours until it hummed back to life. Then, notification after notification popped up on the screen, one after another. Missed calls from Antonio. Missed texts from Bryce, and even one from David. Emails from the network. Her heart started to beat faster as she scrolled through everything, finally clicking on the oldest one, from that morning. An email, from a source she didn't recognize. The subject line read *Care to Comment?*

In the body of the email, a picture. Of Ava. Dressed in her parka and scarf. Entering the clinic.

"No," she said out loud, the word escaping before she had a chance to stop it. *But that could be anyone,* she thought. *They don't know it's me.* She went back to her inbox and read through the rest of the thread. The same email address, from less than an hour ago, with a link to an article.

Did Ava Hart have an abortion?

She scanned the article quickly. No mention of Antonio, no actual sources quoted, no additional info. There were several other pictures, but most of them were fuzzy, her face hidden. *Maybe nothing will come of it,* she thought. *People don't believe what they read. They know that tabloids are full of shit. Maybe this will all just go away.*

But she stared at the notifications on her phone—47 new text messages, 232 new emails, 22 missed phone calls—and she knew this wasn't going to just go away. Everything she had tried to keep for herself was now out there for everyone to scavenge.

At some point she must have thought this was what she wanted, for the world to pay attention to her. But there was nothing about this kind of attention she wanted anymore. Maybe she never had.

"I was thinking, maybe you could, like, retweet this for me?" Ava looked up and saw the girl standing in the kitchen, holding her phone out. When Ava glanced at the screen, she saw a picture of the girl scrolling through her phone, standing near Ava as she scrolled through her own phone not moments before. "Val took it for me. I think it's super cute, like, the two of us twinning on our phones."

"Get out," Ava said. She picked up a pair of sequinned platform sneakers that obviously belonged to the girl and threw them at her, one at a time. The first one flew past her, out of the kitchen and across the living room, landing in the middle of the coffee table, sending weed flying everywhere. The second one hit her squarely in the head. Ava didn't wait to see her reaction. She just ran to her room and slammed the door.

Once she was in her room, she started to panic. Any minute now, Val would realize his phone was blowing up too and he'd confront her. And then it would be real.

She picked up her phone and started scrolling through her contact list. Not Antonio. Not David. Not Bryce. Not Bob and Tess.

There was no one. She had no one to call, nowhere to go.

She scrolled past Mags Kovach's name multiple times before she actually saw it. Someone who didn't really know her, someone outside of all of this. She had vague memories of Mags talking her down off a ledge once before. Maybe she'd be able to do it again.

A woman answered. "Mags's phone," she said.

"Hi, uh, is Mags there?"

"Mags can't talk right now. Wait, hang on." In the background, Ava could hear traffic. It sounded like they were standing on a street corner. "Hey!" the woman called to someone else. "Take her to 442 Ossington." There was a pause. "No, I don't know the best route. Last I checked, though, Toronto *was* on Google Maps." The woman came back to Ava. "Is there something I can help you with?"

"No," said Ava. "That's fine. I'm fine, thanks."

"Mags, sweetie, text me when you get there, okay?"

"Give me my phone, then," Ava heard Mags mumble, somewhat incoherently. The line muffled, then went dead.

Out in the living room, she could hear Val and the girl laughing over the pounding bass of the game's soundtrack. She knew she could sneak past them and go down the service elevator and through the gated garden next door—her quick exit route that the paparazzi had yet to discover. But she had to do it now.

Her next call was for a cab to take her to the airport.

It was almost four in the morning by the time the cab dropped Ava off at Mags's place, a second-floor apartment above a cupcake shop somewhere in the depths of downtown Toronto. She stood in the street for a few minutes, gazing up at the dark windows, wondering what she was doing there. Would Mags even remember her? Ava shook off her doubts and opened the door. There was no going back now. Not that she even had anything to go back to.

The outside door was open, so she climbed up the stairs to the second floor. At the end of a hallway lined with a few apartment doors, she could see one door propped open by a crumpled figure lying on the ground a few feet into the hallway. As she got closer, she realized it was Mags, naked, passed out on her side, and lying in a pool of her own vomit.

"Shit," Ava said under her breath. Mags moaned. Well, at least she wasn't dead. Ava crouched down next to her, covering her own mouth and nose to block out the smell of the vomit, so heavy with alcohol that Ava could taste it. "Mags? Mags, are you okay?"

Mags mumbled something unintelligible. Ava pushed Mags's hair off her face, took in her closed eyelids, red and puffy from crying, her sallow skin, her colourless lips, the corners of her mouth flecked with dried vomit.

She was too heavy for Ava to lift, so instead she dragged her by one arm into the apartment and shut the door behind them.

TMI Online
News – Sports – Celebs – Watch – Connect

Exclusive: Did Ava Hart have an abortion?
By Sadie Jackson

February 19, 2015 7:47 pm

TMI Online has obtained exclusive photos of a woman who appears to be reality television star Ava Hart entering a private abortion clinic in New York earlier this week. The woman, dressed in a hooded parka with a scarf pulled up over her face, arrived at the clinic by taxi, which, according to sources, originated from the apartment building in Tribeca where Hart currently resides with her brother, Val.

TMI will continue to monitor this story as it develops.

11 Comments

> Harryetta 45 min ago
> The real question is, who is the babydaddy

> guest 2 hours ago
> prob her brother lol they are trash

> Irosele 47 min ago
> Why do you keep reporting on these people TMI no one cares about them

> Jack Dawson 1 hour ago
> Slut

ploiu_rhy 1 hour ago
lol that doesn't even look like her

Kerrie Cass 1 hour ago
garbage TV makes garbage people

Dian Barnette 1 hour ago
I knew you were low TMI but this is really low, give the woman
some peace

SallyO 2 hours ago
The real question is WHAT HAPPENED TO EDEN HART the
network is keeping her hidden because she had DANGEROUS
INFORMATION about their top execs this is the only reason
they could possibly be keeping her off the air FREE EDEN HART

Chaya_lin 1 hour ago
Shut up u freak

JuicyG 2 hours ago
You suck TMI

Peter Smyk 2 hours ago
I am Ava's baby's father

Mags

———◇———

Friday, 6:34 p.m.

M ags woke up in her bed, naked, a drool-soaked towel spread
out across her pillow under her throbbing head, her body
drenched with sweat. She blinked into the light of the morning—
afternoon?—and tried to sit up, gingerly at first, then urgently, as
her stomach started to heave. She barely made it to the edge of the
bed before spewing the contents of her stomach into a garbage can
that had somehow appeared there. Then she rolled onto her back,
staring at the ceiling and grabbing the sides of the bed in a failed
attempt to stop the room from spinning. She tried to focus her
eyes on the table next to the bed, where there was a full glass of
water and a bottle of Advil that she didn't remember putting there.
She was fairly certain she didn't even *own* a bottle of Advil.

When the room slowed down enough for her to get her bear-
ings, she slid off the side of the bed and dragged herself across the
floor to her dresser. She reached up and grabbed her cell phone,
staring at it a moment before turning it on. There was one text,
from Emiko, with two words.

Call me.

It all came back, the way things do the morning after: at once, like a bucket of cold water dumped on your head, leaving you standing there, dripping and humiliated.

All of it. Including the hands. Someone putting her to bed.

She stumbled to her feet, then pushed open her bedroom door, letting it swing wide and bang loudly against the table behind it in the living room. A rush of cold air hit her with so much force that she had to hold on to the door frame for balance.

"Hello?" she called tentatively into the room. No one there.

As she tiptoed out into the living room, which smelled faintly of cigarette smoke, she realized that even though there was no one there now, it was obvious that someone had been in her apartment: empty bottles neatly tied up in a blue bag and placed near the door, throw blankets folded over the arm of her couch, magazines stacked in a tidy pile on the coffee table. She quickly discovered the source of the cold air: one of the windows had been propped open a couple of inches with a flashlight, and a light dusting of snow had drifted in, covering the sill. Had she really been smoking inside? Did she even own a flashlight?

"Dammit," she said. She walked over to the window and brushed her hand along the sill. The snow was so light that it melted as soon as she touched it, cool water dripping down her hand and over her wrist. She pulled out the flashlight and closed the window, the remaining snow flying up from the sill and disappearing in the air, a fine mist raining down to the floor as she stood there, naked and shivering, her bare toes curling against the hardwood.

After she had found a sweater and some socks, she ventured into the kitchen. A stack of clean dishes sat drying on a rack that she didn't even know she owned. The ripped dress was draped over the back of one of her kitchen chairs. The rotten pear was nowhere to be found.

In her hand, her phone vibrated. A text from Emiko.

Front page of tomorrow's National Chronicle!!

Mags didn't have to look; she already knew what she was going to see—all the messiest, most broken parts of her splattered across the page. Instead, she stared hard at those two exclamation points at the end of Emiko's text, those two little vertical lines on top of two little dots, a punctuation mark that she had never seen Emiko use singularly before, let alone doubly. And she began to realize, with a sick feeling, that she might be the only one who thought of Sam's death as a tragedy. Mags turned her phone off, resisting the urge to throw it across the room.

A sound came from the hallway, startling her so intensely that she dropped her phone. "Sam?" she called softly, then immediately felt embarrassed. Too many movies, too much fantasizing. If she weren't so freaked out, she would have laughed.

She came out of the kitchen, her heart thudding in her chest, just in time to see a woman walk in carrying a couple of large paper bags.

"Oh good," the woman said, standing in the doorway, shaking the snow from her hood. "You're up. I brought us burgers. I hope you're not a vegetarian. For a variety of reasons, really, but mostly because I brought us burgers."

Mags stared at the woman, uncomprehendingly, momentarily feeling as though she had woken up in the middle of someone else's life. Then it clicked in, like a lens focusing. Ava. The hands underneath her, putting her to bed.

"I didn't feel like cooking, and I didn't think you would, either," Ava continued, as though they had been having the same conversation for years. "I bought some wine too, just in case. They barely even looked at my fake ID. It's wild here." She kicked off her shoes and walked over to the couch, unzipping her parka.

Mags followed her across the room, her mind still trying to catch up. "What are you doing here, Ava? How did you find me?"

Ava looked startled, staring wide-eyed at Mags, one arm still in the parka sleeve. "I . . . you said to call you."

"*Call me*. Not walk into my apartment and clean while I'm asleep." Mags flopped down on the couch, then picked up the bag with the wine in it and pulled out the bottle, studying the label. "What even is this, cooking sherry?"

"I . . . don't buy wine much."

"At least it's not in a box." Mags cracked the cap and took a swig. She could not handle this right now. All she wanted was for Ava to leave so she could drink this Dubonnet or whatever the hell this crap was and wallow in her hungover misery. "Look, I'm sorry you came all this way for—well, I don't know what you came for. But whatever it is, I can't help you."

"But you said . . ." Ava pulled her arm out of the parka and placed it carefully over the back of the couch, brushing a piece of lint from the fabric. "I just need somewhere to stay for a bit."

Mags ran a hand through her hair, feeling the sticky end where it must have dragged in her vomit. "Thank you for cleaning my apartment. You didn't have to do that. But I feel like shit and I just want to be alone."

"I promise you won't even know I'm here." Ava dropped her gaze. "I don't have anywhere else to go."

Mags studied her. She seemed paler, even more exhausted than she had that night on the balcony. But instead of the sadness and desperation she had recognized in Ava then, Mags saw only defeat now. She thought about Ava's blank slate of a phone, her empty contact list, and knew it wasn't that she didn't have anywhere else to go—it was that she didn't have any*one* else. That was a feeling Mags knew well. She leaned forward, picking up the other bag. "Demon's?" she asked.

"Yeah," said Ava, sitting down next to her tentatively. "I thought it looked okay in there. They're not famous for their health code violations or anything, are they?"

"No," Mags said. "No, they're great." Demon's was one of her favourite places to eat on the street, but the smell of the burger made her stomach turn, and she grimaced, passing the bag to Ava.

"Are you naked under that sweater?" Ava asked as she pulled out a burger.

Mags glanced down. "It seems to be a theme," she said. She took a drink of the wine. It really wasn't half bad. "I *am* curious how you found out where I lived. Am I that easy to track down?"

Ava unwrapped her burger and took a bite. "I called you," she said as she chewed. "Some lady answered. She was putting you into a cab, I think? I heard her tell someone your address."

"Oh, Emiko, probably. My manager. After the show last night." She didn't want to think about the show, or any of the shows that were to come . . .

Suddenly, Mags shot straight up, her heart pounding. "What time is it?"

Ava looked at her phone. "Seven thirty."

"Shit. I'm going to be late." Mags grabbed the burgers and, after a brief hesitation, the wine. "Ever been backstage at Mercer Hall?"

They finished the wine in the back of the cab, then moved on to a flask Mags had in her coat pocket. When they got to the venue, a throng of paparazzi was waiting for them at the backstage entrance. Mags paused with her hand on the door of the cab, momentarily paralyzed, her whiskey-slick mind spinning its wheels as she tried to remember how she was supposed to do this. Any of this.

"Here." Ava untwined the scarf from around Mags's neck and rewrapped it around her face so that only her eyes were visible. Then she pulled an elastic from her wrist and pulled Mags's hair back into a ponytail, tucked it into the scarf, and pulled up her hood. "There," she said. "You could be any random Canadian."

"I can barely see," Mags said, her voice muffled through the scarf.

"You'll be surprised how little you actually need to."

They got out of the car and pushed their way through the crowd, heads down, elbows out. Ava was right—Mags followed the steady beam of light from the door, concentrating on putting one foot in front of the other. She could feel the cameras on her even though she couldn't see them, could hear the shouts of the reporters.

"Mags, is that you?"

"Mags?"

"Who is that with you?"

When they reached the door, she whispered her name to one of the security guards, who pulled them into the venue and rushed them backstage. By the time they got to the green room, it was after 8:30, and Emiko was pacing, cell phone glued to her ear. She threw it down as soon as she saw them. "God, Mags, you haven't even done your hair or makeup yet and you're on in less than thirty minutes," she said, unzipping Mags's parka. "Who is this? And where is your fucking bra?"

Mags pulled away from her, surprised. Emiko never swore. Even in her inebriated state, Mags knew that couldn't be good.

Ava stuck out her hand. "I'm Ava."

Emiko's eyes flicked toward Ava's hand, then rolled briefly heavenward. "I don't actually care," she said, falling back to make room for her assistant-of-the-week to move in with a makeup brush. "I care about this." She flicked one of Mags's nipples, hard.

"What? Fuck bras. I'm a rock star." Emiko glared at her. "Fine. I think I have another one on the bus." She sniffed her armpits. "And another top."

"The bus isn't here, Mags. Jesus." Emiko scraped her nail across the front of her shirt. "There's mustard on this."

Mags glanced down. "Shit."

"You can have mine," Ava said. Her face was flushed, her eyes bright with wine. She plopped down in the chair in front of the vanity mirror, then picked up an eyeliner pencil and began drawing whiskers on her cheeks. "I'm going to be a kitty!"

"Hey! I want to be an animal too." Mags sat down in the chair next to Ava, then reached into her pocket and pulled out her flask.

Emiko scowled at her. "You remember to bring your whiskey but not your bra?"

Mags shrugged. "Priorities." She felt strangely reckless, untethered, all those threads that had begun fraying that night she met Ava finally coming apart. "What other kind of animals can you do?"

"How about a lizard?" Ava said. "I could cover your face in scales."

Shaking her head, Emiko rummaged through her own purse. "Do whatever you want," she said, thrusting a bottle of pills at Mags. "Just take these so we don't have a repeat of last night."

"I thought you said last night was good publicity!" Mags shouted at Emiko's back as she walked out of the room.

Mags and Ava swapped shirts quickly. Ava's top was much too tight on Mags, but at least it kept her packed in. She opened the bottle and popped four pills as Ava touched the tip of the eyeliner to her face.

"What are those?" Ava asked, leaning her face closer, her breath hot on Mags's cheek.

"Dunno," Mags said.

Ava kept glancing at the bottle as she worked. "Can I have one?" she asked finally.

"Sure." Mags opened the bottle and palmed two more pills, throwing back another one herself, closing her eyes, and swallowing. When she opened her eyes again, she studied Ava's face, hovering inches away from her own—the dark circles beneath her clear blue eyes, the wild scattering of freckles across the bridge of her nose. "That was a good trick out there," Mags said.

"Thanks. Avoiding cameras is my specialty. Or, at least, it used to be."

"I remember your show, you know," Mags said. "Your old show. Sam loved it. He watched it all the time. You were always his favourite."

Ava blinked slowly, the eyeliner pencil hovering over Mags's cheek. "That's not true," she said. "I was never anyone's favourite." She touched the pencil to Mags's skin once more, briefly, then stepped back. "There. I decided to skip the scales and gave you a little starfall."

Mags peered at her reflection in the mirror. A spray of tiny, perfectly symmetrical stars of varying sizes rained down from the corner of her eye to her jawline. "It's like I'm crying stars," she said, touching her finger to her jaw just below the marks.

"That was the idea," Ava said, recapping the eyeliner.

Mags opened her palm. "Here," she said. "Open your mouth." Ava's lips parted, and Mags placed the pill between them. Then she handed Ava the flask. "To wash it down," she said.

Ava swallowed. "Thanks."

Then Emiko was back, tall and still in the doorway, her gaze piercing Mags like an icy wind. "Let's go." She glanced briefly at Ava. "You can come watch from the wings if you like."

Mags grabbed the flask as she headed into the hall, and still had it in her hand as she stepped out onstage. She could see Paul glaring at her as she stumbled in a haze to the mic.

"Where the fuck were you?" he growled, leaning toward her.

You were once my friend, Mags wanted to say. *You were Sam's friend.* "Shhhh, it's time to sing," she said instead. She fixed her vision on the mic in front of her as whatever drug Emiko had given her started to kick in, sound and light washing over her like waves. She waited to feel the usual exhilaration, the magic that kept everything else away. But it didn't come.

She took another swig of whiskey as she heard the drumbeat kick in. "Hey everyone," she breathed into the mic. "How . . ." Suddenly, she felt as though she had burst into flames. She tried to

302

focus on something, anything, but the room was spinning, and she was sweating, and she couldn't hear anything, the drum seeming to beat directly into her ears. "It's really hot in here," she said. She clawed at her shirt, yanking it up over her head, and then began trying to worm her way out of her jeans, sticky against her damp skin. But still the heat overtook her, her body a coal burning. And slowly, everything washed out to bright white, and the past, the future, all the answers to the universe were right there in front of her, and as she reached out her hand to touch them they dissolved into sparks of light.

Lashay Bullard
@shayisdeadd
OMG YOU GUYS MAGS KOVACH JUST RIPPED OFF HER CLOTHES
AND PASSED OUT ON STAGE THEN CAME BACK OUT AND SLAYED
FOR 2 HOURS LIKE A FUCKING QUEEN #alignaboveatmercerhall
11:10 PM – 20 Feb 2015
119 Retweets 2,458 Likes

B @a_beew 39 min
Replying to @shayisdeadd
That was the Align Above concert content I have been waiting for

Lashay Bullard @shayisdeadd 38 min
Replying to @a_beew
Right? I live for this shit

Talisha @teebot45 37 min
Replying to @shayisdeadd @a_beew
JFC I *knew* I went on the wrong night #alignaboveatmercerhall

Reiko Redd @thereddening 29 min
Replying to @shayisdeadd @a_beew
TITS EVERYWHERE

Martika @fellinahole23 28 min
Replying to @thereddening @shayisdeadd @a_beew
OMG

Talisha @teebot45 21 min
Replying to @shayisdeadd @a_beew
There better be pics!

B @a_beew 20 min
Replying to @teebot45@shayisdeadd
Just saw this on @chatterfuel

> **Blistering hot shots of Manic Mags at tonight's Toronto show *NSFW***
> We have exclusive pics of the troubled rock star in all her naked glory onstage tonight at Toronto's Mercer Hall ...
> chatterfuel.com

Talisha @teebot45 18 min
Replying to @a_beew @shayisdeadd
THIS IS REAL OMFGGGGGGG I'M DEADDDD

Ava

Friday, 9:08 p.m.

———◇———

A va had never seen anyone go down the way that Mags did. Staggering around the stage, her eyes gleaming, voice roaring, red hair practically on fire, ripping herself out of her shirt—Ava's shirt—as though she were some kind of monster. When Mags collapsed to the ground, Ava thought she was going to burn right through the floor.

"What were those pills?" she asked Emiko, feeling the palms of her hands start to sweat. "Horse tranquilizers?"

"Basically," Emiko said impassively, watching as a paramedic knelt in front of Mags, who was now huddled on a chair backstage, pale and shivering and wrapped in a blanket. "How was I supposed to know she was going to take so many?"

"I'm fine," Mags mumbled. "Let me up. I'm fine."

Ava started to feel dizzy herself. She sat down on a chair and put her head in her hands, trying to steady her breathing. She didn't know why she had taken the pill, just that Mags made it look so easy. *It's all in your head,* she told herself. *You only took one pill. It's all in your head.* She had barely slept that day, tossing and turning on Mags's couch before giving up and going out to get the burgers, which she had hardly even touched. No wonder she felt so lightheaded. "We should go to a hospital," she said. "I mean, Mags should go to the hospital. This isn't normal."

"I told you, I'm fine," Mags said louder. Her eyes were glassy and her lips wet, but her voice was clear. She shook off the paramedic's hand. "Just give me a minute and I'll get right back out there."

The paramedic started to protest, but Emiko dismissed her with a wave of her hand. "Here," she said, handing Mags her clothes, which someone had retrieved from the stage. "You're going to need these." When Mags had finished dressing, Emiko took her hand and dropped three small pills into her palm. "These too."

"Are you serious?" asked Ava, sitting up in her chair. "Did you see what just happened?"

"I see that there are twenty-seven hundred people out there who paid a lot of money for this show."

"Yeah, *Ava*," Mags said emphatically, her body swaying like an alder in a windstorm. She grabbed the pills and swallowed them down. "Where are the boys? I'm ready." She pushed herself to her feet. "Rock and roll," she whispered into Ava's ear and then staggered toward the stage.

Ava sat, rooted in her chair, unable to move. While the show went on behind the curtain, she tried to think of herself as being ensconced in a very large pink bubble, one that put a watery, rosy sheen between her and the rest of the world and muffled all sound to a soft, relaxing drone. She didn't know how else to be in that moment, drunk and high and wearing a mustard-stained T-shirt backstage at an Align Above show in Toronto, and she worried that if she thought about it too much her bubble might burst.

Then, her bubble burst. She felt her phone buzz in her pocket, startling her—she had forgotten she'd turned it back on to call a cab at Mags's place, hiding it away again when new notifications started spilling out onto her home screen like marbles onto the floor. Sighing, she pulled it out and looked at it. Val. She watched his name flash across the screen for what seemed like forever, waiting for it to stop. When it didn't, she gave up, pressing accept and sticking her finger in one ear. "Hello?"

She could barely hear Val's voice over the music. "Where are you? Are you okay?"

"Yeah. I'm just . . . out."

"Out where? *Canada?*"

Ava got up from her chair and moved away from the stage, ducking down a hall and behind some equipment. "How did you know?"

"You're actually in Canada? I was making a joke. Wait." He sucked in his breath, and she knew he'd figured something out. "Is that Align Above in the background?"

"I'm at a bar," she said, keeping her voice low. "They must be playing the album."

"Ava." He paused. "Jesus. I don't even know where to start. That article . . . We're *worried* about you."

"I know." Ava dropped her head back against the wall. "I'm sorry."

"David and Bryce have called a million times. David wants to get the police involved. They think you killed yourself or something. Even Antonio's been here, like, twice today, looking for you."

At the mention of Antonio's name, Ava felt reality slip away from her. *Had* she killed herself? Was this all some kind of puzzling afterlife? "I'm alive," she said. "Yes," she added with more certainty. "I am."

There was silence on the other end. From somewhere out in the hall, she could hear Mags say something unintelligible over the mic, followed by a loud cheer from the crowd. What must it be like, she wondered, to have the people watching you be standing right in front of you? What must it be like to feel their love in the room with you, without the filter of a camera, a screen?

It must be suffocating. It must feel like the whole world is closing in on you.

"Was it you?" Val asked finally.

Ava took a deep breath. "Yeah."

More silence. Then: "Who?"

For a moment, she considered it. But she couldn't bring herself to say the words. "I can't tell you, Val."

"You *can't* tell me?"

Ava pinched the bridge of her nose, trying to quell the headache that was surfacing across the front of her forehead. "No. I mean, it's no one you know, anyway."

"Right." She heard a fumbling on the other end, the click of the vape, a deep inhale. "Well, you need to get back here. Bob and Tess are so psyched up by your newfound notoriety that they've renewed the show and want to start shooting the new season early."

Shit. "Really?"

"Oh yeah. They're creaming their shorts. They were thinking about cancelling before this." He exhaled, long and slow. "You're the new golden girl."

It's happening again, Ava thought, her head spinning. *Except this time the spectacle is me. Me and my broken life.*

"I'm sorry, Val, I can't do it."

"What's with all this *can't* stuff? You're Avalon Hart, you can do whatever you want."

A man pushed past her in the hall, carrying a guitar. She lowered her head as he passed and tucked herself in toward the wall. "Fine, then. I don't want to. I don't want to do the show."

"You don't want to do it now, or you don't want to do it ever?"

Ava stared down the hallway, feeling her eyes pulse with the flickering fluorescent light. "Maybe ever."

Val laughed, then dissolved into a coughing fit. "That's really great, Ava. You talk me into this shitshow and now you're bailing?

I know you hated Gin Harbour, but I actually had a *life* there, a girlfriend, an actual chance at a music career. Here I'm just a dumb New York hipster with a guitar like every other dumb New York hipster with a guitar that no one gives a shit about. And now you're telling me I don't even have a fucking *job*? What the hell am I supposed to do?"

"I'm sorry."

"Sure you are." He inhaled once more. "You know, I wouldn't be surprised if this was all bullshit. The abortion, this running-away crap, threatening to quit, all of it. Just a big old fucking publicity stunt, like the kind you used to accuse Eden of pulling. Oh hey, I know. Eden's back from rehab, they could replace you with her. Her big comeback. Bob and Tess would love it."

The whole room around Ava went silent. She could still hear Mags singing, but it was as if her voice were being transmitted from another universe. "Fuck you, Val," she said finally, and hung up.

She stared into space, her phone still in her hand, her body rocking gently back and forth, propelled by the beating of her heart. Val had been her only ally, and even he didn't understand. Even he had let her down in the end.

Opening her email, she scrolled through what seemed like millions of messages from the network until she found the most recent one.

Dear Miss Hart,

As we have been unable to get in touch with you by phone, we are writing to inform you now that shooting for the second season of *Absence Makes the Hart Grow Fonder* will begin in three days, on Monday, February 23. If we do not hear from you before then with a confirmation of your participation, you will be considered in breach of your contract, in which case the next communication you will have from

310

us will be through our lawyers. There will be consequences
for your actions, Miss Hart, so choose wisely.

Best,
Bob Axelrod
President and CEO
LifeStyle Network

Breach of contract. Lawyers. Her horse-tranquilizered brain
wasn't capable of handling any of this. She walked back into the
wings in a daze and looked out at the stage, where Mags was now
lying on her back, pushing herself backward across the floor with
her feet as she sang. She didn't know how Mags did it—how she
put everything else aside and threw herself into the moment and
was utterly, completely herself no matter who was watching. She
wasn't doing this for the audience. She wasn't even doing it for
herself. Maybe she was doing it for Sam.

Ava didn't know who she had been doing anything for. But she
knew for certain it hadn't been for herself.

After the show was over, Mags stumbled offstage and into
Emiko, who was waiting behind the curtain. Emiko shrugged her off
and passed her to Ava, who bent under her surprisingly dead weight.

"There's a car out back," Emiko said, pulling out a tube of clear
lip gloss and running it over her mouth. "Make sure she gets home.
We leave for Europe in three days, so make sure she doesn't run
off to the butcher's son or something."

"Is that a saying?"

"No, she literally tried to run off with the butcher's son last
time she was home. She went out to buy sausages and didn't come
back for twelve hours." Ava couldn't tell if Emiko was being sarcastic or not. She couldn't read Emiko at all.

Ava and Mags made their way through a darkened hallway and
then out the back door, where they were immediately met by a

wall of people shouting, pushing, taking photos. Ava braced herself against the throng, keeping her head down as a security guard ushered them to the waiting car.

"These buildings need underground tunnels or something," Ava said, once they were safe in the backseat.

Mags leaned her head back against the headrest and let it roll back and forth. "Emiko says the more cameras out back, the better the show." Then she dropped her head onto Ava's shoulder and whispered loudly, "I think some of them are just her friends that she tells to come."

"I hate her," Ava said. "I really think I actually hate her."

"She's okay. She's our manager."

"You still shouldn't let her do that to you," Ava said. "Pump you full of pills like that just so you can perform. It's not right."

"Whatever." Mags stared at her with glassy eyes. "Let's get the hell out of here." But instead of giving the driver her own address, Mags told him to take them to a hotel downtown.

"I'm supposed to get you home," Ava said as the car pulled away from the curb.

Mags pulled the flask out of her purse and took a drink before passing it to Ava. "I thought it would be fun," she said, winking at her, but Ava could see something else in her eyes, something still and distant. She didn't want to go home. Ava remembered standing outside of Mags's door earlier that evening, bags in hand, hearing Mags call out Sam's name into the empty apartment. Of course she didn't want to go back there. She didn't want to confront any more ghosts.

The hotel Mags had chosen was big, opulent, the lobby busy even at midnight. Ava kept her hood down as Mags checked them in under fake names—Cee Cee Bloom and Bertie White, Ava's idea—but still she could feel eyes on her.

As they headed for the elevator, a woman in a parka and toque started running toward them across the lobby. "Ava!" she called.

"Get in the elevator," Ava said, pushing Mags in ahead of her.

The woman ripped her hat off to reveal a head of short, platinum blonde hair. "Ava, wait!"

"Whoa," said Mags. "That woman looks exactly like you."

Ava jabbed at the button, and the doors closed just as the woman reached them, banging her open hand on the outside of the elevator. "Come on, come on," Ava said, and slowly the elevator chugged to life, rising through the floors.

"What the hell was that all about?" Mags peered at herself in the mirrored wall, running her fingers over her starfall, which had smudged into one long, black streak.

Ava put her hand on top of her head. "It's the haircut of the season," she said. "At least it makes my superfans easy to identify."

"I wish my fans came with a warning sign like that." Mags kept staring at her reflection, her face clouding over. "I guess they could all be drunk."

When they got to the room, Mags turned the television on to the Food Network and muted the volume. She was restless, manic, pacing the room, looking through drawers, tearing the paper off the glasses, opening sugar packets. It was as though she were chasing something. Or being chased, Ava supposed. She knew the feeling.

"The view here is the worst, but there's a pool on the top floor that apparently has the best views of the city," Mags said as she flung open the curtains. "Whenever we were on tour and had to stay in shitty guest houses and hostels and stuff, Sam and I used to read about all the fancy hotels on the internet and try to figure out which ones we would stay in when we were rich and famous."

Ava stood by the window, looking out at a view of the building directly across from them—another hotel, she assumed, although it could have been a condo building—and wondered whether the people behind the curtains in the darkened rooms were sleeping, fucking, maybe fighting, or lying in bed in the dark, rehashing all their old grievances at midnight. It comforted her, knowing there were people over there, living their normal lives, being the centre of their own universes.

Behind her, Mags had already moved on to the minibar, emptying the contents onto the bed. "Pick one," she said to Ava as she filled her own pockets. "We can take them to the lobby and try to find that basketball team that was down there, did you see them?"

"Yeah," said Ava, moving over to the bed to rifle through the bottles, choosing a tiny bottle of Beefeater gin. "But I think I'll probably just stay here."

"Oh, *come on*," Mags said. She cracked open a tiny bottle of rum and took a sip. "Are you scared of your doppelganger?"

Ava laughed shortly. "No. I'm used to those."

Mags cocked her head to the side. "Well, what then? You're not still heartbroken over that guy, are you?"

"I . . . maybe. I don't know."

Mags climbed onto the bed, stretching her legs out and scattering the bottles to the floor. "You're . . . what? Seventeen?"

"Eighteen," Ava said, a little defensively.

"Oh, please. You'll fall in love *a million* more times."

"No," Ava said. "I won't. I mean, you only loved your husband, right?"

"True." Mags stuck her tongue into the top of the now empty bottle and then pulled it out with a pop. "You know, I was totally faithful to Sam right up until he died. A lot of people think I wasn't, but I was. Right up until he died."

Ava sat down on the bed next to her, pulling her knees up to her chest. Through the window, she could see that it had started to snow, great big fat flakes floating lazily through the glow of the streetlight. "So, you were always faithful to him, then." Mags raised an eyebrow. "Well, you can't be unfaithful to a dead person."

Mags shrugged. "I don't know. It feels like you can, sometimes."

"But you will only ever love Sam. And I will only ever love Antonio."

314

"*An-to-ni-o,*" Mags said, sounding out the name. It was strange to hear it coming from someone else's lips. "What did he do to you?"

"It's a long story." Ava scratched her fingernail against the ridges on the top of the gin bottle, trying to think of what to say. "He loved me when he shouldn't have. And then he decided I wasn't enough."

"He was married, wasn't he?" Mags said. Ava didn't say anything. "That *scumbag*. I *hate* married men."

Ava finally cracked open her gin and took a sip, the liquid like bile in her mouth. "It wouldn't have been my first choice, either."

"Antonio. Antonio. What kind of ridiculous name is that, anyway?" Mags rolled over to face her. "Look, Ava, I'm going to give you some advice. You can have the most perfect love in the world, and they're still going to leave you." She paused. "Stop loving people. It only screws you up in the long run."

"Sam didn't leave you, though," Ava said. "There's a difference."

"Is there? At least when you fuck someone, you know that you only have them for a brief moment. There's no expectation. There's only that moment."

"Like with Val?"

"Who's Val?"

"My brother."

Mags laughed, but the laughter didn't reach her eyes. "Exactly. Like with *Val.*" She leaned over the side of the bed and picked up another bottle of rum off the floor, then gazed at Ava as she brought it to her lips. "Why are you here, Ava?"

"Because you dragged me here?"

"No, why are you here in Toronto? Why do you need 'somewhere to stay for a bit'?"

Ava stared at the television set in front of her and debated what to say. Finally, she pulled out her phone. *What the hell,* she thought. *She'll see it eventually.*

Mags took the phone from Ava, squinted her eyes at the screen. As she read, her face softened. "Is it you?"

"Yeah."

"Shit." Ava thought Mags was going to reach out her hand and caress her cheek, or maybe push her hair back behind her ear. But the moment passed, and instead she sat back against the pillows, tossing the phone onto the bed. "I *really* hate married men."

Ava put her phone back in her pocket without looking at the screen. "Antonio wasn't that bad," she said. "It was my fault, really. I should have been more careful. I screwed everything up."

"Don't ever let me hear you say that again." Mags sat up abruptly. "Fuck this, we're getting out of here."

"I don't want to go back down," Ava said.

Mags grinned, her eyes shining—with alcohol or tears, Ava couldn't tell which. "Then we'll go up."

They made their way to the roof. The pool was closed but their key cards still let them into the glassed-in atrium, the lights of the city reflecting off the still water. Ava crossed the pool deck to the opposite end, drawn in by the view. She felt giddy, drunk, and high, but also full of the possibilities of all those lights, their bright promise. "Maybe Toronto now is New York seven years ago," she said, or something like it—she couldn't remember the words after they left her mouth. When she turned back around, Mags had stripped down to her underwear and jumped in the pool, the splash echoing through the quiet room.

Ava hesitated only for a second before taking off her own shirt and jeans and diving beneath the surface, the clear, chlorine-tinged water and sterile blue tiles of the pool so far removed from the murky depths of the Atlantic Ocean. She felt clean and whole and strangely happy—until she burst to the surface and saw a security guard standing over them, demanding they get out.

"Do you even know who this is?" Mags shouted, her voice echoing through the atrium as she gestured wildly to Ava.

"I don't care if she's the fucking Pope, you are both getting out of this pool."

"Make us!" Mags screeched, diving back under the water, pulling Ava down with her.

Ava felt her nose and mouth fill with water, her eyes stinging from chlorine, a feeling of calm overtaking her as she let her body go limp. *Maybe this is what's supposed to happen,* she thought. *Maybe I've always been destined to drown.*

But just as quickly, she was being dragged to the surface by the security guard—his hair slick on his head like an otter's, his uniform heavy and dripping as he pulled her to the side of the pool. But Mags had swum away from him, and at the deep end of the pool she stripped out of her underwear, which she flung through the air, landing directly on his head.

"You can't stop her! She's Avalon Hart. From that TV show about the Harts!"

It wasn't until later—after the security guard had called in backup, and Ava and Mags had both been wrapped in towels and sent back to their room to sleep it off, the sun creeping in through the still-open curtains as they lay together on the bed, all wet hair and clammy skin and breath as heavy as smoke—that she thought: *I'm not, though. I'm not from that television show. I'm not from anything.*

Reality Check
Reality TV Writing for Reality TV Fans

LifeStyle Announces New Season of *Absence Makes the Hart Grow Fonder*

Lex Jackson, staff writer
02/20/15 8:34 am Filed to NEWS

Absence Makes the Hart Grow Fonder, the troubled spinoff of beloved reality classic *Home Is Where the Hart Is*, will begin filming its second season next week, *Reality Check* has confirmed.

The show, which had a rocky start this past fall, capturing a measly 0.23 share among adults 18–49, was reportedly on the brink of cancellation before this week's news about Ava Hart's alleged abortion. Now the world is asking, "Who is Ava Hart's babydaddy?" and LifeStyle is banking on viewers tuning in to find out the answer.

But will the mystery be revealed?

LifeStyle CEO Bob Axelrod is playing his cards close to his chest. "Our aim is to document every aspect—both highs and lows—of the lives of these extraordinary young people," he said. "Viewers can take that as they will."

Season 2 of *Absence Makes the Hart Grow Fonder* will premiere Thursday, March 19 at 9 pm EST on LifeStyle. In the meantime, catch the AMTHGF Season 1 marathon this Saturday and Sunday from noon until 10 pm.

TMI Online
February 20 at 1:54 am

Looks like Ava Hart is in Toronto!

> TMI.com
> **Ava Hart Spotted in Toronto Outside Concert Venue**
> **with Align Above's Mags Kovach**
> Only a few short days after photos surfaced of Ava Hart
> outside an abortion clinic, Celebrity.com has received exclusive
> photos of the reality star in Toronto, intoxicated and . . .

👍 34   22 Comments   15 Shares

Like   Comment   Share

Amber Leigh Delacruz via **TMI Online**
February 20 at 2:12 am

I know I shouldn't be doing this, y'all, but I can't sit by and watch while
this piece of trash runs around doing whatever she wants, giving the rest
of us decent, hardworking reality television stars a bad name. She is a
disgrace to reality television and someone needs to say something. Ava,
go back to your family and get back to God.

> TMI.com
> **Ava Hart Spotted in Toronto Outside Concert Venue**
> **with Align Above's Mags Kovach**
> Only a few short days after photos surfaced of Ava Hart
> outside an abortion clinic, Celebrity.com has received exclusive
> photos of the reality star in Toronto, intoxicated and . . .

👍 112   43 Comments   2 Shares

Like   Comment   Share

319

TMI Online
February 20 at 3:22 am

Shots fired!

TMI.com
Librarians of Florida **star Amber Leigh Delacruz Slams Ava Hart on Facebook**
Amber Leigh Delacruz, one of the stars of HBG's hit reality series *Librarians of Florida*, recently took to Facebook to put fellow reality television star Ava Hart on blast, calling her "a disgrace to the . . .

👍 10   12 Comments   2 Shares
Like   Comment   Share

Mags

Saturday, 10:56 a.m.

———◇———

They could only have been asleep for a few hours before they woke to a pounding on the door. Mags surfaced through the heavy layers of unconsciousness and forced her eyes open. Across the room, the television was still on, tuned to a reality show about bakers.

Ava was still snoring, her pool-wet hair stiffened to little meringue-like peaks on her head. As the banging continued, Mags rummaged through what remained of the mini-fridge's contents, looking for something to deal with her hangover. She would have killed for one of Sam's favourite hangover cures—honey, lemon, hot water, ginger, and lots and lots of rum—but had to settle for beer, Clamato, and Red Bull, which she dumped all together in the container meant for ice before she opened the door.

"So, the good news is your first five shows in Europe are sold out," Emiko said, bursting into the room, an impossibly large Starbucks cup in her hand. "But the bad news is they're not charging you with public indecency."

321

"That's bad news?" Mags said. "Wait, how did you find me?"

"Public indecency is your high-speed train to rock stardom. Jim Morrison. Wendy O. Williams. Madonna. Mags Kovach. Not a bad list to be on. Next time you decide to take your clothes off onstage, remember to make some obscene gestures. And I had a GPS tracker implanted in your neck when you were passed out." When Mags reached for the back of her neck, Emiko rolled her eyes. "You sent me a Snap from the pool at, like, one a.m." She thrust the coffee at Mags. "Put down whatever swill you're drinking and take this."

Mags took the coffee, but instead of drinking it, she peeled the top off and put it down on the dresser. "Madonna was never actually arrested," she said, poking through the minibar bottles again and picking out a bottle of Bacardi, which she emptied into the coffee. "They only threatened her with it."

"And Jim Morrison was a narcissistic, misogynist creep," Ava said from the bed, her eyes still closed. "Didn't you see the movie?"

Emiko glanced over at Ava. "Oh, you're still here."

"No charges, then. Got it." Mags took a sip of her drink and hoped she wouldn't throw up while Emiko was there, but she would do what had to be done. After all, Emiko was the one who had convinced her to self-medicate. She shouldn't be surprised when she had to deal with the consequences. "People are just going to have to live with my continued clean criminal record."

"Well, you've got a couple of days before we leave. There's still time."

Mags put her coffee cup down with a shaking hand. Europe had been looming large in her mind since the tour began, a giant monster waiting for her in the dark. Going on a North American tour without Sam was one thing. They had been to all of those cities before, and she had memories of Sam wherever she went— there was their favourite pizza joint in Detroit, the beach in Ocean City where they had watched the sun rise, the bookstore in Chicago whose awning they had stood under, waiting for a thunderstorm to pass. She found having those memories somehow comforting, as though he were still there with her. But thinking about going to Europe without him—a place where she didn't have any memories of Sam to keep her company, a place they had always talked about going together—she wasn't ready for it. Deep down she knew she needed to take a break, that living this way was eventually going to kill her. But she also knew that staying here, drinking and thinking about Sam, that would kill her too. Either way, she was dead. She might as well die singing.

"Hurry up and finish that," Emiko said. "You're going to be late."

Mags put the cup down. "Late for what?"

Emiko sighed. "Your interview. Come on. Where are your clothes?" She scanned the room, letting her eyes fall on a pile half shoved under the bed. "Are those the same clothes you performed in last night? Do you not have anything else?"

Mags shook her head. "What interview? With who?"

Emiko looked at her phone. "Jack Francis with the *National Chronicle*. You agreed to this interview weeks ago."

"No." She tried to comb out her hair with her fingers, but they got stuck in the chlorine-crisped tangles. "I'm not doing it."

"You have to do it. Everybody does it."

Mags began extracting her hand from the bird's nest on top of her head. "If everybody jumped off a bridge, would you make me do that too?"

"If it was essential for your career, yes."

Mags's hand came free and dropped to her side. "Why can't Paul and Zac do it?" Though even as she said the words, she already knew the answer. Paul and Zac were not the ones whose faces were on the covers of the albums. Paul and Zac were exempt from this kind of bullshit. Also, Paul and Zac hadn't spoken to her off-stage since she walked out of the radio interview in Cincinnati. So there was that.

Emiko stood up, her eyes fixed on her phone. "One afternoon. Then you can get back to partying with your D-list celebrity lover."

"Hey!" said Ava, face muffled in the comforter. "I'm a solid C-list."

Mags waved her off. "Look, I'll do the interview, okay? But I don't have to explain my social life to you."

"You do when it's costing me money." She looked up from her phone. "There, I've emailed you some talking points, some nice, neutral things to say about Sam."

"I'm not talking about Sam."

"Of course you are. What else do you think he wants to talk about?" Emiko picked up Mags's T-shirt off the floor and smelled it, then wrinkled her nose and dropped it again. "Go have a shower and I'll try to find you some clothes." She turned abruptly and walked out the door.

"I'm not talking about Sam!" Mags called after her, but she was already gone.

Mags sat down on the bed next to Ava, then flopped backward. Everything hurt, but she knew Emiko would have a pill for that. Or at least something strong enough to ease her hangover and make her coherent for this interview that she did not want to do. So much of being a rock star was exactly the way she had imagined it would be. What was surprising was how much of it she couldn't stand.

"So, you're going to Europe in two days," Ava said, propping herself up in the bed.

"Yeah, apparently."

Ava rubbed her eyes. "I have two days until I'm supposed to start filming again."

Mags stared up at the ceiling, a blank, monochrome wash of white. How could there not be a stain there, a mark, a patch of peeling paint? How could anything be that flawless? "What did you want to be when you grew up?" she asked.

"I don't know," Ava felt around for her phone, which she located under a pile of pillows. "I think I was just always grown-up."

"That is totally not true."

"It *is* true." She started fixing her hair in her selfie camera. "Haven't you read the tabloids? I am completely self-obsessed. I can't conceive of anything outside of myself."

"Liar." Mags paused. "Are you going to go back to your show?"

"I don't know. Are you going to go to Europe?"

"I don't know." Mags traced her eyes along the ceiling from one side of the room to the other, searching for some kind of crack. But there was none.

—◇—

Jack Francis folded his hands on the table in front of him. "So. Tell me about Sam."

Mags felt her whole body tense up as she shrunk down in her seat. She had known this interview was a mistake from the moment she walked in and saw his smug, generically handsome face, his too-blue eyes, his hair stiff with styling products. She immediately disliked him, but she also knew she was too fuzzy and too worn down by pharmaceuticals to keep her guard up.

He had suggested this bar at the last minute, some try-hard hipster place that was just a nameless black room with bike parts and old mannequin pieces stuck up on the wall, a ceiling hung with industrial wire woven together to look like a giant nest. She had kept her body stiff as he hugged her, whispering in her ear that he had already ordered her a gin and tonic, that he had read somewhere it was her favourite drink. It wasn't even remotely true, but she downed it anyway and ordered another before they'd even started.

The first part of the interview was a blur as the gin picked up her heartbeat, which had been slowed by whatever pills Emiko had given her. She vaguely remembered him asking her about the

325

band's origins, about their songwriting process, about favourite shows they'd played. Now, Jack Francis was looking at her with what she could only assume was meant to be an expression of fatherly concern, and asking her about Sam, and she was immediately pulled back into the room. She supposed it was inevitable, although now the words she had practised on the way over—that she missed him, that the band would never be the same without him, that in the future they would be going in a different direction, that she hoped he would be happy with the album—were impossible to say.

Instead, she asked, "Can we talk about something else?"

"Absolutely," Jack said, regarding her over the rim of his pint glass. He was drinking a draft stout, something dark and syrupy. All the older music guys did—as though the darker the beer, the more you could prove your masculinity. Sam had always laughed at that. Sam only ever drank Coors Light. "But tell me . . . I'm curious as to why you decided to release the album and tour so soon after his death. You had only been married a few weeks. Losing him must have been very difficult."

A few weeks. Mags took a sip of her own drink, trying not to smash the glass on the table. As if they were newlyweds still working out which side of the bed to claim. As if the preceding six years didn't mean a fucking thing. Which maybe they didn't. Maybe, Mags thought, she had just made it all up in her head—all the first times and the trying out and the talking and talking and talking, late-night jam sessions and morning coffee, backyards and basements, scars and freckles, their bodies pressed together in bed, Sam's fingers winding through her hair.

"It's important to us to keep working," she said.

On the other side of the room, over the top of Jack's head, Mags could see Ava sitting on a barstool, legs crossed, back straight. She was wearing a Toronto Raptors toque and scarf, and a huge red hoodie with a maple leaf in the middle, all of which Emiko had bought in the gift shop at the hotel. "At least no one will recognize me," Ava had said. "I look like a Swedish tourist. All I need is a fanny pack."

Mags herself was wearing a Blue Jays T-shirt under her coat, which she had left zipped up, one last line of defence against Jack. But it didn't seem to be working.

"How have fans responded to your husband's death?" Jack asked.

"Oh," said Mags, jabbing her straw into her drink, trying to break up a big piece of ice. "Everyone has been kind. Everyone's been super positive. We love our fans." The rote answers were coming back to her. In her former life, she had been great at interviews. "We have the greatest fans in the world." Ava gave her a thumbs up.

"And what about Josh Falco? How have things been going with him?"

"Who?"

"Josh Falco. Your new bassist."

"Oh, right. Yeah, he's great. He's super talented. He's bringing such a fresh, new sound to the band. It's really been great working with him."

Jack sat back, crossing his arms. "It sounds like the future only holds good things for Align Above. You've been taking advantage of a difficult situation and making it work in your favour." He held his pint glass to his lips and drained the rest of his beer, then set the glass back on the table gently.

Mags watched the beer suds slide down the side of his glass. Jack waited patiently to see how she was going to respond, but Mags just sat there, mesmerized by the slow trickle of liquid, until she couldn't even really remember the question anymore. After what she realized must have been an eternity, she said, "Oh, yeah. It's great. Really great."

"Your performances throughout this tour have all been, well, pretty dramatic, to say the least. But I think it's fair to say that with

327

last night's show you took things to a whole new level." He raised his eyebrows questioningly. "Was that planned?"

The suds began to pool on the table as everything went quiet in Mags's brain. "All part of the act," she said.

"Of course. People are paying good money to see your . . . act."

Mags felt her body go cold. "I'm just trying to do my job," she said, finally tearing her gaze away from the glass and meeting his eyes. "I'm just trying to do what's right for the band. I'm just trying to sing."

"True. But surely you're aware that your ticket sales are based on much more than your *singing*." He raised an eyebrow, a slight smirk on his face that made her skin crawl.

"No, I was not aware. Please, enlighten me." She clenched her fists beneath the table. "What else are they based on?"

Jack gazed at her levelly. "Nothing, of course, you're right," he said breezily. He reached for his tape recorder, tucking it into his satchel as he slid out of the booth. "I think that's a great place to stop. Thanks so much for doing this. I know that some of this stuff must be hard to talk about."

"Hard?" She dug her nails deeper into her palms. "Are you fucking serious? *Hard?*" But Jack didn't respond, only squeezed her shoulder on the way out the door.

Mags slammed her fist on the underside of the table. "Of course he had to have the last word," she said as Ava slid into the booth across from her. "Of course he's going to piss me off then walk away like a fucking psychopath."

"What a d-bag," Ava said, pushing his glass away. "Condescending, self-important little prick."

"I want to set his whole world on fire," Mags said. "I mean it, Ava, I want to burn it all down."

"We should," Ava said, taking another sip of her drink, some tall pink thing in a glass rimmed with sugar. She took her phone out and stared at the screen, but kept it turned off. "All of them are vultures, picking at the bones of our various tragedies. Feeding on our fucking souls."

A woman approached the side of their table. "Excuse me," the woman said to Mags. "I'm sorry to bother you. I just wanted to tell you that I'm such a huge fan of your work. I've been listening to Align Above since your first EP came out."

Mags smiled broadly even as her stomach knotted. "Great! Always nice to meet a fan."

"I was so sad to hear about your husband," the woman went on. "I hope that with a little perseverance and God's love you can get through this time of turmoil and get back out there and make some music."

Mags's smile began to waver. "Oh yes, for sure," she said. Ava stifled a laugh. Mags kicked her under the table.

As the woman left, Ava leaned toward Mags. "There's your answer," she whispered. "All you need is God's love!"

Mags slid down in her seat, trying to keep herself from throwing up. "Yes. That's what God wants. For Mags Kovach to get back out there and make some music." She downed the rest of her drink. "Come on, let's get the hell out of here."

As they stepped out into the street, she heard someone call her name. She turned and was surprised to see Paul coming toward her. "What are you doing here?"

"Emiko said you'd be here." He turned to Ava. "I need to talk to Mags for a second."

"I'll go back inside," Ava said.

"No, you won't," Mags said, grabbing on to Ava's arm and holding it. "What do you want, Paul?"

"Fine." Paul shoved his hands into his pockets. "You need to get your shit together, Mags. This tour, this album, hell, *everything* we do right now is incredibly important. Our entire future depends on what happens in the next few weeks. We can't have you running around onstage naked or getting kicked out of hotel pools or whatever the hell else you've been doing that has gotten your face plastered all over the internet."

"You still have that stupid Google Alert for the band on your phone, I see."

"Yeah, I do. It's been going crazy now for weeks. And do you think any of it has been about the band, Mags? No. It's all been about you and your ridiculous antics, your desperate bids for attention. It's pathetic."

"Oh my god, not this again." Mags let go of Ava's arm and dipped her hand into her pocket, rummaging for her smokes. "Sorry my being fucked up by my husband's death has been so bad for your ego."

"Come on, Mags. How long are you going to use that as an excuse to do whatever you want?"

With trembling hands, Mags lit up a cigarette. "I honestly don't know why you think this is any of your business, Paul. We're not friends, we're colleagues. And as long as I do my job, you shouldn't care what I do, or what excuses I use."

"Exactly. I want to make sure you do your job. We're not some kind of circus sideshow, we're *musicians*. Do you want people to come to our shows to see you sing, or do you want them to come just to see what kind of crazy shit you're going to do?"

"Jesus Christ," said Ava, backing up and leaning against the wall, as though the sheer force of Paul's words had pushed her there. "This is your bandmate?"

"It's fine," Mags said through clenched teeth. "You know, Paul, there wouldn't even *be* a band if it weren't for me and Sam writing the songs. Or did you forget about that song you wrote in fucking *Klingon?*" But she knew he was right, that Jack Francis was right. She and her *act* were on the verge of becoming a joke. Paul was only protecting his dream, which had once been her dream too. "Look, I know you're worried, but I'm going to be okay. I had a rough couple of days, but I'm over it now. I'm going to get back to work."

Ava stared at her. "Do you hear yourself? You are grieving. You are *sick*. These people pushing you, drugging you to keep you going, they do not have your best interests at heart." She turned to Paul, her eyes glinting with rage. "How could you do this to her?"

"Who *are* you?" Paul asked. "What do you know about any of this? We are on the brink of having everything we ever wanted, and I'm not going to let anything screw that up."

Mags felt something tear open inside her, some wound that had barely healed, that she had been trying to keep together through sheer force of will. "Everything we ever wanted? *This* is everything you ever wanted?" She lunged toward Paul. "None of this matters! None of this even fucking matters without Sam!" She began slamming her fists against his chest, until Ava finally pulled her back and Mags collapsed against her, shaking. She was crying again, but she couldn't stop. She couldn't control anything that was going on in her body, not the pain, the fear, the anger, the violence that bubbled up from the very depths of her. "Nothing matters without Sam," she said again.

"Okay, we're going home," Ava said, reaching her arm out to hail a cab. Mags climbed in the backseat and leaned her head against the window.

As the cab pulled back out into the street, she watched Paul, still standing outside the bar in the snow, growing smaller and smaller as they drove away.

Madeline Boudreau
@mads4cupcakes
Name a more iconic duo . . . I'll wait.

Busted! Mags Kovach and Ava Hart's Nighttime Skinny Dip Adventure
Not only did Mags and Ava break into a hotel pool for a little evening swim *au naturel*, they Snapchatted the whole thing, according to these anonymous screencaps . . .
chatterfuel.com

5:32 PM – 21 Feb 2015
458 Retweets 8,441 Likes

Bianca @beeeew 22 min
Replying to @mads4cupcakes
Like literally anyone?

Geo Jazz @jlb_789
Replying to @mads4cupcakes
Me and your mom

Jewel Medeiros @jewel_medeiros
Replying to @mads4cupcakes
Oh my god, I love this! I wish I had a BFF like that.

Karl Neel @neel565
Replying to @jewel_medeiros @mads4cupcakes
They're not BFFs, they're dating. TMI has video of them kissing.

Madeline Boudreau @mads4cupcakes
Replying to @neel565 @jewel_medeiros
Karl I think you mistook your dream last night for a video.

Brandon Frawley @frawls101

Replying to @mads4cupcakes @neel565 @jewel_medeiros

But have you seen them together tho? They are totally fucking

Jewel Medeiros @jewel_medeiros

Replying to @frawls101 @mads4cupcakes @neel565

WHY DO GUYS ALWAYS THINK GIRLS ARE FUCKING THEIR FRIENDS JFC

Karl Neel @neel565

Replying to @jewel_medeiros @frawls101 @mads4cupcakes

Cause it's what we'd do if it were us

alignaboveofficial   Follow

alignaboveofficial We're coming for you, Europe! Align Above's first ever European tour kicks off in Dublin on February 24. For tickets, check link in bio!

Load more comments

abukex Can't wait to see you in London!!!

greebo90 Got my tickets for Frankfurt, pls play "You're the Only One"! 😍

magskovachfan_56 I love you soooo much!! I am your biggest fan in the entire world!! You are beautiful and precious and just an amazing person!! My entire room is filled with posters of you and I have been to your concerts 2 times. I can't explain how much I love you!! 😂😂😂😂

lovelykierstennnn SHAME ON U

iammelodyjane Mags! Repeat after me "one body one life." That is a very powerful phrase for me and maybe it could help you. . . . sending love and light and peace. Forgiveness of ourselves and love and keep it moving, god loves you 🖤🦋🖤🦋🖤🦋

riachantika_gh please mags will u take ur cloths off in lisbon hehehe

zuhrodewi_x take off your clothes in France

dyc.ahonana You fkn Crackhead 😂😂😂😂 getfukt

alecavalcantec ✦ quítate la ropa en barcelona ✦

budcu4zenginI I don't understand why people are not happy with there life, especially someone like Mags. You've got everything you want but still . . . Yo, remember some people have very hard life. I actually love Align Above but it's . . . you know what i mean.

steph.mara89 togliti i vestiti a Roma 🖤🖤🖤🖤🖤🖤

fransiskochaerani30 TAK YOUR CLOTHES OFF IN MY ROOM

334

Ava

Saturday, 4:30 p.m.

———◇———

Mags didn't want to go home.

As soon as the cab pulled away from the curb, she jolted back to life, defibrillated by the sharp U-turn. "It's so early," she said, bouncing up and down in her seat. "We can't go home yet. Oh!" She slapped Ava on the shoulder, hard. "Do you like over-priced, watered-down beer and cheesy country music?"

Ava narrowed her eyes. "No," she said. "Does anyone?"

"Hey," Mags said, leaning forward to speak to the driver. "Can you take us to Parkdale?"

"What's in Parkdale?" Ava asked. But Mags just grinned.

The Butcher's Son, it turned out, was a bar. All the staff seemed to know Mags, and she went to the bar to order while Ava sat in a sticky booth with a pile of peeled-off beer labels stacked in the middle. As she sat there waiting, exhaustion crept into her body, and she could feel herself on the verge of a comedown, from the drinking and the after-effects of the pill and the adrenaline of being around Mags. But she didn't want to stop. She needed to not stop.

"Okay," Mags said as she stumbled toward the table. She slammed two shots down, amber liquid sloshing everywhere, followed by two beer bottles she procured from the pockets of her coat. "Vodka shots and beer chasers." Mags picked up a shot glass and held it out for a toast. "Sam and I always came here and ordered them after terrible interviews."

"Well then, I guess I can't say no." Ava lifted her shot glass, then tipped it back, a flash of fire skidding down the back of her throat. "What else did you and Sam used to do after interviews?"

Mags grinned. "Nothing you can help me with," she said. Her eyes flickered over Ava's shoulder. "But maybe those guys can." She leaned across the table conspiratorially. "Want to go talk to them?"

"I don't think so."

"Oh, *come on.*" Mags traced her finger in the condensation from the beer bottle, little wet trails snaking across the table. "You need to fuck someone else. You need to get whatshisname out of your system."

"I just . . . I don't know." She couldn't even imagine being with anyone but Antonio—not because she felt guilty about it, but because the thought of anyone else's hands on her felt wrong. She had never wanted anyone except him. That didn't change because he didn't want her anymore.

Mags shook her head. "Fuck this. You need shots. We need shots." She stood up on her chair. "We need shots!" she yelled, and everyone in the bar let out a cheer.

A group of guys at the next table—hockey players drowning their sorrows following an afternoon trouncing—obliged Mags's request, and bought them Tequila Poppers and Jaeger Bombs, Snake Bites and B-52s. Things got hazy, hazier, Ava's thoughts like sediment swirling, refusing to land. She found herself watching Mags, mesmerized by the way she transformed herself, the way every interaction became a performance—touching their arms and leaning in close, letting them think she was there for them, one more shot and one more shot and one more shot and she'd be theirs for the taking. Ava untucked her hair from behind her ears, thrust her shoulders back and leaned forward against the table, just like Mags did, her tongue darting out between her lips, trying to copy Mags's wet-mouthed pout, her feverish breath, her heavy-lidded eyes. But that only lasted a second before she started to feel like an idiot, and then she went back to sitting tall and aloof on her stool, her collarbones rigid under the soft fabric of her ridiculous Canada hoodie.

It wasn't until she spilled her drink on her jeans that she split away from everyone, going to the bathroom to wash the smell of vodka lime out of the fabric. Then, sitting on the toilet, her phone in her hand—because she couldn't help it, even now, when she was trying to forget everything—she checked her notifications. She scrolled past the texts from Val and Antonio and clicked on her texts from Bryce.

Can you give us a call, please?

Just text us to tell us you're okay.

We're worried about you, Ava.

Ava, we know we haven't always been there for you in the past, but let us be here for you now.

"Nice try," she said out loud, but her voice trembled, a lump forming in her throat. She had never expected an admission of culpability, not even from Bryce. She stared at her phone, her finger hovering over the reply button, trying to think of how she might respond, when a new message lit up her screen.

Hi.

It took a moment for her to realize it was from Eden. Her hands started to shake as she stared at the one word, the first word she had heard from her sister since that night on the pier. Eden, who she had been trying so hard not to think about. Eden, who had been the architect of all her misery. Eden, who was still her sister, and who she sometimes missed so hard her whole body ached with sorrow.

Ava stood up and pulled up her jeans, still staring at the screen. She let her phone fall to the ground, only hesitating a second before bringing her foot down on it, over and over, until she felt the screen crack under her heel, the phone becoming a mangled and useless mess on the floor. Then she opened the door and walked away.

Back in the bar, the Pogues' "Fairytale of New York" was coming through the speakers, as if she didn't feel wretched enough.

"Hey you." A man appeared in the hallway, grinning as he came toward her. He might have been one of the guys from their table, but she couldn't really be sure, all of them a blur of baseball caps and graphic T-shirts and mildly attractive facial features. "Where'd you go?"

"Just to the bathroom," she said, backing up against the wall. Instinctively, she felt in her pocket for her phone before remembering it wasn't there. "Is it my round?"

"Maybe." The guy leaned in toward her, snaking his fingers along her waist. "But we could also just take off, if you wanted."

"Take off?" She blinked at him uncomprehendingly, his face coming in and out of focus, moving closer toward hers until his lips were on her neck. "Oh," she murmured softly.

He pressed himself up against her, and she felt herself go limp inside, everything else melting away, leaving nothing but a blur of wild hands and wet mouths and the rough stubble of his chin. Then his breath was in her ear, his tongue snaking along the lobe, and he whispered, "I can't believe I'm making out with Ava Hart."

Ava froze. "Get your hands off me," she said, grabbing his arm and twisting it, hard. She felt his muscles yielding under her hand, softened by alcohol and surprise.

His reaction was delayed but still effective. "What the hell?" he yelled, wrenching his arm free. Then, seemingly without any effort at all, he pushed her, sending her stumbling backward down the hall and into the bar, where she crashed into a table, knocking several pitchers of beer onto the floor.

When she stood up, she saw Mags suddenly fly into her field of vision like a slingshot. "Don't you dare touch her!" she screamed. She grabbed a bar stool and swung it though the air, hitting the guy in the shoulder. He toppled over to the ground just as Ava made it across the room.

"Mags!" Ava said, grabbing her arm. "Stop it! I'm fine!"

But Mags wasn't paying attention. She threw the bar stool off to the side and jumped on the guy. It took three of his buddies to pull her off. "Let go of me!" she growled, twisting and biting, kicking and scratching, all teeth and claws and hair. "You fuckers think you can do anything you want!" She wrestled her way free with a knee to a groin and sprung back on the first guy, singularly focused on going in for the kill. Ava watched, mesmerized by Mags's fury, while around them cell phones circled and bobbed, lenses like eyes, seeing all.

Finally, a bouncer dragged Mags off, and she let herself go heavy as he carried her to the back door. Ava stood in the middle of the bar for a few seconds, watching the guy roll around on the floor. His buddies were yelling at her, but the blood rush to her ears was too loud for her to hear them. Eventually, she found her feet again, grabbed their coats, and floated to the back of the bar as though she were being pulled along on a current.

Outside, Mags was sitting on the ground, small and spent in an alley between the gawping buildings of whatever city they were in—which Ava remembered was Toronto. She had been in Toronto for less than forty-eight hours, time stretching and condensing like a jellyfish undulating through the salty sea. In the distance, a police siren wailed. To Ava, it sounded a little like a clanging mast.

"We need to go," Mags said, climbing to her feet as the sirens came closer. Then she grabbed Ava's hand and they started running.

They ran until the sirens died to a whimper behind them, and still they ran, Mags leading her through alleys, across parking lots, under overpasses, until finally she pulled her into a park and they both collapsed on a bench, gulping for air.

"I haven't run like that in a long time," Mags said. She fumbled in her pocket and pulled out her cigarettes, staring at the packet. "I don't even know if I can smoke one."

"Do you really think they were coming for us?" Ava asked. Even though it was cold, she was sweating, heat radiating in waves off her cheeks.

Mags lit a cigarette, the smoke mixing with the vapour from her breath. "Maybe. I wasn't going to risk it."

"Sorry if I ruined your chances of getting laid."

Mags laughed, then started to cough. "Don't worry about that," she said, her voice wet, raspy. "Actually, the only person I've slept with since Sam is your brother."

"Really?"

Mags nodded. "I know most people assume otherwise. But I can't bring myself to."

She held her cigarette out. Ava stared at it, then reached out and took it. *Well, why not?* "Our show's producer was the one who got me pregnant," she said. "He's the only boy I've ever slept with. I mean, man." She took a drag, feeling the heat of the smoke filling her lungs. "I guess he's a man."

"That's debatable." Mags took the cigarette back. "Are you going to go back to do the show?"

"I don't know what else I would do. Are you going to go to Europe?"

Mags shrugged. "I don't know what else *I* would do." She pulled out her flask and unscrewed the top, peering in. "There's a shot left for each of us."

At the sight of the flask, Ava's stomach heaved. "You can have it," she said. What she really wanted was a glass of water. A shower. To sleep for a million years. But Mags didn't seem to want to go home. And Ava . . . well, she wasn't sure she even had a home anymore.

From down the street, Ava could hear music drifting out of one of the pubs. After a while she realized it was "Barrett's Privateers"—the same song that had been playing the night Antonio took her to the pub. The memory brought an unexpected lump to her throat. Not because she missed Antonio. She was sad for fifteen-year-old Ava, who still thought everything could turn out okay.

Mags rolled her eyes. "Fucking Nova Scotians and their TERRIBLE FUCKING MUSIC."

"Aren't you a Nova Scotian? Haven't you played this music all your life?"

"Yes. Yes, I did. And I had to play my fair share of jigs and reels, let me tell you. I paid my dues." Mags stretched her legs out in front of her. "And then I get to Toronto and what happens? I realize it's full of FUCKING IRISH PUBS."

Ava tucked her hands in her pockets. "You can't escape it, no matter what you do."

"No, you really can't," Mags said, tilting the flask back to excavate the dregs of the whiskey. Then she turned to Ava. "We should just embrace it. Go back there. We can move to Rum Cove or wherever it is you lived."

Ava laughed. "Just what I always dreamed of. We can marry fishermen and pop out a bunch of kids."

Mags shook her head. "No, no. Fuck that. We live together. We buy a cottage by the ocean and live off the grid. We raise chickens and goats, and preserve vegetables, and make our own soap, and we put up weird sculptures in the front yard and all the neighbourhood kids will be scared of us."

"I like that idea better."

"Me too." Mags put her head on Ava's shoulder. Ava was surprised by the weight of it, the warmth that she felt even through all the layers of winter clothes. Eventually, Mags raised her head and said, "Let's go."

They walked out of the park to the street. It was only 8 p.m. and it was still busy, crowds of people trudging through the snow with gym bags, dogs on leashes, little hand carts full of groceries, the lights from the storefronts casting the frozen sidewalk in an eerie glow. Ava felt oddly invisible, slipping into the silent throng— her body enveloped in layers of down, her Raptors toque pulled low over her ears.

The feeling didn't last long.

"Ava Hart!" she heard someone yell from across the street. People around her raised their heads from their hunched positions, curious about the commotion. "Ava Hart!"

"A friend of yours?" Mags asked.

"Oh yeah, sure. Meet my old pal Tina Celebritystalker," Ava said.

"Ava Hart! You're a fucking whore!"

Ava stopped, shrinking down in her coat, unable to move or speak. Mags turned toward the source of the yelling. "Better a whore than a cunt!" she yelled back. Then she took Ava's hand and ducked down an alley, weaving in behind a building.

"Thanks," said Ava. "You never think you're going to encounter an internet troll in person."

Mags pulled out another one of her smokes and lit it. "Do you get a lot of internet trolls?"

"Of course." Ava gave her a sideways look. "Don't you?"

"I guess. Probably. I don't really go online much."

"I wish I could be like that." Ava stopped, reaching into her pocket for her phone. Mags puffed her cigarette, watching her. "Shit, I lost my phone." Then it came back to her. "Shit. I smashed my phone."

"Maybe I should do the same thing," Mags said. She flicked her cigarette into a snowbank and pulled her phone out, twirling it in her hand.

"Come on," Ava said. "Throw it. Join me in the light."

Mags tossed the phone in the air and caught it. Then she wound up and hurled it against the side of a building, where it shattered into pieces on the ground.

They exited the alley. Ahead of them, a basset hound tied to a bike rack gave a raspy howl and Ava stopped and bent down. "Hey, buddy," she said, scratching behind his ears. "Where's your person? Why did they leave you out here in the cold?" She took off her mitten and let the basset sniff her hand. He raised his head and looked up at her with big, wet, droopy eyes, and she felt as though he were staring right into her soul. "I think we should take this guy home," she said. "It's freezing out here."

"Ava, we are not stealing a dog."

"It's not stealing. Someone left him here."

"*Someone* is in that electronics store buying a new alarm clock. Plus, I mean, what are you going to do with him when you go back to New York?"

Ava stood up and put her mitten back on. "*If* I go back to New York."

Mags gazed at Ava intently, considering her words. Then she bent down and petted the dog tentatively on the head. "I guess we could use a dog at our beach house in Whiskey Inlet," she said.

Ava peered in the window of the electronics store, looking for someone who might belong to the dog. She didn't really think they were going to take the dog, but it was exciting to think that maybe they could. But instead of the basset hound's potential owner, she was surprised to see her own face distorted by the glass. She assumed it was just a reflection or a trick of the light, but then she realized that her face was on a television screen in the window. *Maybe it's a rerun*, she thought. *LifeStyle trying to capitalize on all this free publicity.*

But then she saw Antonio's face next to hers, and the world around her fell away.

It wasn't a rerun. It wasn't the show at all.

343

She could hear Mags calling her name behind her as she was pulled into the store by some invisible force, guiding her through the door and to the back where the rest of the televisions were on display. Every single one of them tuned in to an image of her face. Sitting in Antonio's van.

No, Ava heard her own voice say. *It feels like nothing.*

She felt suspended in time, simultaneously living in this moment and a previous one. Or that everything that had happened since that conversation was just a dream, and she had never come to Toronto, never gotten away, was still sitting in the front seat of that van, talking to Antonio.

Across the bottom of the screen, a line of words appeared. At first, it was as though she were reading them in a foreign language, until slowly her brain caught up and translated them.

Young Reality Star Gets Caught in Sex Scandal with Producer

Then the pieces all came to her, rushing into place with a resounding click. The dashcam, the one that Antonio had set up in the van for extra footage. It had been on when he picked her up from the clinic. He had been filming the worst experience of her life, the moment when everything broke apart, the moment he had promised he wouldn't film.

She could feel people's eyes on her, whispering to each other behind their hands as they stared, their cell phones raised up to silently capture her transition from confusion to fear. Vomit rose in her throat, but she swallowed it down, blinking her eyes as they watered from the burn. *Fuck them*, she thought. She wasn't afraid anymore. She was angry.

Calmly, she walked over to the first television on the shelf. *You want a cool video?* she thought. *Here's something for you.* With one hand, she reached up and tipped it forward, the TV flipping once before smashing on the ground, pieces of plastic and glass and metal firing off in all directions around her feet.

"Ava," she heard Mags call from across the store, although she could have been standing right next to her for all it mattered to Ava. She walked to the next television and toppled it to the floor too. *This one's for you, LifeStyle.* She could hear footsteps behind her, people shouting, but no one stopped her as she moved down the line of televisions, bringing them down one by one to the floor. *This one's for Bob, this one's for Tess. This one's for David and Bryce. This one's for all the girls who copied my haircut. This one's for the guy at the bar. This one's for the woman on the street.*

When she got to the last one at the end of the row, a huge 50-inch that was mounted to the wall, she paused. *This one, this one's for you, Antonio.* She picked up a display DVD player and hurled it into the screen, which wavered and wobbled but didn't break, her own face warping under the force before reassembling itself as the waves came to a stop. She picked the DVD player back up and threw it again, but the same thing happened, the television mocking her with its unbreakability, her face and Antonio's face staring out at her resolutely as the clip kept playing.

Then someone's hands were on her, wrestling the DVD player away, and suddenly she was on the ground, someone's weight pinning her there, and a security guard was holding her hands together behind her back.

"Stand up," the security guard said, her breath hot in Ava's ear. When Ava didn't move, the guard grabbed her by the arms and pulled her to her feet. "I said stand up."

Ava kept her head down, aware of all the phones turned on her. She knew the media frenzy that was about to come, the joy that the world was going to take in her breakdown, but she didn't care. She was done with playing the part they wanted her to play, with letting everyone manipulate her, with watching passively as her life was reduced to a punchline on a late-night talk show. She was done with all of it. Antonio, David and Bryce, Bob and Tess—they had taken everything from her. She didn't owe them anything anymore. She was free.

But as they dragged her away, it wasn't Antonio she was thinking of, or her fathers, or the network. It was Eden. Was this how she had felt that night on the pier? Had pushing Ava been her own last, desperate bid for freedom? She remembered the relief she saw on Eden's face, distorted through the currents as she sunk deeper into the ocean. Ava had always assumed it was relief at being rid of her. But now, she knew. It was relief at being rid of a life that had spun completely out of control.

"Hey."

Ava opened her eyes to find Mags standing in front of the 50-inch, with the DVD player in one hand, smiling. She raised the player in the air and then pounded it into the centre of the screen, over and over again, the corner of it making contact with Antonio's eye until a small hole appeared. She continued to smash the television until the screen was a mangled wreck. When they finally took her down, she let out a breath of air, but she never broke eye contact with Ava, and the smile never left her face.

The store manager was an Ava Hart fan.

"I won't call the cops," he said, leaning back in his desk chair, his hands behind his head. "You can just pay for the televisions. And let me take a selfie."

"Of course she can do that," Mags said when Ava didn't respond, nudging her with her foot.

"Oh. Of course, you want a selfie," Ava said, only dimly aware of the manager's gummy grin, his clammy hand on her shoulder as he moved in for the picture.

Once they were driving away in a cab, Ava watched through the window as the city flew past. She felt sick inside. "Did you see it?" she asked Mags as the cab pulled up to a stoplight, her eyes still fixed out the window.

"So that was Antonio?" Mags asked.

"Yeah."

Outside the window, a woman in a black parka struggled with a basset hound barking at something on the other side of the street. Ava wondered if it was the same one she had become friends with earlier. The woman hauled the dog back and when her head came up she and Ava made eye contact. Then the woman looked quickly away. *At least the dog doesn't know*, Ava thought. "I thought there were some parts of my life I could still keep to myself. I guess I was wrong."

Mags reached over and grabbed her hand. "There are *always* parts you can keep to yourself. They can never get all of you."

"You don't really believe that," Ava said. Mags didn't respond. The light turned green, and as the cab pulled away, Ava watched the woman staring after them through the back window, her phone in her hand, pointed at Ava.

After a few minutes, Mags told the driver to stop. "We'll actually get out here," she said.

"Where are we going?" Ava asked, as she stepped out of the cab.

"Come on!" Mags led her under the overpass, running across the street against the red, cars honking as they whizzed past. They kept running, but all Ava could see was darkness ahead of them, as though they were running right into an abyss. Suddenly, everything came into focus and she realized they had reached the waterfront. The abyss was Lake Ontario, stretching out in an inky blackness punctuated only by a few scattered lights from the islands. Like the pinpricks of stars in the night sky.

Once they were on the boardwalk, Mags slowed. "I used to come here when Sam was in the hospital," she said. "Sometimes I just needed to look at something really big. Like bigger than my life."

"It looks like the ocean," Ava said. At the thought, her throat closed over, the taste of salt thick in the back of her mouth.

"It pretty much is. Except it's fresh water." Mags climbed up onto the edge of the boardwalk. Ava's heart rippled in her chest, a

347

tiny tremor that sent needles of adrenaline through her veins. Then Mags threw her head back and screamed, long and loud, the sound echoing across the lake through the vast darkness. She turned to Ava. "Now you."

Tentatively, Ava climbed up next to her. Beneath her, she could see the black water swirling. But she found she was not afraid.

She tipped her head back and screamed.

Kyle Percival
3 hrs

OMG you guys won't believe what just happened . . . I was out with some of my buddies in Parkdale and my buddy Cody got the shit kicked out of him by Mags Kovach lololol!

👍 4,687   456 Comments   234 Shares
Like   Comment   Share

Dwayne Niles Bahahahaha **Cody** what the fuck did you do
Like • Reply • 3h

Cody Markovitz Dude she's fuckin crazy I had to get like six stitches in my fuckin face
Like • Reply • 3h

Dwayne Niles Lol
Like • Reply • 3h

Janay Cotter Holy shit
Like • Reply • 3h

Terrell McNeil Yo Cody, man how's it feel now the whole internet knows u got beat up by a girl
Like • Reply • 3h

Fiona March Wut
Like • Reply • 3h

Nikki Vanburen My dude
Like • Reply • 3h

Alissa Jean This is wild! I hope you're okay!
Like • Reply • 3h

Kellen Peyton I saw her and Ava Hart walking down Spadina like ten minutes ago

Like • Reply • 2h

Jade Leger You mean she's not in jail?

Like • Reply • 2h

Kellen Peyton Famous people don't go to jail, Jade, come on

Like • Reply • 2h

Chantay Keefer They have literally been all over Toronto in the past 24 hours. My friends saw them at Laundromat earlier

Like • Reply • 2h

Elisha Soriano My friend just saw them on Queen West and said they tried to steal her dog!!!!!!

Like • Reply • 1h

Align Above
Daily Update • February 21, 2015

NEWS

Align Above's Mags Kovach delivers "shocking" performance at Mercer Hall
The Toronto Herald
Rising Canadian music stars Align Above played their second of two sold-out shows in the city this week, but the band's stellar musical performance was overshadowed by the onstage antics of Kovach, who . . .

"It was like she didn't even realize we were there": Align Above strips it down – Toronto Today
Mags Kovach of Align Above bares it all at Mercer Hall in Toronto – Google Entertainment
Align Above's Kovach was "always hard to handle," according to estranged sister – TMI Online
"Disgusting" display at Align Above show a sign of the permissive (and promiscuous) times –New Canadian

Full Coverage
Share   Flag as irrelevant

Life, Death, and Rock and Roll: The Tragic Story Behind Align Above's *Nothingview*
Music Magazine
The tour has been notable for the increasingly erratic behaviour of frontwoman Kovach, but the album is marked by something even darker—each track is anchored by a bassline that has been written by a dying man.

Share   Flag as irrelevant

Concert Review: Align Above
The Times Ledger
What stage of grief is "capitalizing on your husband's death in order to make a name for yourself?" Because we think Mags Kovach might be stuck in that stage forever.

Share   Flag as irrelevant

Show more results / Edit this alert

Mags

Sunday, 8:30 a.m.

———◇———

A fter Sam died, there had been so many times when Mags had desperately wanted to believe in ghosts. Every strange coincidence, every misplaced object, every random sound in the night, she tried to convince herself was him, communicating from beyond the grave. She knew it wasn't true—even if Sam were a ghost, he would never deal in cryptic signs. If Sam were a ghost, he would take over a radio signal, he would appear in her television screen, he would find a billboard to announce his presence. HI MAGS, IT'S SAM. I'M A GHOST NOW. BOO! He wouldn't leave anything up to chance.

This is why she was sure—as she sat by the edge of the frozen lake, a bruise blossoming along her shoulder where she had landed when the bouncer threw her out—that the light drizzle that had begun falling from the sky wasn't a message from Sam. He would never have been so subtle. He would have made it pour.

The sun was struggling to rise, a pale light pushing through the grey. Mags didn't know how long they had stood by the lake screaming themselves into exhaustion, until they fell to the ground, unable to move. Eventually they had crawled to the lifeguard station and broken the lock, curling up against each other under a blanket on the hard floor. Next to her, Ava was tucked up in the fetal position, her eyes closed.

"Are you asleep?" Mags asked.

"Yes," Ava said.

"We should go before it really starts to rain." She didn't want to leave, and she didn't want to go home. But she had run out of options. It was time.

Mags pushed herself to her feet, then held her hand out to Ava, hoisting her up too. Then she brushed the sand off her coat, letting out a sigh. The lake sighed back in response, the ice cracking along the shoreline, restless for spring, for change, for renewal.

If only it were that simple, Mags thought.

When they got back to the apartment it was freezing. But it wasn't just the air making the room cold. It felt hollow and unfamiliar now, as though she were stepping into a stranger's apartment. That feeling lasted only a few seconds before the old, familiar grief began snaking its way back into her system, as comfortable as an old sweater. She suddenly wished Ava wasn't there, so she could be alone with it, slip it on, wrap it around herself.

She went directly to the kitchen and took out a bottle of rum from inside the microwave—one of several hiding places she had around the apartment. When she came back into the living room, Ava had taken off her parka and was sitting on the couch with the copy of the *National Chronicle* that Mags had picked up on their way home, from a box outside the Tim Hortons when Ava had run inside to use the bathroom. She had skimmed it, keeping her eyes half focused, not wanting to linger too long on any of the words. But now, the thought of Ava reading it filled her with a gnawing dread.

"What are you doing?" she asked.

Ava unfolded the paper. "I need something to do with my hands," she said. "Is the Jack Francis article in here?"

"No," said Mags, snatching the paper from her. "Just leave it."

"Sorry." Ava stuffed her hands into her pockets. "Do you want to go get breakfast or something? I'm starving."

"I don't think so. I need to start packing for Europe."

"You're actually going?"

"Of course," said Mags. She took a swig of the rum and immediately felt the warmth spreading through her body, the comforting embrace of an old friend.

Ava stared at her. "Mags, you can't. It's going to kill you."

"I have to." Mags put the bottle down and cleared her throat. "I have to keep singing."

"So just sing. Forget Europe. Forget all this big tour media bullshit. Just sing."

"What are you talking about?"

Ava sat up excitedly. "You could go out to some small bar and just play your guitar, and it would be this amazing moment, like a redemption moment, but it would be on your own terms. People would be talking about it for days."

Mags studied Ava's face. There was something fractured about her, two versions of herself superimposed over one another but slightly askew, like a photograph taken as someone is moving, so Mags was never quite sure which one to focus on. "This is reality, Ava, not some stupid television show," she said. "Life doesn't have redemption arcs, it just has people who fuck up and then have to live with the consequences. There is no beautiful resolution, and you can't script one. When you lose everything, all you have left is yourself, and the decisions you make."

"Why not?" Ava asked. "You're infuriating. Why are you so attached to your pain?"

"Why am *I* attached to my pain? I have never met anyone more attached to her pain than you." She clasped her hands to her chest.

"Oh, Antonio, I miss you so much! I'm going to fucking throw myself off a balcony because nothing matters without you. If it hadn't been for me, you'd have ended up splattered all over the street."

"Oh. I get it, you think you're my saviour now, do you?" Ava narrowed her eyes. "When I first got here, you were passed out naked in the hallway outside your apartment."

"I was not." But Mags knew it was true. She took a drink of rum as flashes of memory came back to her, gripped the bottle to keep herself from decking Ava in the face.

"What is going on with you right now?" Ava asked. "You've been acting weird since we got back here."

"Oh, I'm sorry, I didn't know you had the monopoly on tragedy," Mags said. "Or did you forget my husband died?"

"How could I forget? You've been using it as an excuse to drink yourself to death."

"Jesus Christ, Ava, it's not an excuse. I need to keep performing."

"No, you don't. You don't need to keep doing anything that hurts you."

"Yes, I do. I need to go to Europe and do this tour, and it needs to go well."

"You don't have to keep doing this to yourself, Mags. You can quit."

"Like it's so easy to walk away. I mean, I know it was easy for you, but you don't give a shit about anything or anyone but yourself. The rest of us, we actually care about things, you know. We make commitments to people and we keep them. We don't just give up because we're sad or because things get too hard." She brought the bottle to her lips, taking a deep drink. "Maybe if you stuck it out more, you wouldn't have to turn to a stranger for help."

"What is wrong with you? Why are you being so mean?"

Mags could see the hurt in Ava's eyes, but she didn't give her an answer because she didn't have one. She felt as powerless as she did when she was fifteen and the rage would build up inside

356

her and she didn't know where it came from or how to control it.

"You know," Ava continued, "where you see commitment, I just see you letting Emiko walk all over you. No manager should be prioritizing a stupid tour over your health and well-being."

Mags laughed. "Oh, right. Like Antonio prioritized *your* health and well-being. Let me ask you, Ava, did you ever think he might have slept with your sister too? Is that why she pushed you into the ocean?"

Ava paled. "Fuck you," she said, but her voice was shaking, and Mags knew she'd done it. She had found the perfect spot for her knife.

"You're so obsessed with Antonio, with your ridiculous childish heartbreak. But I've never even heard you talk about your sister once. Not once. Did you think I didn't know about her? About how she tried to drown you? I read up on you, Ava, after you tried to throw yourself off that balcony. I know all about your sister in rehab. Do you even know if she's still alive? She could have died of an overdose months ago and you wouldn't even have noticed, would you?"

Ava's lip trembled, but she didn't cry. "Well, if she had, at least I wouldn't try to capitalize on it."

Mags sucked in a breath. "Get out," she said. "Get the hell out of my apartment."

Ava stared at her in disbelief. Then she grabbed the parka and walked out the door.

After Ava left, Mags went into the bathroom and stood in front of the mirror for a long time, watching as her reflection waxed and waned as she focused and unfocused her eyes. *How can I do this?* she thought. *How can I go out there and do this alone? What kind of monster am I?*

In the shower, she calmed herself by watching the water swirl down the drain, taking with it the coating of sand from the beach, the alcoholic sheen, the chlorine smell of the pool, the dried blood from the guy she had hit, the high-frequency buzz of her heart slowing with every layer of grime that fell from her body. The calmness, she knew, wouldn't last—it would disappear the second she shut off the water, no matter how much she tried to hold on to it. So she stayed in the shower until the water got cold. Then she found herself standing naked and dripping in the middle of the kitchen, staring at the toaster, thinking about Sam. She tried to remember him in that room, the way he had turned the dials on the stove, the way he had placed his hands on the cupboard handles. The way he made toast—how much he had hated their toaster, how he could never get the settings exactly the way he wanted, and instead of just being able to toast his toast he would have to stand there and wait until the perfect moment and then make it pop up himself, because there was no setting on the dial that was his perfect toast setting. His perfect toast setting did not exist outside the realm of his own imagination. But she couldn't picture it—did he stand on the left-hand side of the toaster, or the right? Did he lean against the counter, or did he bend down, hands on thighs, peering into the slots? She couldn't remember.

She exhaled slowly. It had been seven months since Sam had died—of course she was starting to forget things. And not just the things that she'd purposefully forgotten through the drinking, but things she had assumed were so ingrained in her memory that she would never lose them: the sound of his voice in the mornings, when he woke her up with his mouth on her ear to tell her the coffee was ready; the shape of his body as he moved around the apartment, his bass hanging from a strap around his shoulders at all times, like an extra appendage. The smell of his soap, which she still washed with, the scent changing with the chemistry of her own skin, so that it didn't even come close to smelling like him anymore.

The feel of his hands on her body, which she had known since she was fifteen, the way they traced around her edges, reaching with their softness the places she could never reach herself.

These things had all started to fade, and she had noticed and yet hadn't noticed, the drinking muting everything, including the noticing. And when she did notice, with the drinking, it didn't matter. The feeling of Sam's memory slipping away was floating in a bubble at the edge of her peripheral vision. She could watch it floating there with a detached curiosity, but it didn't touch her. It didn't reach into her gut and pull everything out onto the floor.

She thought about those first days and weeks after Sam died. Those had been the worst months of her life, and she knew it was the fear of returning to that place that had kept her on the road, kept her running. But she suddenly felt an aching nostalgia for those months, for a time when there was nothing standing between her and her pain.

She spent ten minutes looking for her phone before she remembered smashing it in the alley. So she went into the bedroom and opened Sam's drawer, which she hadn't touched since he died. His phone sat on top of his pajama pants, the ones he'd been wearing when she took him to the hospital. She closed her eyes, reached in, pulled out the phone, and slammed the drawer shut.

When she turned it on, she discovered it still had battery life, which momentarily stunned her, a choked sob rising up from her chest. At least there were no new notifications. She wasn't sure she would have been able to handle that.

"Jesus, Mags, you almost gave me a heart attack," Emiko said when she answered. "I thought you were Sam phoning me from beyond the grave."

If Emiko were actually having a heart attack, Mags thought, *would anyone even notice?* "I've changed my mind. I need some time off," Mags said. "I can't do this right now. I'm not ready."

"You had time off," Emiko said coolly. "You had two days. That's the length of a weekend, which is what most normal working people get. How much more time could you possibly need?"

"I don't know. I need some time to get better." Mags lit a cigarette, hand shaking, and moved toward the open window. She had given up on not smoking in the apartment. "I don't want to keep living like this."

Emiko sighed. "What do you want me to do, Mags? Cancel the tour?"

"Yes, I want you to cancel the fucking tour!" Mags said, although she hadn't known that was what she wanted until she said it out loud. "You shouldn't have planned the tour in the first place, Em. You should have known it wasn't going to work."

"If you do that, you kill the band."

"At least it's better than killing myself."

"Is it?"

"Jesus, Em." Mags pressed her forehead against the window, feeling a cold ache spread across her skin. "I feel like everything is spinning out of control."

"Save it for your shrink." Mags could hear water running on the other end of the phone, and she tried to imagine Emiko standing in her apartment, washing her hands, pouring a glass of water, filling a sink with water to do dishes. But she couldn't picture it. Mags had never seen Emiko's apartment; she didn't even know if she lived in an apartment. As far as Mags knew, she lived in an airtight pod. "We are not cancelling the tour. You have a contract. If you don't show up to the airport tomorrow, the rest of the band will sue you. Do you understand?"

"Perfectly," Mags said, and hung up the phone. She stubbed her cigarette out and lit another immediately, not even bothering to blow the smoke out the window. What did it matter anymore?

February 22, 2015

Quiz: Are You a Mags or an Ava?
Because everyone knows that BFFs are always a binary

By Stella Stewart

Pick an ice cream flavour
☐ Vanilla
☐ Rum raisin

Pick a movie
☐ *Knocked Up*
☐ *Ghost*

What feature do you like most about yourself?
☐ Your hair
☐ Your boobs

You're stranded on a desert island. How do you get rescued?
☐ Using a seashell as a horn, you call your lobster minions to ferry you across the water in a seaweed chariot
☐ You flash your boobs at a passing helicopter

What's your favourite kind of spider?
☐ Diving bell spider
☐ Red widow

What did you have for breakfast this morning?
☐ Lobster benedict
☐ A cigarette and two shots of whiskey

The year is 2057. The robots have risen up and taken over the Earth. What are you doing?

☐ You're in cyberprison for murdering several televisions

☐ You flash your boobs at a passing robot and they make you their queen

13 Comments

Mari Jarvis Mags!
Like • Reply • 8 min

Annie Yee Mags
Like • Reply • 8 min

Rachel Billingsly Mags
Like • Reply • 8 min

Colleen Olsen Ava!! Yay
Like • Reply • 7 min

Cassandra Dwyer I got Ava! lol
Like • Reply • 6 min

> **Kyla Roland** oh cass you are such an ava
> Like • Reply • 6 min
>
> **Cassandra Dwyer** Right? Vanilla forever.
> Like • Reply • 6 min

Michael David What is even the difference? they're both trashy rich white sluts with too much time on their hands and not enough supervision
Like • Reply • 5 min

> **Shenika Savoy** They're not children
> Like • Reply • 5 min
>
> **Michael David** They might as well be
> Like • Reply • 5 min
>
> **Pete Knudson** They are two grown-ass women who should know better
> Like • Reply • 4 min

Cordie Rauch I got Ava but I'm sure I'm much more of a Mags
Like • Reply • 3 min

Natalia Huggins an Ava in the streets a Mags in the sheets
Like • Reply • 3 min

Ava

Sunday, 11:56 a.m.

———◇———

A va stepped out onto the street. Her entire body was humming, as though she were trapped in the hollow of a ringing bell, all sensation obliterated by the vibrations. She watched the cars driving by in front of her without hearing them, dug her feet into the snow on the edge of the sidewalk without feeling the cold. A few lazy snowflakes drifted down from the sky and landed on her eyelashes, melting into drops of water that trickled over her cheeks and fell onto her parka in dark splotches like tears. She reached up to wipe her face and realized they *were* tears, hot and briny on her hands. She hadn't even felt them at all.

Without any place to go, she went into the cupcake store beneath Mags's apartment, ordered a red velvet cupcake, and sat at a table in the back corner. She had wanted something sweet to take the edge off, but she could barely taste it as she chewed, the cake dry in her mouth, the frosting sticking in the back of her throat. How long she sat there—staring straight ahead, trying not to think about Mags's words—she didn't know. Eventually, she tried to kick her brain into gear, to figure out where to go from here. She hadn't thought about much in the past few days except surviving in the gravitational pull of Mags's orbit. Now that she had broken free, she had no idea what to do.

As she stepped back out onto the street, she heard a voice call her name.

"Thank god," he said as he got closer. "It is you."

She stood there staring at him, stunned. He looked dishevelled, his chin shaded with stubble, his hair standing away from his scalp on one side. *Breathe*, she told herself. *Just breathe.* "Antonio. What are you doing here?

"I drove here. From New York. I needed to talk to you, and you weren't answering my calls."

It had only been six days, but it felt like six years. The enormity of this only fully hit her when she heard his voice. How something could be so strange and so familiar, as though he were speaking to her from a memory, or a dream. "I lost my phone," she said. "How did you find me?"

Antonio shrugged. "You're not exactly keeping a low profile. I called in a favour at Align Above's label and got Mags Kovach's address." His eyes travelled down her body, then back up again. "You look different."

I am different, she wanted to say. "Okay," she said instead. "Here I am. Talk."

He was silent for so long that Ava wondered if he was going to say anything at all. She watched him inhale and exhale, his chest rising under his down vest. *He's making himself breathe too*, she thought.

Finally, he ran his hands through his hair. "Now that I'm here, I don't know what to say."

"That doesn't sound like you."

Antonio gave a short laugh. "I honestly didn't think I would get this far. I thought you'd punch me or something."

"Yeah, well," she said. Her mouth dry. "I still might."

"I'd better say something good, then."

"You should have written something down."

He patted his pocket. "I did, but I'm not going to read it. It's unreadable. Seriously. It's ten pages."

Ava smiled. It was so easy with him. To fall into the same banter, to backslide into the same roles. Then, in a sudden flood of memory it came back to her, all the reasons why she had left.

"Go fuck yourself, Antonio."

"Yeah," he said. "I was wondering when that was coming."

"No, seriously," said Ava. "Take a long, sharp, jagged object and swiftly and thoroughly fuck yourself with it. Then get back to me and tell me how it feels."

Antonio moved closer to her. "I didn't do this," he said. "You have to believe me. The van was broken into. Someone stole the camera. I need you to know I didn't do this."

"But you did." Ava took a step back. She couldn't risk him getting too close to her, close enough to touch, close enough to hurt. "Maybe you didn't release the tape, Antonio, but everything else—that was you."

"You're right." His voice bent under the weight of his breath.

"I gave you everything."

"I know, all right?" he shouted. "I know. I know. I know." He leaned against a telephone pole, letting his head fall back briefly. "This is bad for me too, Ava. Molly is leaving me. I think I'm about to be fired. And if anyone finds out how long this has been going on, I'm screwed."

"Are you here to cover your own ass, Antonio? Is that it? You want to make sure I don't tell anyone about how you took me to a pub and had your hands on me when I was fifteen? Or about how after I left the hospital, you came back to the house, knowing I'd be alone and confused?"

Silence. Then: "You're not going to, are you?"

365

Ava closed her eyes. "Get the hell away from me."

"No!" She felt his hand on her arm, and her eyes flew open. "Look, if that were the only thing I wanted, would I have driven all this way? I slept the whole night in my car, Ava, waiting for you to come back here."

"You're only here because you want to make sure I keep all your secrets. Every time I turned around, there you were, telling me the things you knew I wanted to hear, making me think that you cared about me. But you didn't give a shit about me then and you don't now."

"That's not true." His face was inches from hers, his eyes dark and pleading. "I miss you. I want you to come back. Not for the show. For me. I want us to be together, like a real couple. I want to be good for you." He lowered his eyes. "I want to be better."

Ava didn't know whether to laugh or scream. It was such a perfectly calibrated performance, so desperate in its Hollywood earnestness, a rom-com cliché. And yet, somehow, it was working. She felt as though she were on the brink of falling, without anything to grab on to, without any safe place to land.

But then, miraculously, something caught her. "She isn't going back to New York." Mags stood in the doorway of her apartment building, in bare feet and pajama pants, her hair wrapped in a towel, an unlit cigarette pinched between her fingers. "For the show, or for you."

"I think I'd like to hear that from Ava," Antonio said, keeping his eyes focused on her.

"Okay," Ava said, without hesitation. "I'm not going back to New York. For the show or for you."

He clenched his fists by his sides, and she briefly feared that he was going to hit her. She remembered how she used to love to try to make him angry, to crack that impenetrable exterior. It never worked. He had always stayed calm, in control, no matter what she threw at him. But now, the exterior wasn't only cracked, it was split open, and she could see everything—every last dark corner of his soul, frantically clawing for purchase now that everything around it had shattered.

"What are you going to do, Ava?" he asked, stepping away from her and putting his hands in his pockets. "You can't *do* anything. You have nothing without us."

When you lose everything, she thought, *all you have left is yourself*. She knew she would be all right. She couldn't say the same for him.

"*Us*? Who is *us*?" she asked. "You don't have anyone left. You are the one who has nothing." She stepped up onto the stoop next to Mags. "Goodbye, Antonio. If you ever come near me or my family again, I promise you I will be on the phone to TMI and Zoe Conrad and *The Cynthia Show* so fast you won't even know what happened. And if you think you have nothing *now*, wait until you see how much more you can lose."

Antonio stood there, glaring at them, the anger on his face never wavering. Then he turned and walked back to his car. Ava watched him go, her entire body growing lighter with each step he took away from her. She knew she wouldn't see him again, but instead of the pain she expected, all she felt was relief.

Mags lit the cigarette and leaned against the doorway. "You didn't get very far."

"No, I didn't." Ava paused. "Thanks for saving me. Again."

Mags smiled at her. "You saved yourself."

She held out her cigarette. Ava shook her head, but then took it anyway, letting the smoke fill her lungs, waiting for the dizziness, the head rush. But it didn't come. That was how she knew. She really was a different person.

—◇—

They went across the street for breakfast, some faux-'50s rocka-billy diner with a jukebox at every table and eggs served on plates shaped like different states. Ava ordered the two-egg breakfast with a side of pancakes, which came served on Montana. She couldn't remember the last time she had eaten a real meal.

Mags watched her devour the pancake stack with bemuse-ment. "Where do you put it all?" she asked. She had only ordered a bagel, plain and untoasted on a saucer-sized Rhode Island, and had barely touched it beyond a couple of unenthusiastic nibbles.

"Existential angst makes me hungry," Ava said, shoving a piece of bacon into her mouth, whole. "I am filling the void inside me with breakfast foods."

Cocking her head to the side, Mags regarded her with tired eyes. "You're not letting that toolbox get to you, are you? There are plenty of things you're good at."

Ava wiped some bacon grease from her chin with her hand. "Name one."

Mags gestured to the window, where a girl with a platinum pixie cut was walking by, oblivious to her style guru sitting on the other side of the glass. "Well, you inspired the hairstyle of a genera-tion. That's something."

Ava touched her hair. "I didn't plan it. I just cut off all my hair on a whim and everyone did the same thing."

Mags laughed. "Seriously?"

"Yup."

"Jesus." Mags began picking creamers out of their bowl and stacking them on top of one another. "Was it a breakdown or some-thing? Some kind of Britney Spears head-shaving thing?"

Ava pulled on a lock of her hair, remembering the hospital room, the man with the scissors. "Actually, a stranger cut it for me. In the hospital. The night my sister tried to drown me."

There was a brief flash of shock on Mags's face, there and gone before Ava could even be sure she had seen it. Then Mags reached forward and tucked a loose tendril of Ava's hair behind her ear. "Well, whoever it was, he did a good job."

Ava flushed, and cleared her throat. "It felt like it was weighing on me. I guess I thought that if I could cut away the hair, maybe I could cut away what happened with Eden. It's stupid, I know."

"Do you ever talk to Eden?"

Ava shook her head. "I didn't hear from her the whole time she was in rehab. And then yesterday she texted me, and that's why I smashed my phone." She traced her finger through a drop of syrup on the tabletop. "I was so mad at her for so long. I mean, she tried to *drown* me. But now, when I think about all the ways I wasn't there for her . . ." She trailed off, licking the syrup from her finger. "Well, I would have tried to drown me too."

The creamer stack was now as high as Mags's chin. She balanced another one on top, steadying it as it wobbled. "I have a sister," she said.

"Really?" Ava couldn't remember Mags ever talking about a sister. "What's she like?"

"Stubborn, angry, lost. A lot like me, I suppose." She let the creamer go and suddenly the entire pyramid came crashing down, scattering over the table.

Heads turned at the sound, but no one seemed to have recognized them. Still, Ava leaned in toward the wall, shielding her face with her hands. "You're not lost. You're just *sad*, Mags. There's a difference." She pulled a creamer out of her coffee and took a sip. "I've never met anyone with as clear a sense of purpose as you. You're not lost."

"Yeah, well. Frankie is. We haven't spoken in years." Mags swept the creamers back into the bowl, and then straightened up. "I would kill to get a text from her. Even after everything she's done."

"What would you say to her?" Ava asked.

Mags focused her eyes on a spot on the table. "I'd tell her that I know how she feels, why she's angry all the time," she said. "I'd tell her she fucked me up really good, but I'm going to get help, and I'm going to get better." She paused. "I'd tell her that I forgive her even if she doesn't forgive me."

Ava tried out the words in her mind. *I forgive you even if you don't forgive me.* "That seems about right." she said. She raised her eyebrow. "Does this mean you're not going to Europe?"

"No, I'm not." Mags lifted her gaze to meet Ava's, bringing her coffee to her lips. Even though her hands were trembling, for the first time since Ava had been with her in Toronto, she seemed clearheaded, sure of herself. "I'm going to check myself into rehab. I promised someone I could look after myself, and now I have to prove it." Her eyes flicked to the next booth, where someone had left a copy of the *National Chronicle* open on the table. She reached over and grabbed it, pushing it across the table toward Ava. "But there's something I have to do first."

That Thing She Does
Align Above's Mags Kovach

By Jack Francis

It's a Saturday afternoon, and I'm sitting in a pub in Toronto's Parkdale neighbourhood waiting for Mags Kovach, the enigmatic frontwoman of the nation's new indie rock darlings, Align Above. Outside it is snowing, and the floor of the pub is covered in a grimy slush, and parka-wearing patrons are slumped over their stouts at the bar, looking like they might stay there all winter.

Kovach is late and I'm nervous. It's my first time meeting the singer, and we're on her home turf. We're meeting at the Nest, a place where she and her band played frequently when they first moved to Toronto in 2013, and a few blocks from the apartment she shared with her late husband, Sam Cole, Align Above's long-time bassist. Cole passed away on July 22, 2014, from complications from bone cancer, at the age of twenty-one. As if that weren't tragic enough, while Cole was able to complete recording the band's first major label record, *Nothingview*, sadly, he didn't live long enough to see its release. After years of moderate indie success, with *Nothingview*, Align Above has had a meteoric rise to fame. The album was an instant success, and broke the band into the U.S. market, with the title track hitting number 5 on the Billboard charts and landing them a rotation of performances on late-night talk shows, including *Late Night with Zoe Conrad*, as well as a musical guest spot on *Saturday Night Live*.

It sounds like a terrible thing to say, but it's what many have been thinking: ultimately, the tragedy of Cole's death has been a boon to Align Above's career and to Kovach's fame.

But although rumours have been swirling about Kovach's struggles performing many of the songs from the new record, many of which she co-wrote with Cole, the band has just wrapped up a successful three-month

371

North American tour, with Josh Falco, formerly of Roofpuppy, filling in on bass. The band is on a brief hiatus before jumping across the pond for several tour dates in Europe. It's during this break that Kovach agreed to speak to me.

I'm also nervous because, well, it's Mags Kovach. Known to most as just "Mags," she is a bona fide rock star, and—I'm sure my wife won't mind me saying this, because it's true—she's hot as hell. The first time I saw Align Above perform, it was in a dingy basement bar in Halifax known for breaking local bands, and the bar was packed—I mean packed—with local scenesters, many of whom had been following the band since their first EP in 2010. There were at least two forgettable opening acts, both of whom the crowd tolerated, but by the time Align Above came out, the crowd was tired of waiting, and ready for the main act. As soon as Kovach stepped onstage, wearing a tight black dress and thigh-high black boots, her hair a red flame around her head, the crowd lost their minds. I somehow made my way to the front of the stage, and at one point Kovach looked right at me and flashed me a peace sign. We had what I like to call a "moment," one unlike I've ever had in my 20 years of music journalism. Of course, the rational part of my brain told me that I wasn't special, that it wasn't a "moment," that she was out there making every man in the audience feel like the only man in the room. I didn't care. I was instantly in love. And that was when she slowly and seductively pulled her scarf off from around her neck and dropped it into my hands. It was like she was dropping manna from heaven.

I still have that scarf, hanging on the wall in my study. I had considered bringing it to the interview, but I was selfish and I didn't want to have to give it back. I'm wondering whether Kovach would remember this encounter as the door to the bar opens and the singer herself appears, stamping her boots in the doorway and pushing back her hood. All the heads in the bar turn toward her. She's a regular here, but she still manages to cause a stir. She's wearing a grey coat and fur-lined black winter boots that look like something one might wear on an Arctic expedition, but I can tell that underneath it all she is quite petite, much smaller than she appears onstage. With her hair pulled back into a ponytail and no makeup, she still looks gorgeous. Personal tragedy or not, whatever she has been doing in the past few months looks good on her.

372

"Sorry I'm late," she breathes, in that trademark husky voice. "A fight broke out on the streetcar and I had to walk."

And this, right here, is what sets Kovach apart from all her other teeny-bopper counterparts: a bona fide rock star, and the girl still takes public transit.

She orders a gin and tonic, even though it's mid-afternoon, and sits down across from me. The first thing I notice when I make eye contact with her is that she holds it—she's not one to shy away from intensity. Eventually it's me who looks away, and I can feel myself blushing. In that instant, my mind is full of all kinds of fantasies, most of them variations on the idea of us running off together, starting a new life on a beach somewhere in Jamaica. But when I look back, I see that Kovach is blithely checking her phone, the straw of her drink nestled between her pillowy lips, and I realize that the sexual tension I felt between us was possibly all in my imagination. But what can I say. Kovach has that effect on people. And now that she is newly widowed, the allure only grows—clearly something that she has made work to her advantage in the past few weeks of touring.

Her manager has already warned me to stay off the topic of Cole, so instead I ask Kovach about their two-night stint in Toronto. "I was there for the first show, which was incredible. But I heard the show last night was, well, pretty epic," I say.

Kovach's eyes grow distant. "Yeah," she said. "I mean, I love playing in my hometown, of course." She tosses her straw around in her drink. "I wasn't feeling well, so . . . I was worried. But it turned out to be great." She smiles behind her phone, a secret smile that makes me wonder what she means by "great."

"The success, it's been pretty overwhelming," she says, and I wonder if I am catching a slight waver in her voice. "But it's what I was meant to do. This is what I was meant to do."

Thinking back to that show in Halifax, I ask her if she remembers it. But my details are fuzzy, and it's clear she has many blurry memories of dingy basement shows in Halifax to sift through. "Maybe you remember me," I say. "I was standing near the front. You caught my eye at one point and flashed me a peace sign."

"Oh," Kovach says. "Yeah, I remember." She holds my gaze for another long moment, still sipping her drink. And it occurs to me that I will never know if she does remember, or if this is just something she says to everyone, if this is just that thing she does that makes every man feel like the most important man in the room. And I realize I don't care. This is part of the mystique of Mags Kovach. This is what we keep coming back for. And this is what will keep taking her band to the top of the charts.

Mags

Sunday, 4:45 p.m.

I t didn't take them long to figure out where Jack Francis lived. He was in the phone book, for Christ's sake. Some cul-de-sac in Scarborough, where all sad old scenesters go to die, apparently. They took public transit, huddled in the back in hoodies and sunglasses and toques, the newspaper still clutched in Mags's hand.

"He didn't even get the details right," Ava had said, at the diner. They'd spread the paper out on the table, and Mags had watched Ava's face as she read it, her eyes growing darker as the words sunk in. "What is even the point of making up stuff about your drink?"

"I guess it fits better with his idea of me." This was the part that killed Mags—that to people like Jack Francis, her life was just fuel for their fantasies, something to manipulate however it suited them. "Why do people think they can say whatever they want about us?"

"We're public property," Ava said. "People think our stories belong to them."

Mags looked down at the paper, thinking about how many people had already read it, how many more people were now claiming her story for themselves. A scream caught in her throat, a scream that was still echoing inside her, gaining momentum the longer it stayed trapped.

"This is it," Mags said now, standing in front of a brick house, Christmas lights still twinkling even though it was almost March, snow piled in perfect snowblower lines on either side of a driveway. The Christmas lights were on but the house was dark. No car in the driveway, no shadows moving anywhere. "What do we do now?" she asked. She still had the newspaper in her hand, hadn't let it go the whole time. She wanted to stuff it down his throat. She wanted to make him choke on it.

"We ring the bell," Ava said. "We ring the bell." But she just stood there, staring.

Finally, Mags pressed the doorbell. They waited, but no one came. "Come on," she said. "Where are you, Jack?"

They tried the door, but it was locked. Then they made their way around to the back door and tried that too. Nothing. No signs of life anywhere. Clearly, neither of them had thought this through at all.

"There's got to be a way in. Even if there's an alarm, we can beat it." Mags felt reckless, invincible. They could outrun an alarm. They could outrun the police. They could outrun anything.

Ava took a step back. "You want to break in? And do what?"

"I don't know!" Mags began pounding on the door. "All I know is we're in fucking Scarborough and I am really fucking angry and I am not going back until I do *something*."

Ava bit her lip. Then she turned and started walking through the garden, focusing on the ground. Before Mags could say anything, Ava had picked up a rock and smashed it through the window of the back door. Mags braced for an alarm, but nothing came.

Nothing but silence and a dog barking off in the distance. Ava reached through the opening, unlocked the door, and walked into the back porch.

Mags followed her. "What now?" she whispered.

"Let's find his office," Ava said. "That's a good place to start."

They walked through the house in the dark. It was a strange thrill, to be inside someone else's home when you weren't supposed to be. It made Mags want to go through his cupboards, see what she could steal, just for the sake of stealing it. They felt their way along the hallway until they got to what looked like it could be Jack's study. Ava flicked on the lights. Behind his desk, there was a picture on the wall of Mags, in the middle of a performance, her mouth open, her face dripping with sweat. She knew it was probably a media photo, but in that moment, Mags felt Jack Francis had taken the last piece of her soul.

As she took in the rest of the room, she realized there were similar pictures lining the walls, all of different female musicians, each captured mid-performance in that moment of pure, exultant joy that Mags knew so well, when they were giving all of themselves to the music, to the audience, when they were at their most vulnerable, their most open. Of course, she hadn't been the first. And she was certain that she wouldn't be the last. Jack Francis would keep getting published, and so would all the others—the ones with their names at the tops of the mastheads and captioned under the photographs, the ones in control. They would move on to the next bright young thing and chip away at *her* self-worth until she came to believe what they believed about her—that she was nothing more than tits and ass and a smile.

A wildfire of rage swept through her, obliterating everything in its wake. "Fuck this," Mags said, and ripped the picture off the wall, throwing it on the floor in the middle of the room. Then she knocked everything off the desk, including his computer, smashing it to the floor. She started going through drawers, pulling out note-books, boxes of papers, memory sticks, and throwing them all into the pile, building it higher and higher toward the ceiling like a funeral pyre for Jack Francis's career.

"Here," said Ava, throwing a stack of papers on the pile. "These were from that file cabinet over there."

Soon, they had a looming stack of papers in the centre of his office that was almost as tall as Mags and Ava. One man's life's work, smugly telling other people's stories as though they were his to exploit however he wanted. The thought of it made her sick.

"You know what the worst thing is? I do remember," Mags said, staring at the pile, her brain suddenly clear, pin-sharp and focused. "I remember the show he's talking about in the article. There was blood on my scarf from when Sam hurt himself falling down the stairs, and I couldn't stand to look at it. Couldn't stand to have it on me. So I threw it away. I'm tired, Ava," she said. "I'm just really, really tired." She gazed down at her hands, which were covered in newsprint. How easily these words could smudge, she thought. How easily they gave the illusion of disappearing.

"What do we do now?" Ava asked.

Mags didn't say anything as she pulled a Zippo out of her pocket and struck the flint.

"Wait," said Ava.

Mags's hand vibrated with tension, the flame dancing in front of her eyes. "Don't try to stop me," she said.

"Of course not," said Ava. From the wall, she pulled down a piece of fabric that Mags immediately recognized as her scarf. "I just thought you should add this."

Mags took the scarf and tossed it on the pile. For a moment, she hesitated. Something felt off, like even fire wasn't enough.

Mags moved the flame of her Zippo back and forth, her eyes trailing behind. Suddenly, she felt a vibration in the back pocket of her jeans. Sam's phone. She was sure she had turned it off. But when she reached back and pulled it out, the screen was glowing and open to the video camera.

Mags smiled. She knew he wouldn't be subtle.

She pressed record. Then she tossed the Zippo on the pile.

burn it all down

4,176,683 views

👍 85K   👎 1.3K   SHARE

Mags Kovach   SUBSCRIBE 8.7M
Published on February 22, 2015

You want to watch us set ourselves on fire.
We're not going to do that anymore.

It's your turn, motherfuckers.

—Mags and Ava

Comments have been disabled for this video

Ava

Monday, 12:34 a.m.

———◇———

The plane back to Halifax had been late, and by the time Ava had convinced the woman at the Hertz desk to rent her a car, it was already past 10 p.m. She hadn't driven since she had gotten her licence in Season 4, Episode 14, "Tell It to My Hart," and the roads were slippery after a warm spell followed by a deep freeze, so she drove slowly and carefully and didn't get to the B&B until after midnight.

She knew she didn't have much time.

The lights were off in the front of the house, but when she stepped up onto the porch she could see a glow coming from somewhere down the long hall, hear the faint sound of music wafting through an open window into the winter night. The front door was unlocked, so she stepped inside, following the light and sound.

David and Bryce were in the kitchen. David was making pancakes—"Pancakes at Midnight," they used to call it back when they lived in New York—dropping batter in a pan and then topping it with banana slices as the butter sizzled around the edges. Bryce stood next to him, phone clutched in his hand, his shoulders slumped, his eyes downcast. She couldn't hear what he was saying, but when he was finished, David stared at him a moment before pulling him close, kissing his forehead.

"Hey," a voice said behind her. She turned to find Val standing in the hallway, in bare feet and pajama pants, a pair of headphones hanging around his neck. "You came home."

"Yeah," Ava said softly. "So did you."

Val shrugged, grinning. "You know what they say."

"Don't," said Ava, raising an eyebrow, a smile playing on her lips. "Don't you dare."

"Trust me, I wouldn't dream of it."

A peel of laughter came from the kitchen, piercing the silence of the house. They both turned to watch Bryce and David, who were now sitting at the table, eating the pancakes. "They look so old," Ava said.

"Well, you're not twelve anymore either." Val paused. "She's upstairs, you know."

"I figured." She turned back around to look at Val. She wanted to say something to him, to tell him how much he meant to her, to fill in all those gaps in every conversation they'd ever had. But he had his headphones back on, his eyes focused somewhere else, and Ava realized it didn't matter. She didn't need to fill in the gaps with words. With family, they filled in with something else.

She moved toward the stairs, tiptoeing down the creaky hallway to the staff door. She had no idea if the B&B was actually running, if there were any guests there, real or pretend, but she didn't want to find out. Finally, she reached Eden's room. The door was ajar, and Ava could see Eden sitting on her bed, propped up with pillows, a book in her hand. When she closed her eyes she saw Mags's face, her eyes reflecting the glow of the flames licking the ceiling, her lips parted in a soft smile as black flakes of ash fell around her hair like snow.

Ava took a deep breath. Then she knocked gently on the door and went inside.

Acknowledgements

First and foremost, thank you to my editor, Anita Chong. I honestly don't think I will ever be able to properly express how much your support means to me and how much you have helped me grow, both as a writer and a human being.

I'm grateful to the extraordinary team who have helped make the book you're holding possible: my agent, Chris Bucci; my publicist, Ruta Liormonas; Jared Bland, Joe Lee, Kimberlee Hesas, Erin Kelly, and the rest of the team at M&S; as well as Kelly Hill, Gemma Wain, Heather Sangster, Tyson Erb, and Ali Eisner.

Also huge thank yous to Andrew F. Sullivan, Naben Ruthnum, Rudrapriya Rathore, Kris Bertin, Ashley MacCuish, Kevin Hardcastle, Jenna Illies, Kirsti Salmi, Sarah Ramsey, Nancy Jo Cullen, Peter and Natalie Smyk, Jeff Nichols, Laura Hanson, Tova Rosenberg, Jen Davidson, Jess Taylor, Taslim Alani-Verjee, Matthew J. Trafford, Trevor Corkum, Chantal Mittag, the Canada Council for the Arts, the Ontario Arts Council, the Joneses, the Sullivans, and, of course, Iggy.

Discussion Questions
for *Every Little Piece of Me*

1. The novel weaves together the compelling stories of two wilful young women who are often forced to conform to other people's rules at great personal cost. In what ways is *Every Little Piece of Me* engaging with current conversations about what it means to be a woman in the world?

2. How did the shift in time between the book's prologue and the first chapter affect your reading experience? Did you make any assumptions at the beginning of the novel that were later overturned? Were there moments that surprised you in the trajectories of the characters?

3. In the opening chapters, David and Bryce seem like loving, doting parents. But once they sign on for *Home Is Where the Hart Is* without the consent of Ava, Val, and Eden, their role in their children's lives quickly begins to shift. What motivates David and Bryce as parents? What responsibility do they bear for the people Eden, Val, and Ava become in their teenage years?

4. Mags is an orphan who, after falling out with her sister, Frankie, finds a tenuous home with Sam, whose own parents are far removed.

Through her involvement with Sam, Mags becomes part of another "family" unit—the band. What parallels can be drawn between the relationships within the band and the sibling relationships depicted in the narrative? Which scenes in particular suggest similarities or points of divergence?

5. Antonio is an adult and Ava is in her early teens when they first meet, and he has a powerful influence on her life and career. Yet Ava often defies Antonio, and she is not without agency in the events that unfold between them. Is Ava a victim of Antonio's? Why or why not?

6. The symbol of the deer, or the hart, threads throughout the novel. What does the hart represent? What do Mags's encounters with the deer, in the van and during the rainstorm, portend?

7. Ava and Eden play fictionalized versions of themselves on television. For Mags, singing is a transcendent experience, and when she's on stage she's "nowhere and everywhere all at once." All three women have complicated responses to the public attention they receive from their success. Describe their respective relationships with fame. Also, given what we know about Sam, Paul, Zac, Val, David, and Bryce, what distinctions is the novel making between the effects of fame on men versus on women?

8. Ava initially resists participating in *Home Is Where the Hart Is*, and then feels resentment and envy at Eden's burgeoning fame when she plays by the rules of reality television. Through Mags's involvement with the band, she quite literally finds her voice; and yet, as the front woman of Align Above, Mags struggles to be truly seen by the public and by her fellow bandmates. At different times in the narrative, both Ava and Mags find themselves unwilling participants in the stories that are being told about

them. Are their perceptions of themselves as such accurate? Why or why not?

9. How do social media feeds, email memos, and other online content function in the book? If these voices are like a twenty-first-century Greek Chorus, what are they saying about the fears, hopes, and judgments of the average person?

10. In their own ways, both Ava and Mags become influencers. What has the greatest influence over Ava and Mags, respectively? How do external forces shape their stories?

11. Mags is in the throes of grief when Jack Francis interviews her. How does the narrator's description of the interview differ from the account in the *National Chronicle* article? What are the similarities in the dynamic between Mags and Jack and that between Ava and Antonio?

12. Jack Francis and his article are a microcosm of the larger societal forces that have generated Mags's and Ava's particular notoriety. Arguably, Mags intends their visit to Jack Francis's house to be empowering. How did you react to what they discover in his office and their response to it? What are the possible outcomes to their radical act?

13. The last social media post in the book is authored by Mags and Ava. What is suggested by their video post, and by their disabling of the comments function?

14. Near the end of the novel, Mags and Ava are completely isolated from their families—blood relations or otherwise. What do they learn from each other about being sisters, and about being themselves?

15. What do you think Ava is planning to say to Eden at the conclusion of the book, and what do you imagine Eden would say in response?

16. What does the future hold for Mags and Ava? In the last chapter, why does Ava know that "she doesn't have much time"? What do you think is her final destination?